A Big Fan of Yours

SPEAKING VOLUMES, LLC
NAPLES, FLORIDA
2023

A Big Fan of Yours

Cover design by Hannah Linder

ISBN 978-1-64540-578-8

A Big Fan of Yours

Tina Murray

Acknowledgments

I would like to thank Erica and Kurt Mueller and their colleagues at Speaking Volumes LLC for this revised edition of A Big Fan of Yours. Thanks, also, to the people, living and deceased, who were instrumental in the completion and original publication of this work of fiction: Joanna and Robert Gelinas, Dr. Mark Ewald and associates; Zena G. and Leon B. Murray; Cindy and John M. Murray, Nancy B. and James Rugen; Erlene Tubb; Wayne Walker; Ryan Tubb; Linda Driver; Claudia S. Murray; Stacy and Michael A. Murray; Gwendolyn, Irene, and Alton C. Griffith; Stephen "Tivo" Lifschitz; Patricia H. Quinlan; Robert Hendon; Mitch Johnson; Candace Minter; Oluwakemi Elufiede; Destiny; Rae Monet and company; Bob Bair; Lisa Jo Brightman; Maryanna Clarke; Carnegie Writers; Linda B. and J. C. Arlington; Heather Burch; R. Scott Anderson, China Grove Press; The Pat Conroy Literary Center; Dorothy Brown; Sonja Miller; Judy Hawks; Sallie Wood Mayne; Elva Bertram, Steve Jones, Barbara Jordan; Lisa Aschmann; Charles Holt; Lance Hoppen; Collette Divine; J. Karen Thomas; Sandy Ramos; Bonnie Boyd Troxel; Dayle Savage; Ted Crockett; Mr. Hess; Monjue Lindt; Charlotte Rae, Lurene Tuttle, Orkney Taylor; Beth and Mona, gracious employees of the Hermitage Hotel. In addition, I thank my dear pet, Miss Kitty Lovey Cat, also now deceased.

Most of all, I am grateful for help from the Creator.

Although I have matured in understanding since I first wrote this novel, I have left intact the spiritual ideas I included in the original text. They represent a phase of my journey. They may be of interest to readers who wrestle with life's big questions. Certainly, they are vital to the story.

Tina Murray

"Art is the lie that enables us to realize the truth . . ."

Pablo Picasso

"The word hypocrite ultimately came into English from the Greek word hypokrites, which means "an actor" or "a stage player." "

Merriam-Webster.com

Chapter One

"I am so hot for Damian Velasquez," whispered Winner Demming. "I might burn up and disappear into smoke. Like—-spontaneous combustion. Poof!" Blonde and beautiful, slender and stacked, the 19-year-old actress pouted in frustration—until her pent-up passion erupted. "I want to sleep with the man!" she shouted, pummeling the throw pillow next to her on the window seat. On impulse, she seized the pillow and flung it across the living room. Landing with a thud on the hardwood floor, it had narrowly missed the china cabinet. Startled, but relieved, Winner burst into laughter. She felt embarrassed. Yet no one had heard or seen. Alone, inside her family's New York apartment, she had been venting aloud to herself—*and why not?*

She had no one in whom she could confide, no one she could trust to understand her intense desire for a sexy older man—except maybe her best friend since childhood, Felicia Garcia, who, for some unknown reason, wasn't replying to texts these days. For now, the torrid romance with publicity-shy Damian was a big, juicy secret. Winner wanted the whole world to know.

I could throw a surprise party—to announce our engagement. I could even surprise Damian.

Outside her window, overlooking Central Park, an overcast sky promised overnight snow. Thankfully, she had survived the first semester of design school. Next semester, while she worked on the pilot, her courses would be online, except for the fashion internship. Encouraged, she popped another anti-depressant pill and washed it down with a sip of sugar-free, fat-free hot chocolate. It curbed her loneliness.

I miss Florida. I miss Damian. I can't wait to be with him!

The more she thought about throwing a surprise party, the better the idea sounded. She would get the ball rolling today. Her personal assistant, Millie, could do the groundwork in secret.

And we can have the party at the Southern Seas Resort. I'm going to be there anyway . . .

Beside her, like a companion on the window-seat, her smartphone cried out for attention. She grabbed it. "Damian—?" *No. It's not his ring. It's—*

Answering, she sighed. "Hello, Ezra."

"Hello, beautiful. How's my girl?"

Winner replied in monotone. "I'm not a girl. And I'm not yours." Guiltily, she imagined Ezra's puppy dog eyes.

"Sure. Whatever." As usual, he sounded preoccupied. Something was on his mind.

"Got your bags packed, Win?" His New York accent was right at home.

Winner sipped warm chocolate. "I haven't unpacked from my trip to Naples at Thanksgiving."

He snorted. "Over a week. The help must be slacking off. Want me to straighten 'em out?"

She bridled. "I don't need you to watch over me, Ezzie. So, but out. Please."

The shot hit home. Sulking, Ezra fell silent, then spoke up. "I should never have made you take those Karate lessons."

"You had to. My character knew Karate."

"Yeah, but I created Princess Daphne. I wrote the script." He sounded petulant. "I could have changed her."

Winner felt she had hurt him. "Ezzie, I'm sorry. I know you try to make up for my Dad's abandoning me—us—"

Ezra snorted. "Are you kidding? Look, college girl. I have a lot more to worry about than your skinny ass. I have a new series to direct."

"Uh, yeah. I know. Why did you phone?"

"To make sure—you are—ready to roll. Has Millie made your plane reservation?"

"She chartered a jet for me."

"To Orlando, right?"

"Right." *And beyond . . .*

Ezra's tone became lighter. "Too bad for all those airline passengers in First Class. They won't get to sit beside the prettiest lady in the entire universe. In my humble opinion."

Pleased, Winner chewed her lower lip. "Not like your biased or anything."

"Heck, no."

Amused, Winner twirled a long strand of hair. She knew she was extraordinarily lovely. People had been telling her so since birth. For better or worse, she had inherited the world-class good looks of her once-iconic father. Over and over, she'd heard the same mantra. "You have Heston's silver-blue eyes. And his perfect features. You have his height. His slender build. His elegance. His grace. But you got the blonde hair from your supermodel mom." All her life, she'd heard it. From everyone, but especially from gushing fans. Funny, that no one ever mentioned his acting ability—

But I don't want to act. I want to be a wife and a mom. I want to be Senora Velasquez, with five little Velasquez-ettes.

Envisioning her future, Winner pondered what family life with Damian would be like. She thought fondly of the baby dolls in her collection back home in Naples. She loved kids, even inanimate ones. Returning to the present moment, she realized Ezra was speaking. "All the roles in the pilot are cast, except one. We still haven't cast the professor role."

"Really?"

"Yeah. And you know who'd be perfect for that part, Win?"

"Who?"

"Your dad."

"P-f-f-t. Good luck finding him."

"Adair and Hailey proposed the idea. They think I should track Heston down."

"No one knows where Dad is. Not even Poppy—and she's still married to him." Winner's tone was as frosty as the branches beneath her 10th-story perch. She looked out over the wintry park. "I hope you're not planning to do that, Ezra. It would be—uncomfortable for me."

"It's not really my call, Win." He exhaled. "We'll work it out this weekend in Orlando. The Champlain kids arrive there tonight."

"Adair and Hailey aren't kids, either."

"They are to me, Winnie. Just because I gave Hailey a new title, "Producer," and I cast Adair as our leading man, doesn't mean I think of them as grown-ups."

She wagged a finger at the phone. "You're not that much older than they are, Ezra."

"Well, me and those kids go way back."

She knew what he meant. Ezra Gold and Vivian Champlain had been long-time lovers, until Vivian had died several years ago. Hailey and Adair Champlain had been Vivian's stepchildren. After the recent death of their father, Truett Adair Champlain III, Adair had inherited billions.

"Ezzie, you're a terrific director, but you're too complicated," Winner confessed.

His voice reflected a grin. "Heady praise."

"I'll see you in a few days." She hesitated, then said. "By the way, I have a surprise."

"For me?"

"For everyone."

He chuckled warily. "Uh oh. What is it?"

Winner sat up straight, placing her empty cup on a nearby bookshelf. "You'll find out." Standing, she turned on the floor lamp and adjusted her scarlet cashmere pullover.

"That's what I'm afraid of. Look, nature calls. Gotta go. Take care of yourself, Blondie. Go easy on the anxiety meds."

Inwardly, she groaned. "Goodbye, Mr. Gold."

"Bye, Win. Study your role. And stay out of trouble."

Winner turned off the phone and gazed out the window. Snowflakes were descending. Marveling at their fragile perfection, she recalled the family Christmas in Vail when she had been six years old. Her abusive real mom had vanished from her life by then. Daddy and Poppy had been happily married—and so much in love. The twins had been babies. Kipp had still been alive. Dakota hadn't been born yet. Winner sighed.

Ancient history.

Better to think forward, to imagine the magic her future held in store. In a few days, she would be sleeping at the Southern Seas Resort in Orlando, Florida. Most thrilling of all, Millie had assured her that the hotel overlooked the Enchanted Palace. Winner was determined to go to that palace with Damian. A romantic proposal at the world-famous theme-park castle had been her secret fantasy since childhood. All she had to do was survive one more night in the Big Apple.

The room had become too warm. Winner pulled the sweater off over her head. She folded the sweater neatly, caressing its softness. Folded garment in hand, she gazed out the window. Her vision blurred. She couldn't help but wonder.

5

Where is my Daddy now?

***

"Hey, Tom! There you are!" yelled DeAngelo Dickinson, a post-adolescent vagrant dressed in raggedy denim dungarees. "Everybody's looking for you, man!"

Huddled in contemplation, Heston Demming heard the young man's booming voice.

"Where you been hiding?" DeAngelo yelled. His voice sounded closer.

Rousing from deep reverie, Heston responded silently

In plain sight—for years.

"Wake up, Tommy!" DeAngelo barked as he zoned in on Heston, who was seated, seeking sanctuary, on the old church steps.

Wearily, Heston sighed. As his awareness of the physical world returned, he opened his eyes and shifted his weight. Now in his early fifties, he felt stiffness in his limbs. He had been sitting for so long, on the top step of the entrance to St. Mary's of the Seven Sorrows, that the hard, cold stone had warmed beneath his buttocks. Reluctantly, he responded to the approaching youth.

"DeAngelo, what's up?" he said indifferently, blinking his eyes against the intrusion of morning sunlight. Looking down the front steps, which led to the church's main portal, Heston found himself surrounded by a motley crew of street people, seated alone and in pairs. A few of them he knew by name. The city sidewalk adjacent to the steps was bustling with office workers and tourists.

Just then, Heston caught sight of his pursuer. The pom-pom atop DeAngelo's knit cap bobbled irreverently as the agile young man sprinted up the steps and squatted down beside him.

"Wake up." DeAngelo jostled his shoulder.

"Hey, man." Heston yawned, releasing the prayer in silence.

"Hey." DeAngelo barked rapid-fire, "Rudy's been looking everywhere for you. He's got big news to tell you. Real serious stuff."

"Yeah?" Casting his gaze downward, Heston regarded a plump pigeon as it waddled near the foot of the steps. The lavender-gray bird pecked repeatedly at the dirty sidewalk.

"You asleep, man?" DeAngelo poked him with a bony forefinger.

"Not anymore." Heston tossed the cold remnants of his breakfast sandwich to the cooing pigeon. "Guess I've been dreaming about seagulls."

"Well, while you been daydreaming, Old Rudy's been hobbling around town, hunting you down, man."

"Yeah? I've been right here—all along." Feeling lost inside a grimy, second-hand sweatsuit, Heston shuddered in the autumn chill. Today was another gray day in Nashville—sky, church, office buildings, sidewalks, faces, all varying shades of shadow. He missed the bright colors—and the warmth—of Florida and the Caribbean, his home base until a few years ago.

"I'm wise to you, man," said DeAngelo. "You were praying, not sleeping."

"Was I?"

"You're wasting your time on this religious bit," DeAngelo observed. "Dog eat dog, Tom."

My name isn't Tom! Heston yearned to cry out but did not.

Instead, he shrugged. Deep down, he had grown tired of the charade. By now, he had learned what he'd needed to know about real life— hadn't he? He was tired of pretending to be someone he wasn't—for free. At least, as a movie actor, he had been paid to pretend to be someone else. If it weren't for Montsey Flynn—*I'd do what? Head home?* Heston squinted up at his companion. "So, what's the big news, Dee?"

Reeking of last night's beer, DeAngelo dropped down beside him on the steps. "Don't know, man. Ask Rudy. He knows. He's over yonder at the bus station." He thumbed northward. "I can call him. Got a phone, Tom?

Lying, Heston shook his head. "Nuh-uh." *If nothing else, I'm still a good actor.*

"Me neither," DeAngelo spoke bass *staccato,* as if words were firing from his tongue. "Hey, check this out." DeAngelo pulled a crumpled twenty-dollar bill from his pocket. "I found this bill, man. Down on the riverfront. Bet some drunk hayseed dropped it. At that cracker concert last night."

"Probably." Heston yawned, brushing breadcrumbs from his hands. "That crowd was raucous. I could hardly sleep."

"Yeah?"

"Tossed and turned—all night long—on my bench."

DeAngelo grinned from ear to ear, still admiring his treasure. "Can you believe this?" Gingerly, he snapped the twenty-dollar bill.

Heston cracked a smile. "You're a lucky man, Dee."

"Ain't I though?" The young vagrant shot up to full height and scanned the city streets. "Rudy's message is from Reverend Bill. That's all I know." Abruptly, DeAngelo charged down the church steps and hit the sidewalk running. 'See you back at the shelter, man," he called, sprinting southward on Fifth Avenue North. "Hey, don't be late for supper! Tonight's hot-dog night!"

Great.

Rising to his feet, Heston shook out his limbs and sauntered down the steps of St Mary's. His knees creaked. He felt anxious, all of a sudden. If the message was coming from Bill, it could be serious.

Immediately, he spotted Old Rudy hobbling across the intersection of Fifth and Charlotte. The elderly veteran's halting gait was unmistakable.

Rudy saw him. "Tom! Tom Roberts!" Rudy croaked, waving, as Heston strode towards him.

At the street corner, Heston greeted Rudy, who had stopped, short of breath. The old man was leaning against a lamp post. As the traffic, both human and automobile, flowed around him, Heston confronted Rudy, face to face.

The toothless old man was panting. His stringy, white hair framed a bearded, flushed face. "Bill sent me to find you. Pronto."

"What's the message, Rudy?"

Rudy's gaze fell to the sidewalk. Then he looked up at Heston, pale eyes watery and filled with regret. "It's Montsey Flynn, Tom. They've taken her to Hospice."

As if slugged, Heston staggered backwards. "When?"

"Late last night. She's there now." The old man grabbed for Heston's sleeve. "Bill said to hurry."

"Thanks. man," called Heston, who was already dodging honking cars as he crossed the busy intersection, against the traffic light. Once safely across, he ran through the doors of the Music City Central Bus terminal.

Inside the massive, open-air building, he slipped into a familiar, grimy corner. Taking out his phone, he called for a ride. Pretense no longer mattered. He had to say goodbye to Montserrat Flynn. In his youth, Montsey had been the woman of his dreams—decades before her stroke, her drug-dependency, and the early onset of Alzheimer's. As he pocketed his phone, emotion overwhelmed him.

Blinded by tears, Heston waited anxiously for his ride to arrive.

***

Three days later, Heston stood, poised for flight, in the doorway of Rev. Bill's homeless shelter in Nashville. Dejected, his fingers numb with cold, he buttoned his woolen navy peacoat and took in one last look. The clean, but humble shelter was located eight blocks south of the downtown bus terminal. It had been his home for the past few months.

"I meant to thank you for the nice funeral service," Heston said. "You did Montsey proud."

"Good. Are you going back to your wife?" Bill asked, walking towards him, arm outstretched.

Heston remained mute. Stepping forward, he grasped and shook the strong, warm hand of the Reverend Doctor William Erskine, his sponsor for the past two years. Rev. Bill—a spongy, blond, bespectacled man of 39—squeezed Heston's hand quickly before letting it drop.

"Are you?" Bill gazed at Heston, as if seeing him for the first time. "I got that impression just now, Tom—I mean, Heston—that you miss your wife."

Essentially, Heston realized, Bill *was* seeing him for the first time. Ten minutes earlier, inside Bill's private office, Heston had spilled the proverbial beans, confessing his true identity to the astonished Midwestern minister.

At the moment, Bill was still reeling from the shock. He gawked at Heston. "Man, I still can't believe you're—a celebrity."

Feigning modesty, Heston shuffled his feet. "I was. Years ago." *Before my world fell apart.* Poised in the open doorway, he centered himself, spiritually and emotionally. Saying goodbye was never easy. He had felt valued here at Bill's shelter, while living in masquerade as a homeless derelict. Now, his life was about to change forever—once again.

In a few short minutes, he would be walking back onto the world stage. In previous decades, he had had been one of the planet's most popular movie stars. Now, surely, he had been all but forgotten by the world—which was fine with him because his consciousness had changed. He had no desire to return to acting.

Stardom was the arena he had abandoned, at the zenith of his career. In fact, he had walked away from his entire life a few days prior to his fiftieth birthday, not long after receiving his second award for Best Actor; amidst worldwide adoration and acclaim. Not until yesterday, in the aftermath of Montserrat Flynn's funeral, had he realized how isolated he had become during the past few years.

"So, are you?" Bill nudged him with a rounded elbow. "Going back to your wife and kids?"

Heston shrugged. "Here's the funny thing, Bill. Of my three legal wives—and all my lovers—it's my current wife, Poppy, I miss most. And I don't know why. I've known Poppy since we were kids together in grade school. She's a drifty, freckled thing with wide-set eyes. Amazing, isn't it?"

As Heston spoke, a cold wind whipped through the streets of downtown Nashville. He felt its sting, as it swept into the church-shelter's office, bringing with it the metallic smell of bus exhaust. Shivering, he peered into the interior of the storefront reception room, watching the downtrodden interact with compassionate staff members. Unconsciously, he gnawed a fingernail, then caught himself, and stopped, drying his finger on the woolen pea coat.

Bill contemplated him. "It can be hard to loose the ties that bind."

"Certainly, it can be." Heston contemplated Bill in silence. *I will miss you, Doc.*

Bill cleared his throat. "Families need fathers. That famous daughter of yours—the Wild Child. She's yours, right?"

"Her name is Winner." *My little Ladybug.*

"Well, she could use a guiding hand."

"Win's had rough go. Abused as a toddler. Kidnapped in adolescence. Abandoned by her father. Raised by her stepmother—more like fairy godmother, really."

Bill glanced up the street, then looked back at Heston. "Does your wife, Poppy, still love you, Heston? Sounds as though you're still in love with her."

"I shouldn't have mentioned her." Heston glared at the man. "You're relentless."

Bill blushed and looked away. "Sorry. Guess that was presumptuous."

"Bill, I just don't know—the answer—yet." He glanced up the street. *If she'll have me.* "Poppy Sue Craft. That was her name back in grade school. Brown eyes and red pigtails. She stammered a lot." He smiled fondly. "But she was red-hot, even then."

Bill pointed at the sky. "I get it. Red hair, red flower, Poppy."

"Actually, 'Poppy' is short for 'Penelope.' "

"Really?" Bill studied him. "The original Penelope was the wife of Odysseus—in Greek mythology? Did you know that?"

Heston stared blankly at the former professor. Obviously, Bill was not a film buff.

Drawing up his chest, Bill explained. "Odysseus—the mythical hero of *The Odyssey* by Homer You've heard of him, right?"

Heston found his footing. "Yes. Of course. I played him once—in a film. Huge hit." He thought better of admitting that the film had been entitled, *King Odysseus: Alien Space Warrior.* Nor did he voice his usual editorial comment: that his early success in a different space film had red-carpeted the way for his ascendance to the stellar role of King Ody.

Bill looked skeptical. "Well, then you know the story. Odysseus sailed the ancient world. Battled monsters. Lost his men. Vanquished every woman he met. Then returned home, in the guise of a beggar, to a wife who'd been chaste for years. Eventually, he regained his crown as King of Ithaca—by killing Penelope's many suitors."

Heston stared, deadpan "Suitors?"

"Yeah. Gird your loins, man. Your wife may have a new boyfriend."

"I should be so lucky." Heston's Groucho Marx impression fell flat. His Brooklyn accent was rusty.

Oblivious, Bill scanned the brooding sky. "I've just realized something else."

"Yes? What?"

"A few years ago, a rock star died in a plane crash. Crashed into the Caribbean Sea. The bodies were never recovered. The rocker's name was Kipp Demming. He was your son, wasn't he?"

Heston braced himself. *Help me here.* "Kipp is my son." He measured his words. "It's a long story, Bill. My father had enemies. They came after me and my family. I had to protect—"

Bill shook his head, horse-like. "I sense a justification coming on." He eyed Heston tenderly. "You want to come on back inside? Get out of this weather?"

Ignoring the invitation to confide, Heston explained briefly. "My wife threw me out—after the plane crash."

"Oh. That's rough, buddy." With the toe of his oxford, Bill scuffed the sidewalk. "One of my converts had been a big fan of Kipp Demming and The Demonsong."

Heston felt uncomfortable. "Look, Bill, I'd better be off. To discover what my own future holds." He caught Bill's twinkling eye. "Thanks for not betraying me, Bill."

"Only you can do that, Heston."

Glancing up the street, Heston smoothed a forelock and pocketed his chilly hand. "Give my regards to—"

"Broadway?"

Heston laughed. "No, I mean, give my love to everyone here at the shelter. Will you, Bill? Explain everything—"

"You betcha." Bill cut to the core. "You're really a multimillionaire, aren't you, Heston?"

Heston dug his hands into his pants pockets. "Something like that—yes."

"Whew." Bill's eyes rolled. "Well, I guess you had your reasons." Reluctant to part, he regarded Heston's stuffed pockets. "Need a pair of warm gloves to take with you? How 'bout a can of ginger ale for the road?"

Heston shook his head. "Save them for the next fellow. Won't need 'em where I'm going."

Bill said, "What you will need is the Good News—of our Savior's love—which you already have. He's just waiting for you to receive it."

"So you've been telling me." Heston glanced both ways, up and down the street. *It's time.* "Well, goodbye, Bill."

"Goodbye, Tommy Roberts, whoever you were. Hello, Heston Demming, beloved child of the Most High."

Heston avoided the frontal assault. "It's my real name, Bill. I was christened Sean Heston Demming—and, believe me, I *will* remember you—and this haven—in more ways than one."

Bill gleamed. "Do what you got to do."

Heston shivered. "I shall indeed. Check out the shelter's bank balance tomorrow."

"Okay."

"See that DeAngelo attends trade school. And that Rudy goes home to his sister in Texas."

Beaming, Bill nodded. "Bless you, Sean Heston. Just remember. I'm still your sponsor. Always will be—'til they lay me down. And I don't care a whit if you ain't got a dime, bro."

Heston blinked rapidly. "Thanks, man." He raised a fist. Bill met it with his own, in a farewell fist-bump.

"Give me a hug, movie star," Bill said suddenly. Quickly, he embraced Heston.

Quickly, Heston returned his embrace, slapping Bill's warm, solid back. "I love you, man." Breaking free, Heston trudged up the sidewalk, feeling more than a twinge of guilt.

"Goodbye, Tom!" Bill called, as two middle-aged tourists waddled by. "Text if you get work!"

Laughing hoarsely, Heston looked back, saluting his guardian angel. Turning, once again towards the future, he steadied himself. Braced, he walked slowly to the nearest street corner.

Someday I'll tell Bill—and Poppy—the whole truth about Kipp— when it's safe—if it ever is.

Rounding the street corner—and now out of Bill's sight—Heston hailed an idling limousine.

"Hermitage Hotel," he commanded the chauffeur. Climbing into the vehicle, Heston offered no explanation for his seedy attire. Preoccupied, he rode in silence to the city's historic five-star hotel. As he rode the pot-holed streets, he planned his agenda—for his own personal transformation.

First, he'd make a pit-stop at the hotel's famous black-and-green, art-deco gentleman's room. Then, he'd register as a guest, under his real name. Then, after a shower and a massage, he'd have lunch brought to his suite—and then, a tailor—*and, for crying out loud, a barber.*

Once settled, he would locate Poppy and insist that she take him back, suitors be damned. Hell, no, he wouldn't go home disguised as any beggar. He would return as king, triumphant.

He clenched a fist, as the limousine pulled up in front the luxury hotel.

I want my wife. I want my family. I want to go home.

Chapter Two

Far south, on the edge of the North American continent, the elite, seaside city of Naples, Florida, glistened prettily, awash in golden dawn. Inside the yellow-stucco mansion at 1708 Galleon Drive in Port Royal, Poppy Demming stepped hesitantly onto her bathroom scale.

Naked and trembling, she opened one eye and peered down at the digital numbers between her two big toes. Her heart thumped in exultation. Hopping off the scale, she squealed in excitement. On impulse, she performed a shameless happy dance upon the gleaming marble floor.

Only one more pound to lose!

Elated, she clucked softly to herself. She was proud of her figure again, and proud of her hard work, which had paid off, at last. Her nutritionist would be pleased, too. So would he personal trainer. She would text them both, right after breakfast—a protein shake and black coffee—because she was famished. Abandoning her happy dance, she pressed a key on the wall display.

"Lissette, where's my food?" she asked urgently. "And my phone?"

"I'm coming," Lissette's voice replied. "Relax."

Slumping against the wall, Poppy couldn't stop smiling. Her life was going well, for the first time in ages. Not only was her make-over complete, but also her first book, *Collecting Florida Art,* had just been published, happily, in time for Christmas sales. Inwardly, Poppy gloated.

Who needs Heston Demming anymore? Not I!

She was finished with the past. She was on the cusp of something new—but what?

Six months earlier, she had made a decision—to switch from drinking lattes to skinny lattes—and she had never looked back. Most certainly, she looked better now—more like her old self. Not that she would ever be that naive girl again. But she was no old crone, either, even though, recently, she had passed childbearing age.

Bah! Who cares? Four babies are enough.

Proudly, she studied her nude reflection in the full-length bathroom mirror.

Not too shabby, lady. If only . . .

Suddenly, sadness flickered in her heart. Throwing on a terry robe, she sat down, overwhelmed.

It always comes back to one thing, doesn't it?

During the eight years Poppy had lived with Heston as his wife, she had found happiness, intermittently. After she and Heston had separated legally—an event foreshadowed by the tragedy of Kipp's plane crash—she had fallen into a morbid funk. The memory of those three deaths was still too great to bear, even now, eight years later, and it still separated her, emotionally, from her husband.

In the ensuing years, grief had been her constant companion. After separating from Heston, she had stopped working out, gained weight, and concentrated on raising their kids. For years now, she had avoided any social or romantic entanglements.

Worse yet, she had even ignored her own health. A recent cancer scare had brought her to her senses. Since then, she'd realized how lonely she had become, now that all the kids had flown the nest, all safely ensconced in boarding schools. Win, of course, had been living in New York.

Abruptly, Poppy's stomach growled, bringing her back to reality.

"Lissette!" she cried loudly. "Get a move on, hon!" She could hear feet padding down the hall.

Returning to the dressing room, Poppy skimmed through her voluminous racks of clothes. A certain dress caught her attention. The figure-hugging, teal-colored cocktail frock had been one of Heston's favorites.

I wonder if it fits me now.

***

Moments later, Poppy's aging domestic servant, Lissette Garcia, toddled into the bedroom. "I been dusting Winner's doll collection," Lissette panted, a breakfast tray balanced in both her hands. "Two of the dolls are missing."

"Missing?" Poppy removed the phone from Lissette's breakfast tray and tossed it onto the king-sized bed. "Which ones? Not the Hopi kachinas her Uncle Banks sent her? Those are priceless."

"No, not those." Halting, Lissette huffed, "The Princess Daphne Doll—in the flowy gown."

"The one with the pearls and sapphires—and the tiara of golden leaves?"

"*Si.* The one Ezra Gold had made special for Winnie." Setting down the breakfast tray, Lissette groaned.

"Have a seat, Liss," said Poppy. She pondered. "Hmm. That action figure is a collector's item—one of kind, valuable in and of itself, aside from its gold and jewels." Mildly alarmed, but unconvinced of foul play, Poppy asked, "Which other doll is missing?"

Lissette drew up a chair. "That old Greek doll of Heston. The one in the short skirt."

"You mean the vintage action-figure of King Odysseus?"

"I guess so."

"It's a collectible, too. That version of the Odysseus doll was never mass produced. It was a prototype, but now it's a one-of-a-kind, too. He's wearing a space tunic, by the way, not a skirt."

"Whatever it is, it's gone." After seating herself, Lissette handed a brimming glass to Poppy. "Your breakfast shake, lady."

19

Poppy took the glass and guzzled. Taking a linen napkin from the tray, she said, "Heston gave that doll to Winner for her eighth birthday. She used to treasure it. Lissy, are you sure the dolls are gone? Not simply misplaced? Accidentally?"

"Well, that Heston doll was here at Thanksgiving. I saw it when Winner showed it to my daughter and the kids. Felicia made a joke about Heston's cute legs."

Poppy dabbed her lips. "Win probably took the dolls back to college with her. I'll phone her."

Rising, Lissette panted slowly. "Win says it's not 'college.' It's 'design school.' " But Lissette's round, brown eyes popped as she realized that her employer was wearing the tiny teal frock.

"It fits!" Lissette clapped her plump hands together in approval.

Gratified, Poppy beamed, turning in place, displaying the sexy little dress. "Yes, it does."

Deftly, Lissette brushed away a stray piece of lint from the hem. "Wait 'til your kids see the new you! Did they get in touch with you last night?"

Poppy nodded vigorously. "Yep. All travel plans are on schedule. We're all meeting in Orlando this coming Monday."

"Good."

"Dakota and Sage texted me. They're booked on the same flight. Tegan phoned. She's looking forward to the theme parks. We had face time. She's practically giddy." Poppy grimaced. "Tegan's a silly goose, but I miss her. I miss them all." *Especially Kipp, my lost boy.*

Intuiting Poppy's thought, Lissette frowned. "Dakota, Sage, and Tegan—they're alive. That's what matters. Will they be going to Winner's party, too?"

"No," Poppy replied. "They won't arrive in time. Certain you won't join us in Orlando, Lissy?"

"My husband needs me here." Lissette scowled at the floor.

"So he claims." Poppy sipped her shake significantly.

***

Annoyed, Lissette turned her attention to Poppy's wardrobe. Busily, she straightened unruly clothes hangers. "You ought to continue that book tour. You're in demand, Lady Author," she called from inside Poppy's dressing room.

Entering, Poppy snorted. "I? No. Not really. Mrs. Heston Demming is in demand. Mrs. Heston Demming's art book is popular." She stared into the dresser mirror. "I don't exist. Sunshine House only published the thing because I'm still married to Heston."

"No—"

"Yes, Lissette. Haven't you noticed? Whenever I'm interviewed on a talk show, that's all they ask about—Heston. How is he doing? Is he planning a comeback?"

"They do ask some stupid questions."

"Is he still painting? Do you know where he is? Is he still living like a hermit—on that tropical island? Or is he in the Himalayas? Or the Andes? Is it true that he's become a monk?"

Playing along, Lissette lumbered a rhythmic jig. "Has he gone crazy?" she uttered, singsong.

Watching her, Poppy chuckled. "They never ask that. But they insinuate it."

"Well, there's one question they always ask: Why you and Heston never get a divorce?' Needling, Lissette leered at her. "You don't answer that one so quick, *Senora.*"

Poppy hitched a hip in defiance. "Lissette Garcia—"

"Yes?" Catching her breath, Lissette fanned herself with the hem of her apron. "The whole world—and me—wants to know the answer to that question, Lady. Your man was a big star. What else can you expect?"

"He's not my man. Not anymore." Poppy frowned. *Lissy wants me to admit I still love Heston. Well, I won't. Because I don't.*

"So why don't you divorce him? Money? Kids?"

Poppy waved a hand dismissively. "Too much trouble, I suppose." *Obviously, the man no longer cares whether I live or die.*

Lissette needled her. "You don't fool me. I've known you too long. You want him back." Breath recovered, she picked up the coffee cup from the breakfast tray and offered it to Poppy.

Inhaling sharply, Poppy glared at the rotund housekeeper.

"You know what, Lissy?" she exploded, waving away the cup of coffee. "The time has come."

"What time?"

"It's time for Heston and I to make our split legal."

Scandalized, Lissette goggled at her. "No way!"

"I mean, look at me! I've shed twenty-five pounds. I'm like a sculptor, carving out my own future. I'm ready to live again."

Lissette gasped. "Oh, no, you're not—"

"Oh, yes, I am. Thank you for making me realize it."

"Me? I didn't mean—"

"Next time I see Heston, I'm asking him for a divorce."

"I don't believe it."

"I promise you."

"Oi-yeh!" Lissette moaned, sad faced, then added philosophically, "Then it's a good thing he's disappeared off the face of the earth."

"Why so?"

"Because if you never see him, you can't ask him for a divorce."

"Oh-ho! Well, I should try to find him, then, shouldn't I?"

"No! How?"

"Easy. Heston's still alive somewhere. Otherwise, I would have heard. His attorney will know where he is."

Shedding the old frock, Poppy slipped back into her bathrobe. Lips pursed, Lissette retrieved the frock and placed it neatly on its hanger.

"Lissette, give me that phone!" Poppy demanded, snapping her fingers.

Scurrying, the worried servant located the phone and handed it over.

However, instead of placing a call, Poppy gawked at the phone's small screen.

"What is it?" Lissy asked nosily. "What's wrong?"

"A text message."

Instantly, Lissette's eyes widened. "Not from Heston—?"

Poppy shook her head. "No. Worse. From Jim. James Talbot."

"Your first husband?"

Slowly, Poppy nodded. "Jim says, 'Meet me for cocktails. Starfish Grille. 5:00 p.m. Tonight'."

"Whoa."

Legs wobbly, Poppy sank down on the bed she once had shared with Heston. She'd had no contact with her first husband, Jim, for—*how long?* Mentally, she did the math.

It had been one year, to the day, since Jim's second wife, Cookie, had passed away. Jim had married Cookie Lee, the proprietor of Rainbows on Fifth Avenue South, downtown, years earlier. He had married her on the rebound, after Poppy had abandoned him to marry superstar Heston Demming, her childhood playmate, high-school sweetheart, and secret "baby-daddy."

Now, suddenly, Jim was back. Her life had come full circle.

Worried, Poppy stared at the text message. How was she going to respond?

***

High in the Florida skies, Winner Demming sat enthroned in luxury, the lone passenger aboard a small, chartered jet. While in flight, she was video-chatting, deep in conversation, at last, with her dear childhood chum, Felicia Garcia. As children, Winner and Felicia—the daughter of the Demming's housekeeper, Lissette Garcia—had grown up in close proximity. These days, they kept in touch. Most recently, they had seen each other in Naples, during the Thanksgiving holidays.

Although attractive in her own right, Felicia, unlike Winner, was no great beauty. A columnist had written, "La Tropica is a cute girl, but Winner Demming is a beautiful young woman." Even so, the two remained fast friends. At one time Heston's protege, Felicia had launched a singing career of her own and now, was fast becoming a famous pop diva, known worldwide by the stage name Tropica. Tropica's spicy songs now topped the Billboard charts, but she was also versatile. In a recent gig, she had appeared as a no-nonsense judge on a reality-TV talent show. Currently, she was on tour in Spain. At the moment, however, she was giggling over Winner's latest conquest.

"He's a wealthy *Latino?*" Felicia cried, a tiny moving image on Winner's tablet device. "So, Win. You're marrying one of us? Win, la *Latina.*"

"Wait until you see Damian Velasquez, Felicia. He gorgeous."

"He's old."

"He's hot!" Winner giggled, then blurted it out, "Oh, Fe! He's so hot!"

A smile framed Felicia's words. "Why am I not surprised?"

Winner laughed.

"Is this Damian Velasquez on the plane with you now?"

"No!"

"Didn't think so. Is he already at the hotel in Orlando? Waiting for your tight little bod?"

"No. He'll be driving up from Key Largo, day after tomorrow. He works at a club down there. He had to work today and tomorrow. So, I chartered a jet to Key Largo. So I could be with him."

"Yeah?"

"I'll fly up to Orlando tomorrow. Poppy's joining me tomorrow, too. My sibs arrive Monday, so they'll miss my party. But I'll do the theme parks with them."

"Fun times."

"Tegan's such a baby still. She loves The Mouse. So does Dack, but he won't admit it."

"What about Sage?"

"Sage doesn't believe in fun. She's is all 'science this' and 'science that.'"

Felicia snickered. "At this very moment, your lover-man's probably somewhere on Largo, looking up at the sky, wishing he was with you right now."

Smiling, Winner exhaled plaintively. "I definitely miss him. Even when we're apart for a moment. The thing is, Felicia—Damian doesn't know I'm throwing this party—to announce our engagement. He thinks it will be just the two of us, alone together at the resort—lovebirds on a romantic holiday."

"Winston, you haven't told this guy he's about to meet your step-mom? Not to mention the Demming brats. And two hundred of your closest friends and associates?"

"No. I'm springing it on him. It's a surprise . . .?"

"I'll say."

"Come on, Fe. It'll be fun."

"Win, what would your dad think about you marrying an old guy?"

"The thing is, Felicia. Damian isn't just any 'old guy.' He's special. I feel as if I've known him all my life. I felt that way the moment I first laid eyes on him."

"About your dad—"

"You know very well Dad's dropped off the planet."

Felicia leaned forward into the camera. "Well, guess what? Heston's turned up."

Winner bolted upright. "What? You're kidding, Fe."

"Nope. That's why I phoned you this morning. To break the news."

"I don't believe it."

"See that TV over there? I'm watching him—on the entertainment news—right now."

Disbelieving, Winner shook her head. "It must be an old movie."

"Win, it' not! See for yourself!" She aimed her camera phone towards a nearby TV set.

"I can't make it out. Where is he?"

"Don't know. Sound's off."

Anxiety growing, Winner sat, perplexed, absorbing the implications of her father's return.

Felicia seemed sympathetic. She turned her phone's camera lens back towards her own face. "Win, let's change the subject. Go on. Talk to me about Damian. Your party. Your wedding plans."

Winner was silent.

"Hear me, babe?"

"I hear you." Winner cleared her throat. "Well, Millie invited everyone secretly—to the party. Fe, I do have really big plans. First of all, I going to have the most fabulous website for the wedding—"

"Cool." Felicia interrupted. "Win, what does Mr. *Machismo* do for a living?"

"You mean Damian? I'm not totally sure. He's sort of a developer. He and his partners own tennis resorts in Italy and Spain or the Caribbean or somewhere. All over the place. Right now, he's working as a tennis pro—just for security and benefits and stuff like that."

"Whoa, Win. You mean he's a tennis bum?"

"He's not a bum, Felicia."

"Oh, yeah? Who pays?"

"Felicia—!"

"You do! I thought so. Is he at least good at tennis?"

"Killer, even at his age. Crushes me at singles every time. He's in great shape."

Felicia scoffed. "Give me a break, Winner. You let him beat you. I know your ass."

"You do not."

"You know what Damian means?"

"What?"

" 'Tame.' "

Winner burst out laughing. "His mom didn't have a clue."

Without disturbing her, a flight attendant placed a fruit smoothie on the table in front of Winner.

Dismissively, Winner mouthed "Thank you." She toyed with the straw. "I don't have to play games with Damian. He's genuinely tough. In fact, he can be scary, sometimes."

"Yeah?" Felicia sounded wary.

"In a good way, Fe. Damian's got that bad-boy thing goin' on. When I'm with Damian Velasquez, nobody messes with me."

Felicia mused, "Still got a thing for bodyguards, don't you? Even after what happened to you when you were kidnapped?"

Winner gasped. "Shut. Up."

Quickly, Felicia apologized. "I'm sorry, Win."

"You should be, girl."

Felicia snorted. "Yeah, right. Hey, did you get that cute stuffed manatee I sent you? I sent it to your New York address."

"I did. Thanks. It's absolutely adorable. What was that for?"

"Saw it. Felt like it."

"I hadn't gotten any new stuffies or dolls lately. Not since the one Ezra brought me, when he came back from China."

"I keep an eye out." Felicia said softly.

Winner hesitated. "He wants me to go with him next time."

"To China? Ezra does?"

"Mm-hmm."

"The man's in love with you, Win."

"Come on, Felicia." Gazing out the airplane window, Winner watched the clouds drift by. "Can we change the subject again, please?"

"Sure." Felicia paused in silence, then spoke. "How about this subject? Would you call me 'Tropica,' please, from now on?" urged Felicia. "I have an image to maintain. I left fat-freak Felicia behind in summer camp six years ago."

Winner smirked. "And now you're Tropica, the trimmed, toned trollop?"

"Nice, Win."

Winner laughed. "I couldn't resist. What does it mean, anyway?"

"Nothing. I just made it up."

"Trashy Tropica takes—"

"Just don't post that mess on social media, please. It wasn't funny when the tabloid published that lurid story, Winner—and it wasn't true. I'm a good girl. I just dress and gyrate on stage like a slut."

Winner winced. "You're still a good girl? I'm pretending to be."

"If the tabloids ever find out you're faking it—"

"Shut up, will you?" Aghast, Winner looked around at no one. Oblivious, the flight attendant was seated at the rear of the cabin.

On screen, Tropica snickered. "This connection is secure."

Sipping her smoothie, Winner reconsidered. "You know the old cliché—there's no such thing as bad publicity."

"Right. Tell that to my pop."

"Your Dad's okay with the money you're making, isn't he, Tropica?"

Felicia grunted. "I'll say. He's my business manager, Win. I hardly see a dime of what I earn."

Winner winced. "I can't touch all of my earnings, either. Not 'til I'm twenty-one. But it's protected. My folks can't even touch it." Pushing away thoughts of her father's return, she took an anxiety pill and sipped her fruit smoothie.

Strawberries, yum!

Watching, Felicia veered off the map. "What about your real mom? Did Millie invite her, too?"

Taken aback, Winner shook her head. "No one knows where that woman is—except Uncle Banks, and he's not telling. By the way, he's coming to the party, too."

Tropica sighed. "Maybe Banks thinks he's protecting you—from his evil sister. After what she did to you when you were a little kid. The way she abused you. And *mira,* you haven't heard a peep from her in fifteen years."

Winner caught her breath. "If she's even alive. Look, Tropica, I've got to go."

Felicia sucked air. "Win, I'm sorry. I've said all the wrong things today."

"Forget it. So, are you coming to my surprise party this weekend or not?"

"Of course, I'm coming. I'll hop a plane in Madrid ASAP."

Placated, Winner sipped her fruit smoothie. "My ears are popping. I think we're descending." She signaled the attendant. "Gum?"

"Just yawn. Winner, look, I'm very sorry I said that about your real mom—"

Winner bit her lower lip. "Sorry enough to perform at my party, Tropica?" Accepting a stick of gum from the attendant, Winner yawned. "Thanks."

Meanwhile, Felicia cried, "Why not? It'll be my wedding gift to you. I have a great new set."

"Of what? Boobs? Teeth? Bongos?" She chewed the spearmint gum, popping it expertly.

"Songs to perform, you geek. Who else is coming? I guess you had to invite Hailey Champlain?"

Winner frowned. "Well, she is our producer. Besides, I wanted to. Little Hailey's a hoot. I invited her brother, Adair, too. He's our star. Interested?"

Felicia laughed. "In Adair Champlain? Naw. But my teenybopper fans idolize him."

Winner laughed. "That's because they don't know him."

"Seriously. Listen, I did a gig in Vegas. Adair showed up at the venue. All the girlies were crying and sobbing and tearing at their clothes and screaming over him. I don't see it. The guy doesn't do it for me."

Winner looked out at the cloud cover. "Who does do it for you, Felicia? Are you seeing anybody?"

"Nope. No time." Felicia chattered on too rapidly. "The teenyboppers say Adair is weird—in the bedroom department. Like, if they go back to his hotel room, all he does is play with their boobies. Then he sends them home in a limo." She stopped for breath. "Maybe he's gay."

Winner shrugged. "Maybe so. But he bragged about his—sexual exploits with women—to me last week."

"He was hitting on you?"

"If he was, I turned him down flat. Once he meets Damian, he'll know why."

The flight attendant approached Winner. "We'll be landing soon, Miss Demming. Please turn off your device and fasten your seat belt.

Winner nodded in compliance. "Oops, got to go. Luv ya, Fe." Then she paused, realizing her mistake.

"Tropica!" the two friends screamed in unison. Both giggled amiably.

"You win, friend," said Win. "From now on, I will call you Tropica."

"I just wish my mom would," Tropica smiled. "Talk to her, will you? Hey, is she coming to the party?"

"I invited Lissette. But Poppy told me your dad put his foot down."

"As usual. Hey, Win. Do me favor, okay?" She hesitated. "Be careful. I don't know—I've got a bad feeling."

"About what?"

"I don't know. I'm just glad you've got your security details with you."

Winner hesitated. "Actually—I don't. I ditched them at the airport. I'm all alone in the big, bad world. And I'm loving it. Got a short, dark wig in my bag."

Raising her brow, Felicia exhaled. "Be careful, Winner. Keep your eyes open, babe."

"Okay."

"Thanks. Bye, Win."

As her screen went blank, Winner ended the call. Disturbed, she drained the dregs of her smoothie and buckled her seat belt.

So, Daddy's back.

She watched as the flight attendant prepared for landing at the Key Largo airport. She handed him her empty glass.

Is he coming home?

As the plane touched down, Winner felt frightened. She would take some more meds in the airport bathroom, don the black wig, and leave the real world behind. Soon she would be kissing her hairy, hard-bodied lover, pressing her pelvis to his . . . in just a few, short minutes . . .

Touch down.

Chapter Three

At the Demming home in Naples, Poppy was preparing to make a phone call of her own. She was about to phone Heston's attorney. She needed to get in touch with her husband. It was time to talk.

Seventy-two hours had passed since her first husband, James Talbot, had texted her, asking for a date. Finally, she had agreed to meet Jim at the Starfish Grille, a fish-tank filled eatery located in the upscale Waterside Shoppes. Over drinks and dinner, to Poppy's surprise, Jim had declared his intention to woo her. He was still in love with her, he confessed, and always would be. He had forgiven her for leaving him, he said. Although unsure of her own feelings, Poppy had returned home that night invigorated and empowered. Incredibly, instantaneously, she had become a desirable woman again, one pursued by an eligible widower, albeit a dull one.

This morning, phone in hand, she was seated at the breakfast table. Nearby, in the kitchen, Lissette, was crooning at the top of her lungs, singing while scouring the double sink. It was obvious that Lissette's daughter had not inherited her mother's voice. Cupping her own ears, Poppy grimaced. "Shhh!" As silence fell, she looked at her phone. It rang. The caller's name was not listed on the screen.

Poppy answered. A familiar accent rattled her eardrums. "Inez Vega speaking. Is this Poppy?"

"Hello, Inez." *You psychotic harridan.* She switched on the speaker phone.

Inez's voice filled the room. "Poppy, dear. It's been ages. What's new? I thought, perhaps, you might be thinking of selling your house?"

Poppy played coy. "Which house?"

Inez laughed. "Well, I'm open. But I was referring to your Port Royal place—on Galleon Drive."

Cruelly, Poppy toyed with the eager real-estate broker. "This house? Why? Interested in listing it?"

"Well, darling, I—might be. Suppose we start with a market analysis. How's the property holding up?" Inez sounded vulnerable. It had been years since her return from the mental hospital.

Relenting, Poppy retracted her claws. "Honestly? We had plumbing problems at Thanksgiving, when all the kids were here. Workers in and out. Otherwise, fine." Intent, she refused to meet the concerned eyes of Lissette, who now stood over her, arms barred at chest level, toes tapping insistently.

Ignoring the bad vibrations, Poppy responded to the broker's question "Sure, Inez. Why not? Do it."

"No!" hissed Lissette.

"Do the market analysis." Rising from the table and walking into the kitchen, Poppy focused on Inez's gooey prattle. The experienced negotiator hemmed and hawed. "All right, Poppy. I will. Depending on the outcome of my market analysis, I might be persuaded to take your listing—if it seems worth my while— although I am quite busy at the moment. Frankly, I half expected you to call me."

Poppy frowned. "You did? Why?"

"Honestly? I had a hunch you might want to sell the place. I assumed you and Heston were divorcing—finally. Thought I'd save the trouble and get the ball rolling myself."

"Why did she assume that?" Lissette whispered hoarsely.

Just then, the front-gate bell sounded. Lissette went to view the security monitor. "Right on time," she called to Poppy. "Your hairdresser is here."

Quickly, Poppy addressed Inez. "Why did you assume that Heston and I are divorcing?"

Inez's snide attitude became visceral. "Well, dear, because—Heston's back—and he looks as dashing as ever, I must say."

"Back?"

"Yes. Heston has resurfaced. Didn't you know?"

"How do you know, Inez? You've seen him?"

"Not in person. But his handsome face is plastered all over the morning news. And I spoke to his lawyer this very morning. Hess is showing his age, but he looks distinguished."

"You what? Did the attorney tell you Heston was divorcing me?"

"Well, not in so many words, but—"

Poppy was speechless.

Inez tore flesh. "You see, I phoned Heston's attorney. He didn't phone me."

"Okay, Inez. I'll bite. Why did you phone Heston's attorney?"

"Because, dear, I presented an offer from a buyer. This buyer made an offer on Heart of Fire Key. I'm waiting, right now, to hear from Heston himself. Literally, as we speak."

Flabbergasted, Poppy croaked the words. "Heston listed the island for sale?"

"Not exactly." Inez coughed. "But, sweetie, I certainly hope he will—with me."

"So, you'll receive two commissions, right?"

"Realtors call it a home run." Sniffling, Inez blurted out, "The offer includes that old tub of a sailboat Heston cherishes so much. What's it called—the *Spindrift?*"

Poppy bristled. "You mean, his sailing yacht, *Windswept?*" *The one you snuck aboard when you tried to assassinate him.*

35

"Yes. That's the one. My buyer's offer is contingent. They want the old tub thrown in. Non-negotiable."

"Go figure." Poppy was becoming agitated. "Maybe the buyer is a big fan of Heston's. Maybe they want to own a piece of his life. So many people do. People like you."

Inez retaliated. "Confess the truth, Poppy. You don't care if Heston sells that island or not."

"I don't?"

"No. A little bird told me you hadn't wanted any part of that place—after, well—all the bad memories: Winner's kidnapping, Kipp's death and all. Your youngest boy shooting the bad guy and all that jazz."

"Yes, Inez. I know what happened," said Poppy, voice low. "I was there." *Almost.*

"We have that in common, you and I. We both buried a son of Heston's."

For a split second, Inez sounded almost human. Unable to respond, Poppy watched as Lissette ushered the stylist into the kitchen. Eager to staunch the bloodletting, Poppy purred guardedly. "Inez, so sorry. I have an appointment. Keep in touch, will you—."

Inez seized control. "One more thing, Poppy—about Heston. I believe—he may have realized that, well—he still has feelings—for *me.*"

Poppy's heart thumped. "What makes you think that, Inez?"

"Well, for weeks now, he's been sending flower arrangements to Franco's gravesite."

"He has?"

"Yes. And they all say, 'Our beloved son.' The one that came yesterday said more. It said, "Rest in peace, beloved son. The wrong done you will be undone." Isn't that sweet? Heston must have sent them. Who else? I'm going to thank him as soon as—"

Conflicted, Poppy wavered. "Heston did love Franco, Inez. He always felt guilty about causing the boy's death—even though it was an accident. But I don't understand the part about undoing the wrong. Do you?"

A beat of silence followed.

"Listen, Inez—"

"Can't. Sorry."

"Huh?"

"Adios. Incoming call. I'll be in touch."

Poppy's phone went dead. Numb, she dropped the device onto the kitchen table.

"Come on," she said off-handedly to the waiting hairdresser, leading her towards the master suite. Once again, the phone rang.

"Grab that, will you?" she said to the hairdresser.

Obliging, the hairdresser handed her the phone. Poppy stared at the screen, astonished. Then she waved frantically at Lissette, beckoning her, as the ringing continued.

Rapidly, Lissette approached. Poppy thrust the phone in her face. "Okay, Lissy. You don't believe I'll ask Heston for a divorce?"

"Que—?" Agog, Lissette read aloud the caller's name: "Heston Demming."

"Shall I wait in another room?" the hairdresser inquired discreetly.

"Don't move," Poppy barked, accepting the call. "Hello? Heston?" she snarled into the phone.

"Hello, Poppy. I—"

At the sound of his deep voice, her heart palpitated. "Heston Demming, I want a divorce."

Placing a hand over the phone's mouthpiece, she barred her teeth at Lissette, who was lingering in the doorway. "Howdaya like them potatoes?" Poppy whispered triumphantly.

Lips pursed, Lissette slunk away, shaking her head in disapproval. Embarrassed, the hairdresser followed in Lissette's footsteps, as Poppy resumed the phone conversation with Heston.

***

On Key Largo, Winner waited, stranded at the airport. Damian had not come to meet her. Nor had he answered her phone messages. After waiting a solid hour, she decided to act on her own.

In masquerade, and armed with fake ID, she managed to rent a car. With the help of the car's GPS, she located the Silver Cypress Club condominium development, where Damian both lived and worked. She had been to Damian's condo before. She knew he kept a spare key hidden under a ceramic planter filled with succulents. She parked the car. Found the right door. Knocked. No answer. She located the planter.

The door key was there for her, even if Damian was not. She let herself in. Quietly, she cried.

An hour later, she found herself waiting impatiently on the tiny lanai of Damian's studio-apartment condo. She was languishing in the heat. Her bare legs dangled over the armrest of a patio chair. Shielding her fair skin from the intense rays of the South-Florida sun, a bamboo shade flapped against the screen enclosure surrounding the lanai. Warm wind gusted sporadically.

Her phone rang. *Not Damian's ring tone.* She answered. "Hello."

Ezra Gold's familiar voice greeted her. "Winnie. Got a shocker for you, babe. Sit down."

"I am sitting down. I know he's back, Ezra. I heard."

The edge left Ezra's voice. "Okay. What you don't know is that Heston just phoned me."

"He phoned you?"

"Yeah. He asked about you."

"I don't care if did or not."

"Well, he did. And guess what? I asked him to play the role of the professor in our series pilot."

"You what?"

"He turned me down. So now I want you to ask him."

"I don't want to ask him."

"Do it anyway, will you, kiddo? Look, this wasn't my idea. It was Hailey's, and she's our backer. Adair agrees with her. Money talks. So do contracts."

"Oh. I get it."

"Excellent. I'm going down in the *Lady V 2* this afternoon. Nick's going with me. To Heart of Fire Key. Heston's there now but keep it under your hat."

"Okay." Resigned, she agreed to contact her father.

Relieved, Ezra gave her the private phone number of her father's mobile phone and rang off. Sullen, Winner composed a text message to the man she had not seen in four years. So intense was her concentration that she almost forgot the oppressiveness of the midday heat and humidity. At last, her composition completed, she re-read her text message prior to sending it:

> Hello Father,
> Please play the professor in our pilot.
> Our first cast table read will be Monday in Orlando. BTW
> I'm throwing a party there Saturday night. You're invited.
> Regards,
> Winston Demming (your daughter, in case you don't remember me)

Less than enthused, she fired off the text to her father. Secretly, she hoped he received it and would reply, although, she told herself, she didn't really care anymore what her dad did or didn't do. Obviously, he had stopped loving her long ago.

A thought crossed her mind.

I wonder if Poppy knows that Daddy's come out of hiding. Should I phone her?

Her decision made, Winner dropped the tablet into her designer bag. Perspiring in the muggy, afternoon heat, she was growing tired and edgy. A serious chat with Poppy would be too intense at the moment. The sudden shock of her father's return—along with Damian's indifference and neglect—and the heat—had left her emotionally exhausted. She couldn't face confronting Poppy with the news.

Not right now.

The effect of the meds Winner had taken in the Largo airport bathroom was wearing off. Worse, she missed her security team. At least those guys would have kept her company. Although grown men, they had reacted like babies when she'd ditched them at the Miami airport. Rolling her eyes, she sighed. She hated making scenes in public, almost as much as she hated waiting.

Stardom is a crazy, lonesome bitch.

Retrieving her tablet, she launched the application for entertainment news. Unable to staunch her growing curiosity, she viewed various videos of her famous father's triumphant "return." Checking his official fan gage on the Internet, she started to believe. He was back, all right. The site's webmaster, Cecily Hodges, wouldn't post lies.

Winner studied the large head shot dominating the screen. All she knew, was that this man—her father—had walked out of her life cold— out of all their lives—and now, poof! He was back, like magic. Only he looked older. He was still in shape, though. She would give him that much. The old man hadn't let himself go.

There's hope for me yet.

She knew that, as a beauty queen, the life expectancy of her career was short. Not that age mattered to her. It didn't. Damian was 25 years older than she was.

Her anxiety accelerated.

Perspiring, she fumbled through the contents of her bag and fished out a tube of strawberry lip gloss. The melted gloss had become a sticky goo. "Ew!" She grimaced, applying it to her lips anyway, but it was gross. Clicking her tongue in disgust, she closed the tube and tossed it back into her bag.

Ten more minutes and I'm out of here.

Although her lips were sticky, the inside of her mouth was dry. Was there bottled water inside the apartment? Perhaps—

Lazily, she tapped the heels of her stiletto pumps against the Mexican floor-tiles. Maybe she should wait a little longer. Damian was always late—but, she reminded herself, *El Tigre* was worth waiting for. Damian Velasquez was the sexiest guy on the planet. Definitely hotter than that ridiculous Adair Champlain, her new leading man. Adair was convinced *he* was the world's sexiest man. His sister was convinced of it, too.

Not a chance. My buff tennis pro is the world's hunkiest hunk.
And he loves me—for me, not for my image.

So, why couldn't she shake the feeling that something was wrong— somewhere? It was all Tropica's fault. She had the planted the idea.

Stop it. It's just nerves.

Or sexual tension. Velasquez was the only man in the world who kept her waiting like this. Everyone else jumped to do her bidding. Rising from the rickety lounge chair, she groaned. Petulant, she paced the chipped floor tiles of the lanai. Clutching her tablet, she considered phoning Damian again. What if something had happened to him? What if he were injured? Torn, she rested the device against her chin.

It will piss him off.

She decided against phoning her fiancé. Nagging was a no-no. She had seen Damian angry once. Once was enough. She did not need any more drama—or pain—in her life. All she wanted was a passionate love life—and the privacy to enjoy it. That was another problem with stardom. It brought lunatics out of the woodwork.

Earlier that day, at the Miami airport, her security people had warned her about the dangers she faced without them—from criminals and obsessive fans and opportunists and fortune hunters—simply because she was a popular celebrity—and wealthy. No one knew that better than she did, but she was sick of living in fear. She'd had to get away from them. They were smothering her.

Why couldn't she have a few days to herself? It wasn't fair. Once her engagement went public, she might just chuck her entire career. She hadn't confessed that, not even to her childhood shrink.

Speaking of which—

Groping inside her purse, Winner located the pill bottle and clasped hold of it. Opening the bottle, she tapped two capsules into her palm and swallowed them dry, expertly. She could handle things. She'd even stopped seeing the shrink—but nobody knew that, either. Uneasy, she glanced around the half-shaded lanai. The breeze felt refreshing, but not refreshing enough.

The pills stuck to her tongue.

Water.

Rising, purse in hand, she smoothed her dress and strode through the back door into the air-conditioned interior of Damian's studio apartment. Opening the fridge, she located a bottle of water and opened it. Sipping, she found relief as the pills went down. Leaning against the counter, she took in her surroundings.

Definitely, a man's place. *A bachelor pad,* as Ezra would say. He was always quoting old movies. No doubt about it, Damian's one room was a mess. Yet the familiar scent of cigars and spearmint, mingled with sweat, aroused her, as did the sight of the unmade bed. So, weirdly, did the disorder of the sloppy room. Obviously, Damian needed looking after.

And I'm the woman for the job. He needs me.

Glancing around, she shook out her hair and snorted in contempt. The man she married wouldn't live like this for long. She rifled through his jumbled closet. Or dress like this.

Once we're married—

Suddenly, a latch clicked. Startled by the sound, Winner whirled around, facing the front door.

"Damian? Is that you?"

She listened. All was still. Had she really heard someone at the door? Or had the sound come from *inside* the unit?

"Damian? Are you in here?" Her gaze roamed the room as she set down her purse and inched towards the door. A thought occurred to her.

What if it isn't Damian?

The unit had been empty when she'd arrived an hour ago. So she had assumed. Now, sensing movement in the room, she tingled, looking around.

"Damian? Tiger? Is that you?" she sang out playfully.

A muscular arm encircled her neck, choking her, cutting off her wind.

***

Heston still couldn't believe it.

Poppy wants to divorce me . . ..

Alone on his private island, Heart of Fire Key, he gazed at the ruins of the island's old chapel. To him, the crumbled walls symbolized his entire life. Turning, he stared down a desolate stretch of the heart-shaped island's tropical shoreline. He felt as if he were staring at a blank canvas.

Now what?

Squatting in the sugary beach sand, he braced his sunburned fore-arms—thatched with salt-and-pepper hairs—atop his bare knees. In his right, hand, he clutched an unopened, sand-coated bottle of scotch, which he had unearthed, five minutes earlier, from beneath a small coral monolith near the shore. The newspaper swathing the bottle stank of decay. The bottle itself was the last remnant of his hidden horde. It was very old.

Absorbing the shock of his wife's words, he grappled both with an-ger and a sense of futility. Montsey's death in Nashville had hit him hard, but Poppy's total rejection of him had finished him off. He wanted to kill the whole world, and then die, himself.

His thoughts floated back to Montsey—and her death in Nashville. He had not arrived at the hospice in time to speak to her. She had died an hour before he'd shown up. There had been no good-byes. No fare-thee-wells. Montserrat Flynn had died as she had lived, oblivious to his emotions.

Squatting, he felt the heat of the late-afternoon sun on his back. On hands and knees, he crawled into the shade of a nearby slab or coral and sat. Surrounded by the dilapidated walls of the island's small church, which he had once used as a family theater, he contemplated his options, methodically.

He was working to remain sane. Seeking relief, he pressed his spine against the cool slab. Seeking order and clarity, he focused on the present moment.

So, what is on my agenda for today?

After a time of quiet cogitation, he knew. Essentially, he had four big decisions to make. Mentally, he listed them, finger by finger. First, should he drink the last bottle of scotch, or not? Second, should he sell Heart-of-Fire Key, or not sell it? Third, should he accept the acting role Ezra and Winner had just offered him? Fourth, should he grant Poppy a divorce or not? Four problems to solve, in order of difficulty.

It's time to man-up. Hit 'em head on.

First, the bottle of Scotch. Should he drink it or not? He had been sober for two full years, with the help and support of Rev. Bill. Why destroy his good record? But was he up to facing reality? Poor Montser-rat was gone. Nothing could change that. Filled with hope of reconciliation with Poppy, he'd left Nashville only days ago, grief-stricken, and now here he was, back in his sun-saturated paradise—*yeah, right. Poppy despises me still. For lying to her so many times—*

How much she would hate me if she knew the whole truth? The whole truth behind my lies . . .

Bleary-eyed, he glanced skyward, dazzled by the huge orb of orange sun dribbling down a blue-yellow sky and spreading out in a fiery stream along the horizon. The molten gilding shimmered across the lapping surface and gave him the urge to paint.

Like all appearances, the scene was deceptive. The once-pristine body of water was now impure, toxic with unseen oil, leaked during a huge oil-rig explosion in the Gulf, a toxicity made worse by the chemicals used to disperse the oil. Still, visually, the seascape reminded him of the Mediterranean, which he had sailed on *Windswept,* in his travels prior to Nashville.

His life had been an extraordinary journey. Had it all been a waste of time?

Desperately, he fought the urge to drink alcohol. Should he contact his sponsor? Rev. Bill had phoned him yesterday, making sure he was still on the straight and narrow—

This is not Bill's decision to make. It's mine.

Angrily, Heston glared at the sun. The sun glared back at him. His morning run around the perimeter of the island had left him weary—and with weakened resolve. He longed for the freedom of his youth, the vigor—*honestly, the glory*. Only the sun itself had rivaled his own youthful majesty.

I had the world at my feet.

Now envious of—and, thus, challenged by—the sun's ageless, radiant majesty, he decided that his only superiority was the moral one. The sun could not choose. It could not act, but he could. Quickly, he opened the bottle of Scotch and poured its contents, to the last splatter, onto the ground.

Good riddance.

Aiming for a low-cruising pelican, he flung the empty bottle into the sea, where it plopped, splashing into the breaking waves. Watching, he became aware of dull roar of the gently pounding surf.

Missed again. On purpose.

Standing up, he straightened his khaki shorts and wiped the grit from his hands.

Problem Number One, solved.

Now on to his second decision. Should he sell this island to a heartless, gutless international corporation who would develop it into some grandiose tourist trap? It would be like selling a piece of his own heart. So much had happened here—good and bad. A decade earlier, the island had been his artistic haven, but he had not painted in recent years. The thought of paintings—of art—now brought back crushing memories.

Ruminating, he made a radial scan of his property, and realized: *Every inch of this infernal sandbar—is haunted.*

Here, on Heart-of-Fire Key, there could be no escape from his past. Ever. So, was he going to accept that corporation's colossal offer? Should he? Perhaps. Yet he wondered. Why was the prospective buyer offering him so much money? Far greater than market value—

It's a magnificent offer.

Whatever the reason, he had only four days left, according to the contract, to notify Inez of his decision. Happily, that first wife of his was back in the real-estate business. It was incredible, too, because Inez had once tried to shoot him to death, out of rage and jealousy. Her license reinstatement had his doing, however, a fact known to few, other than himself.

He felt he owed Inez. He did not blame her. He had caused the death of their only son, Franco.

Heston knew Inez's mental collapse had been his fault, ultimately. So, eventually, he had pulled strings on her behalf, after her recovery.

How old would Franco be today—had he lived? 27? 28?

Inez had always been a pain in the ass, but she hadn't deserved what had been done to her—or to Frankie, as she'd called the boy. Her second husband, Rogelio Vega, had been a good man. However, Rogelio's son—Inez's stepson—had been a blackguard of the first order. That guy had been in real-estate too, at one time, and a plague on their house that neither Rogelio nor Inez had merited.

What was the son's name again? David? Daniel?

Yes, that was it: Danny Vega. He had been little Sasha Bassett's brutal beau. What a loathsome pair those two had made. Cretins, both. Now Sasha was doing life in prison. Long before that incident, Danny Vega—

he was athletic—he had beaten Poppy's first husband, James Talbot, nearly to death. The cops never caught Danny, though. Danny Vega had escaped, apparently eluding the law for years.

Last I heard, Danny Vega was still at large. Like Winner's former bodyguard.

Don't go there.

Returning to the matter at hand, Heston pondered. Why not sell? He had no problem with helping his first wife to earn a few bucks in commission. What's more, listing his property with her would allow her to get a double-dip commission. He should list it with Inez now, retroactively. Inez was getting old. She'd been a devoted mother and a hard worker. She ought to retire wealthy.

The Bard had pegged it. Life is. ' . . . but a brief candle . . .' or something like that.

His decision was suddenly made. He did not belong here on the island now. There was nothing left for him, here in this isolated, abandoned wilderness of wind-ravaged weeds. No reason to hang onto the past, good or bad. No love, nor hate, nor anything but bleakness and shadow would meet him here in these ruins. He knew he could not live here alone again.

Not like this.

Inwardly, he was not the same man who had purchased the island. That man had been in the prime of life—in love with his wife, his family, his work—and with himself. But time and experience had marred him since then.

Outwardly, he now appeared to be his dapper self again. His beard had been clipped; his hair, shorn. His resort wear was freshly pressed and of the highest quality. His expensive toys, including *Windswept,* and his stable of vintage European sports cars, were in working order. He'd even had a job offer—from his own daughter, albeit. He was ready to move on from Heart of Fire Key—and all it had meant to him, Originally, he had purchased the island for Poppy, as a Valentine's Day gift. She hadn't wanted it. Now she didn't want him.

Involuntarily, his thoughts returned to the distant past, to events which had taken place on the island. Vividly, he recalled the violent scene which had unfolded on this very ground seven years earlier. Unconsciously, he whispered something like a prayer for his eldest son, Kipp, and for his grandson, Shawnee, and for bossy, little Beryl.

Only I know the truth behind those events . . .

Seven years earlier, Kipp, Shawnee, and the Demming family's British nanny, Beryl Northgate, had been presumed by the international media to be lost—lost in a plane crash in the Bermuda Triangle, after taking off in a seaplane from this very spot. They had been lost to the world, but not lost to him. For Heston, the trio were alive and well, even now. Yet he felt a stab of remorse. Guilt. For he had allowed Poppy to suffer all these years. He'd had to make a difficult choice. Had he made the right one?

What would Poppy say if she knew the truth?

Bah! The point was moot. His wife would never learn the truth now, certainly not from him. He knew he would never be able to face her with it. Eight years ago, Poppy had left him because of his lies, his web of deceit, his inability to tell fact from fiction—a professional hazard for actors—even though his only motivation had been to protect her. Knowledge of the truth about Kipp, Shawnee, and Beryl might make her homicidal.

Blast it!

Fighting tears, he punched the palm of his hand. Decision Number Two was made. He would sell the island. Vacate this ancient rock.

Two decisions down, two to go.

49

Shaking the pain from his hand, he moved on to Problem Number Three—the prospect of his making a career comeback. He had to admit it. Ladybug's cold email had wounded his heart.

He had not yet replied. He had not seen his glamorous teen-aged daughter in two years. He knew she was fast becoming an icon of her generation, and he knew why. He had seen photographs of her. While traveling abroad, he'd seen a publicity layout of hers, in some third world-country magazine.

Her beauty was extraordinary. She had become a stunner— grown-up, stylish, and sophisticated, but wild—and deep down, he knew in his heart, sweet and unassuming. Her could see traces of his mother, Kay, in Winston, as well as the influence of his own crazy father.

But Ladybug looked too much like her own mother, Maude. Worse, he could see himself in Winner, too—and he didn't know which inheritance was scarier—for Win's sake, poor kid.

Now, suddenly, here was his beautiful child, sending him a half-assed request to join her on the set of Gold's new series pilot. Heston winced.

TV series? Face it, Demming. You're a snob.

Heston looked around, scanning a semi-circle of choppy sea at hazy sunset. He scoffed at his own folly. What else was he planning to do with the rest of his life?

I'm a snob without a job.

Perhaps Ladybug was reaching out to him in the only way she knew how, although he sensed Gold's manipulative hand in her invitation. How to respond? What to reply?

'What's up, Ladybug? How's tricks?'

Heston rubbed his throat. His fingers lingered, nudging his own loose flesh, feeling for the reassuring squareness of his jawbone. Despair watered his eyes. No wonder Poppy wanted a divorce.

Once upon a time, I was a perfect physical specimen. Not everyone can make that claim.

Now he was an old-timer—and still searching. He had found a path and followed it. He was still following it because—

Something vital was missing from his understanding of life. What was the great secret he had overlooked? Hadn't he become what society deemed a success?

Professionally, yes. Financially, yes. Personally? Well, I went forth and multiplied. Other than that, it's been pretty much a fiasco. Which is why I went out searching for . . .

He stared into a flaming sky. He had been searching for so long now.

What was his score in life? Was he a great success? Or was he a dismal failure? Both? Neither? Did it matter? He thought about the roles had played—great men doing great deeds, some of them.

Who would I have been if I hadn't become an actor? Who the hell am I now? What if I had chosen a profession in which I'd actually DONE something, instead of pretending to do things. What MIGHT I have accomplished on this earth? What am I supposed to do now?

Now that I'm too old to be the idol of millions?

An odd sensation came over him—a conviction. His flesh tingled. The answer was *coming.*

He could sense it. It was out there, somewhere, just beyond horizon's edge, right behind the setting sun. A feeling of becoming had been with him for years. Now he felt a portending. This feeling was new. Was this new feeling ominous or pregnant with possibility? He couldn't tell, it was so vague; disturbing, yet fecund.

Whatever the answer was, it was *spiritual.*

He heard a distant engine. Vexed, he exhaled, his body on alert. Disgruntled, he shook the sand from his beat-up leather deck shoes. He looked southward, towards the coast. Filtered by amber haze, the shiny cabin-cruiser *Lady-V 2* was approaching the far end of the island's long dock, her white bow splitting the shimmering seawater.

As promised, Ezra Gold was arriving—apparently with his old friend, Nick Townsend in tow. Smiling, Nick—a balding, African American G-man, recently retired—waved at Heston from the *Lady V 2's* trim stern, as Ezra brought her alongside the dock.

Bringing Nick along had been a shrewd move on Ezra's part. However, not even the silver-tongued Nicholas Townsend could talk him into doing a series, daughter or no daughter.

I am a movie star.

Resolved, Heston shook his head in defiance. Armed with resistance, he trudged down to the beach, towards the long, wooden dock. He stopped in his tracks.

He had made up his mind—to refuse Ezra's offer.

No matter what shenanigans Ezra tries to pull, I will not star in an episodic series.

Now only one question remained.

How do I handle Poppy's demand for a divorce?

And only one answer:

By refusing it, that's how. I'm damned if I'll let her go. I'll win back Poppy's love—and her admiration—even if it kills me. Suitors be cursed.

But first he'd give Ezra and Nick the bad news.

Chapter Four

Winner clutched at the strong arm choking her neck. With both her hands, she grasped the arm and thrust it upwards, over her head and jumped away, escaping. Whipping around, she heard familiar throaty laughter. Quietly circling, the swarthy man came up behind her. Gently, this time, his muscular arms enfolded her. His callused right hand found her tender left breast, cupping it possessively.

"Gotcha," he said seductively, squeezing gently. "Miss Tae Kwon Do."

"You scared the life out of me," she said, not moving, relishing his touch, his scent, his warmth. "Where were you hiding?"

"Behind the bamboo screen."

"Oh."

"I was teasing you. You're so easy, Winner." Damian embraced her tenderly, his hands roaming her torso. Melting, her body became pliant. Terror turned to delight. She let Damian wrestle her onto the couch. He dropped his weight on top of her belly. His dark eyes mocked her openly.

Catching her left wrist, he pinned it down against the cushion. She did not resist. Slowly, he opened her hand, finger by finger, as if her fingers were the petals of a tender blossom. Gently, he wet-kissed her palm, then turned her hand over and kissed the back of it.

She watched him, in fascination. She felt as if she might die from her desire for him.

Fondling her ring finger, Damian focused on her diamond.

"My, what a beautiful ring you have," he teased. "The better to marry you with."

"Silly." But, freeing her hand, Winner held it aloft and wiggled her fingers, sighing as her engagement ring sparkled. *It's 12+ carats if you count the halo.*

Rolling off her, Damian reclined alongside her, closer than close. Smugly, he purred, taut and tantalizing. "Any trouble losing your goons this time?"

"No." She could intuit his feelings. Silently, he was taking credit for his woman's great pleasure. She watched him, as he unconsciously thumbed his own empty ring-finger. "We belong together, baby," he said scratchily.

Wrapping her arm around his muscular neck, Winner planted a kiss on his scarred cheek. "I love my ring Damian," she whispered into his ear. "But I love you more. I've missed you. Six weeks is a long time— when a girl's in love."

"My lady," Damian whispered, pulling her to him, his lips opening, his teasing tongue finding its warm, wet way. "My first natural blonde— I think—I won't know for certain until—" His mouth overwhelmed hers.

Moments later, she breathed, speaking as her lips lingered upon his. "First? You mean, last."

"Isn't that what I said, *chica?*"

"No."

"It's what I meant."

Coyly, she nudged his nose with hers. "It had better be."

Or I'll murder you.

She toyed with a strand of his hair. A few fascinating gray hairs sprouted along his hairline. His rugged skin was deeply tanned. She kissed the pulsing vein in his sinewy neck. "I can't wait for my family to meet you." She felt his whole body stiffen.

"Why? You need your famous daddy's okay? He released her from his embrace.

"I didn't mean him. I meant the others." She fell back, disconcerted. "I guess you heard. He's turned up again?"

"Who hasn't heard?"

"My dad's had a lot of problems—"

Damian squirmed. "Sure he has. He's rich. Buff. Handsome. Talented. Women for the taking. Millions of fans. It's a hard life, eh? But somebody's got to live it, right?"

Winner recoiled. "Don't you want to meet him?"

"Maybe. Someday."

"Not now? Not before our wedding?"

"Why bother?" Eyebrow arched, he added, "Look, Win, Heston showing up like this—it's a new development. He wasn't part of our original deal, you and me. The others weren't either." He took a breath. "You heard from him?"

"Not yet." No reason to reveal her recent text.

"You expect to?"

"I suppose so." She stared at him, confused. It had never occurred to her that Damian might not want to meet her family, prior to marriage. True, Damian had refused her invitation to visit the family home in Naples at Thanksgiving, but she had assumed he would want to meet her family eventually. Her feelings were hurt. She turned the tables.

"Don't you want your family to meet me?"

"I've got no family."

Which explains why I couldn't find them—to invite them to the party. She gawked. "You think we should elope?"

He shrugged. "Yeah. Why not?"

"Damian, I want you to meet my whole family—my little brother, Dakota, and the twins, too, not just my stepmom, Poppy and Daddy if—"

Damian's eyes narrowed. He mocked her words. "Pop-py—Daddy—"

"Yeah. Even Lissette, our housekeeper. She's like one of the family. And there's Fe—I mean, Tropica." She glowered. "Is there some reason you don't want to? I don't get it."

He, too, was angry.

She could feel it. *Back off.*

"Why should I? So they can examine me—under a microscope?"

He rose from the couch and strode to the bar. He splashed Mescal into glass and gulped a swallow, then coughed.

"They'll love you!" she cried, rising on one leg, the knee of her other leg braced on the couch cushion. "That's why I want them to meet you."

He poured another drink. "Is that why?"

"It is."

"It's not so that they can pass judgment on me?"

"What?"

"Give me the official stamp of approval before you take the plunge?"

She hesitated. "Damian—"

"That's what I thought."

"If—"

He slammed his glass down onto the bar and strode to the sliding glass doors. He stared out. "You aren't sure of me, Winner."

She dashed to his side. "I am."

"Then prove it. Marry me first. Introduce me to you family later on." He slid one arm around her waist, pulled her groin to his, and nuzzled the top of her head, liquor on his breath. "Prove your love for me."

"Damian—" Her pulse was racing.

"What, you think you're better than me? Because you're wealthy? Got a famous daddy? Because you got millions of followers on the social-media networks? Big deal. Big f-ing deal. I can get any woman I want, understand me? I don't need you, baby cakes."

Wounded, she whimpered. "Does all of that really matter so much to you? Believe me, I don't want any of it. I just want you, Damian. But I want it to be—"

"The way you want it. A fantasy wedding. Admit it."

She hedged. "Okay, look. I admit I've designed my own wedding dress! I'm having it made—"

"See?" He pushed her away. "You aren't willing to accept my terms? Then it's off."

"Off?"

"Our wedding. It's off. I'm not marrying a woman who doesn't obey—I mean, respect me."

Panic constricted Winner's throat. "Of course I respect you. I don't understand—"

He fixed his eyes on hers. "If you love me, Winner, you'll respect my wishes. I need that from my wife. If you won't respect my wishes before we're married, you won't do it after. Prove you are my woman— or this wedding is off."

Her heart was ripped open. Her desire for him overpowered reason. She collapsed against his hard chest. "I love you, Damian Velasquez. I'll do whatever you ask."

He lifted her face. Playfully, he slapped her cheek.

She flinched but did not protest. Her cheek was stinging.

Relenting, he embraced her affectionately, squeezing her waist softly. "You are my woman?"

"I am your woman."

He yanked her towards the couch, cast her down onto the cushions, and fell solidly on top of her. "Say it again," he rasped, his breath hot with Mescal. He kissed her deeply, intrusively.

Overwhelmed, she savored him. "I am your woman."

"Then let's get married."

"Whenever you say." She felt loose and pliant as a strawberry mousse.

He grinned. "What's wrong with now?"

She wiggled. "Right now? In this outfit?"

"Oh! Hah!" Damian laughed deeply, rolling off her, holding his sides. "Women!"

"What's so funny, please? You think I'm being superficial." Incensed, she hopped up, placing a fist on each of her hips. Fashion was everything to her, and he knew it. "I have a serious side, you know. I care about the environment—and other stuff."

"Corazon." He pulled her back down onto his chest. His lips traced her throat, collarbone, shoulder "You—are—exciting—so—so innocent. I adore you. I worship—at your altar." His white teeth nipped at the nipple sheathed by her silk bra. His hand slid up her leg. His lips grazed her abdomen.

She gasped in fear and pleasure. "Damian, please." She pushed at his strong, insistent hand. His wet fingers interlaced hers. He extracted his hand.

Reluctantly, he rolled off her. "I know. I know. You want to wait."

"Yes." She flushed hot, confused, breathless. She swallowed hard and rose, fumbling to straighten her clothes.

He rose, too, and embraced her tenderly. "That's why I want to marry you, Winston."

She clung to his solid chest. "I do want to please you."

"In time, my love. We will make love in ways you have never even imagined. I promise you. You will please me over and over and over again, to your heart's content."

She quivered. Her fingers toyed with the collar of his athletic shirt. "I want to have your babies."

Damian rolled his eyes. "You will."

"I know you think I'm acting like a kid. You're so much more experienced than I am—"

"I like it that way." He smiled sweetly, his dark eyes soft and baiting. "They don't call me *El Tigre* for nothing. I's not only because of the tattoo on my back."

She sighed as he moved away. She ached for him.

He stopped at the door and turned back to look at her. "Let's get married next week. In Cancun."

She genuinely wanted to please him. "I can't. We start rehearsals on Monday. Maybe you and I should wait—until we have more time to spend together—"

He ignited. "Excuses! More of your BS, Winner." He grasped her upper arm. "I don't think you want to marry me."

She whined. "I want to be your wife more than anything in the world."

His breath singed her ear. "Then your wish is my command, *Senorita* Demming. Mind what I say, and you will become *Senora Velasquez.*"

Wincing in pain, she answered tensely, "It's the money, Damian. I've signed a contract. If I don't show up—or if I blow off the gig—

He thought for a moment and released her arm. "Okay. Okay. We'll wait. But not a word to anybody. You understand me?"

"Yes, sir," she lied, worried as he ambled away.

He spoke over his shoulder. "Hey, I left my equipment on the bench by the fountain. Back in a sec." His lips tossed her an air kiss. She returned it. Worried, she watched him slip out the glass doors and trot down the sidewalk leading to the tennis courts

I would do anything for you, Damian—anything. Except cancel the party. It's too late for that.

She shuddered. What would Damian do when he discovered her deception? Would he forgive her? Everything was arranged—and already under way. It was too late to cancel. She had invited everyone she cared about—except for her childhood psychiatrist, but she didn't want him there. He wouldn't understand Damian's power over her.

"Winston, you can do better than a third-rate tennis pro," Doc would say. "You're degrading yourself." She could just hear him now. "The relationship is toxic. The jerk slapped you, for crying out loud. That's a warning sign, Win. How many times have we discussed this? Stay out of abusive relationships—of any kind. Remember what I told you? It's all about self-respect. Yours." No, her shrink just wouldn't get it.

But I do. I'm in love.

She was proud of landing Damian Velasquez. *El Tigre.* How many other girls had tried? How many women had Damian had? She was dying to know, but he wouldn't tell her anything about his past. It had been that way, ever since they'd first met at that bar in Playa del Carmen two months earlier.

For her, it had been love at first sight. She felt as if she had known Damian all her life. He was so much older and more worldly than she was. And this concerned her. What if she couldn't measure up to his expectations in bed? Would he understand? Teach her, like any good husband?

She hoped she was doing the right thing by accepting his terms and waiting to have sex with him. She wanted him to believe she was a virgin. On their very first date, Damian had told her how important virginity was to him. She couldn't let him know about the indiscretions of her adolescence, especially the ones with her first bodyguard—her kidnapper—six years ago. Ram had been her lover, but she had chosen to please him, if only to stay alive. That man would have raped and killed her, otherwise. She knew that then and she knew it now. Her father had known it back then, too. It had taken her years—years of therapy—to recover from that ordeal, once combined with the abuse she'd suffered in childhood. After her brother, Dakota, had shot him, her bodyguard had disappeared into the ocean and never resurfaced.

Had her kidnapper drowned in the sea, that fateful day on Heart of Fire Key—or escaped? To this day, neither she, nor anyone else, knew whether the man was still alive. He'd be older now, too.

A general ring tone sounded from her tablet-phone. Automatically, she located the device.

Is it Daddy? Replying to my email?

Eagerly, she read the new text message on her screen. Horrified, she dropped the device onto the floor. Her ancient terror rose like a mummy released from a sarcophagus.

That sickening message hadn't come from Daddy—unless Daddy had morphed into a monster.

***

As *Lady V 2* approached the lengthy dock, which jutted out from Heart of Fire Key into deep water, her droning engines died. Against the backdrop of sunset, her brilliant white fiberglass gleamed prettily. Watching from the beach, Heston cupped his hands around his mouth.

"Go home!" he bellowed from his diaphragm. "Save yourselves the trouble! I won't do it!"

In the twilight, he watched in vain, as two men, one white and one black, moored the gleaming_cabin cruiser alongside his own weary 56-foot sailing vessel. After *Windswept's* recent short journey from Fort Lauderdale, where she had been in dry dock, she now rested snugly at the far end of the long, planked walkway, which jutted out into deep sea.

Aboard *Lady V 2*, Ezra Gold spotted Heston and waved. His buddy, Nick Townsend, tied a mooring line. Both men appeared jovial. Each looked older than Heston remembered. Ezra was 36 or 37 now; Nick, in his 60s or 70s? It didn't matter. Both men needed to depart.

Annoyed, Heston anchored his hands on his hips, unwilling to greet the visitors, shake their hands, unwilling even to entertain the ridiculous notion that he should resume his acting career. He had abandoned show business on purpose. Nothing they, nor Ladybug, could say would convince him to return. He loved his daughter, but he too old for playing childhood games of pretend—like acting.

He didn't want to make the career comeback they were offering him. He felt a TV series was beneath him. Indignant, he stroked his clipped beard. *Can't blame them for asking, I suppose.*

He knew, that—even at his age—he looked better on his worst day than most people did on their best. *Ho hum. Fact, not vanity.* But it wasn't good *enough.* In his youth, he had been a world-class male beauty, the idol of millions. Because of it, for two decades—in his 20s and 30s— he had been an international superstar—until life had gone wrong—until his consciousness had evolved—grown up.

He was uncomfortable now with the fact that he had modeled so many wrong behaviors—for public consumption— committed what Bill would have called 'sins' on film. In sermons to the homeless in Nashville, Rev. Bill had defined 'sin' as a Greek archery term that means 'missing the mark.'

Bill had told his congregation that sin is really an error in judgment, an act which seems good at the time, but which leads to death and destruction in the end—acts of lust, gluttony, sloth, envy—what were the other three again? Much like what he, Kipp, and Perfecto Logue had discussed in Santa Domingo that time. But wasn't this viewpoint too simple? Surely, there was something more, not yet revealed.

Whatever his sins were, he had committed them all on screen, during his years as an actor—for money. He had committed many off-screen, as well, but those were his own private affair. He wanted to put those years—and those pretend acts of violence, promiscuity, lying, cheating, drug-dealing, and mayhem, that evil trash had made him wealthy and world-famous—and in need of absolution—he wanted to put all of it behind him, not continue on with it, corrupting a new generation of fans.

Nowadays he longed to influence people for good, rather than bad. But the entertainment industry did not allow its human commodities to have a conscience. It hadn't in his day, and, as far as he could tell, it didn't today. To be a player meant to be a purveyor of vice to the masses. Now he was being asked to take up where he'd left off years earlier, several notches down.

Even if I did make a comeback someday, it wouldn't be in TV series, Unless the part were really, really good, really outstanding. It would have to be—

"Heston, old buddy." Ezra Gold climbed out of the *Lady V 2* and stepped onto the dock. "Sweet little island you got here." Approaching Heston, Ezra slapped him on the back and offered a handshake. "Great to see you. Been a while, man." Up close, Ezra *had* matured. Wisps of dark hair straggled from beneath his Yankees cap, which neatly hid his receding hairline. His jawline was still tight, but his crow's feet had hatched. Obviously, a man of means, Ezra was well-dressed. His boating attire was hip, casual, and costly. His resemblance to his mother—who, until her death, had been Heston's theatrical agent—was pronounced, his facial features regular and pleasing. His bright, brown eyes belied contact lenses, but his charming smile was infections.

"We've been trying to find you for a long time," said Nick Townsend, the sturdy, now bald African-American senior citizen clad in navy shorts who followed Ezra up the long dock. "What've you been doing with yourself, Heston?"

Deadpan, Heston eyed Nick, his old fishing buddy. "Been thinking about growing a beard." He wiggled his chin mischievously and set a hard countenance.

Nick feigned fierceness. "Well, when you going to start doing it?" Seemingly hostile, the retired FBI agent locked eyes with him.

A mock eye-duel ensued. Heston did not smile. Neither did Nick, although his lips twitched significantly.

Amused, Ezra cracked up. "You guys."

Nick's fierce expression collapsed into a grin. "Shit."

Snickering, Ezra tugged at Heston's short facial hair and yanked him by the arm. Wheeling him around, he wrapped Heston's shoulders with a friendly arm. "You're expecting us, right?"

Squirming, Heston nodded. "Winner texted me. But you're wasting your time."

"The hell you say," Ezra balked. "You're a born star, man. You've still got your hair." He tapped the bill of his cap. "Something not all of us can say."

"You always had a fine head of hair, Heston." Nick gripped Heston's hand and shook it. "Plugs here is envious."

Heston glowered, refusing to be amiable. "But now it's gray."

Ezra studied him in the dim evening light. "Just at the temples."

Heston snorted. "Please. Do not insult my intelligence with that 'distinguished' claptrap."

"Ever heard of hair dye?" Nick ran a hand over his own glossy pate. "They make beard dye, too, now. So they tell me."

Heston chuckled, in spite of himself. "Fat lot you know about it, Slick." Nicholas Townsend had been a dear friend to him, both during and after the Gabe Cade debacle. Nick had become a fishing buddy *par excellence.* How long had it been? Four years at least since their last deep-sea expedition together, and almost six years since Nick had discovered him passed out and senseless, and had pulled him to safety, as the island's main house had gone up in flames.

"I could use a beer." Ezra indicated a caretaker's cottage, located down the shore from the dock.

Heston frowned. He was being tested. "None there. I only arrived last night." Heston pointed. "I'm camped at the cottage over there."

Ezra's head swiveled. "It's okay. We brought some."

Nick asked coolly, "You never rebuilt the main house?"

"I've learned to live without luxuries."

Nick gave him the arched eyebrow. "How the mighty . . ."

"Yes. Whatever."

"Are you alone here?" Nick sounded anxious. "Where's your security equipment? Your cameras?"

"Got none," muttered Heston. "Just satellite surveillance—of the island as a whole."

Staring at a large mound in the distance, Ezra scowled. "Wasn't your art studio inside the big house? You'd moved it from your Naples home."

Heston shrugged. "Don't need one now."

"Since when?" Nick asked.

Again, Heston shrugged. "Lately."

"You're not painting anymore? Why not? Your paintings sold."

Heston snorted. "They sold because I painted them, not because they were good paintings. I'm a mediocre painter, at best." *That's why I started the inferno.*

Lugging a heavy cooler, Ezra followed him down onto the sandy shore. "Since when do you listen to the critics?"

Heston ignored the crack. "What's in that thing?" He indicated the cooler. "The beer."

"Yeah, and—" Nick shuffled alongside him. "Your favorite food—shrimp. All set to barbeque."

The actor in him unable to resist, Heston mimicked an Australian accent. "Shrimp on the barbie." He trotted up the steps, stopping at the cottage door.

Huffing, Ezra looked askance. "You've got an outdoor grill, right, Heston?" He shifted the load and climbed the cottage steps. Nick dogged his heels.

"Used it last night," Heston said, flinging open the screen door and ushering the men inside. The door slammed shut behind the three of them. "Generator's working now." He indicated the kitchen area. "Plying me with food and drink won't change my mind. But go ahead. Give it your best shot."

***

The room was cool and dim. It had an unlived-in look about it, empty of personal belongings.

"You mean you ate something? You're skin and bones, Heston." Nick stood looking at him. "You and your daughter both."

Ezra dropped the cooler onto the kitchen counter. Opening the lid, he removed a cold six-pack.

"How is Ladybug?" Heston asked nonchalantly, eyeing the beer. "We've had only one electronic encounter, and one-way, at that. Nothing face to face yet."

"Skinny," Nick interjected.

"Fragile. Delicate," countered Ezra. "And troubled."

"About what? The usual? Maude? The Gabe Cade kidnapping?"

Ezra rubbed his eyes. "I'm not sure—yet. But something's up with her."

"Isn't she still seeing her psychiatrist?" Heston tried to sound casual.

"I think so. She was."

Nick accepted the beer Ezra offered. "Troubled about her broken home, most likely. Are you in touch with Poppy at all?"

"No," Heston lied. A knot formed in his stomach. *She hates my guts, but I aim to change that.*

Sitting down on the sofa, Ezra wiped dripping ice-water from his beer can. "Why's that?"

Heston played hurt. "Aren't you going to offer me a beer, Ezzie?"

Ezra and Nick exchanged glances.

Discreetly, Nick took his beer outside, opening the sliding glass doors and stepping onto the deck, which fronted the ocean. Night was falling. Finding a wall switch, he flicked on the porch light. The glare startled him. He shielded his eyes and then moved out of Heston's line of sight.

Inside the house, Ezra faked a smile. "Sure, Demming. Help yourself. I'll be your enabler."

"Only because you want something from me." Grasping a beer can, Heston popped it open and followed Nick out onto the deck.

Ezra trailed after him. On the deck, Nick and Ezra again exchanged glances.

"Now watch this carefully, both of you." In a theatrical gesture, Heston poured his beer over the deck railing, watering the scrub brush below. He did not want alcohol, but he needed to establish his freedom to choose.

"Bravo, Hesty," said Nick, examining the outdoor grill. " 'Cause you'd have to stop drinking—if you were to take the part."

Ezra nodded. "For the duration of the shoot. For insurance purposes." He smiled guiltily. "We had to know—what you would do."

Challenged, Heston played along. "Forget it. I'm not doing the pilot. I'm my own man. If I want a drink, I drink. If I don't, I don't." *A little bravado never hurts.*

"Too bad." Nick pursed his lips.

"Have a little faith, will you?" Heston closed his eyes. "I've learned about faith in recent years." *But it's still a mystery to me.*

***

"You should at least consider my offer, Heston." Ezra brought out his laptop computer. "I have a copy of the first script. It's right here." He tapped he device. "You can read it tonight."

Heston opened his eyes. "I told you, Gold. I'm not interested in making a 'comeback.' Man, I'm old. I'm freaking *passé.*" *I'm not perfect any more, you knucklehead!*

Wandering back inside, Nick called out, "You've been in self-exile for years now, Heston. Your fans want you back, baby."

"My fans . . ." Heston muttered, unconvinced. "Don't make me laugh," he bemoaned, melodramatically, then chuckled at his own theatrics.

Undeterred, Ezra exploded into his sales-pitch. "Yes, Heston. Your fans. They're out there. Millions of them. Big fans. Wondering where you went all those years ago. They want you back!"

Heston laughed. "They don't want me. They want the man I once was. Correction: they want the outer shell of the man I was twenty years ago. That shell has shattered."

Ezra snorted. "You're underestimating them, Heston. Your fans still love you. Your fan club members keep up your website, your social media sites. You know how many 'likes' you have? How many millions of followers? Okay, it's come down some."

"By how much?"

"Ask Cecily Hodges. She's still your webmaster, as far as I know. Running your fan club, too. I know she runs Winner's."

"Mine and Kipp's. My attorney saw to everything."

"Cool. Then you're making money hand over fist, just on your image copyrights. Your fan club has created apps and videos of your movies."

"Who cares? I don't need the money."

Ezra slapped his own forehead. "Would you wise up already? *Everybody* needs the money. Bill Gates needs the money."

"Wise up? I'm washed up."

"You're not. That's my point. You still have your looks."

"Of the more mature variety," Nick acknowledged. "Still got those cute legs, though." He double-clicked his tongue irreverently.

"Shut up."

Nick chuckled.

Ezra changed tactics. "Just think about it, Demming. No rush."

"Except that we're heading out in the morning," Nick asserted. "With or without you."

"Without me." Heston crushed the empty beer can and tossed it into the recycle bin.

Score.

Nick stared at him, disdainful. "Heston, you're going back to Orlando with us if I have to club you over the head and stick you in a gunny sack. Hear me?" Angered, the old-time G-man clattered down the steps and strode out into the sand.

"Now see what you've done?" Ezra arched his dark brows at Heston. "Between you and me, he's got a thing for Hailey Champlain. He wants to please her by reeling you in."

"What's she got to do with it?"

"Don't worry. I'll explain."

69

"Fog's rolling in," Nick shouted from the ocean's edge.

Heston sighed. His old friends meant well. Uncertain in his own mind, he left Nick to cool off on the beach and followed Ezra as he stepped back inside the caretaker's cottage.

***

"This is a great project, Demming. We've been in pre-production for a while." Ezra patted the sofa seat. "Sit down. Look at this." He brought his script file to the screen of the laptop. "Please."

Reluctantly, Heston sat down beside Ezra, who thrust the laptop into his hands. Heston studied the script's first page. *"Monster Mania?* That's your title, Gold? It's lousy."

Ezra laughed. "That was my working title. It's a joke. The official title is *The Stone of Blood*—or *Make My Stake Rare.* I haven't decided which."

Appalled, Heston glared at him.

"Lighten up, dude. That's a joke, too. The real title is *Forbidden Mysteries.* Sort of, horror meets fantasy meets sci-fi."

Heston rolled his eyes. "My daughter's involved in this crap?"

Patiently, Ezra explained, palms up. "Winner is my leading lady— the cool blonde. Her leading man is Adair Champlain. He's all the rage. He's the new you—" Ezra fell silent.

Heston squinted, one eye closed. "The new me? Is that you meant to say?"

"No." Ezra went on the offensive. "And, by the way, my script is not crap. I don't write crap."

Heston refused to let Ezra off the hook. "Gold, you mean to tell me—you cast Vivian Champlain's vapid stepson in the lead role— opposite Ladybug?"

"Why not? Adair's young. He's popular with the teens and 'tweens. He's handsome," Ezra defended, shoulders pinched, palms re-upped. "And he's edgy."

"Say it, man. He's me, twenty-five years ago."

"Touché, Heston." Nick said coolly, reentering the house through the sliding glass doors. "Most important, my man, he's the only son of a recently deceased billionaire. And he's financing us."

Heston slapped a knee. "Now it all makes sense. Follow the money."

"So, let me get this straight." Heston glared. "Adair Champlain is both series star and financial backer?"

Nick grunted. "Yes, Heston. And he—more specifically, his sister, Hailey—wants you on board," Nick clarified, dabbing his sleek dome with a handkerchief. "Savvy?"

"Oh, I understand. "

"Then try to understand Ezra's position," Nick cajoled.

"When Adair was a baby, Hailey was, sort of, 'the hand that rocked the cradle.' " Ezra said. "She holds sway over her bro." He cast a knowing glance at Nick. "Among others."

Nick ignored the jibe. "The Champlain kids love Ezzie from way back—back when he was their stepmom Viv's—uh, main squeeze."

"You're going to love 'em, Heston," Ezra noted. "Winner does. Hailey and Winner have become great pals."

"Really."

Nick pocketed the handkerchief. "They're like Mutt and Jeff."

"Stay in the 21st century, Townsend, please." Ezra sat back, completely exasperated.

" 'Curiouser and curiouser' " Heston said sarcastically, purposefully quoting a 19th-century novel. "Their old man was a world-class art collector, you know. Old Truett once tried to buy my horde of early Cedric Spicer canvases. Right after Cedric died. I told him flatly, 'No.' "

Nick laughed. "Probably pissed the old guy off. But everyone knows those paintings aren't for sale.

"Not while I'm alive." Heston said emphatically.

Ezra spoke up. "And everybody knows you hid them somewhere. But no one knows where—except you, Heston."

And Poppy. Heston replied evenly. "Cedric seduced Maude, while she and I were married. I took his works of art off the market. Permanently."

Nick eyed him. "Aw, forgive and forget, man."

"That's not the point, Nick."

"Isn't it? Now that you're enlightened?"

"I've never claimed to be enli—"

"You played that religious guy in India. They gave you another naked-statue award for Best Actor."

"Man, I was *acting*—"

"Then how come you chucked show biz right after that?" Ezra asked.

Nick stared. "All I know, Heston, is that you changed after you played that part—"

"Maybe. Maybe I just grew up." He settled back. "Now I'm passing the baton. Let the boy billionaire take his best shot—without my help."

Nick caught his eye. "He don't need your help. He's already a star. Girls love him. Adair's got it all—looks, smarts, charm, and youth—he acts peculiar, sometimes, but—"

Heston fumbled. "If you're implying that I should simply accept—"

Nick shrugged. "Time moves on. Don't have to be bitter about it."

Intercepting the ball, Ezra ran with it. "Look, man, about my offer. We're all set, money-wise. Rest assured, we're *not* paying you union scale."

"Rest assured," Heston said, cocking his head. "You're right."

Ezra's brown eyes flashed. "And, trust me, this is a great story. It's a horror story, but it's also an epic adventure—and historical. It's about a lost stone carving—Greek temples—fabulous caches of gold treasure, exotic locales. We'll be shooting locations in Athens—all around the Greek isles—"

"Greece?" Heston shook his head. "I'm tired of traveling."

Ezra dived for the save. "I exaggerated. Most of the background will be computer graphics. The bulk of the acting scenes will be shot on a sound stage—with green screen."

"Stop, please." Heston shook his head.

Ezra persevered. "Picture this: Prehistoric Grecian priests—caught up in wars of conquest, see?"

"I do not see."

Ezra made a lens-frame with his hands and looked through it, into his imagination. "We open with one lone dying oracle, a priestess who manages to save and hide the sacred codex inside a Greek vase. She buries it in a mystical grotto, see? She petitions the Greek deities to protect it, even after her death—but nobody knows about it, see, until 2,500 years later, when this beautiful American anthropology major at an Ivy League university—"

Heston rose and entered the kitchen. "Winner's role, no doubt." Searching the fridge, he located a bottle of ginger ale. "You're coaching her personally?"

Ezra flushed. "Nah. Win's doing just fine."

"Although, she could use some coaching," Nick chimed in. "To keep away the woodpeckers."

Leaning in, Ezra angled his head. "Okay, look, Dad. Between you and me, your daughter could use a little help with her acting technique. She can be a tad wooden."

"No kidding."

"As the director, I can only do so much. *Capeesh?* Heston, your expertise—your guiding hand—would be welcome. Based on your past accolades— the major acting awards you've won—"

Fidgeting, Nick balked. "Stop shoveling, Ezzie. Get on with your story. Tell the man."

Glaring at Nick, Ezra cleared his throat. "See, Winner discovers this hidden codex inside the Greek vase—and bam! All kind of hell breaks loose. Vampire spirits, and bad guys and evil museum curators. Buried galleons, pirate ships—tempests at sea—the works! Oh, it's going to be a great first season!"

"I'll bet."

"You've got to read my script, Heston." Ezra stared into space. "In Episode Five, I reveal that Winner is the priestess, reincarnated."

Heston raised a hand in protest. "Oh, I think I have the idea." Poker-faced, he pondered Ezra's words. He *could* give his daughter some valuable advice about acting. More importantly, it would give him an opportunity to become reacquainted with his eldest daughter. He looked at Ezra.

"Ezra, why horror? I no longer feel right about dwelling on the dark side. I don't think Win should, either. Nor you."

"It sells. We're in business. Remember?"

"People eat it up, Heston," said Nick. "Say, do I detect a chink in your armor?"

Heston turned to Ezra. "Winner claims she has a surprise waiting for me in Orlando. Any idea what it is?"

Nervously, Ezra shook his head. "She told me the same thing." He jabbed Heston affectionately. "Come with us and find out!"

Heston eyed him.

Sensing blood in the water, Ezra groveled. "We need you bad, Heston. And I need you to do more than just act and coach Win."

"Oh?"

"I want you to take over as producer. Little Hailey just doesn't have what it takes. I love her to death, but I'll be honest. She's the zany type—sophisticated, but silly."

"Hailey's the producer?"

Sheepishly, Ezra nodded.

Nick twitched. "Hay-Hay is an airhead. Cute as a button, though. Needs to get laid." He added drily, "Got no boyfriends that I can see. It just ain't natural."

"Knock it off, Nick." Ezra scowled. "Look, Heston, Hailey's willing to accept your help. As a matter of fact, she suggested this arrangement."

"You don't say."

"I'll give you an executive producer credit if you'll take the helm. And do the cameo." He sighed, eyes bright.

"Cameo?" cried Heston, affronted. "What's my part? I thought I would be—"

"In the pilot, you have a cameo." Ezra gnawed a lip. "Later on, your part becomes the most important re-occurring role in the story. You play the girl's father. You're an archeologist. A professor. You try to save her and the codex. Unfortunately, you get sacrificed."

Heston sneered. "And turn into a vampire?"

"More like a walking cadaver. You'd actually be featured in two scenes—in the pilot episode. After that you reoccur every third episode."

Heston faltered. "I don't have to bite Ladybug, do I?"

Grinning, Ezra shook his head. "Read my script, man."

"Well, I might. What's your log line?"

Ezra cleared his throat. "In *Forbidden Mysteries,* an epic adventure slash horror thriller slash romantic comedy, Marcia Blaine, a beautiful archeology student at Yale must save her fiancé, a handsome archeologist, from the clutches of an evil museum curator, who, with her unwitting fiancé's help, has uncovered the secret of eternal youth, in the form of an ancient Greek codex, guarded by Greek deities down through the centuries against the onslaught of an evil cult of the undead." He beamed with pride. "Well?"

Heston cowered. "Great Scott."

"See, the undead need the secret of eternal youth. Get it?" Receiving no response, Ezra pressed on. "Okay, granted, Heston. It's not the role of a lifetime. Not the way the artist Paul Gauguin was for you, ten years ago. Or the way the *'Visionary Star'* flick was for you five years ago."

"Worse, you're asking me to play third fiddle to my own daughter."

Ezra shrugged and sighed. "You might as well know the whole truth. In Season Two, Adair Champlain will be playing a young Odysseus."

"What?" Heston cried. *That should be my role!*

"Yeah. He gets transformed by the cult." Ezra pursed his lips. "And, yes, don't ask. I do recall that you played Odysseus in a film once, which is why I'm telling you. But, hey! Here's the upside. We can use that fact for publicity."

"More upside," said Nick "Now you may win an Emmy—as Best Supporting Actor."

"What for? My masticating technique?"

Ezra grimaced. "Droll, Demming. Man, I know you think doing a series is a comedown. But it's not! Not anymore. Think of it this way. It will introduce you to a whole new generation of worshippers."

Nick nodded. "See? You've found the secret of eternal youth already: reinvent yourself—and keep showing up."

Ezra drove the point home. "Heston, you've got to keep up with the times, buddy." He placed a hand over his heart. "Look it, the show is a major risk for me, too. I'm willing to take it. Take it with me. Kipp would have wanted you to." Sitting back, Ezra let his words sink in.

Heston inhaled deeply. "That's low, Gold."

Ezra sighed. "But it's true—and you know it."

"I know no such thing. You don't know how Kipp feels." Heston stopped speaking. He made a course correction. "How he felt."

Nick rose, adjusting his navy-blue shorts, and ambled to the cooler. "How 'bout Ezzie and I start dinner? You start reading, Legs. You only have twelve hours to decide. We sail for Orlando at sun-up."

Pinching the bridge of his nose, Heston lolled his head against the sofa back. "Ezra, I sold you my production company for this very reason. So I wouldn't have to be bothered by all this nonsense anymore."

"Excuses, excuses," Nick murmured. Opening a kitchen drawer, he withdrew a pair of metal tongs.

Heston cast a wary sideways glance at Nick. "What exactly is your job title?"

The tough man grinned. "Easy. I'm CEO of Security."

"Ah." Heston toyed with the laptop in his hands. "Ezra, I have one important demand."

"Shoot. pal."

"If I did throw in with you, my word would have to trump my daughter's. I assume she still has you wrapped around her pinky? You can't back her over me."

Balancing a platter of kebobs, Nick guffawed, nearly tripping, on his way out to the porch.

Face flushing, Ezra feigned innocence. "Do you really think I would do *anything so lame* - just to please Winner?"

"In a heartbeat," Nick called from the lanai. "Damn, this fog is thick!" he added.

"Like your slick head," Heston called affably.

Before Ezra could respond, Nick poked his sleek dome inside the doorway. "Say, Hesty. Is this island haunted?"

"What do you mean?"

77

"Well, I see—I think I see—a ghost ship, out here, bobbling in the fog. I can't make it out, whatever it is. Something's floating out there. Come and see."

Alert, Ezra stood up. He looked quizzically at Heston. "Are the paparazzi chasing you again, man? We did our best to keep this visit confidential."

"Not these days." Heston's throat tightened. "Possibly." Clutching the tablet, he rose from the sofa and strolled nonchalantly onto the deck outside. Nick was tending the grill.

Ezra joined them. The three men gazed into the fog.

Heston spoke first. "Since my return, the press has referred to me— as Winner Demming's father." *It used to be Kipp's.*

"You are Winner Demming's father," Nick noted. "You're also a great actor."

Ezra pointed. "Who is that out there, do you think?"

"Haven't a clue," Heston lied, heart racing. "Possibly, no one. I don't see anything. You, Gold?"

"Can't even see the ocean," Ezra replied, squinting.

The three companions peered into a dense haze. In the heavy, moist air, the aroma of sizzling shrimp, onions, mushrooms, and garlic hung, suspended. The pounding of the surf hypnotized Heston.

"Whatever it was, it's gone now," Nick said, at last.

"Probably a mirage." Turning, Heston patted Nick's shoulder.

"You've been hallucinating again," Ezra chided Nick affably.

"I tell you, I saw a boat."

"Relax, you two," said Heston, relieved. "It might have been the new buyers."

"Buyers?" Ezra and Nick asked in unison.

"Yes. I've decided to sell the island. I've had a handsome offer."

"From who?"

"International corporation."

Ezra sighed. "Well, it's the end of era." Turning his attention to dinner, he jabbed a forkful of salad greens onto his plate and into his mouth and chewed. "You're some kind of chef, you know that, Special Agent Townsend?"

Nick harrumphed. "Gold, I'm a practical man. I have practical skills," he said, accepting the compliments uneasily. "Trouble is, hanging with you flighty, artistic types—even my imagination tends to run away with me—at times."

"Like when you see ghost ships in the fog?" Ezra grinned, munching. "Hey, Heston, how much do you know about archeology professors?"

"Very little," he replied candidly. "If I did accept the role, I'd have to do research."

Eyes twinkling, Ezra raised a beer can in a smug toast to Nick, who popped open a beer can of his own. "Mmm-hmm," hummed Nick, raising his can in return.

"Don't get cocky." Recalibrating, Heston forced a smile. The threat of exposure had passed. Kipp was safe—for now. *If the ghost ship had been Kipp's sloop . . .*

Somehow, he would have to let Kipp know about his decision to sell the island.

He felt nervous and the need to take action—of some kind. Any kind.

Excusing himself, he stepped inside to the kitchen. Quickly finding his phone, he typed out a message, not to Kipp, but to Winner. *"OK, Ladybug. I'll consider it. No promises."* He hit the send key just as Nick entered the house.

"Texting your Miss June Bug?" smiled Nick, carrying a plate of shrimp kebabs in hand and offering it to Heston.

"Ladybug," Heston corrected, refusing the plate. "Told her I'd consider taking the role."

"You're not a fool, after all."

Heston bristled. "Don't call me a fool, Nicholas. I dropped out of show business because of insanity like this –this ghost-ship and stalking hoopla."

Nick looked skeptical. "That's not why and you know it."

"Why then?"

"You tell me" Nick said. "And while you're at it, tell me what the hell you've been doing for the past few years. I'd really like to know."

Exhilarated, Ezra bounced into the kitchen. He grinned at Heston. "Just got a text from Winnie. She said you agreed to consider the role."

Heston nodded. "And I will think about it, Ezra. Overnight. I'll read your blasted script and then—I'll give you my answer in the morning."

"Good enough," Ezra, beamed. "Now, will you eat a shrimp already?"

Obliging, Heston unskewered and swallowed a jumbo shrimp. "Your mother wouldn't approve of your eating shrimp, Ezzie. She kept Kosher."

"She did, indeed." Ezra, set down his plate. "May she rest in peace."

"I could use some sleep myself," said Nick, yawning.

***

Near midnight, on Heart of Fire Key, a slender figure, shrouded by foggy mist, stole silently along a broken-tiled pathway. It was a pathway leading to nowhere. It ended abruptly at the scorched foundation of the mansion that had once graced the highest point on the remote private island. Upon reaching the foundation, the figure climbed atop a mound of blackened rubble and surveyed the scene below.

Beloved Planet Ithaca. Noble fortress. I am happy to return to my kingdom.

The king surveyed his misty domain. Barely discernible, down along the shoreline, was the caretaker's cottage, its windows dark. Beyond it, more audible than visible, was the sea.

No sign of the enemy. We are safe. I hope my faithful minion will be safe, as well.

Resolved, the king shifted the weight of a waterproof backpack. The pack was not heavy.

Returning to the broken pathway, the king started downhill on foot, then veered off into sandy brambles and trudged cautiously towards the seashore. At last, the caretaker's cottage appeared, looming in the dissipating haze.

Breathing calmly, the king approached the cottage stealthily and touched it, pressing a hand against an exterior wall of the small beach house.

Rest a moment.

Unzipping the wetsuit, the king drew out two items: a package of nicotine gum and a tiny flashlight. Chewing a piece of the gum, the king shined the flashlight down the dark shoreline. The sounds of sloshing waves echoed across the night.

A light appeared suddenly in the open window above the king's head.

Someone inside is awake.

Prudently, the king ducked out of sight, pressing as close as possible to the exterior wall of the cottage. At last came the sound of running water. The light went out.

Too risky. Move on.

Stealing away from the cottage, the king trekked along the sandy beach. Stumbling over a glass bottle, the king reached down and retrieved it. The bottle was empty. The king turned on the flashlight and examined the bottle's label. In days gone by, the bottle had contained Scotch whisky. The king turned off the flashlight and glanced back at the darkened cottage.

I mustn't drink. I am a recovering alcoholic.

The king's wary eyes scanned the foggy darkness, reaffirming solitude. Tossing the bottle into the sea, the king made a decision.

Somewhere else.

High above, a seabird cackled in derision.

Don't panic.

The abrasive sound was not repeated, but the wind blowing in from the ocean was growing stronger. The dull roar of wind and surf was drowned out by a troublesome pounding in the king's ears.

It will pass. It always does. And then the voices of the Ancients come.

With intimate knowledge, the king wandered quietly along the shoreline, exploring nooks and crannies, remembering, until at last . . .

The boat dock—

The king knew what must be done and who must do it.

I alone must do it. I have been chosen.

The king's chest swelled with pride.

I am Odysseus, Protector of the Known Universe. It is my duty.

Unstrapping the backpack, the king walked down the long pier. Reaching a tall wooden piling at the end of the dock the king unloaded the backpack and set to work.

Time passed, unnoticed until . . .

Proudly, the king stood examined the result by crouching down on the boards and pointing the flashlight. It was an impressive night's achievement. After a moment, the king turned off the flashlight and peered down the beach. It was impossible to see the caretaker's cottage now. Thick fog had settled, once again, over the entire island. The pounding in the king's ears had ceased.

Suddenly, an alarm beeped. It beeped repeatedly, at five-second intervals. There was no time to waste now. The voice of his minion spoke through the device.

"Sunrise in one hour, Your Majesty. Return to the mother ship is imperative."

Taking one last glance around, the king dashed into the murky, tropical pre-dawn stillness. The fog was lifting. Down along the shore, the beachfront cottage remained dark and quiet, as did the vessels docked nearby. As the king scrambled through the brush and brambles, voices of the Ancients assailed him.

"Well done," they praised, over and over.

Up the coast, deep in the underbrush, a black raft sat waiting, poised at the edge of a deep, hidden lagoon. The king, dragging the raft into the water, was joined by a second figure, also clad in a full-body wetsuit. Together, king and minion paddled out to a waiting submersible. As they entered the tiny craft, the menacing caws of breakfasting seabirds streamed to shore on the first rays of sunlight. Ithaca was stirring to life. The gulls were feeding, diving and ascending, in calculated chaos, as dawn broke over the eastern horizon.

Chapter Five

As sunlight spilled across the Demming home in Naples, Poppy drew the draperies in the second-floor media room. She was still sleepy and wanted to block the intrusive light of sunrise. As she waited for the airport limousine to arrive, the home's land-line phone rang.

'I've got it, Lissy," she called downstairs to the housekeeper. Entering the media room, she picked up the receiver. "Hello."

"Poppy?"

"Winner? It that you?" Her stepdaughter sounded frightened. "What's wrong?"

"Poppy, it's the most disgusting thing I've ever read," Winner said, panicky." I couldn't believe someone could write something that filthy, that sick."

Poppy's mom-alert was triggered. "What was, honey?'

"The text message. Some maniac has been sending me horrendous messages. I tried to put them out of my mind. But I can't. Poppy, I'm scared."

"Since when? How many?"

"Yesterday afternoon. Three." Silence. "I tried to ignore the first one. But I had nightmares about the second one. But today I received the third creepy text. Actually, it's worse than creepy. Creepy would be better."

Alarmed, Poppy tried to calm her own fears. "Did you inform your security detail, Win?"

"I'm going to."

"Good girl. You should have done it immediately. Are they with you? Where are you now?"

Poppy looked up as Lissette entered, carrying a cup of skinny latte on a festive breakfast tray. Warm cup in hand, Poppy sipped the sweet, bracing fluid. She could hear Winner's fear.

"Poppy, it's kind of hard to explain. I need privacy right now."

"You're alone?"

"Temporarily."

"Where are you?"

"I'm at the airport in Orlando. In a secure lounge. Right now, I'm alone in here, except for the two airport security guards on duty."

"Thank heaven they're there." Urgently, she felt the need to grill Winner, but, under pressure, the girl might end the call. It had happened before.

"I don't feel so good." Winner sounded like a tiny child.

"Have you eaten breakfast?" Spoon in hand, Poppy picked at the pink grapefruit nestling in a bowl on the breakfast tray. Distracted, she shoved it aside. She would take the protein shake with her in the limo to the Naples airport. Silently, she signaled her plan to Lissette, who took away the tray.

"Gag me! I couldn't eat!" Winner added, "I tried, but I threw up."

Worried, Poppy searched for words.

Winner went on. "The texts were so creepy. The whole thing is so gross."

"Oh, honey—"

"I haven't told anyone else but you, Poppy."

"Your team would have notified the authorities, as matter of course. They should. We pay them enough. In fact, I'll make certain they do. I'll contact them myself."

"No!" Winner cried, near hysteria. "Please don't. I must have privacy—until my party. I'll explain when you get here," she pleaded, subdued. "Please, Poppy. I just wanted—someone—to know."

Poppy inhaled deeply, trying to think rationally. "Maybe you ought to cancel the party this weekend. It might not be safe. Come home if you want. I know you'll be safe here—with me and Lissette."

"No! I can't. The party's all arranged. Everyone's already at the hotel, practically—except you—and me—and a couple of other—important people."

Poppy could hear the movements of Lissette, who was busily hauling suitcases to the foyer downstairs. "My jet leaves Naples in two hours, Win. I'll be in Orlando by lunchtime."

"Okay. We'll meet."

"Be extremely careful, Winner. I'll be there soon. We can figure out what to do."

Winner's tone became lighter. "Don't worry, Mommy. If any assassins appear, I'll use a couple of moves on 'em."

"Why am I not reassured, Winston?"

"Bye, Mommy. I love you."

"Winner, wait. Have you heard the news? Your father is—"

Winner tone changed again. "Yeah. Fe told me. I texted him."

"Did he reply?"

"Sort of. I'll explain everything when you get here."

"You bet your life, you will. Bye, sweetie. Love you, too."

Troubled, Poppy put down the smartphone. *I've got some explaining of my own to do.*

How would Winner react to the news of the divorce?

First things first.

As soon as she arrived in Orlando, she was getting some solid food into that girl's stomach. Hopefully, Winner would keep it down. For several years after the kidnapping, Winner had struggled with bulimia. Although regular therapy sessions had helped her control the condition, she sometimes relapsed, when stressed.

Poppy felt she had to do something to help Winner cope. *But what? If only Heston gave a whit.*

She had heard nothing from Heston, nothing at all, since demanding a divorce. Where could she turn for wise counsel? A thought struck her. Maybe she should contact Jim Talbot. He might know what to do. Their second date, at Maxwell's on the Bay, had gone well. During dessert, Jim had presented her with a single red rose.

The old curmudgeon is still in love with me. Should I phone him for advice? Jim's level-headed. That's why his accounting firm is successful. He'd jump at the opportunity to advise me . . .

Weighing her options, she decided not to involve Jim in her step-daughter's affairs. Not yet. The best thing she could do for Winner, right now, was to get her own fanny out to the Naples airport and catch that flight to Orlando. She glanced at the time.

Scrambling, she gathered her personal things and headed downstairs to the foyer. The airport limousine would be arriving at any moment. She found Lissette, sitting and panting, near the front door.

"Don't forget to ask Winner about the two missing dolls," Lissette reminded her.

Poppy slapped her own forehead. "Yes, yes. Of course. I don't know why I keep forgetting to ask her." Five minutes later, she was on her way to the airport.

***

On Heart of Fire Key, Heston stood alone, barefoot in the strip of cool beach sand that ringed his private island. The fog had lifted, revealing a squall of feeding sandpipers, Deep in rumination, Heston reconsidered his third decision. How much could it hurt—to take one final acting role?

Maybe I should take a stab at acting—and producing. For Winner's sake, if for no other reason. I owe her that much, after all my neglect. She isn't much of actress. I could guide her, teach her craft.

A series of small, crashing waves provided ambient noise. Heston watched as, one by one, the tiny birds took flight. Watching, he caught sight of Ezra and Nick tramping slowly towards him from the caretaker's cottage. Waving, Ezra shouted at him, but he could not make out the words. The sandpipers seemed to hear, squawking in reply above his head. As the ocean waves crashed, he watched the two men approaching on foot along the shoreline.

What am I going to tell Ezra? And Ladybug?

Since before dawn, he had been contemplating this question. He knew himself to be like the island's dilapidated chapel. Once thriving, now, abandoned, both he and the crumbling ruin were hanging on to fading, former glories. He shook his head in dismay.

What legacy would he leave as a testament to his strife and glory? A body of work—movies, the remaining paintings—ghostly images collecting dust in a vault somewhere? Or on some obscure or obsolete Internet site. What difference did any of it make? To anyone, but him?

What is true success?

These days, he was plagued by the question. Was there really any such thing? Had international stardom been worth what it had cost him personally? As a man? Were power, fame, and glory worth any sacrifice? Any cost, in human happiness and lives?

Or did every life end the same way, in crumbling ruins, no matter what? Or was there another dimension to life, one he had only begun to glimpse during his lonely sojourn around the planet? He had been searching for years, to little avail. How much did he care now? Did anything really matter?

Last night, he had read Ezra's script. Obviously, the vacuous TV series was destined to be a mega-hit. He himself could be part of it. But it was so dark in content. Ten years ago, that wouldn't have bothered him, but his recently raised consciousness rendered it distasteful. What to do?

Was he willing to compromise his new-found integrity to regain his starry crown? Or sacrifice his principles for the sake of spending time with his daughter? He had been willing to do anything, in his youth, to climb the pinnacle of success. Now he had suddenly developed values? Wouldn't it be easier to live out his life in a drunken stupor in this isolated earthly paradise? It certainly would be simpler. Probably, more fun, too. Maybe it was too late for him to worry about scruples.

He knew, no matter what happened, he would continue to search, sober or not, for something beyond the obvious physical reality—if it were real, and not entirely an illusion. His heart yearned to transcend—into the mysteries, to "shuffle off this mortal coil"—well, maybe not quite that.

Dying would be too drastic. He wasn't ready to die. He just wanted to glimpse Ultimate Reality, and to preserve a sliver or dignity for the sake of posterity.

The way Kipp and I discussed it in Santa Domingo.

Or should he put his foot down? Resist everything that was being offered to him? He could do that. And yet, he felt strangely compelled—as if the universe wanted him to make a definite move . . . as though it were important, somehow . . . for him to accept the role in the series pilot.

Looking down the beach, Heston saw his two chums rounding the sand dunes. At close range, Nick appeared sleepy. Ezra looked hungover, but jovial.

Suddenly, Heston's skin tingled. It was that feeling he had experienced the day prior—that feeling of portending . . .

"Hooked?" Ezra called to him from across the dunes. Heston could hear the man's voice now.

"What?" he yelled in return. Zero hour had arrived.

Prayerfully, Heston flipped a cosmic coin. It came up heads.

***

"On my script idea—are you hooked?" Ezra beamed, putting his best salesman's foot forward.

Nick squinted, rifling his flip-flops through a bed of seashells. "Good opportunity for you, Heston. Ought to take it."

"Is that so?" Heston did not want or need advice. "Face it, Nick. You hate retirement. You're happy to have a job hassling people. You want to hassle me."

Nick scoffed. "No, Heston. I want you to find yourself."

"You think I'll find myself in play-acting? In another make-believe situation? Pretending to be an archaeologist?" He knew he sounded bitter.

Nick turned, facing him. "It's a start. Better than hiding."

Ezra was losing his battle with cool. "Admit it, Heston. My pilot script is fantastic."

"Modesty, thy name is Ezra Gold," quipped Nick sardonically.

"Look, I admit I am partial to it because I wrote it. Still—"

Tired of toying with fate, Heston lowered his head. "Frankly—"

Both the movie director and the former G-man regarded him expectantly. Above their heads, the sandpipers circled and cawed, as though in anticipation of an oracle's pronouncement.

Heston looked up at the clouds, and then addressed his companions. "Frankly, my dears, I *do* give a damn. The script's adequate—no offense—and it's sensationalist. But I want to do it—for my daughter's sake. I want to do it because Winston asked me to—when she didn't really want to. I believe her heart may hold a spark of love for me yet." Stern-faced, he picked up a flat piece of shell and hurled it across the water's surface. "I'm in—on one condition. Cannibalism is out. Totally. You must agree to reimagine that aspect of the story."

"Hey-Hey!" cried Ezra, leaping in victory. "We'll work it out. Welcome aboard!" He grasped Heston's hand, pumped his arm, and quickly released his hand.

Nick clasped Heston's open palm. "Good move."

He almost smiled. "Thanks."

Reaching into his pocket, Ezra spouted, motormouthed. "It's the perfect opportunity for you, man. You won't be sorry. This will be the greatest comeback in history of comebacks—"

Heston dug a heel in the sand. "As long as I'm not mistaken for one of the ancient relics uncovered in the script—"

Nick cackled. "Oh, Hesty, my man. You slay me." He, too, skipped a broken shell along the surface of the water. "Good fishing out here. 'Member that time we caught the big grouper?"

"Yeah." Heston's salty, dry lips cracked into a grim grin.

"You'll never regret this, man. I swear it." Ezra busied himself with his phone.

Frowning, Heston rubbed his own bearded chin and cheek. "I might need a facial. I haven't had one in years."

Ezra and Nick exchanged glances.

"Couldn't hurt," said Ezra, obviously suppressing a horse laugh. He pocketed his phone.

Again, Nick cackled, shaking his head. He pointed to Heston. "You mean there's a face under all that mess?"

"A face?" shouted Ezra, frightening the birds. "One of the world's great faces, that's all."

Nick aimed a forefinger. "Those famous bee-stung lips are pouting—under that fur somewhere."

"Knock it off." Heston's phone chimed. He pulled out the phone and read the message aloud.

"Hi dad C U tonight big surprise win"

He glared at Nick. "She knows already? That I accepted the role? How could she?"

"Ask him," Nick said, indicating Ezra.

Ezra beamed. "I just sent her a text. What do you think her big surprise is?" he asked, too casually.

Hands in pockets, Heston pondered. "Don't know."

"A new boyfriend, maybe?" Nick suggested impishly.

Whipping around, Ezra gaped at Nick, horrified.

Nick belly laughed. "It's bound to happen someday, Ezzie. Right, Heston? How old's Miss Ladybug now? Eighteen? Nineteen? She's marriage material. Rich *and* beautiful. Sweet as pie. Better ask her quick, Gold—before the competition does."

"Bastard."

"Ease up, Nick." Conflicted, Heston stifled his amusement. He hoped he was covering his own discomfort with the subject. He was the girl's father, after all. And he was sorely feeling the need for a drink. He licked his dry lips.

I won't.

Studying him, Nick squeezed his shoulder. "You're staying strong, man. Hang in."

Heston nodded, grateful for the support. "Think I can handle it?"

Nick cocked his head. "Your world's about to change—and that's good. Thing is, the world's always changing. Sometimes, though, we get to decide on the changes. This time it's your choice."

"Think so?"

"Absolutely. In my opinion, man, you've made the right decision." He slapped Heston's shoulder. "Buck up. Let's head on back to the cottage. That coffee ought to be brewed by now."

"You're scary, you know that?"

"You don't know the half of it," said Nick, sauntering away up the beach.

Loping after Nick, Ezra shouted to him, needling him gleefully. "I don't know how the FBI is managing without you, you old buzzard."

Stung, Nick bristled as he walked away. "I told you. I keep my hand in, now and then."

"Yeah, sure, G-man." Ezra jogged back in Heston's direction. "Hey, let's get a move on. Pack your bags. We leave for the mainland by noon." Pup-like, Ezra circled back, nipping at Nick's heels.

"Always in a rush." Nick barked over his shoulder.

"Time is money, G-man," Ezra cried, catching him up.

Apparently forgotten, Heston trotted after his two bickering buddies as they headed for the cottage. Even the sandpipers had scattered, uninterested, to higher ground. Perhaps this was to be his first lesson in being a has-been.

I wonder what Poppy will say when she hears about my comeback.

Far ahead of him, Ezra and Nick turned, waved, and resumed walking towards the cottage. Picking up speed, Heston jogged ahead to catch up with them.

***

Splat!

Ezra's rubber soles slammed solidly onto the deck of the moored *Lady V 2*. The impact jarred Ezra. He straightened his sunglasses. A flaming sun was scaling the sky now, east of Heart of Fire Key. Two hours had elapsed since Heston agreed to accept the role.

Gaining his balance on the gently rocking boat, Ezra looked back towards the tropical island. What was the history of this place—before Heston bought it? Some islands in the part of the world had been plantations or pirate hubs. Despite this island's beauty, there was something disturbing about it.

My own bad memories, probably.

He himself had been here the day Kipp died. He didn't blame Heston for selling.

I'll be doing the old guy a favor, hauling him back to civilization.

Scratching himself, Ezra yawned, arms outstretched. As he did so, he caught sight of something *odd* in the baking sunshine.

What the hell is that?

Curious, he focused in on the object. It was propped atop a nearby wooden piling.

Intrigued, he climbed out of the boat and pocketed his sunglasses. Focusing in on the strange object, he ambled down the pier towards the piling. As he grew closer, the hair on the back of his neck rose. The strange object was a battered and bloodied *doll,* about 18 inches tall. Something about it seemed familiar: white silk, pearls and sapphires, the tiara of golden leaves—the long, blonde . . .

It looks like—that Princess Daphne doll—the one I gave her—

Revolted, Ezra refrained from touching the tortured toy. Instead, he studied it closely, his skin crawling. The action-figure's torso and limbs were contorted weirdly; its Grecian-style clothing, purposely tattered. A noose of twine encircled its neck. The figure was streaked with red— *something . . .*

Oh, shit.

He backed away. On guard, Ezra scanned the surrounding terrain. His gaze roamed the shoreline, searching for a lone lunatic running loose. Seeing nothing suspicious, he scanned the waters beneath the dock, then the seascape behind him.

No bobbing heads. No ships to be seen.

Again, he glanced towards the island. This time he saw signs of life. Nick was striding towards him, approaching down the long dock. In the distance, Heston was locking the front door of the cottage, a bulging, blue-green canvas duffel bag parked beside him on the stoop. Ezra's gaze returned to the tortured doll on the piling. Unable to resist, he reached out a hand.

"Don't touch that," he heard Nick bark behind him.

Ezra froze.

"Good man," said Nick, eyeballing the mutilated action figure.

Ezra watched closely as Nick drew out a smartphone and photo-graphed the disturbing toy. "I'm sending these shots to the lab," Nick said. "You text the Coast Guard." He indicated the doll. "Has Heston seen it yet?"

Texting, Ezra shook his head. He looked towards the house. "Heston's coming this way now."

Toting his heavy bag, Heston strode briskly down the dock towards them. Calculating, Ezra stared at the clouds on the horizon. A bolt of fear shot through him. On impulse, he texted Winner.

Everything okay there?

Waiting for a response, he fondled the phone in his hand. The phone vibrated, but the response was from the Coast Guard, not Winner. Dismayed, Ezra fretted.

We could be delayed for hours.

Meanwhile, quickly and expertly, Nick examined the doll. "This is gruesome."

"No lie."

"It looks nasty, but it's only red nail polish." He fished in his pocket. "I've got an evidence bag. I always carry plastic."

Producing latex gloves, along with the sack, Nick grimaced. "I'll try to keep some integrity. I can drop this nastiness off at the lab once we're back in Miami. What about the Coast Guard?"

Ezra watched as Nick methodically deposited the battered Winner doll into the clear container. "They're delayed. Can't get here for hours."

"It's okay. I'll put 'em wise. They can comb the scene on their own. It would be better now, but—"

"You want to tell Heston about this?"

Nick shrugged. "He deserves to know."

"It's going to mess with his head."

"What is?" Heston asked, joining them, duffel bag in hand.

"That." Ezra pointed to the desecrated doll.

Heston beheld the doll. "What the—?"

Ezra exchanged glances with Nick. "It's a Princess Daphne Action Figure."

"A what?"

"It's a Winner doll, Heston. From *Laurel,* the first picture she and I made together, four years ago. You signed the marketing contracts. While you were underground, we sold a bajillion of these babies. Sold them all around the world."

"Ah, yes."

"But—I had a special one made, just for Win—real gold leaves, real stones. I think this might be it."

Heston absorbed the implications. "Where did you find it?"

"Up there." Nick indicated the top of the piling. Then he pointed. "Our caller left a card."

On the backside of the piling, a slip of paper fluttered in the breeze. The ragged note had been stabbed, by a fishing knife, into the wood. It dangled from the sharp knife's blade.

Carefully, hands still gloved, Nick steadied the note against the piling. Moving his lips in silence, he read the scrawled words to himself.

"What does it say, Nick?" asked Heston, tossing the duffel onto the deck of the boat. Nick sighed. "It says, 'To Orlando fly, or Ladybug will die.' "

"Like hell," muttered Heston, ripping the paper away from the knife.

"You shouldn't have done that," Nick said.

"Yikes," said Ezra guardedly, reading over Heston's shoulder.

"Who could have left this? Who else is here?" asked Heston, glancing around.

Nick waved his arm 90-degrees. "Anyone could be on this island. Anywhere. Wait, I'll access the satellite images." He turned his attention to his phone.

"Maybe you have squatters," Ezra suggested to Heston. "Psychotic squatters—living in the cottage, and you put 'em out. Or maybe they're docked in the lagoon. Or camped out somewhere."

Nixing the idea, Nick motioned to Ezra. "How could squatters get hold of this doll—if it's the one you think it is?" Nick said and then returned to his call.

"How the hell should I know?" Ezra muttered.

"Great. Just great." Heston was livid. "Back in the public eye, and I've already endangered my daughter's life." He threw up his hands. "Now I don't know what to do—leave or stay."

Ezra bridled. "What do you mean? How can you even think about staying here?" The device in his hand vibrated. Instantly, he read the message, relieved. "Winner's fine," he said softly "For the moment.

Everything's okay in Orlando." He held up the device so his companions could see the screen.

"Did you tell Win about the doll?" Nick asked. "Or the note?"

"No. I didn't know about the note."

Disgusted, Heston handed the note to Nick, who bagged it separately.

"I can't risk being around Win now—not if a stalker's after me." Heston crossed his arms.

Angry, Ezra growled. "The stalker's not after you, Heston. He's after your daughter."

"Really? Then what was he doing here?"

"Someone was here. I saw that boat in that fog, y'all." Nick scowled.

"Blast it!" Heston said. "Now I don't know what to do. I can't let some lunatic think I'm catering to his demands."

Suddenly, Ezra saw Heston's point. Relenting, he listened in silence to Heston's rant.

"Nor do I like being bullied." Heston said. "Maybe I should decline your offer, after all. Stay here. Stand my ground."

Ezra eyed Heston. "If you do that, who will protect your daughter?"

Heston's face went slack. "Another low blow, Gold."

Lowering the phone, Nick frowned at Heston. "Hell, you can't stay here. Not now. Not after this." He pointed to the doll. "What you got here is—a bad combo: a nut on the fringe of sanity who's running loose on an island on the fringe of civilization. Uh-uh. Too dangerous."

"Did you access the satellite images, Nick?" Ezra asked.

"Yes. Nothing. Nobody. Nowhere. We're it, at the moment."

"What about last night?"

"I'll keep checking."

Ezra shook his head. "Nick's right, Heston. We can't leave you here alone. I won't do it. You'd be a sitting duck." He felt penitent. "Look, sorry for the crack. I know Win has the best security people money can buy. And I know your money buys it." He held out a hand.

"Accepted." Heston shook his hand.

Nick held up the transparent bags and wiggled them. "See these? We're getting you off this sand spit just in time. The kooks have found the Demming clan."

"Let's get out of here," Ezra suggested, heading back to the *Lady* V 2.

"Wait a minute." Heston stared at the doll made in his daughter's image. "Is this a prank? Did you two jokers plant this doll here? To scare me into going with you? In case I refused the role?"

***

"Are you serious?" Nick shook his head. "Please, man—"

Guiltily, Ezra grinned. "I only wish I had thought of it. But I didn't."

"There are practical jokes," observed Nick, "And there are practical jokes. This isn't one."

Ezra rubbed the side of his neck. He pointed to the piling. "Some-one—not us—left it there for you to find. I happened across it, but, obviously, it was meant for you."

"Someone twisted," Nick added, his deep brown eyes locking Heston's shimmering silver-blues. "But who?"

"You've been all over the news lately." Ezra eyed Heston. "Maybe it was—a big fan of yours."

"How would a fan know about Orlando?" Joining Ezra, Nick hopped into the boat.

"Will you stop already with the questions?" Ezra griped.

"Come on, Heston." Nick pursed his lips.

As Heston boarded the *Lady V 2,* Nick stared down into the translu-cent, green water swirling around the boat's hull. He seemed uneasy.

Taking the helm, Ezra did his job. "Put these on." Tossing life jackets at each of two passengers, he engaged the boat's engines. His buddies obeyed.

Life vest strapped on, Heston saw the bags in Nick's hands. "I didn't recognize Winner's action figure. I myself had plenty. The Odysseus in Space series was huge hit. I haven't seen one in years. Not since I lived in Naples, when the kids were little. Win had one in her doll collection."

Self-absorbed son of a bitch. Ezra kept his cool.

Nick sighed. "Maybe next time you'll believe me when I talk."

On edge, Heston laughed. "It wasn't you two pranksters? Was the doll part of your devious plot to draft me? Gold, did Ladybug loan you the action figure?"

"Come to think of it, how did—whoever it was—get hold of the doll?"

"Maybe it's not the original." Nick tightened his belt strap.

Heston smiled. "You two are pulling my leg."

Nick yowled. "Do not, under any circumstances, take this thing lightly, Heston. Y'all know there are some people who can't tell fantasy from reality? And some people are just bullies, thieves. We don't know what you're dealing with yet. But I see real, active hostility here, Heston."

Heston blanched. "Maybe so."

Ezra chimed in. "Who would go to the trouble to do something like this? Anyone you know?"

"You mean, who harbors hatred for me and my daughter?" Heston frowned. "I can think of any number of people, Townsend. You've met some of them. Remember my father's nemesis, Gabe Cade?"

"That old geezer died in prison," Nick said. "For kidnapping Winner when she was a 'tween."

"But no one knows where his kids are. Winner's bodyguard was never seen again."

Ezra expounded. "The culprit could be someone you don't know, Heston. Some goon from nowhere. Some publicity hound or some— some huge fan obsessed with you and your life. Remember how Lennox Cordova had that secret fan room devoted to your worship?"

"Yes. I do."

"A stalker," Nick whispered. "That's what my instinct tells me."

"Comforting," said Heston, at the mooring line.

"Ain't it, though." Ezra prepared to cast off. "Orlando, here we come." He snarled, firing the *Lady* V *2's* big engines. "We'll reach port in Tampa. Then on to Orlando by limo," he yelled above the roar.

Standing on n the deck of the roaring *Lady V* 2, Nick waved the two bags. "Well, men, we'll know more after we get the lab results on this evidence. "For now, let's blow this iceberg."

"Casting off," Ezra shouted. Eagerly, Nick and Heston scrambled to unleash the mooring lines. Ezra turned the *Lady V* 2 towards open sea. The large, white boat sped northward.

***

For a while, the three boatmen traveled without conversing, each lost in his own thoughts. As waves from the wake of a passing fishing boat slapped *Lady V* 2*'s* hull, Ezra maneuvered expertly.

Wind in his face, Nick tapped Heston's shoulder. "Hey, man! What happened to your beard?" he barked. "It's gone."

"Shaved it off," Heston barked in reply, adding, "Don't worry, fellows. I've been thinking. A little thing like a homicidal maniacal hasn't dampened my enthusiasm. If anything, I take it as a challenge." He smiled suddenly. "Besides, I know you guys did it. I've realized you set me up."

"You're crazy!" cried Ezra, appalled. *Maybe Heston has gone crazy.*

Heston grinned. "Come on, Ez. You're a prankster from way back. You're a Hollywood legend."

"Heston, you don't have the sense of goat," Nick called.

"That's my man," shouted Ezra.

"Come on!" Heston yelled louder. "It's odd."

"What's odd?" cried Nick.

Heston said, "That our homicidal maniac knew I might go to Orlando. That he knew my pet name for Winston was 'Ladybug.' "

"He or she," Ezra countered at the top of his voice. He cast a brief glance at the freshly shaved movie star. *Dammit, I was right. Heston's still a handsome devil, even in his old age.*

His thoughts flew to Winner and then to Vivian.

In his youth, Ezra had been involved with Vivian Champlain, a married woman and many years his senior. Despite all, Ezra and Vivian had bonded, forging a complicated history of love, passion, betrayal, and guilt. Until Vivian's illness had impacted her reason.

Eventually, Ezra had forgiven Vivian's vicious assault on his aged mother, that long-ago night at the Ritz-Carlton Hotel in Naples. When Vivi had died—not long afterward—from a congenital heart ailment, he had mourned her passing. Even now, he missed her, and he knew he always would.

But he was madly in love with Winner Demming. Since her adolescence, Winner had been the focus of Ezra Gold's fantasy life. He worshiped at her altar. He felt unworthy. But he would kill any maniac who tried harm her or any member of her family, including her itinerant father, Heston.

Fiercely, he stared at Nick, who sat studying the coastline.

Nick looked up and caught him staring, then looked at Heston, who still stood, smirking.

"Here's another idea," Heston shouted. "What if the guys who want to buy my island are trying to scare me off it? In case I might not agree to sell?"

"What I want to know," hollered Nick, "is why you won't face facts."

"Maybe you yourself planted the doll, Heston," Ezra shouted. "You knew about Orlando. You had access to the doll, at some point."

"Why would I have done it? Got no motive," Heston cried.

"To save face." Ezra accelerated the boat's speed. "So you could go slumming—do a series—"

Heston grinned. "Good try, Gold."

"Or maybe you've gone nuts, and we don't know it yet."

"Get real!"

Annoyed, Nick shook his shimmering head. "Ain't no laughing matter, Heston. Ain't no laughing matter."

Grinning, Heston shouted a reply, but his words were swallowed by the ravenous wind.

Chapter Six

Poppy nestled quietly in the first-class cabin, dozing lightly, her eyes shut. She hated flying—ever since the deaths of Kipp, Shawnee, and Beryl—but the jet's droning engines had lulled her into quietude. While boarding the plane, she had felt agitated, unnerved. Her resolve to move on, however, remained intact. Now, in the comfort of first class, she dreamily contemplated her future plans.

She was determined to help Winner, and she was determined to file for divorce from Win's father in the coming weeks. Nothing could stop her. Yet her recent phone conversations with both Heston and Winner had been unsettling. Heston had seemed stunned by her request for a divorce. She had agreed to give him time to think it over, but she was determined to get him out of her life, once and for all.

She had spent a lifetime in emotional tumult and turmoil over the man—loving him, losing him, loving him again, losing him again. His presence, like his absence, was woven into the fabric of her being. Perhaps if she had been a stronger, better, more forgiving woman . . .

When we were kids, I forgave Heston everything, always.

Half dreaming, she found herself drifting back in time . . .

. . . standing in the cool shade beneath the City Pier of Naples, her bare feet sinking into the wet sand. Small waves lapping the bright, white shore . . .

In recent years, she had stood, sometimes, on that very spot, alone, waiting for Heston—waiting for a man who might never return to her, and all because she had sent him away. That spot, beneath the Naples pier, had been their secret meeting place since elementary-school days.

How long had she and Heston rendezvoused there? When had it all begun? That first time, it was under the pier . . . *right over there . . .*

What she had learned about Heston, when first they'd met, was how badly he had needed a friend. She had needed one, too, and so their alliance had been born. But—

Exactly when did I fall in love with him?

Her thoughts drifted farther back, into the distant past . . .

***

At assembly, in the gymnasium of Lake Park Elementary School, seven-year-old Poppy Sue Craft could feel the presence of the new boy sitting behind her. She had seen him for the first time day before yesterday, from her bedroom window. He was her new neighbor. She had noticed him at school yesterday—the day he'd enrolled—at lunch in the school cafeteria. His name was Heston . . . Something. It was a weird name.

Suddenly, from behind her, this Heston-boy tugged at her pigtails.

She swatted his hand away. "Stop it." She did not turn around, but paid attention to the principal, who was speaking to the assembly of young students.

Putting a finger to her lips, the teacher caught Poppy's eye. Alarmed, Poppy shuddered in fear. Moments later, she felt something tickling the nape of her neck. Slapping her palm against the back of her neck, she whirled around angrily.

"Quit it," she whispered, spying the ballpoint pen in Heston's hand.

Feigning innocence, Heston shrugged, pointing to the boys sitting on either side of him.

"Poppy!" her teacher whispered. "Shush!"

Not fooled by Heston's denial, Poppy huffed quietly and faced forward in her seat. Feeling, once again, the point of a pen rolling along the skin of her neck, she sat motionless this time, afraid to make a sound. The point rolled but did not hurt.

"It's okay," she heard Heston whisper in her ear. "I'm just connecting your freckles." He smelled like oranges and—something . . .

The 3:00 p.m. bell rang. The principal dismissed all the assembled children, who filed out one by one, escaping into the afternoon sunlight. They piled into waiting cars or buses or began their short walks homeward.

Walking home, Poppy carried her book satchel in one hand and wiped the back of her neck with the other. Blue ink smeared her fingers.

"Hey, wait up!" Trailing her, Heston ran, overtaking her. On his back was strapped a blue-green-colored knapsack.

"You're that new boy," she scoffed, walking on.

"You're Penelope Susan Craft."

Surprised, she stopped, then kept on walking.

He beamed. "I asked the crossing guard. Carry your books?" He indicated her satchel.

Studying him, she realized how cute he was. He was much cuter than the other boys at school.

"Okay." She handed him the satchel and walked on. She decided not to yell at him—because he was the new boy. He didn't know any better. "Your name is Heston?"

"Sean Heston Demming."

"They say you sing good."

He followed. "Well. I sing well. Says who?"

"The choral-music teacher."

"Yeah?"

"She t-told our c-class about you."

"Yeah? C-C-Cool."

She ignored him, her feelings hurt.

On cue, he burst into song, delivering loudly the first two lines of The Star-Spangled Banner. He sang as they walked onward.

Impressed, she forgave him. "I can't sing."

This pleased him. He fell in step beside her. "You sure have a lot of freckles, Red. I'm calling you Red. It's easier than Penelope."

"I know it. Everybody calls me Poppy."

He grabbed her wrist. "Got a pen, Red? I want to connect more dots." He turned her bare arm over, examining it.

She jerked her arm away. "All I have is a pencil." Quickly, she trotted away from him, heading for US 41, also known locally as the Tamiami Trail. She had veered off her usual course. The major highway was the main ground route between the coastal cities of Tampa and Miami. It passed through downtown Naples.

Running, his sneakers slapping the pavement, Heston caught up. "We just moved here—from Illinois." Panting, he looked around as he followed her along the sidewalk. He pointed to the restaurant at a nearby chain motel. "Ever go to this Howard Johnson's for ice cream?"

She nodded. "Yes. Uncle Mel likes the fried clams." She looked straight ahead. They were approaching Four Corners. She wasn't allowed to cross the busy intersection of US 41 and Fifth Avenue South, where a liquor-store building loomed. A den of sin, the building featured dancing-feet, shod in oxfords and high-heeled pumps, painted around its top ledge. They had ventured into territory forbidden by Uncle Mel.

"Clams are okay." Heston thought a moment. "I prefer fried shrimp. Do you?"

Walking on, she said nothing.

"Hold it a minute," Heston said, setting down the satchel and opening his knapsack, He touched her arm, stopping her in her tracks. "Want to see something?" He took out a spiral notebook.

For the first time, she looked up into his face. Heston was really cute. He had the sparkliest eyes she'd ever seen. She felt shy. "S-Sure." He was so much cuter than other boys she knew.

Opening his notebook, Heston revealed a drawing of a monster.

"You drew that?" she asked, heart pounding.

He nodded, closing the notebook, embarrassed. He tucked the notebook inside his rucksack and drew the flap shut.

"I like to draw, too," she confessed. "But mine aren't as good as yours."

Heston's jaw dropped. He looked at her. "You think I'm good?"

"Yes." She felt funny—all squirmy. It was time to go home. Turning on her heel, she started back towards her street.

Heston grabbed the satchel and trotted along beside her. "Got a bike?"

"Yes, I have."

He pulled ahead of her, facing backwards as he trotted. "Want to ride bikes after school?" He moved fast, almost dancing. "Tomorrow."

"I don't know—" She stumbled on a pebble.

He caught her elbow, preventing a fall. He smiled. "Pretty please? With sugar on top?"

"Well . . ." She couldn't help it. When he smiled, he was really, really, really cute. "Okay."

"Okay." He brushed back his dark-brown bangs. "Whew."

As they walked, he pointed to a small house. It was painted light green. "I live here. But I'll walk you home. Where do you live" He yanked the book satchel from her hand, determined to carry it for her.

"Over there." She pointed to the house next door, then walked on in silence, studying her new friend. He was so tall. Tall and thin. He walked faster than she did. She couldn't think of anything else to say.

As they arrived at the walkway leading to her house, she halted. The entrance was flanked by pink and green hibiscus shrubs and rows of dark-green monkey grass "See you tomorrow."

Heston halted, too. "Okay."

She pointed to her book satchel. "That's mine."

"Oh, yeah. Right." He handed her the satchel.

"Thank you for carrying it for me, Heston. It's pretty heavy."

"I'm strong." He flexed his bicep for her approval.

"Oh, wow. Well, goodbye." She started towards the front door. At the door, she turned around.

Heston was still there. He waved.

Feeling awkward, she waved in return.

He called to her. "We can bike down to the pier."

"Okay. If I'm allowed. I'll ask. Bye."

Heston shrugged, then suddenly dashed up the walkway and kissed her on the cheek.

Abashed, she looked into his eyes, then looked down at her book satchel. "Thank you, Heston." She raised her gaze, uncertain.

His cheeks glowed like neon apples. "Anytime, Poppy Sue." Thrusting his hands into his pockets, he sauntered away, whistling, then skipping. He did not look back, his attention, apparently, focused elsewhere.

She watched him go. He was tall for his age and scrawny, like he didn't get enough to eat at home. She would fix that. That night she packed a brown bag of four small apples and a sack of ginger candy for their bike ride the next afternoon.

Her father didn't come home until late that night. She never asked him for permission. She knew he would say 'no.' She had never done such a thing before, but—

On the following day, an hour after school let out, Heston showed up at the house. He was perched atop a beat-up bicycle that had once been blue but had, at some point in its rugged history, been spray-painted in spots with glossy black paint. Its rusted metal basket, bolted onto the handlebars, was bent out of shape. The black-wall tires were bald, and the rusty spokes were rimmed in sand. Dangling from the handlebars was a squeaky horn, powered by a black rubber ball. The chrome on the handlebars was flaking off.

She felt embarrassed because her bike was new and shiny. It was spotlessly white, trimmed with pink. Pink and white plastic tassels dangled from the end of the handlebars. The seat was covered in pink and white striped cloth. Two brown, woven-straw baskets hung attached, one on either side of the back wheel. She had pasted several pink and yellow daisy decals on the bike's fenders.

"What a stupid-looking contraption," Heston laughed, pale arms crossed at his chest.

"Yours is more—broken in," she replied tactfully.

"Does yours have gears?" He squeezed the metal clamps attached to his handlebars.

"No."

"Mine does. Watch. I can peddle backwards." To prove it, he peddled in place.

Shifting gears, he took off, riding forward down the street. "Come on, slowpoke," he yelled, turning back to wave her forward. Whipping around to face the road, he honked the horn repeatedly, to egg her on. He laughed in delight.

She giggled in excitement. Fumbling to raise the kickstand, she finally succeeded and hopped onto her bike and sped after him. Following him, she marveled as his thick, dark hair flouncing each time his bike took a bump in the road. She was amazed at his speed and agility. She felt slow and uncoordinated, but she did her best to keep up with him. He led. She followed.

They rode their bikes across Tamiami Trail then over to Eighth Street, then down past the school and onto Third Avenue South until they reached 12th Avenue South. Stopping, they parked their bikes at the Olde Naples City Pier, which jutted out into the placid Gulf of Mexico.

"Let's sit under it," Heston suggested, picking out a spot.

She followed him, picnic brown bag in hand. She felt as if she were entering a cave or a, dark, secret tent. Together, she and Heston plopped down, surrounded by pilings, in the cool, shaded sand.

"What you got in there?" he asked, tearing the bag from her hands and opening it. He began to devour the food. Within minutes, he had consumed three apples and half a bag of candy.

"What is this stuff?" he asked, nearing the bottom of the candy sack. "It's hot."

"Candied ginger. Haven't you ever tasted ginger candy? Uncle Mel buys it at that Gourmet Shoppe on Third Street South."

"Eat it all the time. You like it, too?"

"Yes."

He smiled, crinkling his nose. "One of my favorites. Bring more next time."

"All right, Heston." She watched him quietly, while munching, herself, on the one remaining apple.

He caught her gaze. Leaning in, he kissed her mouth, his bee-stung lips sticky with apple juice, hot with ginger. Tenderly, he touched a hand to her cheek . . .

***

111

Seated in the cabin of the plane, Poppy touched a hand to her cheek. So long ago now—

Had that been the moment . . .?

Perhaps.

A rumbling bump of turbulence scared Poppy awake. Her eyes popped open. Recalibrating, she gazed out the window at the clouds flying past. There had been something magical, enchanted about Heston, even in childhood. All the little girls—even the grown-up girls—had been obsessed with him. Sometimes, they would gather around him, and she would just wait, off to the side, until, at last, he rejoined her.

She hadn't known what she was seeing then, but she had recognized that Heston was a special person, not like anyone she had ever known. For one thing, he'd had those incredible silver-blue eyes, and, for another, a smile too bedazzling for an elementary-school boy. She hadn't known such words then—or the word "charisma" or the phrase, "star quality"—but she'd had felt them all the same. Uncle Mel had taken a dislike to Heston instantly upon meeting him, telling her, on more than one occasion, that Heston had "too much charm for his own good."

Mostly, she remembered thinking what a big show-off Heston was, but she had liked him, so it was all right. She hadn't minded. In the years that had followed, he was always doing something zany or dangerous—like skateboarding or wind-surfing—and each time yelling, "Hey, Red! Watch this!" She only minded when he asked someone else to watch, instead of her. Even back then, he had tested her limits. From the very beginning, he had been able to drive her mad with jealousy.

It would be another ten years before he proposed marriage to her—and then dumped her before she could even reply, running off after that teen-aged vixen Montserrat Flynn. And then, nothing.

I didn't see Heston again for two decades.

Abandoned and pregnant at sixteen, she had borne Heston's first child, a son born out of wedlock—in secret and in shame—in Tampa, in a home for unwed mothers. Uncle Mel had made the arrangements, but he had been cruel to her. It would be another nineteen years before she and Heston, at last, said, "I do" to one another, and reunited with their firstborn; and then, another eight years before they lost that first child tragically and separated.

Mind fuzzy, she did the math. That meant she had known Heston for something like forty-five years. Could that even be possible?

Sometimes, she missed him so much—it felt as though she were missing the biggest piece of herself. All those nights of intimacy, after their marriage, had seared the bond between her and Heston—until she had lost faith in him and sent him packing.

All in all, she had borne the man four children. Obviously, something about the union was meant-to-be, or had it already been? Was what they had together really over forever?

Oh, Heston. I should have forgiven you, that day eight years ago. I never should have sent you away. But it's too late now—

Her weary heart ached.

What would that seven-year-old Poppy advise her to do now? Admittedly, that child knew the real Heston Demming better than anyone in the world. She's the one he fell in love with, all those many years ago. She didn't dump him because he was fickle, and a fabricator—a fickle fabricator—even then—

What am I saying? I'm babbling. To myself.

As the plane began its descent into Orlando, she came to her senses and put away the past. Yesterday was gone. There was only today. There was only now.

At the moment, all her attention needed to focus on keeping Winner safe and healthy. Realistically speaking, the Heston Demming of her childhood was now nothing more than a phantom. She was better off without him, and his adult counterpart. And yet—

Had she had been a fool to leave James Talbot for Heston, fifteen years ago? She might even have been better off— had she taken Rogelio Vega up on his sordid proposition. It would have served Inez right. Pulling herself together, Poppy stared out the window of the airplane as it descended.

Maybe I do still love Heston. Maybe I always will. Perhaps I should have forgiven him then.

It was too late now. The die had been cast—and she had cast it.

***

"All roads lead to Orlando, baby."

Singing his words, Winner's mature, athletic beau—sizzling, smug, and sassy—eased his bronze Jaguar along the Tamiami Trail. He was driving alone, listening to reggae from his music play list. After leaving Key Largo that morning, he had avoided taking the Florida Turnpike— too many tollbooths and too many cameras. Instead, he had driven westward across the southern tip of Florida. Soon he would pass through his old hometown, Naples.

Driving across the Everglades, he noticed cypress trees, cabbage palms, and tourist rest stops, as they drifted by, outside his car's tinted windows. An historic road, the Tamiami Trail snaked its way through the huge swamp, once a pristine wilderness, but now endangered by development.

Naples, Florida, had grown like wildfire. As he entered the city's outskirts, known as East Naples, he recalled an incident from his child-hood. He'd been around twelve years old.

He'd been riding in the car with his stepmother, Inez. They had pulled into a fast-food joint in East Naples. As they'd approached the drive-through window, hungry for burgers and fries, they'd seen four huge, scary vultures roosting on the corners of the restaurant's big garbage bin. Panicking, Inez had driven away. He had thought it was so cool, the whole thing. He laughed, just thinking about it.

I remember my childhood like it was yesterday.

But it was today, midday, and he was a grown man, driving into the Naples of today, a much larger town than the Naples of his youth. Tourist hotels, gas-stations, and mini-marts had taken the place of swampland. Too bad he was hiding from law and could no longer sell real-estate.

Cautiously, he drove the Jag at a moderate pace, into downtown Naples and through the traffic light at Four Corners. This morning, as every morning, he took care not to arouse the cops.

Like a model citizen.

Driving past old haunts, he couldn't help thinking about Winston Demming and her breathtaking young loveliness. Gloating, he congratulated himself on landing the world's most beautiful meal ticket.

It takes a certain talent, you know? Finesse. To seduce a girl like that.

Yes, his experience with women had paid off. He laughed. This 'pretty baby' had even leased this car for him! What's more, he was on his way to the most expensive resort in Orlando—and she was paying for his stay! And her own! Happily, he danced in his seat, thumbs tapping rhythm, against the steering wheel, to the music he loved.

From now on my whole life will be an easy ride.

Winner. *What a name, eh?* In the game of love, he was the real winner, even if—in the game of tennis—he had become a second-rate player. *Only because I haven't applied myself—*

So what? He was a victor in the sexual arena and always had been. That long-ago screw-up with Sasha Bassett had been—well, a screw-up. *Just a blip on the screen.*

And he'd be having more women, too, down the road. After a couple of years of bedding the delicious actress, he would begin to play the field, quietly. By then, he'd have money out the wazoo. For now, he'd go on pretending to be a one-woman man. Again, he laughed out loud, adjusting his shades against the sun's heated reproach. *Man, I am good.*

Seriously, if I wasn't laying low from the law, I might've become an actor myself.

Pretending could be a lucrative racket—a great racket, if you hit it as big as Heston Demming had. *Better than the tennis racquet.* He snickered, delighted by his own wit.

Lifting his shades, he glanced at the digital clock on the dashboard. He'd made good time from Key Largo. As he continued north on the US 41, he felt an impulse—to visit his father in secret.

What the hell.

Half a mile later, he turned left into Bay Colony. Locating Rogelio's and Inez's old street, he drove slowly down it, looking for the Vega home. He saw it, up ahead, and pulled into the driveway.

The house was vacant. A tiny *For Sale* sign in the front yard told the story—Inez's realty firm, of course, so she must be back in biz. For a silent moment, he contemplated his old residence, then backed out of the driveway and ventured onto Pelican Bay Boulevard.

I'm bummed.

He'd wanted to tell the old man about his forthcoming nuptials— about winning Winner Demming—and why he couldn't invite him to the ceremony. Give him a heads up, so his pride wouldn't be hurt. And—

I can admit it. I am not ashamed. I miss the old guy.

As a young man, he'd given old Rogelio a lot of headaches, heart-aches, and regrets—ever since being born, really. After the Jim Talbot fight, he'd stayed away. He hadn't contacted his father in years. His father knew the score, so it was okay, but still—

Fear seized him, as he steered the car back onto the Tamiami Trail.

What if the old man is dead?

Of course, he had considered the possibility, but now that he'd seen their empty house—

My old man's close to seventy. Inez would be over fifty now.

What to do? Beating back fear, he drove on, but hit traffic on the Trail near Pine Ridge Road. The road became clogged with SUVs, driven, mostly, by gray-haired snowbirds. Slow, old people drove him crazy. The Jag became a snail.

At last, he was able to pull into a parking lot, off Vanderbilt Beach Road. Once parked, he got online and made an electronic search of county records.

Pay dirt.

He sighed in relief as he located the new home address of Rogelio and Inez Vega. He entered the address in his GPS and started the Jag. The Vega's new abode was on Pelican Bay Boulevard, in, one of the gated communities within the large, ocean-front development.

Just about a mile from here.

Heading back south on the Trail, he turned west into Pelican Bay. Driving slowly, he spotted the condo's gleaming white-tiles—and then, the main gate, manned by an electronic gate.

How the hell do I get through?

Intent, he watched expectantly as a delivery truck approached the gate. The truck's driver entered a code on a stationary keypad, and the gate opened noiselessly. The truck entered the complex, the gate closing again once the truck had passed through.

The technology was dated, but the truck driver's actions gave him an idea. As a real-estate agent, he had once had a universal passcode. The passcode might work in this old system. It would be worth a shot.

Why not try it?

Driving up to the keypad, he punched in the magic numbers.

Poof, as Winner would say. It worked.

The gate slid open. Accelerating ever so slightly, he eased the bronze Jaguar through the open gate, cruising onto the driveway that snaked through the condominium complex. Reducing the Jag's speed to a crawl, he searched for the Vega's house number.

There it is.

Parked in the driveway of the townhouse, he got out, quickly glancing around. Nervously, he knocked on the door. *No answer.* He knocked again. Still no answer.

Should I leave a note? No! I'll come back—another time.

He knew he was being videoed by security cameras. If only he could text or phone or email his folks. But he could not. It was too dangerous. These attempts could be traced back to him—unless he used the disposable phone.

Do I still have it? He slapped his pockets. *Where is it?*

Dashing back to the car, he flung open the front door, searching frantically for the missing phone. *Ahhh . . .*

He spotted it; it was peeking out from under his bag of tricks.

Quickly, he hopped behind the wheel and revved up the car. Slowly, he drove out the main gate and away from the complex. But, this time, he headed south onto Gulf Shore Boulevard. As long as he was in Naples, he might as well make one more long-overdue visit.

Another blast from the past.

***

He had always wanted to return to the scene of his crime—the reason for his change of identity—Rainbow's Coffee Bar on Fifth Avenue. He drove south on beautiful Gulf Shore, eventually turning left onto Fifth Avenue. East a couple of blocks—

The building's still here.

The coffee shop was, too. *Sort of.* It had changed. Apparently, it had morphed into an upscale foodie hangout. The last time he had sat at one of these outdoor tables, he had been chatting up Poppy. Her last name had been Talbot then.

My future mother-in-law, no less.

Winner had no idea he had known her step-mommy, Poppy, 15 years ago. Or that Poppy and Sasha had been best friends—until Sasha had tried to steal Jim Talbot. Poppy had gotten wise. Bent on revenge, Sasha had ended up in prison.

Forget about Sasha. Focus on Winner now.

What Winner didn't know wouldn't hurt her, including the fling he'd had with her own birth mother, Maude Winston. He remembered the first time he had ever seen Winner Demming. It had been at Heston's house in Port Royal, just a few days after he'd purchased it. Little Winner had been around four years old.

That, Winner will never know. Besides, nobody has any idea where the hell Maude is.

Slowing down, he entered the alley behind the eatery. This was the spot he really wanted to revisit. Afraid to stop and get out, he guided the Jaguar past the place—where he had beaten Talbot to a bloody pulp— because the pervert had been kissing Sasha. Frenching her right there in public. He couldn't let the fat bastard get away with it—

Danny's fists clenched. He pounded the steering wheel.

"Hey, watch it, buddy," a female pedestrian yelled.

He swerved to a stop. His breathing was shallow. Like he had just done the deed, all over again.

Maybe it hadn't been such a good idea to come here after all. He started the car, drove down Fifth Avenue South, and headed back towards I-75 North. He hadn't realized he still had feelings for Sasha Bassett, the poor, dumb kid.

What's the f-ing point of it all?

Veering the car north onto US 41, he drove back through town one last time, then, remembering, turned westward on Vanderbilt Road. Quietly, he drove about a mile—almost to the Gulf of Mexico—and then he sighted the cemetery. Driving onto the grounds, he edged slowly towards Franco's grave. Oblivious to the world and blinded by tears, he stopped the car and got out.

For a time, he stood, weeping, beside the grave of his stepbrother, Franco Demming. Twelve-year-old Frankie been killed in a road accident. He'd been chasing a soccer ball, one kicked in anger by his own father, Heston Demming.

I will never forgive that SOB for causing your death. But I will avenge you. I'll start by knocking up his daughter. Controlling his fortune. I got other plans in the works, too. Wait and see. Frankie. I'll destroy his ass.

At last, he wiped his eyes and returned to the car and drove swiftly away. A few other cars were parked in the cemetery's lot nearby. He assumed they belonged to other unlucky souls who'd lost somebody close.

Turning eastward, he stopped for gas, and then entered I-75 via the north-bound on-ramp. Burying his memories, he drove on, in silence, bound for Orlando and his budding bride-to-be. She was so hot for him. He laughed.

What a deflowering I have planned for you, baby cakes.

He had all the meds she would need—just in case.

Driving towards Orlando, he did not notice the small Chevrolet hatchback now tailing his gleaming bronze Jaguar. The economy car had been following him ever since leaving Rainbow's in downtown Naples. As he focused on the road ahead, he activated his play list.

Drowning his feelings, he lost himself in music. Outside, the afternoon was beginning to wane. Far behind him, in clandestine pursuit, the unseen Chevy followed, remaining a safe distance away from the sleek, purring Jaguar.

Chapter Seven

"Our staff serves at your pleasure, Miss Demming," said the well-groomed manager of the Southern Seas Resort. "Confidentially, we're all big fans of yours. But we won't let it show."

"Thanks." The elevator arrived the 18th floor of the five-star hotel's main tower. Winner added, "I'm excited about my party tomorrow night. You've done a good job of keeping it secret."

The elevator door slid open. "We are proud to serve you and your guests. Quite a few have arrived already," he added, stepping out of the private conveyance. "This is our Royal Suite. Welcome home, Miss Demming."

The deferential man ushered Winner and the other two passengers, Hailey and Adair Champlain, into the immaculate living area of the spacious penthouse suite. Entering her new accommodations, Winner—her engagement ring hidden away—glanced back at Hailey and Adair. Both seemed right at home. As was she, the Champlain siblings were accustomed to luxurious surroundings. Adair yawned. as he entered the spectacular suite.

The manager resumed his subtle spiel, directing his attention to Winner. "You'll find that the Royal Suite has all the features and amenities you required: expansive rooftop terrace, private pool—"

"And a romantic master bedroom and bath?" Hailey asked, strolling around. She seemed curious, if unimpressed. "If I were you, Winnie, that would be my top priority."

"She's not you, slut," said Adair, a slender, broad-shouldered man in his twenties. Aloof and disinterested, Adair straightened the sleeves of his tailored blue blazer. A finely crafted leather bag dangled from his left shoulder. On his feet, alligator pumps gleamed sedately, as though still alive, lying in wait for prey upon some fallen log in a swampy bog.

Shaking off the fanciful image, Winner studied Adair's handsome face. Evidently, today was one of Adair's lucid days. She never knew, at any given moment, what to expect from the eccentric young actor. Among his fans, Adair's peculiarities were legendary.

I guess he took his meds this morning.

"Curb your tongue, wretch," Hailey said to her brother. "Or else." She waved a small fist.

"Never mind, Hailey." Winner said. She had no worries. Her own personal assistant, Millie Wong, had surveyed the territory in advance, sent her a secured link, and recommended a virtual tour. At the moment, Millie was hard at work, furtively welcoming guests, several floors below.

"Winner's a nymph, not a nymphomaniac," Adair said to his sister. "Unlike some people."

"Stow it." Hailey, a diminutive young woman, jabbed her elbow into Adair's hip.

"Hay-Hay, why so brutal?" Adair whined, rubbing his hipbone.

"That was for insulting me," Hailey replied smugly. She grinned toothily at Winner. "In front of Winnie and the help."

Doubtfully, Winner returned Hailey's platinum smile. As she did so, she caught sight of her own and Hailey's reflections in a large, gilded mirror on a far wall. Win almost laughed out loud.

What a kick.

She studied the mirror images. Like her, Hailey Champlain had long blonde hair, plus she was wearing clothes nearly identical to Winner's, crafted by the same designer. Winner giggled. What made the scene comical was that Hailey was twelve inches shorter than Winner. Placed side by side, Winner and Hailey appeared to be large and small versions of the same fashionista.

They say imitation is the sincerest form of flattery.

Yet, personality-wise, she and Hailey would never be clones. She, herself, was feminine and elegant, while Hailey, at thirty, was chunky and attractive—in word, cute. They were different in other ways, too. She herself was reserved and quiet, whereas Hailey was bubbly and talkative.

Tearing her gaze from the mirror, Winner recalled Ezra's comment about Hailey.

"She's a speed-demon in stilettos, that one."

About that, he was right. Little Hailey was constantly on the go, clip-clopping around everywhere, "trying to be sexy, and trying to be tall," Ezra had observed snidely. "And all that yammering! It's like she wants to irritate me."

Unlike Ezra, however, Winner enjoyed Hailey's outspoken spontaneity. She knew that Hailey's bold, brassy manner was the result of upbringing: an unsupervised childhood of unbridled privilege. In her own way, Hailey was endearing. Somewhere in her nature was an underlying sadness.

Arrogant Adair, on the other hand, never seemed sad, although the young heir did seem remote and strangely self-contained. In media circles, Adair was known for his cold sense of humor, occasional histrionics, and often bizarre comments. Yet he was so rich and so good-looking and so popular with fans, that no one cared. Rumored to be on drugs, he provided fodder for gossips and groupies.

"Come over here by me, Winnie," said Hailey. She indicated Adair. "He bites."

"Give it a rest, mister twister," Adair said, unsmiling, to Hailey. "Be nice."

Tactfully, the manager continued the tour of the premises. "Ms. Champlain, I believe I can put your minds at ease. Please step this way to view the master suite."

Winner's heart trembled as she followed the manager into the forbidding boudoir. As she entered, and beheld the room's decor, she said nothing, but the blood pulsed in her veins. The bed itself loomed, enormous, almost cartoon-like in its proportions. She felt—lost—and yet, found. Would this be the arena of her fate? The mattress seemed to undulate before her eyes.

Beside her, Hailey stood transfixed.

Adair broke the silence. "Let the games begin," he said.

Winner gasped.

Hailey giggled.

The manager coughed discreetly. "Allow me to show you the rest of your accommodations, Miss Demming." Ushering the trio from the master suite, the manager guided them into the kitchen. After a brief inspection, he led them back into the great room. A floor-to-ceiling shuttered wall lined the length of the great room.

Halting in front of it, the manager waved his hand, and the shutters began to rise slowly. Sunlight began to fill the room. As the wall disappeared into the ceiling, a rooftop terrace, and the theme-park skyline beyond it, gradually came into view.

Winner caught her breath. "The Enchanted Palace!"

"Yes, indeed. This way, please," the manager urged the trio politely. "As promised, the Royal Suite overlooks the magnificent structure. It's in the foreground, but you can see the entire theme park in the distance."

Thrilled, Winner gazed at the grand fairytale edifice. Its triangular, pennant-like flags waved proudly from myriad spindles and turrets. Around the palace, tourists and theme-park visitors milled like ants. The palace was framed by huge magnolia trees.

"I love it!" cried Winner, clapping her hands like a child.

"How very gratifying," said the manager sincerely. "And from this very spot, you'll be able to watch the fireworks each evening."

"When she's not making fireworks of her own," said Hailey.

"Hailey, give me a break." Winner was well aware of Hailey's reputation for *goofing* on people. She, like Ezra, was known for practical jokes. Still, the insinuation embarrassed Winner.

"Good view," said Adair, at the edge of the 18th floor terrace. A stone railing ran round it.

"Whoa! Back up, Bro!" Hailey cried, pulling Adair away from the edge. "Hope you don't have vertigo, Win."

"I don't have vertigo," said Adair. He fingered the inner lapel of his blazer and extracted an electronic cigarette. Unceremoniously, he vaped.

Watching him, Winner grunted. "All I know about *Vertigo* is that it's one of Ezra's favorite films."

"Ezra's always loved that old Hitchcock thriller. You know, the word 'Vertigo' means, like, a dizzy fear of heights. Do you have a dizzy fear of heights, my dear?" asked Hailey.

"Not really," said Winner guardedly.

"I don't," said Adair. He vaped placidly, emitting steam.

"Ezra is an artistic genius," said Hailey, brows knit. "If he likes a film, I like it, too."

Unconcerned, Adair stretched out on a deck chair and donned his wraparound sunglasses. "I my made my first jump when I was twelve." He waved his e-cigarette at the manager. "Skydiving."

"So did my dad!" said Winner, surprised. "He was in a club. They all went together."

"Very brave of you, sir," the manager replied gallantly. He turned to Winner. "Is everything to your liking, Miss Demming?"

"Yes, I'm satisfied," said Winner to the manager. Her voice was noncommittal, but inwardly she was thrilled. She felt effervescent. Her childhood dreams were coming true. Losing her cool, she gushed. "Actually, I love the whole place! What I really like about the whole resort is, like, when you drive up to it—you see all the mansions and the high-rise hotel itself—all in Spanish-style architecture. The whole Spanish motif—really works for me."

"Si, senorita," said Hailey, studying her. "I wonder why."

Blushing, Winner turned away.

Hailey cannot possibly know who my fiancé is—can she?

Worried, Winner gazed out at the Enchanted Palace. All she needed now was the prince to go with it—and he was on his way right now, driving up from Key Largo.

Prince Damian.

Emotion overwhelmed her. She needed to be alone in her fantasy kingdom. She glanced at Hailey, who was watching her closely. She glanced at Adair. He, too, was watching her, as though she were a bug under a microscope.

"Winnie, you look all in," Hailey said. She looked at Adair. "And you look right at home here, Bro," she said. "But you're not." She whacked the sole of Adair's shoe. "Get up. We have our own quarters downstairs. Right, Win?"

"Uh-huh," said Winner, watching Adair rise and stretch his long limbs. "I put you two in the second-best suite in the hotel. Is it okay?"

"Yeah." Hailey admired the view. "But, to tell the truth, Winnie, I crave your rooftop terrace, almost as much as I crave your height."

Winner forced a smile. "This terrace will be perfect for my party,"

Catching her off guard, Adair slithered up and wrapped his arm around her waist. Like a wet-nosed puppy, he nuzzled her cheek. "Dear child," he whispered.

"Watch the make-up," quipped Hailey. She beamed at Winner. "His—not yours."

"Bitch in heat," Adair snarled suddenly at Hailey, adding sweetly, to Winner, "Her—not you." He stroked Winner's exposed flesh. "You're my favorite." he said, pinching her arm

"Ow!" cried Winner, only half laughing.

The manager, who had been waiting in silence, sniffed softly. "I'll take my leave," he said, smiling.

"Oh, of course. Thanks," said Winner, rubbing her arm.

"Tomorrow morning, we'll set up for the party. We can place the stage right over there—for Tropica's performance." He pointed to a spot at one end of the terrace. "She arrives tomorrow afternoon?"

"Tropica's coming?" Hailey applauded. "She's a hottie."

"Indeed," said the manager.

Hailey buffed her nails. "So I've heard."

"When should I arrive?" Adair asked.

"Doors open at 9:00 p.m." replied Winner, relieved to have escaped Adair's clutches.

"When does your mystery man arrive?" Hailey whispered to Winner, as the two of them followed Adair and the manager to the elevator.

"You know who he is, don't you?" whispered Winner. "How do you know?"

Hailey squeezed Winner's hand. "I'm rich, girlie. Money talks."

"Damian arrives tomorrow," whispered Winner. walking with Hailey, arm in arm.

"Is that his name?"

Winner said furtively, "Damian Velasquez. Don't pretend you don't know it. Hailey, don't you breathe a word to a soul. Hear me?"

"Cross my heart."

"Just not your fingers," Winner warned, fondling Hailey's black-lacquered fingernails.

"I would never betray you, Winnie." Hailey approached the elevator and stood alongside her brother and the manager.

"Naturally, we will do everything necessary to make your stay with us an enjoyable one, Miss Demming," the manager said. "And a safe one, of course. You're only moments away from your friends and family, all of whom are staying on the two floors below you."

"The 15th and 16th?"

"Yes, Ma'am."

"Friends like us," said Hailey brightly.

Miffed, Adair tossed his hair at the manager. "Don't call our Princess Daphne 'Ma'am.' She's just a girl. Apologize."

"My apologies, Miss Demming," said the hotelier evenly.

"No problem," said Winner. "Actually, I'm nineteen now."

"Our Winnie's a growed-up woman child," said Hailey lightly, pushing her brother into the open elevator.

Winner's eyes narrowed. "You don't know the half of it, honey."

"What?" Hailey cried. "Whatever do you mean?"

"Your teasing is unworthy of our princess." Adair yawned, covering his mouth. His hand trembled.

"Princess Winner." Hailey declared. She motioned to the manager, who stepped into the elevator.

"Princess Daphne," her brother corrected, at Hailey's side.

"Both!" Hailey conferred. "Winnie, if your storybook prince doesn't show, I'm moving in with you up here. Okay?"

Winner shushed her. "He'll show, Hailey. No worries on that score." *None that I'll admit.* "Oh! I almost forgot. My father accepted the role. Ezra and Nick are bringing him here tonight."

"Hot damn." Hailey's green eyes bulged. "Heston Demming is mine."

"Heston Demming," said Adair, brushing back a forelock of brown hair. "King Odysseus."

Cocking her head, Winner added, "And even more amazing—my stepmother's coming here, too!"

Hailey gasped. "You wicked girl. Do tell. Have you booked them in adjoining suites?"

Winner tittered. "Not quite. But Poppy's suite is right across the hall from Dad's. 1602-1603, I think. Something like that—"

The manager nodded, hands clasped.

"Do they know it?"

Making a silly face, Winner shook her head. "No."

"That will be a surprise," murmured the manager. He had been waiting patiently while his guests chatted, but he was growing restless. "Ready to depart?" he asked Hailey.

"Wait!" Winner said. "Daddy's even agreed to lend a hand at producing."

Grasping Winner's hands—nearly pulling her inside the elevator—Hailey jumped up and down. "Aayeee! Way to go, girlie!"

Winner pulled away. "Way to go, Ezzie, you mean. Ezra sold Dad on the script."

"I love that man!" Hailey jiggled with joy.

Tapping his leather shoulder bag, Adair mumbled. "I have my script. I'll be ready."

"I know you will." Hailey rolled her eyes at Winner.

"Ezzie's written a good story," said Winner. "It's little dark, but—"

"Who's the fairest of them all?" Adair asked the manager.

The manager glanced at Winner, then Hailey. "I'm sure I don't know, sir."

"Ladybug," Adair said, indicating Winner.

Winner blinked rapidly. "Ladybug? Adair, how did you know my father's pet name—?"

"Oh, he heard it from Ezra." Hailey flipped her long, blonde hair over her shoulder. "Adair, you can be such a toad. Leave Winnie alone." She looked up at the manager. "Let's go."

As the manager pushed a button, Adair whispered, "My darling daughter." He smiled oddly at Winner.

"Shut up, beast."

"But she is—"

The elevator door began to close.

"Shut up, Adair," she heard Hailey snarl.

The elevator door closed completely. The car began its descent.

"Both of you, shut up!" Exhilarated, Winner wasted no time, running straight through the great room and out onto the blazing-bright terrace. Transfixed, she stared in wonder at the glorious Enchanted Palace, the beloved setting of her magical childhood fantasies.

***

One hour later, Poppy found herself sitting across from her adopted daughter, Winner, at a small table in a corner of the hotel's deli. The too-public venue was causing Poppy anxiety. She could not help but notice how many of the shop's customers kept staring at Winner. No one was being obnoxious. However, everyone in the room was aware that a major star was present. To Poppy's mind, each and every person was a potential villain.

Was Winner aware of them? The beauty had so many fans. They came in all ages and from every stage of life. Poppy noticed that Winner was twirling hair, a sure that the girl's nerves were on edge. On the surface, Win appeared chatty and outgoing. If Winner were afraid, she wasn't letting it show. Apparently, she was glorying in the attention today. Her mood was buoyant. The girl's manner had changed considerably since their phone conversation early that morning.

"I'm not frightened anymore, Poppy." Winner sipped her strawberry lemonade. "I've realized I over-reacted to those creepy text messages. I didn't mean to scare you. I'm sorry if I did."

"What changed your mind?"

"I came to my senses. That's all."

"But it's still true—right? Some psychopath sent you obscene, threatening texts?"

"I guess. Yes."

Poppy's ire got the better of her. "Where are your security people, Winner? Why aren't they here with you now?" Poppy looked around the room. "They should be. Any one of these diners could have sent that text."

Winner rolled her eyes. "I just need privacy right now, Mommy." Winner did not scan the room, nor did she lift her eyes to meet Poppy's. "Soon enough, you'll understand why."

"What does that mean?"

"You'll see."

Poppy threw up her hands. "You're playing with fire, girl. You need to get on that phone and let the team know what's going on."

"I will."

"When?"

"Soon. Really."

"If you don't do it soon, I will."

Winner sighed and clicked her tongue in disdain.

Poppy realized she was coming off as the nagging stepmother. Reluctantly, she changed her approach. "Well, we can deal with that later.

I'm famished, sweetie. Have you seen the great things on this menu? What do you feel like? How about seared tuna?"

"I'm not really hungry. This drink is enough."

"Winston, it's important that you maintain your health. You need to eat regularly. You need to make wise food choices."

Winner slapped her own forehead. "Please leave me alone about it." Attempting to calm herself, the girl took a sip of the pink lemonade. "You and I get along so well—until this subject comes up—until you try to manipulate me. I'm not a child anymore."

Poppy was at a loss. "You want me to be okay with your choices? Make better choices. One meal a day and vodka? That's what you said in an interview last month—when that entertainment blogger had asked how you maintain your weight. I'm supposed to be okay with that behavior?"

"That was PR." Winner sipped more lemonade. "Anyway, it's my body. It's my life."

"Are you drinking vodka now?" Poppy bristled, examining the lemonade glass. "You're too young and inexperienced to know what you're doing."

"I know what I'm doing," Winner scoffed, her cheeks flushing. "Are you the big star? No. I am. My public expects me to be svelte."

"At this rate, you won't be svelte. You'll be skeletal."

"You're just jealous because you got fat."

Angry, Poppy gaped." What did you say to me?"

"You heard me."

"Oh, I heard you all right, Missy." Flushed, she leaped to her feet.

Contrite, Winner stood and blocked her path. "Poppy, I'm sorry. Anyway, you lost it all. You look great now. Love your outfit, by the way."

Appeased, Poppy took a few deep breaths and resumed her seat. "Thanks. Losing weight is hard work. Not that you'll ever know much about it."

The blonde beauty shot her a smokey-blue glance. "Yeah, I know."

"Even if I hadn't lost the twenty-five pounds, you have no right to insult me."

"You insult me."

"When? How?" She felt her blood pressure rising again.

Winner pouted in silence.

Poppy exhaled, gathering her purse. "This is getting us nowhere. Maybe I should go back to Naples." She rose.

"No! Wait, please. Stay for the party tomorrow night. I want you to meet—!" Inhaling sharply, Winner cupped both hands over her mouth.

"Whom?"

Winner's angelic countenance lit up. Her hands fell away from her mouth. "He's my big surprise, Poppy."

Realizing, Poppy sank into her chair. Mom-duty called. "A man?"

Nodding vigorously, Winner beamed. "The man."

"That's what's up your sleeve?" Poppy leaned across the table. "That's why you seem so flighty."

"Oh, it's just—everything! I'm so happy."

As if leveling a teaspoon, Poppy measured her response. "Are you already married? Are you—?"

Doubling over, Winner giggled in delighted embarrassment. "No. I'm not expecting. But we are engaged."

"Does your father know?" Poppy whispered slowly. "Of course he doesn't. Silly me. How could he? Out of touch, hiding away—who knows where." A thought crossed her mind. "Does Ezra know? Or is Ezra himself the mystery man? Are you engaged to Ezra Gold?"

"Ezzie?" Winner laughed. "Get serious, Mommy."

"I am quite serious. Ezra's mad about you. Has been for years."

"Please. Ezra's my bud, but that's as far as it goes."

"Well, then who is this—man of yours?"

Winner shook her head, biting her lower lip. "Nuh-uh. No one even knows he exists but you—and Hailey—and Felicia. Fe's performing at my party, which is cool. I told her we'd invited Lissette, but—"

"Who's Hailey again?"

"Hailey Champlain. Adair Champlain's sister."

Memory roused, Poppy pointed a finger at Winner. "Oh, yes. I know who Adair is. Isn't he an actor? Your sisters think he's—the cat's meow."

"The what?" Winner cackled. "You mean hot?"

"Sage and Teggie are too young to think any man is hot."

"No. They're not. They're adolescents."

"I will not discuss your sisters' nonexistent sex lives with you, Winston—"

Exasperated, Winner retreated to higher ground. "Yes, Adair is an actor. He's starring in our new series. He's also our financial backer. Hailey's supposed to be the producer, but she's—learning as she goes. Don't laugh, but they're my new pals. Well, Hailey is. Adair is sort of, there."

Poppy recollected. "Aren't those two kids related to Ezra somehow?"

"No, not to Ezzie. But to Vivian, his old mistress—the one who died. The one who willed him the boat. They were her step-kids."

Poppy remembered now. *Vivian Champlain. Reminds me of that awful business with Lennox Cordova, whose strange mother had a December-May affair with Heston.* "Very rich now, aren't they?"

"Bouncing baby billionaires," said Winner. "Their dad died a few months ago. Left the works to Adair, but Hailey's well-provided for."

Poppy chose her words carefully. "Watch your step with them, Win. People like that—can be ruthless—when the stakes are high."

Wrist limp, Winner waved her hand. "Pfftt!" she uttered dismissively. "They're harmless. Actually, they're kind of sweet—in a pathetic way."

Listening to Winner, Poppy pretended to read the menu. She circled back to the previous topic. "Winner, this man of yours. Have you known him long? Who are his people?"

"Let's just say he's *muy guapo,* Mommy."

Astonished, Poppy sat back, setting down the menu. "You mean, he's Spanish?"

"He's an American—of Hispanic heritage." Winner teased from the corner of her eyes. "Wait until you see him—I mean, meet him."

"Well, when will that be?" She looked around inquiringly. "Is he here at the resort now?"

"No. He's on his way. Driving up from Key Largo. You'll meet him tomorrow night—at my party."

"Oh."

"Mommy, there's something else I need to tell you. There's somebody else who's coming—"

"I'm not sure I can take another revelation before lunch. Somebody else?"

"Sort of, yeah." Winner's silver-blues sparkled.

"Lay it on me." Poppy braced for the worst.

"Hello, precious." A handsome young man said from behind sunglasses. He sidled up to the table. He was vaping leisurely, but his free hand massaged Winner's bare shoulders. However, as he removed the sunglasses, his blue eyes found Poppy's eyes and held them.

"Hello, Adair," said Winner, squirming. "I'd like to you meet my—"

"Wife," said Adair, contemplating Poppy, who lowered her gaze.

"No. Well, Dad's wife. My mom, Poppy Demming."

"You," said Adair, offering his hand, "are the one."

"Am I?" Poppy responded politely, accepting his hand.

Adair fondled her hand for a moment and then squeezed it "Lovely to see you, Poppy. You're looking quite well."

"Thanks. So are you."

"Yes, I know. Have you heard? My legions of fans have found me. They tried to gather on the hotel grounds, but the management ejected them."

"Pity," said Poppy, retrieving her hand.

Winner pursed her lips and leveled her eyes at Poppy.

Amiably, Poppy made a stab at conversation. "I've seen a couple of your movies, Adair. My other daughters—Winner's younger sisters—are big fans of yours."

"Sage and Teggie? I know them well."

"You do?"

"They're ours."

"They are?"

Winner exhaled loudly. "Enough, Adair. Mommy and I have stuff to discuss. We'll all catch up later. Okay?"

"I'll look forward to it. *Hasta luego, Winita.*" Abruptly, Adair wandered out of the coffee shop and made his way towards the pool area.

Winner shook her head. "Great."

"So that was Adair Champlain? What did he mean? About the twins?"

"Who knows? He—um—has issues."

Poppy leaned in. "He seems a bit vapid. Sort of—I don't know, disassociated. But he's very attractive. How old is he?"

"Why? Interested?" Grimacing, Winner waved a hand dismissively. "Trust me. That guy is all talk and no action. Believe me. Adair Champlain is stuck on himself. You should hear the story Felicia told me—"

The train of conversation stopped again, as a petite blonde woman in stiletto heels strutted perkily towards the table. "Winnie, conference call in five minutes. We need to discuss wardrobe with Jaime." She caught sight of Poppy. "Hi, there."

"Hailey, this is my mom, Poppy."

"How do you do?" said Hailey. "It's a pleasure to make your acquaintance."

"Thank you." In fascination, Poppy regarded this vivacious miniature version of Winner. "You are Adair's sister?"

"Adair was just here," Winner explained to Hailey.

Hailey lost her puzzled look. She cocked her head and pointed a toothy grin at Poppy. "Say, Mom, I need to steal Princess Daphne here," she said, attempting charm. "Sorry. Business. You understand."

"I'm helping design the costumes for the production," Winner explained. "Mommy, it counts as an internship."

"Not a prob," said Poppy, rising from the table. "Do your job. Maybe I'll have lunch after a swim. If you both will excuse me, Ladies, I'll make my way to the pool."

"Will you be okay?" asked Winner, looking concernedly at Poppy. "If I go with Hailey?"

"Certainly," said Poppy. "Don't worry about me. As a matter of fact, I plan to take dinner in my room tonight, too. Spa tomorrow." She studied her nails. "Manicure. Pedicure. Party tomorrow night. The kids arrive Monday. Basically, I'm all set—except for our little chat about security."

"Relax. Everything is under control. Right, Win? A rest will do you good," Hailey said to Poppy. "I can guarantee you one thing, you won't be sorry you've had your beauty sleep."

"Everybody's speaking in riddles today." Poppy said politely, as Hailey led Winner away.

But Poppy's bitch-o-meter had switched on.

The two blondes made their way across the floor of the crowded deli. As Winner passed among the tables, the customers broke into spontaneous applause.

Annoyed, yet gratified, Winner stopped, along with Hailey and Poppy, and graciously thanked the crowd for acknowledging her celebrity. Poppy could not detect an ounce of fear coming from her stepdaughter, despite the girl's recent scare. Then she realized.

Anxiety medication overload.

"You're the most beautiful girl in the world," a male customer cried out in Winner's wake. "I love you, Princess Daphne!"

Quickly, Poppy urged Winner and Hailey out the door, and followed them out. "Be careful, Win," she said, placing a hand on the girl's arm. "You shouldn't mingle with strangers, unguarded. It's not safe."

Sighing, Winner halted. Hailey's smile froze in place. "Chill, Mom."

"Win, please get your security over here ASAP," she said under her breath.

"I will, Mommy." Winner kissed her cheek. "I'll do it soon, and then I'll phone you later."

"Looks as though we left just in time" observed Hailey, who took Winner in tow. "Here comes the dessert tray. Run, Poppy!" she called bitchily.

Disturbed, Poppy watched Hailey lead Winner across the hotel lobby.

There's something about that tiny woman I don't trust.

Then Poppy realized why. Hailey reminded her of her old nemesis, Sasha Bassett.

***

Unsettled, Poppy stood wondering about the two oddballs she'd just met. The brother, Adair, certainly had psychological problems. How did he manage to maintain an acting career? She made a mental note to ask Ezra about Adair's condition. Maybe it was Adair's boyish vulnerability that appealed to her. Because something about him did.

She found Adair attractive. She wanted to know more about him. Hailey, she could take or leave—preferably, leave. Still, Poppy was curious.

Who were these people, really? Who had Winner gotten herself involved with? Who was Winner's mystery man? Who had sent Winner the disturbing text messages? And why was Winner refusing protection? And there was—something else—what was it? She couldn't remember.

Too many questions. Too few answers. Poppy dreaded the party tomorrow night. She needed guidance, solace. She wished Heston were here to consult with her—about the welfare of his own daughter. But he wasn't. Inwardly, she chided herself.

That's not going to happen, Poppy. Not in this lifetime. Handle it yourself—or phone Jim Talbot. I mean, why not? At least check in with him. Thank him again for dinner—and the rose.

Finding a lounge chair on the shady side of the swimming pool, she settled in, prior to taking a swim. As an attendant plumped her pillows, Poppy noticed Adair Champlain watching her from behind the glass panes of the air-conditioned lobby. She waved a hand. When Adair realized he'd been spotted, he slipped away, disappearing from view. Her interest piqued, Poppy relished the covert attention.

140

I wonder if Adair is available.

From out of nowhere, an emotional lightning bolt struck: Adair was the same physical type as Heston. No wonder she found Adair attractive.

He's my type.

Groaning, she located her phone and placed a call to her ex-husband and current suitor, Jim Talbot. Jim did not answer. She left him a voice mail.

Then she remembered the other unresolved issue. She had neglected to ask Winner about the two missing dolls. Too weary to text, she made a mental note to bring up the topic as soon as she saw Winner again. Looking up, she spied a server approaching with a bucket of iced champagne and a vase of long-stemmed red roses on a rolling cart.

"Whom are they from?" she demanded to know as he parked the cart beside her.

"I couldn't say, madam," said the second server, setting down the tray. "We wasn't given a name. We were instructed to say, 'A token of affection in spite of your rejection.' "

Oh, great. That narrows it down. Not.

141

Chapter Eight

That night, Maude Winston Demming quarried her prey.

Just after midnight, the tall, rangy middle-aged woman parked her modest Chevy in the visitor's lot of The Southern Seas Resort, Orlando, and entered the hotel. Hiding in plain view, she seated herself in the hotel's grand lobby, watching as Danny Vega used his mobile phone to make a call. He did not look her way. Nor did he approach the front desk.

Rather, after completing the call, Danny pocketed the mobile phone and sat down in a nearby chair, facing away from her and towards the elevators.

Clandestinely, Maude studied his body language. He appeared jittery, exhausted from the long drive to Orlando. During that drive, he had stopped to eat and shop repeatedly, wasting time along the way. He had made several purchases, mostly, apparel. Maude knew what that meant.

Who's the naïve woman footing his bills these days?

Like her unsuspecting prey, Maude was weary from the long drive. She had been following Danny, in her own car, since he'd left Naples that afternoon. There in the alleyway, astonished, she had caught sight of him outside of *Rainbow's* on Fifth Avenue South. He'd nearly run her over. Upon recognizing him, she had hopped into her car and tailed him to the cemetery in North Naples. When he had stopped his car in front of Franco Demming's grave and gotten out, she had been sure of his identity. She had been tailing Danny Vega ever since, apparently unbeknownst to him.

Now, after midnight, in the lobby of this posh resort hotel in Orlando, Maude eyed Danny, off and on, judging his appearance. He had changed, and yet he hadn't. He still moved like a sexual predator, although he had aged ten years, at least, since her last glimpse of him. His dark hair was graying, but his physique was still top-notch, his strong arms, 'cut.'

Still in the tennis racket, I suppose. LOL

The pun had been one of his favorite jokes—

He glanced in her direction. She ducked out of sight. She was planning to approach him, but she wasn't sure when or how. She wanted, first, to know the lie of the land. Then she would move in for the kill.

She corrected herself.

For the confrontation, not the kill. Old habits of thought could be hard to break, even when a person had been redeemed.

Suddenly, an elevator door slid open. A tall, slender, gazelle-like young woman—with silky flaxen hair—strode out into the lobby. Seeing Danny, the blonde strode over to him, took him by the hand, hurrying him back into the waiting elevator.

"Winner," he said. "You look good enough to eat."

Putting her forefinger to his lips, the girl shushed him. Silently, the elevator door began to close, just as the girl wrapped her long, elegant arms around Danny's waist, and he cupped her round buttocks with his two hands.

Maude sat, stunned.

That beautiful apparition been her own daughter.

She would have recognized her namesake anywhere. She had followed Winston's acting career for the past three years. She had collected photos of Winner, videos, even bought four Princess Daphne dolls, each one clothed in a unique ensemble. Yet tonight, in person, her daughter had appeared more beautiful, in the flesh, than Maude could have ever believed possible. Her old enemy, regret, assailed her mercilessly.

Winner has inherited my sense of style and Heston's great beauty. If only I hadn't . . .

Maude's maudlin thoughts were interrupted. Three vigorous mature men, followed by a bellhop piloting a luggage-filled trolley, exploded into the hotel lobby and approached the front desk, apparently checking in as hotel guests. The men paid no attention to Maude. Men no longer noticed her. That was part of the new reality she had been learning how to handle.

"We're with Winner Demming's party," one of the men said to the clerk at the front desk.

The familiar deep voice made Maude jump.

"Name, sir?"

"Heston Demming."

"Of course. We're honored, sir."

Breathless, Maude watched unobtrusively as the desk clerk handed her ex-husband an electronic key card.

"Your suite is on the 16th floor, Mr. Demming."

"Thank you."

"Name, sir," the clerk asked the African-American man. "Townsend, Nicholas."

The third man chimed in. "I'm Ezra Gold"

Maude stiffened. *Winner's mentor, the famous director . . .*

The desk clerk looked up. "I'm a big fan, Mr. Gold. I'm a film student. Anything I can do to—"

"Thanks." Gold took charge. "I believe Townsend and I are sharing a suite?" he said to the fawning clerk.

"Yes, sir. We apologize for the inconvenience."

"No worries. Nick brought his bottle of Snore-No-More. Right, pal?" He grinned at the bald senior, who looked disgruntled.

Gold rubbed it in. "See? I have fans, too. I should have been an actor myself."

Unconvinced, Nick blew air in contempt. "Whew . . ."

Smiling faintly, the desk clerk handed an e-key to each man. "The 16th floor, sir."

Despite the cool air in the lobby, Maude was perspiring profusely beneath her scruffy ball cap, which she readjusted, as resort workers wheeled the men's luggage trolley towards the elevator—but a different one, not the same elevator into which Winner and Danny had disappeared, moments earlier.

Confused, Maude watched the scene unfold. Before entering the elevator, Heston trotted back to the front desk and addressed the clerk, once again.

"Excuse me. My daughter—Winner Demming—?

A smile flitted across the desk clerk's face. "Yes, sir. I know, sir."

"Oh, right," Heston said, flummoxed. "As I understand it, Winner has a big surprise in store. Any idea what it might be?"

"Perhaps, her party, sir? It's to be held on the terrace of her suite, sir—the Royal Suite."

"Royal Suite?"

"The penthouse, sir. Two floors above your suite. But the only access to the Royal is by private elevator. Stairs in an emergency—"

"I see. Thank you." He pressed crisp bills into the clerk's hand. "See that my daughter has everything she needs."

"Certainly, sir."

"So, Win's having a party tomorrow night," said Ezra Gold, rejoining Heston at the front desk. "So what?" Rapidly, he snapped his upper and lower teeth together. "Any idea why?" he asked the clerk.

"I'm in the dark, sir."

"Aren't we all?" Gold responded. He sounded worried. As Gold and Heston joined Townsend in the waiting public elevator, Maude's mind whirled. The men disappeared from view as the elevator door closed.

Shaken, she leaned back in her chair. It wasn't possible. Circumstances could not be as they appeared. Or could they?

What is going on here?

Her radar kicked in, cutting short her train of thought. She sat up straight. The lobby was suddenly empty of guests, but the desk clerk had noticed her and was walking her way.

Tugging at the brim of her cap, Maude sprang to her feet and rushed out the lobby door. Walking briskly to the parking lot, she analyzed the situation. After all her years of struggle, she knew a rat when she smelled one.

And this rat stinks to high heaven.

Danny Vega was pulling another fast one—and nobody knew it yet, but her. Climbing into her Chevy, Maude made a resolution, a promise to herself.

This time, he's not going to get away with it.

It was late in the day, metaphorically speaking, for her maternal instincts to kick in, but kicking in they were. She might not have been able to save herself from Danny's shenanigans, but maybe she could save her beautiful daughter, and in the process, make amends for all the harm she had caused her in childhood. It was worth a try.

***

Two hours later, five miles away, a mysterious figure moved silently around the vacant sets of *Forbidden Mysteries*. The culprit, unafraid, roamed freely and unrestricted, fearing no prying eyes nor camera lenses. Somewhere, high heels clicked-clacked, tapping the hard surface of the sound-stage floor. The sounds echoed throughout the vast room. Like the sounds of clashing swords, they amplified in the mind of the king.

En garde!

Imaginary lightsaber in hand, the dashing figure sliced and slashed myriad imaginary foes, dancing in swordplay around the various sets. Dressed in form-fitting aerospace nylon, aqua and black, fencing mask in place, the king lifted the saber perpendicular to the floor. With grace and lightning speed, he lunged at an invisible opponent.

Heston Demming must die.

Slicing the opponent's space-tunic, the king felt gratified. Driving the sword through the heart of his wounded opponent, the king knew victory.

Turning to an imaginary audience, he bowed deeply, from the waist, and saluted, gallantly, the vanquished challenger, whose face resembled the king's own.

Take him away.

Magically, vassals hauled away the body, and the lightsaber disappeared from the king's hand. In its place, a hand-held microphone appeared. The king stepped up onto the podium. Spotlights swirled, settling on the speaker, now the center of the universes.

"My name is Heston Demming," said the speaker to a packed room of imaginary derelicts "and I am an actor. I am—an alcoholic."

Silent voices spoke. "Hello, Heston. Welcome, Heston."

The speaker continued. "Thank you, my friends. Yes, my journey through alcoholism has been a harrowing one, fraught with many ills and perils. I have been a bad man, a very bad man and atrocious husband and father. I know I deserve to be punished for my shortcomings. And rest assured, my friends, I shall be punished. I shall be. "

Applause.

"Those nobler than I am are seeing to such matters. I thank them profoundly, from the bottom of my heart, because I recognize the fact that I am evil and that I must be crushed—and replaced by a much more worthy self—my true self. My true nature—that of the heroic Odysseus, whom I portrayed so ably as an adventurer in outer space—and in homage to those greatest of actors, Edmund Kean, John Barrymore. and their noble ilk, I welcome my acting awards as deserved. But my stupendous talent does not release me from a greater guilt. For my personal misdeeds, I welcome recompense—as well deserved." The king hung his head in dignity and shame.

"Bravo!" shouted the silent voices of imaginary supporters. The dark angels shined down in approval, prepared to do their part in the well-deserved retribution of Heston Demming. This star had not forgiven himself, nor forgotten the debt he owed. Nor did he begrudge the Justice which must be meted out for the Cosmos to remain in balance.

"And I would like to thank the Academy for this award," said the speaker, now clad in an imaginary tuxedo, speaking at a podium before billions on onlookers. "But I am a bad man, a very, very bad man, and I do not deserve more acting roles. In fact, I refuse to accept it. Instead, I give it to the world's greatest living actor, The Great One who truly deserves such accolades. That fine actor is one whom I envy and adore—and I do mean adore—one without whose support I could never, never excel to comparable heights. I reject my international stardom. Thank you, my love. Thank you, thank you, and again I say thank you."

Holding an imaginary statuette aloft, the king graciously handed it off to an advancing imaginary fellow. As the statuette changed hands, the speaker said, "Thank you, Heston. I, Heston Demming, do solemnly swear that I am the world's best actor and that you, my friend, Heston, are the world's greatest living actor. Take all my fans. They are rightfully yours, to do with as you will."

"Thank you, friend—my inspiration and my executioner."

"You are most welcome, my darling Odysseus."

A crackling noise startled the speaker, who fell silent.

A voice blared over the sound system. "Heston, you are wasting time. Get a move on."

My minion speaks truth.

The king turned to the business at hand. The trap must be set tonight. Now. The bait must be placed on the hook. The goose must be cooked. If all goes well, the work of retribution will be accomplished—soon, very soon.

Then our galaxy will be, once again, safe and at peace. Odysseus will return to reunite with Penelope, and Heston will die. Long live Heston Demming. Long live King Odysseus.

I declare it to be so. If the trap I set tonight meets failure, my resolve will only be heightened, Then the bloody deed will be done, on the steps of the Enchanted Palace.

This then is my decree: until the morrow . . .

Pax Hestona.

***

On the following day. Heston dozed, half awake, in bed, until his phone began to blare incessantly. Irritated, he opened his eyes to streaming noon sunlight. Covering his eyes and cursing vociferously, he grappled for the infernal device, which sat jangling on the nearby nightstand.

"-ello," he murmured.

"Heston? Gold, here. 'We got trouble. Right here in River City.' And it starts with a W, and it stands for your stunning, but evasive daughter."

Heston rolled onto his back. "Stop babbling, Gold. I'm in no mood for Broadway allusions. I'm barely coherent. What's wrong?"

Ezra did not respond. Heston could hear him conversing with a room-service porter who, evidently, had delivered a breakfast cart, one laden with blueberry blintzes and sour cream. As the porter took his leave, Ezra returned to the phone. Mouth full, he chomped at Heston.

"Look it, I tried to make a lunch date for you, me, Nick, and Winner. But the kid put me off. Told me nothing doing 'til after her party tonight."

Heston sat up. "Oh?" Fumbling through his duffel bag for shorts and a T-shirt, he mentally prepared to dress himself.

Meanwhile, Ezra swallowed, then slurped. "I told her it was urgent, that we have something we have to discuss with her. She said she'd phone me later if she could find the time. So now what?" He paused, then blurted out, "What the hell is up with her, anyway?"

Heston located his sneakers and untied the laces. "Let it be until tonight, Ezra. If she doesn't leave her suite today, things should be okay. Tonight, at the party, Nick's people can keep an eye out." After donning athletic socks, Heston slid his feet into the running shoes. "What about contacting her security people? You said you would."

Ezra exhaled. "I did. But they won't show up until tonight, either. She's put the fear in them. Funny, they'd like to keep their jobs," he quipped. "So, they're obeying her orders. Staying away."

"What?"

"She doesn't have any protection right now."

"You're joking." Quickly, he tied his shoelaces. "I'll phone them. Get their asses in gear."

"Okay. Good." Ezra slurped more liquid. "So, you believe me now? That the threat is for real?"

"Let's say I've considered the possibility."

"Have you told Nicky? He's gone out for breakfast. Told me to keep him posted."

"Then do. See what he says."

"Okay."

"I'm going for a twenty-minute run, Gold. I'm taking my phone. Keep me abreast."

"Will do. Hey, keep an eye out. Okay?" Ezra rang off.

Yawning, Heston sat on the side of his bed, his forearms resting on his knees, his hands dangling limply in mid-air. Worry pummeled him.

Had his presence here put Win in greater danger? Who really knew what the best move was, at this point? There was no rational answer, not when dealing with a nut job. Rev. Bill had often remarked, when you're not sure what move to make 'Do the next right thing.' Which would be what?

To pay attention. You can't out-reason an irrational mind. So, pay attention. That would be the very next right thing.

Standing up, he stretched. Muscles loosened, he opened the curtains and stared out at sunny Central Florida.

No sign of any crazies out there.

Preparing to run, he shook out his legs and did some initial stretches. Limbered up, he heard a knock on the door.

"Let me in, Sleeping Beauty." It was Nick's chest voice. "I've brought sustenance."

Sighing in frustration, Heston rose and threw open the door to his suite.

Bright eyed, Nick entered, a Styrofoam coffee cup in hand.

"Good afternoon," he said, surprised at Heston's pose and activity. "Brought you some java. Cappuccino from The Pancake House. It's the best in O-town."

"Put it down and get lost, please. I'm on my way out."

"Testy, testy. Sleep poorly?"

Heston relented. "Slept fine. Awakened poorly. Not complaining, though. I've survived much worse accommodations. This place is luxurious in the extreme."

151

Unexpectedly, Ezra poked his head in the doorway. "What? You mean you've been slumming for the past few years?"

"That's exactly what I mean. Although I wouldn't call it that—"

"Hey! That's just like what Joel McCrea did in *Sullivan's Travels?* I love that film. Heston, who played your sexy sidekick? Who was your Veronica Lake?"

Montserrat Flynn.

Mum, Heston walked out the door into the corridor. "Give it a rest. That's 1940's fantasy fluff."

"It's classic Hollywood, man."

"It's the rich telling the rich about poverty."

"Come on, Heston—"

"You're spoiled, Ezra, and you don't even know it."

Incensed, Ezra followed him out. "Well, I do prefer the best. I don't stay in flophouses."

Heston shook his head. "Even the idea of you in a flophouse is comical." Then he addressed Nick, who had followed Ezra out into the corridor and shut the door to Heston's suite. "Winner won't see us until tonight, Nicky. She's up to something, apparently, and doesn't want to let the cat out of the bag."

"How do you know that?" Ezra asked pointedly.

"Why else would she insist on privacy?"

"Think she'll be making an announcement?" Nick asked, amused at Ezra's discomfiture.

"It wouldn't surprise me." Both men eyed Ezra, whose countenance had fallen like that of a condemned man.

Tickled, Nick said, "No problem, Heston, I'll put my operatives to work around the hotel. As a matter of fact, I would suggest checking up on all your children today. Alert school officials. Make sure everyone's safe. You should contact your wife, too, and tell her about finding the doll."

Reluctant. Heston put his hands on his hips. "Okay. I will."

"Now, what am I going to do with this molten cup of brew?" Annoyed, Nick wiggled the steaming cup.

"Peace, brother," said Ezra snidely, rescuing the cup from Nick's jiggling hand.

"Thanks for the thought, Nick." Heston began to jog in place. "I'm going for a run, and then, room service."

"Better wear your woolies," Nick advised, shaking moisture from his hand. "And watch out for kooks."

Ezra quaffed the cappuccino. "You're not in Kansas anymore, Dorothy. You're in Central Florida. In December. It's 45 degrees outside."

"Even the orange trees are wearing woolies."

Heston caved. "You're both right—for a change." Doubling back inside his own suite, he ransacked his duffel back and donned a sweatshirt and running pants.

Exiting his suite again, he found himself alone in the corridor. Pleased, he began to jog in place. Invigorated, he jogged down the long hotel corridor. Rounding the corner, he bumped smack into a pretty woman.

"Excuse me. I'm terribly sorry. I—"

"No. I beg your pardon," she stammered.

Attractive—middle aged—cute figure— red hair—freckles —wide-set brown eyes—holy—!

"Poppy?"

"H-Heston?"

Riveted, Heston and his wife beheld one another in astonishment.

"What are you doing here?" Poppy croaked, finding her voice, at last.

***

For a moment, Poppy stared up into Heston's eyes as if gazing at a heavenly array of stars. The silver-blue orbs had illuminated many dark nights of intimate and passionate lovemaking, all across her lifetime. They ignited so many feelings, deep in her core.

Oh, Heston . . .

He was still so handsome—but—he was 54 years old now! How could he still be so handsome? It wasn't fair, but . . .

Did he speak?

"What?" she asked him.

"I said, 'Are you here for Winner's party?' " He enunciated too clearly, his voice even more rich and deep in maturity.

"I heard you."

"Oh. I thought you hadn't."

She struggled to take in this sudden shift in reality. She and Heston were standing alone in the corridor, except for a few stray guests meandering to and from the nearby public-elevator alcove. Alert and aware, Heston seemed to be taking in everyone and everything.

Poppy examined him closely. He still radiated that charm, that unusual air of enchantment—and yet . . . he seemed different: mellowed, but distant—almost—what?

What shall I say to this—stranger?

For he was still her Heston—and yet he wasn't. The handsome mature man now towering over her, demanding her attention, was only the latest incarnation of Sean Heston Demming. This version of the man—this gorgeous, graying fellow—looked and sounded like a seasoned king, returning to rule his lost city-state, no longer the adventurous young prince who had set out on a perilous voyage of discovery. This man was the world-weary adventurer, turning homeward, sadder but wiser and aching for solace.

"Who are you?" she whispered unintentionally.

He gaped. "Poppy, are you hallucinating?"

She roused. "What? No, of course not."

"I've changed, naturally. You've changed, too."

She put her hands to her throat. "Have I?"

"You've aged. But you've aged well. You look good."

She breathed again. "Thank you, Heston. So do you, as a matter of fact."

"That's nice to hear. Since I'm starting my career comeback this week."

"You are?"

He anchored his hands to his hips. "Ezra—and Winner—offered me a cameo role in their new production. I took it." He stepped aside to accommodate a sexy passer-by. "To get closer to Ladybug. That's why I'm here in Orlando. Production begins soon. We start scene rehearsals with Ezra. After the first read-through." Tearing his gaze from the sexy passerby, he faced Poppy squarely. "How have you been?"

By now, her anger was returning. Her initial flush of excitement, at seeing him, had been replaced by acidic remembrance. "Great. Never better."

"Yeah?"

"Yeah. Well, I need a quick shower. I just took a yoga class—in the hotel gym. That's why I'm dressed this way."

"Yoga pants. Looking good, Red."

Embarrassed, she tried to move past him and continue down the corridor to her suite, but he blocked her path.

"All right, Heston," she said. "Yes. I'm here for Winner's party. She's making an announcement tonight, Heston. Did you know that?"

"That's what I was afraid of," he said. Seemingly unwilling to unhook Poppy and toss her back, he kept staring at her, too directly. "I'll be there, too, at her party—as far as I know."

"Oh, my. Oh—!" Reality registered in Poppy's mind.

This is what Winner tried to tell me—

"Red, I've been thinking about your request—for a divorce?"

"Yes. I remember that, too, funnily enough"

At that moment, Nick Townsend stepped out of an elevator. He headed their way, joining their conversation affably. "Well, hello, Miss Poppy. You're looking lovely, as ever."

"Hi, Nick. It's good to see you again."

"Congratulations on your book release."

Taken aback by the acknowledgment, Poppy replied graciously, "Why, thank you, Nick."

"Book?" Heston inquired, his tone cynical.

"Yes, indeed," said Nick. He smiled. "Poppy's got a book out."

"My first book," noted Poppy, explaining to Heston. *"Collecting Florida Art."*

Nick's countenance lit up. "You did an interview a couple weeks ago on some show—I heard you. Meant to pick up a copy."

Delighted, Poppy said, "I'll sign it if you do."

"All right then." Apparently pleased, Nick turned his attention to Heston. "I assume you've informed Poppy about—"

Heston shook his head. "I was about to."

"Informed me of what?' she asked Nick.

"Something—disturbing, I'm afraid. We think—your daughter has a stalker."

Poppy gasped, glancing from Nick to Heston and back again. "You do mean Winner, right?"

"Yes. On Heart of Fire Key, we found a defaced—violently defaced—Princess Daphne action figure, along with a note—a death threat."

"Death threat?" Poppy put a hand to her open mouth.

"Relax, Poppy Sue. I still think it may be a prank," Heston said. "I think Ezzie and Nick here may have pulled a fast one to get me on board."

"We did no such thing, Poppy," Nick interjected. "The danger is real."

"What did the note say?" she queried Nick urgently.

"Exact words?" Nick deferred to Heston.

Heston took the wheel. "Said, 'To Orlando fly, or Ladybug will die.' "

Nick said, "The mutilation of the doll suggests serious intent. Even though we high-tailed it up here, chances are, Winner could be attacked, regardless."

"When was this, Nick?"

"This was yesterday morning."

Poppy's face fell. "I was afraid of that."

"What do you mean?"

"I talked to Winner yesterday. In fact, she phoned about it."

"About what?"

Poppy swallowed hard. "She's received threatening text messages. At least two, in the past two days."

Nick pressured. "What did the texts say?"

Shaking her head, Poppy shrugged, palms towards the ceiling. "She wouldn't repeat them. Too obscene." Losing control, she buried her face in her hands.

"And probably too violent," Nick observed.

Fuming, she glared at Heston. "How could you believe it was a prank?"

"Who, other than Ezra, wanted me in Orlando?" he retorted.

"Ezra wouldn't stoop that low. You should have taken it seriously."

"Should have? Hey, I'm here, aren't I?" Heston cried out. "I'm here because I wasn't sure if Winner was in danger. I care about my daughter."

"Oh, yeah. You care."

"I'm here because I chose to accept the role she offered me—which I had already done, for your information, hours before we found the doll and the note."

Nick backed up his story. "He'd already agreed."

Breathing deeply, Heston regained his composure,

Meanwhile, horrified, she connected the dots. She felt almost afraid to tell them the rest. "Two dolls are missing, guys. From Win's collection. Princess Daphne and—King Odysseus, Alien Space Warrior."

Heston sucked air. "What?"

"Lissette told me—days ago. I meant to ask Win about it."

Heston and Nick exchanged glances as Poppy explained. "One of them was Win's personalized Princess Daphne doll. The valuable one, the one Ezra gave her for her birthday, right before the premier of *Laurel*."

"Ezra did that?" Heston asked.

"Describe it," said Nick, but he did not wait for her reply. "Porcelain head and limbs? Grecian dress? Embroidered with pearls and sapphires?"

"Yes. 24 karat gold tiara. Little golden laurel leaves."

"Bingo." Nick turned to Heston. "That's what I was on my way back to tell you, man. Ezra was right. I got lab results. And the lab's analysis matches what Poppy is saying. Those gems are real."

"Oh, no."

"What is it?"

Brow knitted, Nick demanded, "Did you have a break-in at the house in Naples?"

"No. But Win came home a couple of weeks ago. It was Thanksgiving. Quite a few were in and out of house, including all the kids, the plumbers and the caterers and extra help."

"Plumbers?"

"Don't ask. When Lissy told me, I didn't think much about it. Thought she'd just misplaced the dolls, or they'd been moved during cleaning or something. Then I assumed Winner had taken the dolls with her when she went back to New York."

"Maybe she did." Nick looked at Heston. "I'll ask her ASAP."

"Makes sense. It's possible, isn't it?"

"It's also possible that someone else got hold of them in New York—or elsewhere, depending upon Win's movements." Nick cocked his head. "Look, today I've phoned Winner three times. Ezra's tried, too. Each time, her phone goes right to voice mail. I left her messages, texts, warning her—telling her to call me, but I didn't give her any specific details."

"I'll try phoning her, too," Poppy offered. "But my phone's in my purse. I left the purse in my room." She pointed in the direction of her suite.

Nick approved. "Go get it. We may be able to locate Win and put a tail on her, but, in the meantime, she needs to know she could be in danger."

Heston countered. "I think she may still be in her suite."

Nick shook his head "Nope. Hotel clerk saw her leave. Alone. Well, we think it was her. A girl matching her description—only with short, black hair—came out of the private elevator."

"Oh, Heston—!"

159

"Listen to me, Poppy." Heston looked proprietary. "Our other children may be at risk. Phone each of our kids. Phone their schools. Inform everyone to be vigilant—for the next few days."

"No specifics," noted Nick.

Poppy bridled, torn by feelings of desperation and defiance.

Should I take his orders?

She looked up at Heston. He stared into her eyes. He *expected* her to do his bidding. This aspect of him had not changed. He still made her knees weak. *Damn him!*

"All right."

"Good."

She added brusquely, "They'll all be here tomorrow." She saw her words hit home.

That got him.

"Here? You mean, Orlando?"

"I mean, this hotel. In my suite. Which is where I'm off to right now."

Rounding the two men, Poppy trotted down the corridor. She could feel Heston watching her undulating backside. He made her self-conscious, which infuriated her beyond measure, but she was titillated, too, although loathe to admit it.

"What's your room number?" Heston called after her.

"1603," she muttered, opening the door to her suite.

"1602!" He shouted indiscreetly, pointing to his suite door, which was located across the corridor from hers. At the moment, the corridor was empty, except for Poppy, Heston, and Nick, and one uniformed maid pulling a housekeeping cart into a service elevator, at the far end of the corridor.

"See you tonight at the party!" Heston shouted. "Save me a dance!"

"See you later, Poppy!" Nick called, heading for the elevators.

Furious, Poppy ignored them. Escaping into her own suite of rooms, she slammed the door behind her. Hotly, she debated, then opened the door once again and leaned out.

"In your dreams, Demming!" she cried, but, to her great disappointment, Heston was nowhere to be seen. Glumly, she withdrew into her suite and pouted.

Can I really be missing him already?

She decided to forget about him, if possible, and to concentrate on the safety of their children. Entering the bathroom, she switched on the lights. The blaze reflected in the walls and countertops shiny white marble. She reached for her purse—

She saw the doll.

Jumping back, she saw the writing on the mirror. She read it. She screamed, fleeing the bathroom and then, the suite itself.

Frantic, she stood, helpless, looking both ways, up and down the lonely corridor. Fearing for her life, she dashed towards the alcove of public elevators. Running blindly, she ran smack into the arms of Heston, who, followed by Nick, was running towards her. He and Nick met her halfway down the corridor. She ran into his arms.

"What's happened?" Heston cried, grasping her upper arms, prying her loose, steadying her.

"Doll," she managed to utter, pointing in the direction of her suite. "Mangled."

"The Heston doll?" barked Nick.

"Yes!" She panted in fear. She looked up at her husband. "This t-time, it's Odysseus—who's been desecrated. It's you, Heston!"

"Was there a note?"

"Red scrawl. Across the bathroom mirror. I ran."

"What did it say?" Heston shook her gently. "Focus. What does it say?"

Hysterically, Poppy cried out. "He's going to kill you, too, Heston, and—do things—to me afterward—"

"In a pig's eye," muttered Nick, slapping Heston's shoulder and heading for Poppy's suite. "C'mon, man. Let's go take a look. See what our perv's been up to now."

Chapter Nine

Inside Poppy's suite, Nick stood framed in the bathroom doorway. "Man alive." He stared at the jagged red letters scrawled across the bathroom mirror. Behind him stood Heston, who was deciphering the message, mentally forming the letters into words. He spoke the words aloud.

'Odysseus, will I slay. Penelope, will I lay.'

"Oh, dandy." Characteristically, Heston underplayed the moment. He could feel Poppy's presence close behind him. "Well, we have one clue. This scoundrel's no poet," he said. "For the record, my wife's real name is Penelope. 'Poppy' is her nickname."

"I see. Still think it's a prank, Hesty?" Nick growled, waving his hand.

"Maybe." Heston scanned the odd scene, trying to make sense of it. The bathroom mirror bore huge letters, slashed boldly in red ink, screaming the writer's intention.

Below, on the marble countertop near the sink, reposed a mutilated male action-figure, of the vintage variety. In the middle of the doll's forehead was a hole. Simulated blood—probably more nail polish—streamed from it. The limbs of doll had been mangled.

Looking away, Heston shuddered. He would have known the doll anywhere: good old Odysseus, the alien space warrior. Once upon a time, he'd been so proud of that action figure. He had gifted it to Lady-bug when she was little. She had cherished it.

How did it end up here? Like this—

Unlike Winner's Princess Daphne action figure—created in more recent times—this King Odysseus had not sold in the millions. Other versions of the King Odysseus action figure had sold well, but this doll had never been mass-produced. It was a one-of-a-kind and unmistakable.

"Don't touch anything," Nick ordered Heston and Poppy. "Have you let anyone else use this bathroom?" he asked Poppy as she ventured in, still standing close to Heston. "Any visitors?"

"No." Her freckled complexion had gone pallid.

Worried about her, Heston wound his fingers around hers. He exchanged glances with Nick. "Good girl," Heston said to his wife. She did not object.

Nick's eye speared his. "Heston, I have to ask" He pointed to the mirror. "Did you write this?" He pointed to the doll on the countertop. "Or plant this?"

"What? No! Did you?"

"No. Wait here," ordered Nick. "I'll search the rest of the suite. The perp could still be hiding in here."

As Nick scanned the far bedrooms, a knock sounded on the front door of the suite. Heston tensed. To his relief, he heard the voice of Ezra Gold.

"Poppy? You okay? Your door's open—"

"In here, Gold," Heston called.

Frowning, Ezra joined Heston and Poppy at the bathroom doorway. Seeing their faces, his frown turned to concern.

"What's going on?" he asked. "Thought I heard a scream. I was in my room."

"My wife has had an uninvited guest," Heston replied, thumbing towards the interior of the bathroom. "Nicky's—wait, here he comes now."

"All clear." Approaching, Nick saluted Ezra. "Did you see this?" he asked the film director. "Take a gander."

Heston, clinging to Poppy's hand, drew her aside. Ezra walked to the bathroom door and peered in. For a moment, he stared, struck dumb by the ghastly scrawl and desecrated doll.

"Shit," he said finally, stepping back and letting Nick pass through. "This is truly bizarre." He turned to Heston. "I hope you don't think I did this?"

"I'd like to hear it from your own lips," said Heston evenly.

"I did not do this."

"Well, that's out of the way."

"Turnabout is fair play," said Ezra, unsmiling.

Heston rebutted. "Are you insane, Gold? Of course, I didn't write it. This whole thing is ludicrous—not to mention, despicable. And if you've done any of this, I'll strangle you myself."

Poppy spoke to Ezra. "The dolls are from Win's collection. They were stolen."

Ezra's eye grew wide.

"And she's received threatening texts," added Heston.

"Which I did not send," said Ezra adamantly. "This is turning into a nightmare."

"It's an ugly business, all right," said Heston.

Ezra raised he eyebrows. "You're Penelope, right?" he said to Poppy.

"Penelope Susan Craft Talbot Demming," she replied.

"Just making sure I understand the situation," Ezra said.

He fell silent, as did Poppy. From inside the bathroom, Nick's voice filled the empty space. Nick was speaking into his phone. "I'm calling from Suite 1603. Get the house detective up here pronto. We've had a break-in. We'll need the police crime unit."

"Heston, I'm frightened," Poppy whispered.

He squeezed her hand reassuringly.

Ending the call, Nick squatted in place. He looked up at the semicircle of faces hovering over him. "People, this is a crime scene," he said, matter-of-factly. "Let's treat it like one. Everybody out."

Dazed, Heston, Poppy, and Ezra stepped away from the bathroom door and into Poppy's sitting room. As they made the transition, Poppy slipped her hand out of his.

Reluctantly, he let her, but he didn't like it.

Does she suspect me now?

He wished he knew what his wife was thinking. However, his thoughts were interrupted by the sound of a different female voice. He looked towards the front door of the suite.

A tall, blonde beauty stood in the doorway. "Poppy?"

Heston's jaw dropped.

"Winner, where have you been?" Ezra cried. "We've been trying to get in touch with you."

"Out shopping," Winner said innocently. "I had my phone turned off. I'm—screening my calls. But I just listened to the voice mails Nick left me. Saw his texts . . ." Her voice trailed off. Warily, she looked from Ezra to Poppy and Heston. "Hello, Father."

"Hello, Ladybug."

No one moved.

Heston took the lead. "It's good to see you, sweetheart. Can I get a hug?" he asked softly.

Winner looked at Poppy.

Poppy nodded.

Wafting in on a cloud of floral cologne, Winner stopped momentarily, and then edged towards him and hugged his neck awkwardly.

"I've missed you." He returned Winner's embrace, but she quickly eluded his grasp. Filled with wonder, he admired the breathtaking loveliness of the child he and Maude Winston had produced. His daughter was, in fact, loveliness personified.

Observing her, his wonder became tinged with remorse. It was he who had put her—and Poppy and his other children—in danger—his fault that Winner was in such a precarious position.

Silently, he offered a prayer of gratitude for her safety. After all, it was his celebrity that had made them all targets. Wasn't it? Of course, it was. Winner had inherited his legacy, in more ways than one. For the first time, he wished he had never left Nashville—as if he had brought spotted fever with him and, contagious, had infected those he loved most.

Meanwhile, Nick focused on Winner. "Win, you have a doll collection at home. Correct?"

Winner looked skeptical. "Yes. What does that have to do with anything?"

Intent, Nick persisted. "Have you recently removed any of the dolls? Maybe taken them back to New York with you? Or loaned them to someone else?"

Winner scoffed. "No. I haven't. Why do ask?"

Nick caught Ezra's glance but pressed on, treading carefully.

"A few days ago, your housekeeper discovered that two of your dolls had gone missing. We thought maybe you yourself had taken them."

"Well, I didn't. And I have no idea what happened to them. Was there a burglary?"

"Well, I don't know—yet—who took them. But I do know what happened to them. They've both turned up. Your Princess Daphne doll turned up, yesterday morning, on Heart of Fire Key." Nick pointed to the bathroom. "The other one—is in there." Nick walked to the bathroom door.

Heston glanced at Poppy. She looked scared, frazzled, yet he knew she had hidden strength.

Nick poked his nose through the bathroom doorway. "Winner, come in here, please. You need to see this."

"Nick—" Heston protested.

"She's got to know, Heston—unless she already does."

"What does that mean?" asked Ezra, scowling at Nick.

"Know what, Nick?" the willowy girl asked, stepping into the bathroom.

Heston heard his daughter's shriek. Dashing into the bathroom, he threw his arms around her and drew her close to him. Cowering, she did not resist.

"Easy. Easy." He had forgotten how much he loved this child of his.

But, to his chagrin, she quickly pulled away.

"She doesn't know beans about this, Nick. Tell her the rest of it now," said Ezra. "Get it over with."

"Tell me what?" Winner demanded, looking up.

"Win, we're dealing with a nut job—whoever it is." Nick watched her face." "The Princess Daphne was mutilated. Like this one."

"Who did it?"

"Don't know yet. Anyone could have done it. Anyone with access and motive."

"Even you," said Heston to Nick.

"What are you saying, Nick?" Winner cried, uncoupling from Heston. "That I'm the target? Or that I'm the nut job?" Her silver-blue eyes found Heston. "Or what? I'm confused."

"You appear to be a target. So does your dad. Poppy, too."

As Nick was speaking, Heston noticed a large bouquet of red roses in a vase on the coffee table. "Poppy, who sent you the roses?" he asked, nodding.

"I don't know," Poppy confessed. "All I know is what the server told me—when he delivered them to me at the pool yesterday—and it rhymed. Like the other messages."

"What did they say?"

"He was told to say, 'A token of affection in spite of your rejection.' He didn't know who had sent them."

"I can find out," said Nick. "I'll put a man on it."

Striding up behind Winner, whose anxiety had become apparent, Ezra placed a hand on her shoulder. "We'll figure it out. This is the downside of fame." He patted her and stepped away.

"One of many," said Winner, over her shoulder.

"Easy, honey" said Heston, moving to her side. Again, she shied away from him. He must have hurt her terribly—through his neglect. How much he loved this child! She seemed so fragile.

"Tell me what you do know, please," Winner said to Nick.

"Very well. Yesterday morning, at Heart of Fire Key—" Nick began.

"On the dock, when we were casting off—" Heston interjected, "to come here—"

"We found the defaced Daphne doll," Nick concluded. "I bagged it. Got to the lab at Headquarters. Received some preliminary results. I'm compiling evidence."

Poppy coached him. "Tell her about the note, Nick."

Ezra volunteered. " 'To Orlando fly or Ladybug will die.' That's what it said, Win." He looked at Winner. "The implication was that—you, Winner, would be killed if your dad didn't cooperate."

"But who else besides Dad would call me 'Ladybug'?" Winner asked, puzzled.

"Winner," Poppy said. "I told your father and Nick about—"

"About what?" Ezra demanded.

"Mommy, no!"

"No, not that. About the texts—"

Poppy and Winner eyed one another. Looking away, Winner nodded. "Oh. Okay."

"Ezra," said Poppy, "Winner received threatening text messages."

Ezra snapped to attention. "What did they say, Win?"

Winner would not meet his gaze. "They were too gross. He said he was watching me and—that he was going to do—really bad things to me."

"Do you know it was?" Nick asked the girl.

"No idea."

"Nick continued the interrogation. "When did you receive the first text? Where were you?"

Winner hesitated, then spoke. "Key Largo. Two days ago."

"What were you doing on Key Largo?" Nick was taking notes.

"Visiting a friend."

Skeptical, Ezra scowled. "A friend? Which friend?"

Winner turned to Heston. "I thought maybe the texts were from you, Daddy. The timing sure was a coincidence. I mean, you return from out the blue. I get these horrible messages—and now this?"

Appalled, Heston found his voice. "Honey, you can't believe that I would do such things. Why would I?"

"I don't know. It's hard to trust you. You've been gone a long time."

"You can trust me." He stepped towards his daughter, but she backed away. He halted. "Winner, I love you. I would never harm you. I would never harm Poppy, or your brother and sisters. Never. Do you hear me? I may have been scarce in recent years, but I'm not homicidal. Nor am I bent on revenge. If anything, my motives are just the opposite. I want us to be a family again."

Poppy was incredulous. "You do?"

"I do."

Poppy rolled her eyes but said nothing.

"Progress," said Ezra to Nick. Nick turned his attention to Winner. "Winner, I'll need to know more about your activities. Look, are you hiding someone? In your suite?" Nick asked. "I was informed that—"

Winner hedged. "A friend. Same one from Largo. Please don't ask me."

"Maybe he's an enemy 'in disguise.' " Jealous, Ezra spat out the words. "It is a man, right?"

"Oh, Ezzie, don't!" Winner pleaded. "Guys, please wait until the party tonight. Then you'll understand everything." She seemed on the brink of tears. "Please don't spoil this night for me. It's the most important night of my life—so far."

Silence fell.

"What if he's your stalker?" Ezra hissed, snake-like.

Winner freaked. "He's not!"

"Cool it, Ezra," Heston warned.

"Whoever it is, we'll find him—or her," said Nick to the tormented girl. "Chin up."

"Chin up, Nick?" Winner retorted, her fear turning to anger. "Some deranged psychopath is after me and my family? I'm not exactly feeling cozy right now."

As Winner's words died on her lips, the hotel manager burst into the suite. On his heels came two armed policemen.

"The mobile crime unit is on its way, sir," the manager said to Heston. "What's going on here?" He was interrupted by one of his star-struck companions.

"Hey! You're Heston Demming, that movie star, aren't you?" asked the older and burlier of the two officers, as Nick ushered the men into the bathroom to view the crime scene. "The wife and I have seen every picture you ever made." He eyeballed Heston. "You still look pretty good, considering—"

Heston harrumphed. *Considering what? That I'm an old man?*

As the men followed Nick into the bathroom, Poppy moved to Heston's side.

"I don't want to stay in these rooms," she said. "And I don't want the kids here, either. I'm cancelling their plans. I'm going home to Naples."

Winner wailed. "Mommy, you can't do that! You'll ruin everything! My party—the surprise—everything I have planned. I need you here. Everything's so screwed up."

Reentering from the bathroom, Nick caught Poppy's eye. "We'll have a better shot at catching whoever-it-is—if we stay put and carry on as normal. If we run in fear, we could lose, big time."

"You're not using my children for bait, Nick," Poppy stated flatly.

Heston put a hand up. "Maybe Nick is right. If we run, this lunatic will know he's whipped us. Better to stay and fight."

"You'd gamble with our children's lives?" Poppy asked, outraged.

"We'll protect you, Mrs. Demming," said the younger of the two police officers, as he emerged from the bathroom. "We're on the alert now." Signaling Nick, he exited the suite.

"I swear, Heston—" Muffling her ire, Poppy shook her head, palms to cheeks.

Heston balked. "What, it's all my fault now? Why not! Everything else is! Right, Red?"

"Cool heads," responded Nick, palms pressing air, as the manager reentered the room.

"Look, Poppy," Win chimed in. "We'll find you a new suite. On a different floor. Just 'til tomorrow night—for my sake. Okay?" Winner smiled at her stepmother. "Please, Poppy! Just for tonight. Then you can go home if you still want to."

"Bad news, I'm afraid," said the manager. "The hotel's filled to capacity this weekend."

"That's why Nick and I are bunking together," said Ezra. "Remember?"

The manager attempted diplomacy. "Perhaps your mother might stay in the Royal Suite with you—"

"No. That's impossible!" cried Winner. "I can't explain why—"

"Then it's settled," said Heston, stepping up. "Poppy's moving into my suite—with me. So are my other children when they arrive tomorrow. There's plenty of room for all of us in 1602."

"Oh, I don't know—!" Poppy cried.

"Please, Poppy," Winner begged. "For me."

"I'll protect you, Poppy," Heston said quietly. "Give me a chance to prove myself."

"We're beefing up security for the party," Nick promised.

Poppy gave in. "Well, okay," she muttered. "But I want separate bedrooms," she added to Heston.

"Done." He stifled a grin.

Winner threw her long, lean arms around Poppy's neck. "Thank you," she said, smiling. "You won't regret it."

"I already regret it." Poppy eyes were boring into his. "Whatever happens, it had better be worth it." She kissed Winner's cheek.

"It will be," the girl declared, as the manager stepped out into the hall to place a call.

As Heston watched his wife and daughter embrace, a pang for what-might-have-been shot through his heart. "I have such an awesome family," he said hoarsely.

Poppy's facial expression changed. "Speaking of your family—"

"What now?" Nick asked, alerted by her sudden change in manner.

Poppy gulped. "Something Inez told me." She looked bewildered. "Another rhyme."

"What?" cried Heston. "Explain yourself, woman."

"Heston, have you been sending flowers each week to Franco's gravesite?"

Caught off guard, Heston thought for a moment. "No, not weekly. I have flowers sent automatically at Easter, Christmas, and on his birthday, though. Been doing that for years. That's what I told Inez when she asked me about it on the phone."

"She told you? Someone has been sending flowers for weeks. Inez assumed it was you—because the ribbons say, 'Beloved son,' or something like that."

"Yes. But I told her it wasn't I."

"The florists have been busy," Nick observed under his breath.

"The latest one was different." Poppy wrinkled her brow. "Oh, I know—it said, 'Rest in peace, beloved son. The wrong done you will be undone.' "

"It did? She never mentioned that to me."

"Daddy?" said Winner. "You didn't hurt Franco on purpose. Did you?"

"No," said Heston, wishing he were the hero he had played in so many movies. He had never felt more ineffectual in his life. "His death was an accident."

Ezra held up a hand. "Now, listen. I'm no Basil Rathbone—not even William Gillette—"

"Who?" asked Winner.

"Gillette was an old-time actor. He was famous for playing Sherlock Holmes."

"Okay," said Winner. "Whatever."

174

Ezra continued. "Doesn't it seem reasonable to assume that all this bad poetry is coming from a single source? In other words, from the same person?"

"But who, Sherlock?"

Ezra snorted. "Someone who's whacko?"

"Or maybe a couple of whack-jobs," Nick mused.

Heston's gaze flew to Nick, who looked the other way.

What does Nick know that he's not sharing?

As Heston studied Nick's inscrutable face, the younger policemen reentered the suite. "Make way for the Crime Unit," he announced self-importantly. "They're coming down the hall now."

***

Two hours later, dusk had become darkness. Inside the Royal Suite, Winner stood in the doorway of her fiancé's bedroom. She knocked softly and flipped on the light switch. "Damian?"

"What's up?" Rolling over, Danny beheld her sleepily. She was like a vision. The kid was wearing a tight, silver, full-length gown, and she was loaded down with diamonds and sapphires.

"Did you have a good nap, honey? You've been sleeping for hours."

"Sorry, babe." Sitting up, he took her hand in his. Pulling her to him, he kissed her forehead. "Yeah." He yawned. "Those sleeping pills you gave me worked like a dream."

"So to speak." Winner glanced around. His bedroom was littered with garment bags, clothes, men's shoes, jewelry, and leather goods. She sat down on his bed. "You'd better shower and dress. It's almost nine o'clock."

"Yeah?" He was unconcerned. "So?" Suddenly, he noticed music playing. "Where's that coming from?"

175

She smiled coyly, squeezing his hands. "The terrace. Tropica's about to open her set."

His smile petrified. "What are you up to, babe? What's going on?"

"Just—a party."

"A party?"

"Uh huh." She fondled his hands gently. She was wearing the heavy rock on her left hand. "So, here's my big surprise. I'm throwing us an engagement party tonight. Right here, out there on the terrace. For all the world to see. Isn't that wonderful?"

Rage flared. "You're give—?" He was mortified. "Why?"

Fear rose in the girl's shimmering eyes. "Because I'm proud of you. I want my friends to meet you. And my family is here. Poppy and Daddy, anyway. The kids won't arrive until the day after tomorrow, but you can meet them then."

He felt slammed in the solar plexus. "Your stepmother is here? At this hotel?"

"Yes! You can finally meet Poppy tonight. I've told her all about you—"

He slipped the belt from his slacks and coiled it. "What did you tell her, Win?" He snapped the belt. "What have you told Poppy? About me?"

Jumping off the bed, she cried out in fear. "Nothing. Just that I love you."

He toyed ominously with the belt. "Great." He did not believe her.

"Is that so wrong? What's the matter, Damian?"

"Nothing."

Her luscious lips quivered. "I've invited over a hundred people—and the press. Most of them are staying here at the hotel." The tears only heightened his fury. "Millie put the whole thing together—in secret. I wanted to surprise you. I wanted to surprise—everybody."

Shit!

He had to think fast. Suddenly, he doubled over. "I'm sick," he said, grabbing his stomach. "I'm dizzy. I got to lie down. I'm coming down with something."

Winner wiped her eyes. "Sick? Oh, Tiger! Here. Let me help you." Going to him, Winner helped him into his bed.

Moaning, he flopped down, apparently, in agony. "I can't see any-one."

"I'm sorry you don't feel good." She wrung her hands. "People are already arriving. What will I tell them?"

"That I'm sick," he groaned. "Ohhhh . . ."

"I'll phone for a doctor."

"No. You won't" He knocked the phone from her hands. "Get out, Winner. Turn the lights off when you go. I have a migraine. Ohhhh . . ."

She paused in the doorway. "Okay. I'll make your excuses."

"I cannot be disturbed. Not for any reason. Hear me, bitch?" The belt was still coiled in his hand.

"Yes." She inched away. "An engagement party with no groom? What a disaster." She was a shadow in the darkness. "A total disaster."

"You deserve it, Winner. You went against my wishes."

She seemed to contemplate him in the silence that followed.

He couldn't stand it. "I'll bet the joint is swarming. Security? Police?" He had left his gun in the car. "Reporters?"

"It is now. I wanted the whole word to know—how much I loved—you."

He heard the whine in her voice. The pitch of it irritated the shit out of him.

"I don't want your love, bitch. I want your respect. You don't respect me. If you had respected me, you would have obeyed me." His heart hammered inside his chest.

"I'll look in on you later," she said quietly. The door to his bedroom shut softly.

Springing up, he locked the door from the inside. He could hear the band playing on the terrace. Tropica was singing a pop song. There must be quite a crowd of people out there. He could hear the voices of party-goers mingling with the music.

Cornered, hell—like a mad dog. He had to escape, but—how was he going to get out unnoticed?

Chapter Ten

Outside on the terrace of the Royal Suite, the party was on.

The brightly lit terrace was crowded with A-list attendees, all chattering, drinking, dancing. Watching the festivities, Heston sighed plaintively, alone in a corner. He had to admit, he was impressed, and charmed, on a fatherly level. The set-up was a young girl's dream.

Deep-purple night sky. The moon is out. The Enchanted Palace is aglow, in the background. The city lights, beyond. Young hearts aflutter. . . and fireworks thrown in on top of it all. A perfect time for a fiend to strike.

He scanned the trendy, upscale crowd, looking for suspicious characters. Meanwhile, Tropica's band completed a dance tune. The partygoers applauded enthusiastically. On cue, Ladybug—shockingly lovely in a silver gown—walked out onto the small stage and tapped the microphone. In anticipation of her announcement, whatever it might be, Heston steadied himself. Was she about to rock his world?

"Welcome, friends, family, media," Winner said into the microphone. "I had intended for this to be a surprise party—a surprise for all of you, my guests. But I guess the surprise is on me." Winner faltered. "Yeah. This was supposed to be my engagement party. But—guess what? The groom is sick." She was crestfallen. "Yeah. Too bad, huh? My fiancé—yes, world," she smiled sadly as the party-goer's smartphones recorded and their video cams whirred. "My fiancé, Damian Velasquez, is here tonight. Unfortunately, he cannot join us because he's sick in bed." She made a clucking noise. "My poor baby. Yeah."

Her gaze swept the crowd. "He sends you his regrets. Says he can't wait to meet you all—someday soon." She managed to beam proudly. "And I can't wait for you to meet him."

Everyone applauded.

"Thank you," said Winner with a sweeping gesture. "Isn't this band great?"

Again, the star-spangled crowd erupted in applause.

"Please give a big hand to my best friend, Tropica!"

As Tropica stepped forward and bowed, the crowd erupted in cheers. Winner applauded, too, and then addressed her guests. "Please, everyone, go ahead and enjoy yourselves. Eat, drink, and party on—"

". . . for we may die by a stalker's hand tomorrow," said Heston, under his breath. Heart aching, he had listened to his daughter's pitiful speech. Obviously, Winner was devastated by the turn of events. He walked towards the stage.

Velasquez had better be on his deathbed.

When he met the jerk, he'd give him a piece of his mind.

He should have come out in a blasted wheelchair.

"What a pity," he said to daughter, taking her hand as she stepped down from the stage.

"I know." Safely down the steps, Winner dropped his hand. "I'm worried about him, Dad. He's locked in his room. He was okay a few hours ago. All of a sudden, he was nauseated, doubled over."

"Did you call the doctor?"

"He refuses to see a doctor."

"Hard luck, honey," he said, empathetic, although his ire was rising. "Life is that way, sometimes. Things don't work out the way we've planned."

"Like between you and Poppy?"

"Well, uh—"

"Oh, look, Dad. Uncle Banks is here."

Heston looked towards the private elevator. A debonair, ivory-haired patrician stepped out the elevator door. Heston felt revolted. "Banks Winston? It's been an age since—"

The old goat was hot for Poppy, back then, as I recall. And Lennox . . .

Winner cast a guilty glance. "Well, I felt I should invite Banks. He is part of my family."

Reluctantly, Heston agreed, but he remained disconcerted. "Winston, you could have warned me in advance," he chided amiably. "About—everything."

"Would you have come, Dad?"

"Don't be foolish."

Distracted, Heston watched as Poppy and the high-powered lawyer caught sight of one another. Coming alongside Poppy, Billionaire Banks whisked her onto the eddying dance floor. Spotting Heston, Poppy tossed him a wave. As he returned the wave, Winner tugged at his sleeve. A young man was approaching.

"Dad," Winner whispered in Heston's ear. "Here comes Adair Champlain. He can be kind of strange," she warned. "Put a script in his hand, and he seems normal. But impromptu—he can be peculiar. You'll see what I mean on Monday. For tonight, schmooze him, okay?"

Heston grunted. "All right, honey."

"Oh, hello, Adair," Winner said to the fancy young man now standing by her side. "I'd like you to meet my father, Heston Demming. Dad, this is our backer and star, Adair Champlain."

"How do you do, Champlain," said Heston, offering his hand. "Thanks for bringing me on board."

Adair's manner was strangely dull. "Inevitable, it was."

"Excuse me, gentlemen," Winner said, moving away from them. "I need to check on my guy."

Adair responded. "Go ahead, Ladybug."

"By all means." Heston said, astonished by Adair's use of his own pet name for Winner.

No longer alone in the crowd, Heston sized up the young man at his side. Cocktail glass in hand, Adair gave the impression of being one who possessed both wealth and health. However, something about the sleek punk made Heston's skin crawl. Having assured his daughter of cordiality, regrettably, he tried to shake off the bad feeling. However, instinct prevailed, and he threw a verbal punch.

"Well, Champlain," he said, on the attack. "How does it feel to be the new Heston Demming?"

Adair seemed unperturbed. "Fine."

Heston took a second swing. "I heard you could use a few acting tips." *You jackass.*

"I am an award-winning actor."

"You are?"

"I like the name Winston," Adair said, waving to Banks, who had spotted him from the dance floor. No doubt the two men ran in the same circles. Each possessed the fortune of a Titan.

Juggling animosities, Heston tried to regain aplomb, but his irritation increased as he watched Winner retreat into the interior of the Royal Suite.

Blast Velasquez. "It was the only name Maude and I could agree on. That and Kay. Kay Winston Demming. That's her given name."

"Yes, I know." said Adair, who seemed inattentive. He would not look Heston in the eye.

"You know? How do you know?"

"I was there."

Heston detected no acid in the young man's words. "Where?"

"In space." Adair spoke absently, his eyes roaming the crowd. "I abandoned my children—and went trekking around the world. Then I disappeared into space. But I knew where I was."

Hackles rising, Heston felt as if his brains were being scrambled, like loose eggs. "Adair, what are you drinking?"

"Ginger ale. I am a recovering alcoholic."

"Look, man. I don't know what kind of mind game you're playing but knock it off. Okay?"

Adair said nothing. He watched the dancers on the dance floor.

Trying to live up to his promise, Heston offered a half-smile. "Look. I like a joke as much as anyone, but sometimes jokes aren't appropriate."

"I don't know what you mean. We like jokes."

"You and your sister? Yes, I'm aware of that. Like Ezra, your sister has a reputation as a jokester."

"Kings can use the Royal 'We.' "

Adair's jest was becoming tiresome. Heston's temper flared. "Don't goof on me, Adair. Especially in regard to my children." Heston said. "I love all three of my daughters. I love my sons."

A sinister light turned on in Adair's blue eyes, as they met Heston's gaze for the first time. "So do I. Even the dead ones."

Is this fellow pulling my leg? Or am I staring into madness?

Rattled, Heston looked away but spoke directly. "Champlain, if you're not drinking alcohol, what in blazes have you been smoking?"

"Vaping, not smoking." Adair seemed secretly amused as the light in his eyes faded. He became vague again and looked towards the dance floor. "My wife is a good dancer."

"Is that a fact? I didn't know you were married."

"She's a redhead."

Heston snorted. "So is mine. What a coincidence."

Adair prattled nonsensically. "I've planned my work. And I'm working my plan."

"Good for you."

Adair changed course. His looked at Heston, eyes fierce. "I know where the early Cedric Spicer canvases are hidden." He sipped his drink, licked his lips with a snake-like tongue. "Truett collected the work of Spicer and his school."

Heston was floored. "You can't know. No one knows."

"I know. But I never tell."

"Where are they?"

"It's my secret. But I'll find out."

Adair's conversation was baffling. Was the fellow lucid or not? Heston felt as if he were standing on the shifting deck of an alternate reality. His tension ticked up a notch. "I thought your father had passed away."

"Yes. She's amassing the definitive collection of Cedric Spicer's art." Adair tossed his hair. "She wants to possess his entire body of work. She wants to possess everything and everyone."

"Who does?"

"Hailey. She's willing to make a very handsome offer."

An ominous feeling arose in Heston's gut. "No thanks. Not interested in selling," he replied with studied nonchalance. Stifling the impulse to whistle, Heston rocked backwards, onto his heels. Searching for a route of escape, he jiggled the ice in his glass.

Adair flickered in anger. "She collects Heston Demmings, too."

Rocking forward, Heston stared. "Your sister bought my paintings?"

Adair swallowed the dregs of his drink. His smooth Adam's apple bobbed. His blue eyes were glossing over again.

Edgy, Heston faked a laugh. "You mean Hailey Champlain was 'Anonymous Bidder'?"

Adair's dull eyes no longer invited intimacy. "I've won Best Actor twice, you know."

"What——?" Heston began, but stopped, realizing a new possibility.

Does he actually think he's me? Am I looking into a fun-house mirror at a carnival? My own image, but distorted? The idea is preposterous. Isn't it?

Testing his hypothesis, Heston looked around, casually searching for Poppy's whereabouts in the crowd of revelers. "Which ones did you paint most recently? By the way, is you wife here tonight?"

"The cloudburst—and a maritime." Adair pointed. "She's over there. By the ladies' room."

Bullseye. "I must remember to congratulate your sister's taste in art."

"Who?" asked Adair vaguely.

"Never mind, sport," he said. "Sorry I can't introduce you. I haven't met her myself." Sadly, Heston raised his glass in mock conviviality, as a chick in heels approached, dragging Nick Townsend, twice her height, along with her. Stopping for a moment, she snapped photos of Heston and Adair as they stood side by side. For a moment, she fussed with her phone.

"Straight to social media," she said, grinning. "Howdy, Heston. I'm your new drill sergeant."

"Hailey Champlain, I presume," he replied reservedly. "Charmed. I've just been having an unusual chat with your brother here."

"Oh?" Hailey batted her lashes. "Well, don't let him play you. Adair's the jester in the deck."

"Don't be so sure about that." Nick's bald head swiveled as he looked from Heston to Adair and back again. "You two guys look enough alike to be father and son."

"That's why I snapped the photos," Hailey squealed. "Publicity! C'mon, G-man. Move it. Let's find Uncle Ezra. I'll show him the pix."

"Cute as a button," said Nick, as she dragged him away.

"If you like buttons," said Adair. His blue eyes had intensified.

"You're supposed to be protecting us!" Heston called after Nick, who waved. He was about to excuse himself and walk away, but Adair's words stopped him.

"She wants Ezra. That's why we're producing his script. Women. They're all guttersnipes."

Heston lost his battle with cool. "What's up with you, Adair? Tell me the truth."

"I don't know what you mean." Annoyed, Adair left his side, walking into the raucous throng. Gratefully, Heston watched him go. The man was either cruel poison or a pathetic mess.

"If only I hadn't signed the contract for that blasted series—" Heston muttered to himself. Just then, he caught sight of Poppy. His wife was enjoying herself way too much for his liking. Festering, he decided to do something about it.

***

Finding an empty spot near the bandstand, Heston leaned against the wall and steadied himself. After a few sips of ginger ale, his blood pressure returned to normal, but his resolve held firm. He caught a glimpse of Winner, talking to her guests. She seemed safe enough.

His eyes roamed the terrace. Under the dome of heaven, guests mingled with—psychopaths and plain-clothes policemen? Anyone could be lurking in this crowd.

Bless Nick for increasing the security personnel.

Heston drained his glass and set it down. In the early years of his career, people would have swarmed around him at an event like this one.

He felt old, like a has-been. No one seemed to know he was alive, except for—

Poppy was staring at him.

Instinctively, he averted his eyes but quickly looked her way again. She was not looking at him now. Now she was looking at her companion, Banks Winston.

No longer dancing, Poppy was chatting with Banks at the bar. She was wearing a teal-colored gown, low-cut, and chains of gold around her neck wrists. No doubt Banks was enjoying the view. As Heston stared at her, she glanced his way again. He inclined his head. She looked away.

While married to one another, he and Poppy often had played this game of sight tag, when mingling at parties. Tonight, in an updated version of the game, he and his wife had been avoiding one another on purpose, while furtively checking each other out and then catching one another at it.

The only question is: are Poppy and I playing a game? Are we for real?

Involuntarily, his eyes caressed the curves of her body. Feeling his energy, from across the terrace, she turned her head, looking his way. Quickly, she looked away, but not before letting his gaze penetrate. Heston marveled, stirring.

What kind of signals were these? He was too old for such games. On the other hand, was anyone ever too old to play this particular game?

As Heston watched, Banks excused himself and walked away from Poppy. As soon as Banks had disappeared into the restroom, Poppy stood unguarded at the bar. Phone in hand, she appeared to be checking her messages.

A thought flashed in Heston's mind. It was time to reclaim his right to the throne. Taking out his phone, he placed a call to Poppy's mobile phone.

***

The party crowd had become noisy. Raucous music hovered above the din. Relieved that she had ditched Banks Winston, Poppy rose from the bar and walked around, relaxing. As she walked, her phone rang.

"Hello?" She placed a hand over one ear, as she watched Hailey and Adair Champlain leaving together through a nearby exit. She wondered why they were leaving the party so early, but it was really none of her affair. Capturing her attention, a man's deep voice spoke through her phone.

"Hello, Poppy."

"Heston." She sank down into a chair, her legs suddenly unsteady. Glancing around, she spotted Heston across the room and waved. He nodded imperceptibly. Poppy watched him as he spoke, demanding, into his phone.

"Tell me about Winner's new beau." He was not smiling.

Poppy cleared her throat. "Well, Heston. I don't know too much about Damian. Just what Winner's told me yesterday. How much do you know?"

Heston grunted. "I know he's an—and I quote—'amazing' athlete named Damian." Using an exaggerated Spanish accent, he mimicked Winner's high-pitched voice.

Poppy winced. *Still the same old ham. The actor in him never misses an opportunity to perform.*

"She is infatuated," Poppy said aloud into the phone.

"Where'd she meet him?"

"Through friends at boarding school. So she said. I have my doubts," Poppy replied, shrinking as Banks buzzed by her. This time he was dancing the two-step with Tropica, who was taking a break between sets.

"I think he's a rascal. I want to know all about him. I do not take kindly to men who humiliate my daughter in public."

Heston was blustering. She remembered this ploy so well. Tonight, she did not feel like soothing him. Besides, once they were divorced, it wouldn't be her job to do so anymore. She let him have it, straight between the eyes.

"Bottom line? Damian Velasquez is forty-three years old."

"He's what?"

"You heard me, Heston. Damian is twenty-four years older than Win."

"I'll kill him."

Across the room, Heston turned his back to her. His hand, balled in a tight fist, beat the floor of the bandstand. "That freaking bum—" his voice exploded inside the device at her ear.

"Heston, calm down."

"He's got to be a fortune hunter."

"Why? Winner is a stunning girl. Any man would want her." She caught sight of Winner in the crowd. Platinum hair, flowing silver dress—with wings she would pass for an angel.

"Shut your—"

Again, Poppy glanced Heston's way. He was facing her now. Rolling his eyes, he swabbed his face with his open palm. "Have you met this latter-day Valentino?"

"Velasquez, not Valentino. Like the Baroque-era Spanish painter. No. Not yet."

"Why didn't Winner tell me—about his age?"

"Maybe she was afraid to tell you. She was afraid to tell *me*. I had a feeling something was up. I nagged the truth out of her this afternoon."

Heston exhaled slowly. "She's vulnerable still. Worse, she's green."

In spite of her misgivings about Heston, Poppy's heartstrings vibrated. "Well, you could challenge Damian to a duel. Other than that, I don't know what steps you could take."

"I could forbid her to marry."

Biting her lip, Poppy shook her head. "Winner is of legal age. She doesn't need your consent, nor her birth mother's consent, nor mine."

"Why would she marry a man so much older?" Heston fell silent beneath the crowd noise.

Poppy inhaled. *If I'm ever going to say it, the time is now.* "M-Maybe there was something m-missing in her life. Something she couldn't find in a healthy way."

"You mean—?"

"Heston, you've been missing from Winner's life, off and on, for seven years. She was traumatized by the kidnapping. Your leaving made it worse. All that while, she needed attention, care, love from a man she respects. Apparently, she's found a source of love in this fellow, Damian."

"Apparently. What does he do for a living?"

"He owns a couple of tennis resorts in the Caribbean, so Win claims."

"Oh, so he's a tennis bum."

"Not now. He may have been in his youth. Who knows?"

Heston snarled the words. "I'll have him investigated."

"Fine idea. Just don't let Win know. If she becomes angry enough, she might elope. At least this way—meeting him first—we have the hope of changing her mind before it's too late."

"You let this happen."

"I did?" Her heart thumped in her breast.

Abruptly, Heston muttered a word and ended the call.

Furious, Poppy was shaking all over. He could still do that to her. She was post-menopausal—too old to be so affected by a man, any man—even the man whom she considered to be the great love of her life. To her shock, she caught sight of Heston, threading his way through the crowd. He was striding towards her.

Conflicted, she put a hand to her mouth.

She dreaded confronting Heston. Yet she couldn't wait to see him. Watching him approach, she felt sick to her stomach. His form grew larger and large until, at last, he loomed over her like an angry gray cloud of judgment. The only hope for her shone in the silver-blue lining of his faded, mature eyes. However, the words he uttered, as he pressed close, surprised her.

"Poppy," he whispered into her ear. "Cedric Spicer's paintings. Are they all right? Are they still—where we left them?"

Nodding, she breathed a sigh of relief. "Right where you stored them seven years ago. Safe and sound—and secure—as far as I know. I haven't checked on them lately. Why? Has something happened?" She could scarcely think. She heard herself babbling.

"The key?" he asked.

"Safety-deposit box in Geneva."

"Have you talked to Adair Champlain about Cedric's paintings?"

"No. I have not."

"What about Hailey?"

"No."

"Good. Don't." Heston was so close, his torso touched hers. She felt his body heat. She breathed in the old familiar scent of him—orange blossom and myrrh. His moist, warm breath brushed her ear. How well she remembered his deep kisses. His nearness felt like—coming home.

Is he going to kiss me?

The pounding of her heart lessened as Heston moved away from her and walked over to the bar. Finding a place among the customers at the bar, he settled in. A young bartender accosted him.

"Sarsaparilla," he told the bartender. "In a dirty glass."

"Huh?" emitted the metro-sexual bartender.

"It's a joke. An old joke—like me. Pour me a ginger ale, please."

"Sure, Pops. On the rocks?"

"Neat."

Downing the pale-gold liquid, Heston finished it in one long swallow. Then he slung his empty glass, sending sliding down the length of the entire bar. Turning, he flashed the million-dollar smile at Poppy, bowed deeply and saluted her like a swashbuckler bidding farewell to a damsel. It was the sexiest move she had seen in years. Vaguely, she was aware that a second bartender had put out a hand, stopping the slide of Heston's glass before it could crash to the floor.

Bedazzled, she watched her husband saunter away and disappear into the crowd. There was something to be said for being married to an actor.

***

Meanwhile, just off the terrace, inside the Royal Suite, a different storm was brewing.

Suspicious, Winner ventured into Damian's bedroom, as the party blared on outside. She stared down at the masculine form on the bed in front of her. Ignoring her, her fiancé was lying in his bed, covered head-to-toe by a thick down comforter.

She lifted the cover. Exposed, he whined. "I'm sorry, babe. I'm just too sick to meet people tonight."

"Okay. I made your excuses." She placed her hand on his warm forehead.

He grabbed her wrist. "You should have warned me."

She recoiled. "About what?" She looked around for the belt. It was hidden beneath the comforter. She could see the outline of it.

"This party, damn it."

"It was supposed to be a surprise."

Relenting, he released her wrist. "Yeah, I know. I get it." Suddenly, he doubled over, groaning, ostensibly in pain.

Alarmed, Winston rose. "Don't you want a doctor?"

He grabbed her forearm. "No, the pain is passing. I'll be okay by tomorrow. Really. Go back to your party, babe. Make my excuses."

She regarded him dubiously. "I already have."

Dropping her forearm, he fell back into his pillows. "How much security you got out there? How many men?"

"I'm not sure. Some are in plain clothes. A couple are stationed by elevator, inside." She didn't understand his interest. If he wasn't attending the party, why did he care? "Have you changed your mind?"

"No. I told you I didn't want to meet your folks, didn't I?"

"Yes, but—"

"No buts! You did not honor my request. I have told you, Winston, that I will not marry a woman who refuses my commands—"

"I didn't think of it that way, Damian. Honest. I just wanted you to meet Poppy and my sibs—"

His voice softened in the dark. "Look, I would, babe. I would do it for you. You know that. If I wasn't so sick—" He coughed sporadically.

Winner's heart sank. *Damian isn't ill. He's faking.* She might not be an expert on good acting, but she knew bad acting when she saw it.

"Get some rest," she said. "I'll check in on you later tonight." Teary-eyed, she walked out of his room. She felt betrayed and deeply disturbed. More than anything, she felt afraid.

Damian can't be trusted.

What if Ezra was right? What if Damian was the stalker?

What have I gotten myself into?

193

Chapter Eleven

On the grounds of the theme park, a silent figure stood alone, hidden by the nighttime shadows, shadows cast by turrets of the fantastic Enchanted Palace. Visitors to the park, who walked past in pairs and gaggles, did not notice. The evening fireworks had ended. In one hour, the park would be closing for the night. There was no time to lose.

Ignoring the pedestrians as they straggled down the pavement, schlepping from attraction to attraction, the lone figure silently performed mental calculations. Before a plan could be formulated, several questions required answers. That, after all, was the purpose of this clandestine visit to the theme park.

Strategic questions demanded accurate answers.

How far was it from the upper floors of the Southern Seas hotel's main tower to the drawbridge and moat surrounding the Enchanted Palace? What spot, in the vicinity of the Palace itself, provided the best camouflage for assailants? Based upon the surrounding layout, what would be the best way to accomplish the final objective? Gradually, a plan began to take shape.

Yes. It will work.

Gazing skyward, it was possible to see the brightly lit terrace of the Royal Suite, as well as the windows of the 16th floor below it. The rooftop terrace was too far away, however, for one to hear the music and Tropica's singing; but the party appeared to be in full swing.

No one has missed me. No one cares.

Scouting the area for possible pitfalls, encumbrances, or barriers, the lone figure left the shadows and strolled the sidewalks of the theme park. The darkness of evening seemed to exaggerate the carnival atmosphere of the place. Colors appeared more garish. Odors of food and trash were intensified. Chatter from weary fun-seekers irritated the nerves, but it was all for a good cause.

Good for me.

Satisfied with the plan, the lone figure made haste for the park entrance, which seemed much farther away, going back.

I wish I'd been able to change my shoes.

Checking the time, the figure left the theme park and walked back to the hotel. Across the lonely, mostly empty parking lot, the only sound was the click-clacking of heels.

***

By now the party had reached a fever pitch, but not all the partygoers were happy. Eager to avoid Hailey, to whom he had earlier promised a dance, Ezra had slipped away from the crowd. Alone and moping, he now was dawdling in an alcove off the main floor of the terrace. He'd drunk a couple of champagne cocktails, but he still felt downhearted.

Winner is engaged. Out of nowhere.

He had not seen it coming. He felt like breaking something. Instead, he rationalized.

Depression is anger turned inward.

He should have spoken up sooner. He should have said something to her, made her understand how he felt about her.

For years, his late mistress Vivian's poor health had confounded his feelings and inhibited his actions. Even after Vivi's death, he had felt a loyalty to her. Then again, during those years, Winner had been underage. He hadn't known what to do about his growing affection for the nubile teenager. So, he had done nothing. Now it was too late.

Rounding the corner, he swallowed hard.

There, in the next alcove over, was Winner herself, bent at the waist, fastening the strap of her evening shoe. Straightening up, she smoothed her gown and caught sight of him. "Hello, Ezzie. Excuse me. I thought I was alone. I just changed clothes. Enjoying the party?" She began to walk away. "Guess I need to return to my guests."

He blocked her way. "Winner, wait."

She looked radiant. "I can't stay away from my own party."

Desperately, he tried to think of words to say. He caught sight of her diamond. "That's quite a ring," he said, playing for time.

"Yeah. What is it exactly that you want to say to me? Not that I really want to go back—"

Uncomfortable in his tuxedo, Ezra hesitated. In the distance, the lights of the theme park sparkled in the darkness. The Enchanted Palace glowed majestically.

Oh, Winner, baby. What don't I want to say?

The girl was glorious in her shimmering floor-length designer gown of rose-red silk. Her alabaster shoulders and long, flaxen hair glowed. Like an angel, she was luminous, lit from both within and without. She was luminescent, like a film star from the 1940s, in some World War II picture. In soft focus, she seemed all shot through a filter.

His role was that of the madcap-playboy tuned ace-pilot, on a death-defying mission to—

Impatient, she batted her caked, black lashes. "Well?"

Open, bombardiers. "I'm concerned about you, Winner. Thought maybe we should have a little chat."

"So, chat, but make it snappy. My guests are waiting."

"About this marriage business. Do you know what you're doing?"

Crossing her arms, she curled her upper lip. "What kind of a question is that? You're not my dad."

Hell. Ezra licked his lips and began again. "This guy, this Damian Velasquez. How much do you know about him?"

She took a step back. "Why? What have you heard?"

"Nothing. That's not the point. I only meant that you seem to be rushing into a marriage with some man you just met."

"And this is your business because . . .?"

"Because I care what happens to you, Win. Don't you know that? Ever since that day, eight years ago, on your dad's island, when you were just twelve years old. You were in danger. That freak Gabe Cade had you kidnapped—"

"And you and Dad showed up—you were carrying that goofy spear gun. I hadn't known whether to laugh or cry."

He softened. "Yeah. A laugh riot—'til your little brother Dack came out of the bushes carrying a real gun and blew away your demented bodyguard—assuming he never resurfaced."

"Bad times, Ezra."

"My point is, you thought you were in love with that SOB, back then, Win."

"I was twelve years old—and stupid."

"Okay. Then you were just a kid with a foolish crush. But, now—marriage? This is serious."

"What are you trying to say to me, Gold?"

He exhaled and faced the inevitable. "That I showed up to save your life the last time you were in danger. And I'm showing up again to-night—minus the goofy speargun."

Her skin dimmed in the lantern light. "I don't like where this conversation is headed. Tonight was supposed to be a happy occasion for me. Instead, everything is going wrong."

He argued gently. "Is it? Maybe you've got that backwards, Winner. Maybe Fate is doing you a favor."

"How?"

"By trying to tell you something important."

"Such as?"

Bombs away. "Don't marry him. Marry me."

Winner gaped at him, her silver-blue eyes limpid with wonder. Ezra felt he might pass out. If he did, he would kill himself later. He couldn't humiliate himself in front of this fairy princess and continue living.

Obviously uncomfortable, Winner chewed her glossy lower lip. "Ezra, I'm sorry. I had no idea. I don't feel that way—"

He raised his hand. "Stop, Win. Please. Don't say it out loud. I get the picture."

She looked mortified. "I'm very flattered, Ezzie. You know how much I admire you—you're, like, my favorite director of all time."

He cringed. "Please. Don't. Just forget I ever said anything about—me." He took a step back. "You forget. I'll forget. We'll make a pact. We'll both forget. I shouldn't have—"

Winner took a step towards him. "No, really, Ezzie. It's all right. I'm very flattered. It's just that—"

He freaked. "Shut up, Win. Okay? I understand."

She seemed taken aback. "Do you?"

Ezra snorted. "Oh, I get the whole thing. You're the one who doesn't get it, little girl. The guy's bad news. He a gigolo—"

Her icy eyes flamed. "A what?"

He lost control. "Winner, the guy's a money-hungry bum, at the very least. For all we know, he's the psycho who's terrorizing your family—"

Stamping her foot, she turned away. "I'm leaving now."

Grasping her upper arm, Ezra spun her around towards him. The skirt of her gown flared, swirling around her sequined legs. She was livid, and her face—fire and ice—even more breathtaking.

Just keep talking. Say anything. Try to make sense. Make her understand. "Win, the guy is using you. He's a middle-aged tennis bum. Sure, he looks like polo-playing prince, but—"

Her eyes wounded him. "You think he's after my fortune?"

"That. And your exquisite body."

"Ezra!"

"Your body is exquisite, Win. Any man would—would—do anything to have you—as long as you don't starve yourself to death."

"Now you're being ridiculous." Again, she turned to leave.

"Wait. Come back. I—"

Walking towards the door, she turned back to him, crying. "You've gone too far with me, Ezra. Who I give my body to is none of your business."

Shoot me now. "Balderdash, Win." He ran after her, blocking her entrance to the door. "Please hear me out. Listen now, and I swear to you, I will never broach this subject with you again." He crossed his heart, raising his palm in a pledge. "Unless you want me to—"

"Why should I? You've cast—asps—" Her brow furrowed as she searched for the right word.

He nodded. "Aspersions. I cast aspersions."

"You cast them on Damian Velasquez—the man I love. The man I'm supposed to love. I can't just stand here and let you do that." She began to move away.

Placing a hand on her shoulder, he held her in check. Utterly charmed, he gazed into her eyes, mustering as much sincerity as he could, on the spur of the moment. "I'm done, Win. I swear it. I won't mention Damian again. I will cast no more aspersions, on him or anyone else. It's just that . . . oh, Winner, I—" The wide, innocent silver-blues, fringed with black mascara, held him spellbound.

"I'm sorry you want me, Ezra. I mean, I'm grateful and all, but—"

He swallowed harder. *Say it all now. Unload. There is no tomorrow.* "It's true. I care about you deeply—and sincerely. I care about your happiness and your well-being, not just about your beautiful body." *She's blushing!* "I—I love you, Kay Winston Demming." *Am I still breathing?* "I love you."

She placed her hand on his and patted it. "Oh, Ezra. That's so sweet."

Get a gun. But she was listening now. He had her rapt attention. *Pick up the pace.* "If you're really determined to marry this—*man,* which I see you plainly are, then, I thank you for allowing me to declare myself to you. So there can never be any question, in your mind, or in my mind, about what might have happened between us if I hadn't—spoken up."

She was gazing at him, her diamond eyes filled with sympathy, the same sympathy she would show to a wounded puppy dog.

It's all right. I'll take it. I'll take any scrap she wants to toss me. "Your happiness is all that matters to me, Win. If you're happy, I'm happy. End of story." He sensed a blip in her demeanor. "Are you happy?"

"Well, I was. Until—oh, never mind."

"What? Wait!" He ran after her. "Until what?"

Pushing open the doors, she turned face to him one last time. "Until you said all this junk to confuse me." Abruptly, she pushed through the swinging double doors, leaving him standing alone and astonished on the grand terrace.

Transfixed, he stood numb, barely breathing. *Hot shit. This is incredible. Do I actually stand a chance with Princess Daphne?*

Trembling, Ezra leaned against an exterior wall along the terrace. In his mind's eye, he reviewed the scene with Winner. He had blown his big line. He had rehearsed, saying, "I am in love with you," not, "I love you." *Take Two, I'll get it right.*

Regardless, he knew Winner had received his message, loud and clear. *Mission accomplished, Fly Boy.* He began whistling, then commenced a shuffling soft-shoe step, a routine *a la* Fred Astaire. Happily, he danced alone in the dark, beneath a canopy of dazzling stars, an imaginary Winner following, Ginger to his Fred.

***

By 4:00 a.m., the party had ended.

Dressed in tennis shorts and sweater, his best tennis racquet tucked under one arm. Winner's fiancé padded along the chilly first-floor hallway. A while towel draped his neck. Nervously, he toweled rivulets of sweat, He checked over his shoulder. The corridor was empty.

It must be near dawn.

He glanced at his phone. The time was 4:06 a.m.

Once the last party guest had departed, and Winner had gone to her own room, he had dressed in his work clothes and sneaked out of his room. A vigorous night-time workout on the hotel's courts outdoor—that's what he had told the security men who stood guard at the Royal Suite's elevator.

"I'm the bridegroom," he had told them with a smile and a wink. "Late night workout. You fellows understand. Knock a few balls around. Hey, I'm tense." Sympathizing, the guards had let him go ahead, into the private elevator. Sweating like a pig, he had ridden down to the first floor and exited. At the moment, he was wandering an empty hallway. He was looking for an exit door, out of the hotel.

Unexpectedly, he felt a shove from behind and stumbled to a corner. Angry, he wheeled around, ready to explode, raising his racquet to lob. "What the—?"

The sound of a woman's sultry voice stopped him cold. "You belong in hell, *El Tigre.*"

He stepped backwards in his tracks, deeper into the corner, as a middle-aged female crept towards him. He gripped his racquet but, catching hold of his nerves, lowered it. The flickering wall lamps offered little light, just enough for him to glimpse the broad's face.

Ugh. I hope she sued whoever did the work.

Anxious to avoid the ugly woman, he walked forward, pushing past her, but she seized his arm, jerking him around.

"Who are you?" he demanded. "What do you want?"

In the shadows, she appeared grotesque.

"Oh, come on, Vega. Don't tell me you don't recognize me—your old *playmate*?" The familiar voice was low and cautious, His memory passed through the flames of his past.

There is something . . ..

"I recognize that you're old." Possibility slammed him hard.

It can't be.

She got right in his face. "I'm younger than you, *abuelo.*"

"You don't wear it well, *abuela.*" He recognized the eyes. Cold. Blue. With daggers shooting from them. He must protect himself. How? *Stall for time.* "What are you doing here, Maude?"

Her one-sided grin revealed two rows of perfect teeth. "Oh, you do recognize me."

"I never forget a violent psychopath."

"No?"

"No. Just sticks in my head somehow. Wonder why that is."

"I couldn't say." She pressed against him. Grasping his arm, she examined his Rolex. "My daughter's done you proud," she said approvingly. "She has good taste—in jewelry."

He shrugged, as though he had missed her meaning.

"Come on, Danny Boy. Don't tell me you paid for all this. On your meager pittance? I'll never believe you. Unless you say you stole the funds. That I'll believe."

Stepping back, he struck a pose. "What is it, Maude? What you want?" Inwardly, he wrestled, a trainer trying to restrain the tigress of panic.

What if she has a weapon?

Instead of producing a gun or knife, however, the former babe eased her tall, spindly form onto a bench, built into the alcove's whitewashed cement-block wall. She sat demurely, ankles crossing, knees touching. Purse in her lap, she continued to pan the premises. "I want the money you stole from me, Danny. But I want more than money."

He watched her closely. Something was different about her. Not just the outer wear and tear—even her clothes were scruffy—but something in the way she was behaving struck him as out of character. She seemed *tender*—wounded—vulnerable—and that wasn't possible. He had been her playmate for only a short time—just long enough to know that Maude played too rough for him.

In the bedroom, he had to be in charge. *Always.* Their lovemaking styles had been incompatible.

After only a couple of days with Maude, in the Cayman Islands, he had cut out on the sly, leaving her without so much as a goodbye—and robbing her blind. He had felt lucky to escape with his life. And he had been *loco* with worry, ever since falling hard for Winner two months ago—worried that her mom would turn up, someday, under some rock somewhere, at the worst possible moment.

Now she had.

I got to keep my head.

He acted unconcerned. He tried to play along. "What are you doing here?" he asked. "How did you find me?"

She did not answer directly. "By accident. I saw you yesterday, in the alley off Fifth Avenue South. You nearly ran over me."

"That was you? In Naples?" He blinked rapidly. He didn't know what to say.

She continued. "I followed you, Danny. When you blew into Orlando, I blew in, too." She smirked. "I followed you all the way here. To this hotel. When you hooked up with my daughter, I knew I couldn't walk away. So, I camped out in my car for a couple of nights. Snuck in here tonight to use the bathroom. Simple. And so, here I am."

He swallowed his impulse. "Why?"

"Why did I follow you?"

He nodded.

"Naturally, I want my money back. I need it. Counting the cash, the jewelry, and the credit cards, you owe me upwards of fifty thousand dollars. You left me broke and alone in a foreign country. That wasn't very nice."

"Oops?" He tried the schmooze, to no avail. She wasn't buying it.

Handling her purse, Maude snapped it open and shut distractedly. "Today—yesterday now—I followed Winner around while she shopped."

He suddenly felt sick. "Then you know the lay of the land—"

"I want you to break your engagement to my daughter." Her gaze met his.

What did he read there? This surgical-nightmare—this cold bitch—was an unknown quantity, capable of anything. He looked away, extracting an engraved silver flask from his pocket bar. "Would you like a drink?"

"No, thank you."

He bolted a shot of rum. "You look like you need money."

"You look like you're the thieving gigolo you are."

"That's where you're wrong. I'm in love with Winner."

"You're lying, as usual."

"I'm not. She has the heart you ain't got." Inserting the flask into his pocket, he sat down beside Maude on the bench, keeping a safe distance. Running away wouldn't help this time. He would make her see reason.

Contemplating him, Maude chewed the inside of her slack left cheek. "Your feelings don't matter a whit to me," she announced. "I don't care."

He parked his right ankle atop his left knee. "But I do. I care very much." He waved his hand. "Money means nothing to me." He sought her eyes. "I am in love."

She half-smiled. "Then I'm sorry for you."

He leaned in, with attitude. "Yeah? Why?"

"Flask?" she said, hand extended.

He withdrew the container from his pocket and handed it to her.

Snapping her purse shut, she put it on the bench. Opening the flask, she drank it dry, then examined it. "Another expensive gift from my daughter? Monogrammed, yet. Eh, DV?"

"Since when is she your daughter? From what I hear, you nearly killed her as a kid. How come a maniac like you suddenly developed maternal instinct?"

Raising the flask, she aimed it at him.

He ducked. The flask struck a nearby lamp, shattering the bulb and causing a popping sound and a wisp of smoke. On his feet instantly, he strode towards her in the semi-darkness, afraid he might wring her scrawny neck—which was probably what she wanted him to do. *Put her out of her misery.* He felt inclined to do it. But her next move surprised him.

She apologized. "Sorry. I shouldn't have done that." She sighed. "But if you touch me—if you put one hand on me—I'll scream bloody murder and rape and you'll be exposed to the whole world for the fraud you are. Think my little girl would want you after that hullabaloo? She wouldn't . . ."

He let her talk. The time and place were not right—to do what he must inevitably do. He guessed it would come to that.

She poked his shoulder. "Don't get any funny ideas, Danny. I can see you thinking. I know when it's happening because it happens so infrequently."

Die, bitch. "What happened to your pretty face, Maude?"

"Train wreck." Moaning, she brushed past him.

"Give me a break. What happened to your face? You should sue the plastic surgeon."

"Not surgery. Bell's palsy. Ever heard of it?"

"Nope."

"Facial paralysis. Cause unknown."

"Can't you get it fixed?"

"Takes money. The money you owe me."

Instantly, he snatched the purse from her hands. Ripping it open, he dumped its contents onto the bench. He fumbled through her trash—compact, lip gloss, cell phone. Papers. *No weapon.*

"Disappointed?" She still had a snide look on her pathetic mug.

He shoved the empty bag back into her hands, watching, hands on his hips, as she scooped her meager belongings back inside the pouch. As she turned towards the door, he grabbed her by the hair and twisted. She screeched.

"Shut up."

"Stop it," she rasped, voice lowered.

"I'm not going to marry your daughter," he whispered menacingly.

"No, you're not." He twisted harder.

She cried out.

"I'm leaving here tonight. If you try to stop me, Maude, I'll kill you."

"If you kill me, Danny Vega, they'll find my body. I've left a letter explaining everything. Winston will learn the truth, either way."

His teeth clenched. "I don't believe you." Releasing her hair, he seethed. He slapped her face. Her eyes flashed with the old hatred. Stunned, she stopped breathing for a moment, then began to breathe slowly, as the raging fire died away. "I won't fight you—not that way. I don't do that anymore."

"Like hell."

"No, not like hell. Hell is something I'm trying to avoid. I just want you to do the right thing."

"Delete the double-talk. Now you listen to my terms."

"You're in no position to dictate."

"I-I—" *Oh, yeah?*

"You're scared, Danny. That's what you are. I know fear when I see it. Why else would be sneaking out at night, sneaking around in the dark so no one can see you—and recognize you? You're running out on my daughter the same way you ran out on me, you louse. Go back and face her. Tell her the truth. Tell her the truth. It's the only way to be free."

"You're delusional. You need help." *Get away from her.*

"I know you hate Heston—for killing your little brother."

He could not speak.

"Forgive him. I have."

"You have?"

Suddenly, a service worker strode by. Terrified, Danny embraced Maude, pretending to be her lover. She did not fight him. The feel of her sickened him.

As the worker passed by the alcove, he peered in and waved but did not stop. Instantly, Maude pushed Danny aside. "Keep your hands off me. You disgust me."

"Oh, please. Look in a mirror."

She reached out to claw him.

He gripped her writhing wrist, holding her at bay. "Who else knows you're here?"

"No one. But I told you. I've left a note in my car, explaining everything." She ground her heel into his big toe.

He felt a shooting pain. "Shit!" Desperately fighting the urge to strike her, he dropped her wrist and limped to the bench. "I told you I'm not marrying your precious *bebe.* What the hell else do you want from me?"

"I want you to return my $50,000. You have until noon tomorrow—or else."

"Else what?"

"I'll go to the police, Danny. I happen to know there are multiple warrants out for your arrest. Congratulations on eluding the law for so long."

Rubbing his toe, he pretended he didn't care, laughing off her threat. "Please. Let me think about it. Maybe I can come up with the money."

I will teach you a lesson . . .

Maude walked away from him, towards the empty hallway. Turning around, she added, in a low, sly tone, "Just think. I was almost your mother-in-law, Danny Vega."

He humored her. "You sure as hell are behaving like one. But I'm no fool. I know why you followed me, Maude. You had a thing for me. And it burns to you know that I prefer your young daughter. Your *innocent* daughter."

"Innocent? Hah! Don't be too sure. Half her genes came from me. And her father's a rutting beast."

"Winner wouldn't lie—well, not about that."

Ignoring his comment, Maude again checked out the hallway. "The coast is clear," she said. "Meet me tomorrow at noon with the money you owe me."

"Where?"

"At the gas station. Across the street."

"Okay."

"If you don't," she said, "I'll go to the police. I'll tell them all about you."

"I'll take care of you. Count on it."

"You're not beyond redemption, you know, Danny. You can start life again. I can help you. Show you how. If you'll let me." Without explaining, Maude disappeared down the frigid hotel corridor.

Toe smarting, Dan pounded the bench. The woman was nuts. He had to act and act fast.

Now both his toe and his hand throbbed in pain. Hobbling, he left the alcove and found an exit door at the end of the first-floor hallway. Stranded in the hotel parking lot, he mulled over his options.

***

"Are you okay, Miss?" the beefy service-worker asked Winner, as the hotel's main elevator lifted off, rising on its way to the 16rh floor.

"Ye—" The words stuck in Winner's throat. She gulped it out. "Yes. Thank you."

If I die of shame, scatter my ashes in the Gulf of Mexico.

The carriage reached the 16th floor. The door opened. "If I or any of the hotel staff, may be of service, please don't hesitate to ask." The service-worker stopped the sliding door, holding it open.

Winner looked at him. "There is one thing."

"Name it," he said, letting go of the door and pushing the "Hold" key on the elevator console.

Drained of emotional energy, she whimpered. "Please don't tell anyone you saw me tonight."

The man hesitated, obviously disappointed. "Oh. Well, sure. It'll be our secret."

Unnerved, she kept talking. "It's just that I couldn't sleep—"

"That's understandable, Miss Demming"

"You know who I am?"

"Well, you're—famous."

"I just went for walk, that's all."

"Sure. I hear you, ma'am."

"Thanks." Fighting tears, Winner patted her pockets. "Here's some cash. I'd rather not have a digital record of—"

"Not necessary, Miss Demming." He sized her up. "Positive you're okay? You look like you've seen a ghost—if you don't mind me saying so."

Her face twisted in pain. "No! No, I haven't seen a ghost. I haven't! Really!" The anxiety was rising up through her being like a hot, bubbling geyser. "I just went downstairs for a walk. When I got to the first floor, I got off the elevator—and then I changed my mind."

"Sure."

"That's what I was doing when you came walking up. I was just thinking—about whether I really felt like going for a walk—and I couldn't decide— and I was just standing there, and that's when you pushed the elevator button—and I decided to go upstairs and go back to bed. And I didn't see a ghost. I did not see a ghost! Do you hear me?"

"Yes."

"Excellent." Her tears flowed, unstoppable. "Goodnight." She fled down the corridor towards Poppy's suite. Changing her mind, she heard the elevator doors close.

Rushing into the service area on the 16th floor, Winner stopped and stood with her back and sweaty palms pressed against the wallpaper. She breathed rapidly through her opened mouth.

No, I didn't see a ghost. But I did overhear one talking.

Her stomach began to heave. Without her pink bowl, she vomited into a trash can. She no longer wanted to pour her heart out to Poppy. Nor did she want to encounter anyone else. Exhausted, she stumbled towards the Exit stairwell. Once inside the stairwell, she began to climb the stairs.

She would never sleep tonight.

Not now.

In a few hours, she would have to put in an appearance at Ezra's Sunday brunch on the set. Attendance was compulsory. Somehow, she felt comforted. Ezra would be there.

Not that Ezra matters . . .

***

Five minutes later, in the sitting room of Banks Winston's hotel suite, Maude finished resting her case. She had spent the last 10 minutes explaining her absence of fifteen years to her aristocratic elder half-brother, Banks. Not only had she revealed the details of her altered appearance, her wrongdoings, and her recent conversion, but also she had shared her concerns about the relationship between Danny Vega and Winner.

In fact, that was why she had come, to solicit her brother's help in exposing Danny as a con man. She knew Danny would not show up with the money. She did not believe anything he had told her. She did not believe he was abandoning Winner.

Before beginning her tale, however, Maude had sworn Banks to secrecy. To her relief, Banks had agreed, offering to mount a private investigation of Danny Vega, alias Damian Velasquez. Once collected, the facts would be revealed to Winner. Silently, Maude had given thanks.

Then, her concerns abated, she studied the appearance of Banks himself.

Her aristocratic half-brother had aged since their last face-to-face meeting. His shock of thick of white hair had thinned. His white brows had grown bushier. As he had done always, Banks looked down his aquiline nose at her, but tonight his attitude was tinged with bemused compassion. For that, she was grateful. After all, it was her own mother who had been the usurper, who had stolen his father away from his mother. Banks, not she, was indeed the legitimate heir of the Winston family's old-California fortune.

And how he looks the part.

Attired in black silk pajamas and robe, Banks now lounged in the burgundy-leather chair in his suite's sitting room, his long, thin legs crossed at the knee. She had caught him unawares, during his breakfast of tea and toast, when she had rapped, with her car keys, on the door to his suite.

Although surprised by the sudden appearance of his long-lost half-sister, Banks had received her cordially and invited her in, offering her a cup and plate. Yet, confronted with her appearance, he had not masked his distress.

When he had pressed Maude for facts about her disfigured face, she had explained to him that her facial paralysis was revenge of highest order, retribution for the harm she had done to her daughter and others, earlier in life. Fortunately, she had seen the error of her ways.

"How so?" Banks had asked her.

She had sought solace in religion, she had explained.

"But you haven't quite found it yet?" the reserved old gent had asked.

Ashamed, she had not replied, afraid to reveal her true feelings— that she should suffer more to atone for her misdeeds.

"You don't need suffering," he had told her. "You need grace."

Thus, they had arrived at the present moment.

"Why not have work done, to correct your—facial situation, Maude. Surely, a neurologist could do something. I know a superb plastic surgeon who could—" He touched his spindly fingers to her chin, turning her cheek to him gently. Studying it, he winced, as if hurt himself somehow. "I'll pay for it, if that's a concern for you, Sis."

"No. Thank you. I got what I deserved," she said, kneading the cap in her hands.

"In other words, you no longer punish others, but you are not through punishing yourself yet?" he asked.

"That's absurd, Banks." She could not have felt more startled had he slapped her, as Danny Vega had done.

"Then let me help you, Maude. You were a beautiful woman once. Wicked, but beautiful. This—disfigurement—can't be easy for you to bear."

She heard her half-brother's words, but she did not respond. She was too busy wondering whether or not his words were true. She was mulling the word 'grace.'

Unwilling to be ignored, Banks cleared his throat. "Maude? Did you hear me? Or are you lost in your own world of misery?"

That, she heard. She looked up at him and flashed a smile. "Misery? No, Banks. If anything, I'm joyous now."

Banks grunted his approval, adding, "Then why don't we give you a joyous new outside to match your joyous new inside?"

Maude hesitated. "I'll think about it."

"Think about this. The path you're on leads to futility. Forgive yourself, dear. That's the whole point, so they tell me." He watched her as she rose to full height. "Where are you staying tonight?" he asked, rising himself.

She lied to save face. "At a motel. A couple of miles from here."

"Will it do? Is it safe?" he asked. "You're welcome to stay here—"

She held up a hand. "No. I'll be fine. No need to worry about me. I can take care of myself. Been doing it for years."

"Famous last words," Banks said sardonically. "Shall I walk you to your car?" He nodded towards the window. "The sun's not up yet. It's still dark outside."

Placing her hand on the doorknob, she paused. "No. I want to remain *incognito*. But thank you for accepting me as I am—for listening to me and believing me. For not shunning me. For letting bygones be bygones."

His face was in shadow. "I've been through hell, too, Maude. I just wear it better than you do."

"Goodbye, Banks." She opened the door. "I'll be in touch with you this afternoon." One final thought occurred to her. She turned to him.

"Don't mention me to Winner yet. Okay? I'll approach her—when I'm ready."

"All right, Maude."

"Goodnight, Banks." Donning her cap, she exited into the hotel corridor.

"Good morning," she heard him reply as she closed the door behind her and trotted down the corridor to the elevator.

Once inside the elevator, she located the keys to her Chevy and jingled them in her hand. The first thing she had to do was locate her car and get some shuteye. She had fibbed about staying in a motel. For one more night, the back seat of her Chevy would suffice. She yawned.

She was more tired than she realized. Leaving the public elevator, she walked across the hotel lobby. Exiting the main door, she entered the hotel parking lot. Yawning, she did not notice the stealthy figure who tiptoed up behind her. By the time she heard the footsteps, it was already too late to defend herself.

Chapter Twelve

"A third doll is missing," Lissette said to Poppy on the phone at 7:00 a.m.

The housekeeper, who had phoned from Naples, sounded defensive. "I'm sorry to have to tell you such a bad thing, but facts are facts."

Disbelieving, Poppy pressed the phone to her ear. "A third doll?" With the other hand, she towel-dried her sopping-wet hair. "Which one is it this time?"

"It is the Kipp doll. The rock-star doll. Do you remember it?"

Dissolving, Poppy sank down onto the foot of her unmade bed. She put down the towel. "Yes. I remember it." She turned on the speaker phone and placed the phone beside her on the bed. Incredulous, she stared at the device.

Lissette's voice filled Poppy's bedroom in Heston's suite. "It's the doll Winner 'buried' after Kipp died."

"I remember. She gave it a private 'funeral.' "

"She wrapped the doll in silk and put it in a cedar box."

"And placed the box under her bed. Where it's been all these years."

"Until now," said Lissette, her tone ominous. "I vacuumed under the bed. The box was still there, but it was open—and empty. The Kipp doll is gone. I've looked everywhere for it."

Poppy tried calm her own fears. The action-figure's disappearance was a harbinger of danger. "Lissette, who could have taken it? Has anyone been in the house the past few days?"

"Just the pool guy and me and Felicia—*Oy!* I forget. She wants me to call her 'Tropica' now. Me, her own mother! I'm the one who named her Felicia."

"Tropica was in Naples? When was this?"

"She came here yesterday morning, before she flew up to Orlando. She brought me a bagful of presents."

"What were they?"

"An outfit from Paris. I mean, an ensemble. And a strand of Tahitian pearls. Since her success, she's spoiling me rotten."

"Do you think she took the doll?"

"No. Why would she do such a thing?"

"Well, what about the pool guy? Was it Eddie?"

"No, it was a new guy. He did both pools."

"Did you keep an eye on him while he was servicing the indoor pool?"

Lissette coughed. "Excuse me. Most of the time—"

"Great."

Lissette objected. "But why would a pool guy take that doll? What reason could he have?"

Poppy said earnestly, "Even in death, Kipp has a huge fan base. Guys his age loved his music. The pool guy might have been a big fan of his."

"But how would they even know about the doll? It was hidden."

"That's a good question."

A knock sounded on the bedroom door. "Poppy?" Heston called through the door. "Are you ready yet? It's nearly 7:30. Ezra's sent a limo. It's waiting for us downstairs."

Inhaling sharply, Poppy grabbed the towel and rubbed her wet hair. "Coming!" she shouted in the direction of the door. At lower volume, she addressed the phone on the bed. "Lissette, gotta go. We need to report the latest stolen doll to the local police. I'll let Nick know."

"I'll report it." Lissette paused a moment. "Was that a man's voice I heard?" she asked.

Scandalized, Poppy giggled nervously. "Lissy, be careful. I'll fill you in later." For some reason, she did not want to give Lissette the satisfaction of knowing it was Heston.

Flying into the bathroom, she grabbed the blow dryer and went to work on her appearance. Throwing herself together, she had just enough time to dab coral-colored lipstick and blush on her freckled face. She knew from past experience that Heston had no patience with tardiness.

***

Inside the air-cooled SUV limousine, Poppy bubbled over. "Lissette just phoned me," she told Ezra, Nick, and Heston. "Fasten your seat belts—in more ways than one. I have bad news."

"Meaning?" Heston asked drowsily.

"A third doll is missing."

Nick sat up, board straight. "From Winner's doll collection in Naples?"

"Uh huh," Poppy affirmed.

"Crap," said Ezra. He stared out the side window as the limo left the hotel grounds. "Hey, doesn't that put us in the clear? We've been here the whole time."

Poppy shook her head. "No. I thought that at first, too. But think about it. The Kipp doll could have been taken at any time."

Nick acquiesced. "Poppy's right. It could have been taken at the same time as the other two dolls."

"Exactly," said Poppy. "It could have been taken a year ago or five years ago. No one would have noticed. No one ever looked inside the 'casket.' "

The three men regarded her quizzically.

She explained. "Win had buried the doll under her bed. It was a symbolic gesture for her. To cope with her grief—and all she'd been through—the kidnapping and all. Her shrink recommended it. Kind of a closure for her."

"I wish I had been there," Heston said.

Poppy did not answer.

"Listen, you three." Nick pointed an index finger. "Do not mention this new development to anyone. Until I give the okay. No one else is to know about this third missing doll."

Ezra balked. "Not even Winner herself?"

"Well, I'll need to ask her if she took it. Nobody else, though, son. We'll stay one step ahead of our killer."

"Killer?" asked Heston, now wide awake.

Nick's face was somber. "You heard me. The behavior is escalating." He returned to Poppy. "I'll need to speak with your housekeeper, too. Find out who's been in and out of there in past few days."

Poppy brightened. "I asked her already. Just the pool guy and her—and Tropica."

"Tropica?" Nick seemed interested. "What was she doing there?"

"Visiting her mom. Just prior to coming here for the party."

"I got my work cut out for me, people," Nick observed. "I need some breakfast, Ezzie."

"I just hope you know what you're doing, G-man." Ezra checked the messages on his smartphone. "Anybody else hungry? The caterers are setting up at the studio."

Idly, Poppy studied the faces of her three male companions in the limo. Could she really trust these men? What if one of them was wearing a mask? Figuratively speaking. Which one would it be? Feeling guilty, she looked away. No doubt they were suspicious of her.

And she suspected everybody. At this point, even Lissette.

This is what we've come to? Everyone, including me, is under suspicion.

Evil begets evil.

***

After providing a sumptuous brunch, Ezra conducted a tour of the grand movie sound stage, where *Forbidden Mysteries* was to be rehearsed and shot. The tour group —Adair, Hailey, Banks, Tropica, Nick, Poppy, Winner, and Heston, all filled to the gills—meandered around the newly constructed sets, in preparation for the first day of work.

Ezra, as director, wanted everyone involved to get the "feel" of the sets. He was eager to begin work. Indeed, his enthusiasm was contagious. He could feel the energy building inside his actors. Tomorrow, after the initial read-through of his script, they would begin rehearsing the pilot episode. For the moment, he gave them free reign to explore the sets. He drew their attention to the laboratory and the interior of the tomb.

While everyone roamed, Ezra found himself alone, on the living-room set, with his favorite leading lady. He and Winner sat side by side, in the intimate space, watching the others in the distance. Folks milled around, chatting, and inspecting the facilities.

Winner wasn't saying much, so Ezra prodded her. "Did Nick tell you about the latest development?"

"Yes. While he was spooning syrup onto his crepes."

"Do you know where your Kipp doll is?"

"No, Ezra. I don't. It creeps me out that someone is stealing my things."

"Well, it goes deeper than that. Based on what's already happened, the third doll may turn up soon in a very unpleasant way. Have you thought about that?"

"Yeah." Winner did not elaborate. She seemed distant.

He persevered. "Too bad your fiancé couldn't join us for brunch. Is he feeling any better?"

Winner did not respond. Nor would she look at him.

"What's up, Starlight? You still recovering from last night's party?" His focus became riveted on her cleavage, the cleavage of his dreams. He forced himself to raise his gaze. Winner looked worn out. She looked as if she had been crying. He moved as close to her as possible, his gaze never leaving her face. "Clue me in," he cajoled.

"Here's the thing," Winner said. "Last night. Around 4:00 a.m. I missed Damian. I wanted—" She looked at him defensively. "I wanted to be held. But Damian wasn't in his bedroom."

Separate bedrooms. Check.

"So, I went downstairs, looking for him. When I stepped off the elevator, I heard Damian's voice, coming from this—uh, lounge area. Then I heard a woman's voice. They were talking. I stopped, Ezra. I hid. I listened." She broke down, sobbing.

He enveloped her in his arms. "You eavesdropped?"

"I did." She clung to him. Her fingers kneaded his bicep. "I'm so ashamed." Her hair, uplifted in a loose bun, smelled faintly of strawberries. Tiny beads dangled from her ear lobes.

"And what did you overhear?" he whispered, as compassionately as possible.

"My m-mother—!" She cried out quietly, in distress.

"Your mother? You mean Poppy?"

Winner shook her head vehemently. She seemed hardly able to utter the words. "My—birth—mother."

221

He was astounded. "You mean Maude Winston?"

Winner nodded. She brushed stray flaxen strands away from her face.

"The model? The one who—abused you?"

Winner nodded.

Pointing a finger, Ezra fit the pieces together. "Your mother was talking with Damian in the lounge at 4:00 a.m.?"

Nodding vigorously, Winner sobbed, dampening his shirt collar. "Yes," she said, inconsolable. "Except that his name isn't 'Damian'. It's Danny. My mother called him 'Danny.' Ezra, his real name is 'Danny Vega.'"

"Oh?" The name meant nothing to Ezra, but Winner's distress was killing him. Placing his arm around her shoulders, he realized she was paying him a true compliment.

She's confiding in me.

At a loss for words, he drew her close and patted the fluff of angel hair on her head. Stunned by her need of him, he reconnoitered.

How to proceed? If I were directing this scene . . .

"Win, look at me." Placing his hand under her chin, he tilted her face to his. He searched the black-rimmed silver-blues. Wet mascara smudged her ivory cheekbones and, no doubt, the collar of his own favorite jersey-knit.

It is well worth it.

"Want to tell me about it? From the beginning?" he asked kindly. "I'm not your shrink, but I can listen."

Her arms enveloped his mid-drift. Her head nestled against his shoulder. She nodded. "It's like some horrible nightmare, Ezzie," she whispered.

"Come on over here, sweetheart," he coaxed, snuggling. As she nestled into him, he clasped the hand in her lap and held it, resting his cheek against the crown of her head. His fingers toyed with her ruby-red nails.

As Ezra held Winner, she seemed to be drawing reassurance from him. They sat for a few moments in silence. He could feel her body calming—and his own becoming excited. He was grateful for this moment of intimacy—until guilt assailed him.

You're being a jerk, Gold. She's in pain. Help her.

"Talk to me, Win," he encouraged, fondling her delicate fingers, as he had done in a fantasy he'd once had. "What exactly happened? I mean, what were they saying?"

Winner tensed. He nestled closer, holding her in check, inhaling the fragile fragrance of her. "Just breathe, honey. Tell me."

Winner whimpered, burying her face. "They were lovers."

What? Ezra bolted upright. "Maybe you misunderstood. Were you far away?"

"Kind of. But I could hear them okay."

"They said they *were* lovers? Or they *are* lovers?"

"In the past. They talked about it. She—talked about it. She accused Damian—I mean, Danny—of stealing—fifty thousand dollars— from her. He'd run out on her."

Taking a mental victory lap, Ezra willed himself physically to subdue his euphoria. The tennis bum was history.

Handle this right, man.

"That SOB. Did he deny it?"

A beat of silence. "No." Dropping Ezra's hand, she draped her arm across his abdomen, nestling into his chest. Then she raised her head. "Do you have your hanky?"

"Oh, honey! Sorry, no! Let me find you a tissue—"

Quickly extricating himself from the warmth of her embrace, he dashed into the bathroom and yanked tissues from a plastic box. Returning, tissues in hand, he resumed his position on the couch. But Winner was sitting upright and did not nestle into his chest again as he resumed his seat.

Foiled, he handed her the tissues.

Next time bring the handkerchief, schmuck.

"Excuse me," she said under her breath, as she blew her perfect nose and dabbed her eyes.

"You're excused."

Forlorn, she sat forward on the couch, a tissue balled in her hand. "Oh, Ezzie. I've been a fool."

He sat awkwardly beside her. *I should have said no. I shouldn't have gotten up. Lesson learned? Pay attention, jerk. The lady needs a handkerchief. Ma was right. It pays to carry a clean one, "for the ladies."*

"Ezra?"

"Eh? We've all played the fool for love, kid. You've got nothing to be ashamed of."

"Thank you, Ezzie."

Ruminating, Ezra twisted his lips. *What would Humphrey Bogart do now?*

Sniffling, Winner turned to him, lifting one smooth knee onto the couch cushion. "Ezra, thanks for being here—for me." She sniffed daintily.

He made no move towards her. "I'm always here for you, Winner. You know that."

She half-smiled. "Yeah." She dabbed her nostril. "Ezra—"

"Yes?"

"What should I do now?"

He stared at her, agape. *Just like Ingrid Bergman in Casablanca. She wanted Rick to do the thinking for both of them.*

"Ezra? Hello?"

He roused. "All right, I will."

"Will what?" Her expression was sad—and trusting.

"Tell you—what—you should do." *I'm a director. I'm up to this challenge.*

"All right. What?" She rose to her feet. "I should dump him, right? I want to dump him." She shuddered. "It all so horrible. And her—oh, I never want to face her ever, ever. I had hoped she was dead." Her expression changed to fear.

"Win—" Rising, he took her hand and stood facing her. "Why not let me handle this? I can go to this Dan. I'll put the question to him. Were you and Winner's mom lovers in the past? I'll get the truth."

"No. I don't think—" She cast her eyes downward. "I don't believe he'd talk to you. He won't see anyone—now."

"Why not?"

The corners of her mouth drooped and quivered. "Because he's gone," she wailed. "When I knocked on his bedroom door this morning, there was no answer. I went in. His room was empty. He never came back."

"The coward. He'll see me, all right. Because I'm going to find him."

"He agreed to meet—her at noon today with the money he owed her."

"Where?"

"At the gas station across the street."

Ezra rubbed the back of his neck. "I hate to break it to you, babe, but I think he was lying." He aimed an index finger at the glum-faced girl.

225

"Look, you're within your rights to dump that jock. Stop footing the bill for his upkeep. I'll be happy to—"

Standing, she placed her fingertips over his lips. "Shh." She stroked his cheek. "Thank you, Ezra, for understanding. For not judging me."

He gazed at her. *Kiss her now.* As Winner opened to him, he remembered once hearing Lauren Bacall say that—yeah, that was how Bogie had handled her. In an interview, she'd said it . . .

Sometime . . . long . . . ago . . .

As Ezra moved in for the kiss, he heard a woman scream.

Startled, Winner jumped back from him. He could see Tropica, distraught. Others surrounded her, comforting her. Evidently, she had been the one who screamed.

But why?

***

Everyone hovered around Tropica, concerned. No one, except Nick, noticed Heston, who was standing in front of an open cabinet, adjacent to the far wall of the lofty room. Heston's back was to them. He was peering inside the cabinet. Cautiously, Nick walked over and stood beside Heston.

"What the hell's going on?" Ezra bellowed.

Hearing his voice boom out across the sound stage, the spectators reacted anxiously, turning. Jolted by the sound, Heston, too, spun around and took a step in Ezra's direction. At that moment, a heavy light fixture dropped from the ceiling and crashed onto the cement floor, only inches away from Heston, who was thrown off balance as shards of glass flew through the air.

The immense fixture had slammed the floor, on the very spot where Heston had been standing, as he had stared into the cabinet, only five seconds earlier. Reacting to the averted horror of the scene, Ezra gaped in astonishment. At his side, Winner watched, dumfounded.

Quickly, he rushed Winner across the sound stage. "Is anybody hurt?" he cried.

"No, thank heaven," said Banks, "but that's no thanks to you. This is your fault, Gold! Tropica was terrorized. Demming was almost killed. I was only six feet away! I should sue you and your whole, rotten—"

Ezra was not listening to the ravings of Banks. Heston held him spellbound.

Aghast, Heston stood contemplating the smashed fixture on the floor. He was obviously shaken to the core. Winner flew to his side. "Dad? Are you okay?" Her shoes crunched shards, strewn around the crash site. "He'll need a doctor, Ezra," she called. "To check for cuts."

"On it." Ezra said, texting.

Nick approached Ezra. "When I say 'killer,' I mean killer. That light missed Heston by centimeters. He was the target. No doubt about it."

Ezra was skeptical. "How do you know that?"

"Look inside the cabinet," Nick said.

Striding to Winner's side, he looked into the cabinet. Inside, an effigy of rock-star Kipp Demming dangled by the neck from a length of rough cord. Pinned to the doll was a note.

Heston's gravelly voice sounded at his shoulder. "The note says, 'You're in the groove. Now it's my move.' "

"Watch the glass on the floor, man," said Ezra to Heston. He took him by the arm. "At least we know where the third doll is—and who the stalker's target is."

"You mean Kipp?" asked Heston, confused.

"No, man. Kipp has passed already. I mean you, Heston."

"Right." Heston reeled, unsteady.

"You okay, buddy?"

227

"I'd like to sit down."

A stack of folding chairs lined the wall nearby. Hurriedly, Ezra unfolded one of the chairs and set Heston down in it. Meanwhile, Hailey came rushing over to him. As he unfolded a second chair for Winner, Hailey vied for his attention.

"Sit, please," Ezra said to Winner. "Stay with your dad." When Winner had seated herself next to her father, Ezra acknowledged Hailey's presence. He indicated the smashed light. "Big mess, huh?"

Before Hailey could speak Poppy made her way over and stood near Heston. "Are you all right?" she asked her husband. Right behind her came Banks Winston, simmered down and solicitous.

"Here's a chair for you, Poppy," said Banks, gallantly unfolding a seat, which she accepted.

"Uncle Ezzie." Tugging at his sleeve, Hailey got Ezra's attention. She appeared frightened. "I'm so glad you're here—to take charge of things." She latched onto Ezra's arm, but, patting her hand, he gently pulled away. "Watch out for the glass, Hailey." He called to the group. "Everybody! Stay away from this area, please!"

He walked over to check on Tropica. "How're you doing, honey?" he asked the shuddering pop singer.

"I'm okay," said Tropica, teeth chattering. "How's Heston?"

"Lucky," said Ezra.

"Blessed," said Banks.

"Is Heston okay?" Hailey trailed Ezra as he walked away from Tropica, chattering as she dogged his heels. "Tropica almost fainted. She found that horrible doll. That's when she screamed and ran. That's when Heston went over to investigate. And—kaboom!"

"Mind-blowing fun," Adair said, approaching his sister.

"Oh, Adair," Hailey cried out loudly. "What's wrong with you? That's so sick! It's almost as if you wanted Heston to be killed!"

"Cool it, Hay-Hay," said Nick, taking command. "The police are on their way," he announced to the troubled group. "Stick around. They'll be asking you people some questions."

***

Heston's brush with death had upset Poppy. By the time she and Heston returned to their hotel suite, her nerves were shot; her composure, long gone.

"Our children are arriving tomorrow. And a killer is loose. Or do you not care, Heston?"

Heston nipped at her. "I was almost killed this morning. Do you care about that?" he said from behind. The back of his neck boasted two bandages. This was the extent of his injuries.

Exhausted, she stormed into the suite's sitting room. Following her, Heston slammed the suite door behind him—and bolted it. They were alone.

Tossing his passkey onto an end table, he planted himself solidly—legs astride, feet flat—on the pristine rust-and-cobalt tiles. "Let's have it out, shall we, Penelope? Once and for ever-loving all."

Tensed, Poppy spun around. Instantly, her gaze travelled from his chest to his face. She had forgotten how tall he was. She felt inadequate. "It's always about you, isn't it, Sean Heston?"

Heston groaned. "Is that it?"

No, that's not it! "Where have you been for the past four years?" she cried. "Your children miss you."

"I provided well for them—and you" he said patiently. "Has it occurred to you? That I might miss my family? That I might even miss you, Poppy Sue?"

Poppy fought to contain her rage. "Everything occurred to me—every possible horror, every tragedy. Where on earth have you been, Heston?"

"Not on earth. That was the point."

"Gibberish." Her head hurt. Frustrated, she squeezed her temples.

"In a way, I've been on a spiritual quest," he admitted. "I'm still on it." Sitting down, Heston spoke hesitantly. "Look, I gave my attorney strict instructions," he said. " 'Do not contact me.' That's what I told him. I needed to know—something."

"Know what?"

"I don't know yet."

Squealing in anger, Poppy stomped her feet. "Riddles."

Apparently searching for words, Heston rose and walked to the wall and leaned against it. "I know some of it—some of what I was seeking to learn."

"What?"

"How normal people live. What their problems are. How do they survive? How do they make ends meet? How do they find strength and solace? How do they comfort themselves in the midst of tragedy?"

"Oh. Is that all?"

"No. One more thing. How do they live without being physically perfect?"

Surprised, Poppy faltered. "What did you learn about that?"

Grimacing, he replied, "Sometimes they survive. Sometimes they don't." He paused for a beat. "And then I went beyond—to understand the how—and embody it."

She waited for an explanation. He didn't offer one. He didn't need to.

"You're still a very handsome man, Heston."

He took a step towards her. "All right, Poppy. We've addressed my whereabouts. Now let's get down to the heart of the matter."

"Which is?"

"Your feelings of resentment towards me," he said, as if tearing a bandage from her wound.

"I left my husband for you," she stated vehemently.

"I thought I was your husband. Your *very first* husband. And your very last."

She locked eyes with him. She regarded him in pregnant silence. "Jim Talbot loved me."

Heston's body relaxed. "I never cheated on you. Jim did." He stepped back. "I may have been with other women in the past, but not while we were together. Never. Never once did—"

She flinched, stepping forward. "Not even the day you proposed to me? When I was a trusting teenager? Ten minutes later you dumped me for Montsey Flynn."

He bridled. "You're throwing that in my face?"

Petulant, she steamed, unable to come up with a response. "All right. I once said I forgave you. And I do. I did. But then every time I turned around, there you were—revealing some new wrinkle in your past. When Kipp and Shawnee died—when I found out about your old lover—I reached a breaking point, Heston. I didn't trust you then, and I don't trust you now."

Bewildered, he pressed his palms into his scalp. "So, you broke free of me. And took my children with you. Now you want to cut me off totally."

"They are my children, too."

In a flash, an unspoken exchange occurred between them.

Not Winner.

Now who's doubling back? You said she was. You told me I was a good mother to Win.

I did. You're right, I'm sorry. Can't we move on?

Like a smokestack, Poppy spewed speech. "You lied to me! You misrepresented your—sex life. That's the whole point. Of everything. Of our years of separation. You—"

His gaze narrowed. "I what?"

"Your lies led to Kipp's death. And Shawnee's. And Beryl's and the death of our marriage—!" Her gaze fell. She brushed back a fallen strand of hair. It had stuck to the perspiration on her brow.

Heston stood firmly. "Let's not forget the death of your compassion for me," he retorted coldly. "While you're doling out the blame."

Heart palpitating, she dug her heel into the Persian throw-rug. She and Heston were on dangerous ground.

Uncomfortable, he cleared his throat. "Look, Red. There is one more thing I need to tell you. I'm not sure now is the right time, but—"

"What lie are you going to tell me now? I can't take any more. I can't." She turned to leave. "I'm moving on, Heston. I've had other offers."

Grasping her upper arm, he whirled her around to face him. She looked up into the icy blue glare of his disdain.

"Who are your suitors?"

"My suitors, Your Majesty?" she retorted.

"Whom else have you slept with?" he demanded.

"No one, Sire. Yet," she whispered, stunned by his switch in tactics. "I've been on two dates with my first husband."

"The husky accountant?"

"He wants me back."

Battling, Heston squeezed her flesh. "What about Banks Winston? Were you and he finally lovers? Are you lovers now?" He tightened his grip on her. "Who sent you those roses? I have a right to know, Poppy Sue. Who's cheating whom? We're still married, you and I."

"I don't know. Honestly. For an instant, I thought it might have been Adair."

"Adair Champlain? That half-wit lunatic?"

She clawed at Heston's fingers. "Stop it! Let go—What do think this is, Heston? Some Restoration play?" She pried his fingers loose and jumped away from him.

"Adair is an inbred son of a bitch!" He snarled, then laughed. "What a great stepdad he'd make for the kids."

"Why should you care? You've never had our children's best interests at heart."

Incensed, he lowered his voice. "I *had* the kids' best interests at heart. I stayed away because I was *drinking—and murderous*. I didn't want to scar the children emotionally. I didn't want to—abuse them physically." Abruptly releasing her shoulders, he walked away. In a gesture of frustration, he ran his fingers through the thick shock of hair above his forehead.

How well she remembered that old move. She was trembling, breathing hard.

Pacing, he ranted slowly. "I remember what it was like growing up with my own alcoholic father. It was like living in monastery one moment; a house of horrors, the next. I never knew which father I would be dealing with—the remote, aloof, disapproving holy man or the raging, punishing drunk. It was like living with a two-headed monster."

"Heston, I understand—"

"Do you, Poppy? You don't."

"I do. I knew your father, remember. I saw how it was between the two of you. How he treated you—and how—"

"How what?"

"How you treated him."

"Meaning?"

She did not answer. She looked away. "It's all so long ago now, Heston—"

"No, it's not! I can still hear him, Poppy. Screaming at me, dragging me out of bed—in the middle of the night—yelling, "Answer me!" Beating his fists against my back and shoving me around, yelling, "Answer me!" with his stale, rancid bourbon breath. Hell knows, he had his reasons." Heston's icy eyes melted in flame. "Did you want me doing that to our kids? No! That's why I stayed far away. Who knows? Maybe I made a mistake. Maybe what I did was worse. I missed their growing up." He paused, crestfallen. "I miss my children." He looked at her longingly. "I miss you, Poppy." His eyes were dull now, slate-gray in the shadows. "I want to come home."

Silence enveloped the room. His scent was inescapable, as was his pain. At last, she spoke audibly. "You're not acting now. I can tell."

"Can you?"

"Oh, sure. Sometimes, I'm not sure."

He snorted. "Good. Otherwise, that makes me a lousy actor."

She smiled. "I've known you since grade school, Heston."

Without warning, he turned on the charm. "It's nice to be known, Red." He reached for her hand. "Let me in."

"I might. If you can promise me one thing."

"What's that?"

"That you've confessed everything to me—about your past. That there will be no more lies. No more revelations. No more half-truths. And I'll promise you the same."

She was losing the battle. She wanted to lose the battle.

But he turned away. She knew, only too well, what that meant.

"There's something else you've never told me, isn't there? Another lie about the past?"

"How—how—?"

In one final futile attempt to defy him, she exploded. "I know you better than anyone in the world, Heston. Better than you know yourself! That's how!"

His eyes captured her. "You are determined to punish me. Is that it?"

"Yes! I despise you!"

He barked in laughter. "Oh, I don't think so—"

"I know so!"

"You do? Really?"

"Yes!"

As he advanced, her hands clawed the air in front of her. Catching her hands in his, he pushed her back against the wall. Pressing against her, carefully, he kissed her deeply.

Stunned, she let him. She wanted him. And he could feel it. And he wanted her. That was evident.

Oh, I am such a fool. Even after all these years . . .

She pushed him away. "Don't you see? I can't. You've hurt me too much."

"Poppy, for the love of—" His fingertips grazed hers as she pushed past him, to the window.

Wheeling around, she faced him. She had one last chance to say 'no.' "I'm going ahead with my plans for divorce, Heston."

"Are you?"

"Yes." She crossed her arms in front of her chest. "Yes. Yes. Yes."

The taste of him . . .

"You really want to divorce me?"

"Yes." She heard her own lack of certainty.

"Fine. I won't try to stop you. If your own feelings won't stop you, I won't either. Deny what's between us if you want to, Poppy—but you're the one who's lying now. You're lying to yourself. And to me. You're lying to the universe and to—"

"I'm lying to myself? You self-righteous hypocrite! You liar you, you, you y—y-you—*actor!!!*"

He minced theatrically. "Oh, horrors!"

She hiccupped a giggle, in spite of her ire. "I h-hate you I do h-hear me I h-hate y-you."

"Uh-huh. And I'm a monkey's uncle." His eyes sparkled.

"You're a m-monkey's hind end," she muttered, desperately trying not to smile.

"What did you call me?" He started slowly towards her.

Sputtering, she both chuckled and frowned, backing away." Get b-back!" She hiccupped. "Keep away from me, H-Heston. I m-mean it."

Undaunted, he inched steadily towards her. "You mean it? Do you, Mrs. Demming? I don't think you do. I think you—freaking well like it!"

She dashed away from the window, eluding him. Chasing her, he hustled around the couch. Catching hold of her, he laughed out loud at her shrieks of delight, clutching her bodily to his chest, until her panting subsided. Tilting her face to his, he searched her eyes.

"You. Me. Forever."

He kissed her lips once again, gently, this time, and with infinite tenderness. "I need—"

Her arms flew round him. Her head nestled against his chest. His heart was pounding. So was hers, somewhere deep inside. And then—

She hiccupped.

Against her cheek, his chest jostled. She lifted her head.

He was grinning like an idiot.

Again, she hiccupped, raising a hand to cover her mouth.

Laughing outright, Heston hugged her to him.

"Are you laughing at—me?"

He guffawed, releasing her from his clutches.

"The most dramatic moment in our lives—and you get the hiccups! Aha ha-ha, ha-ha!" He doubled over.

"Well, I never get the h—" She smothered another small belch.

He laughed harder, falling onto the couch.

"It's for the best," she uttered stoically, walking to the door so that he could not see the glow in her eyes and the flush of pink across her chest.

'Oh, come on. Be serious."

"I am."

"We're not finished."

"I am."

"No, you're not. It will never be finished between you and me." Slowly, he rose to his feet. "Even if some madman succeeds in murdering me."

She blanched. His energy enveloped her. Her gaze flitted back and forth, between the sexual beast approaching her and the wide bedroom door yawning open, a mere ten *feet* away. Heston's prowess, as well as his intention, had grown strikingly obvious.

A knock on the room door brought him round.

"See who it is," he ordered, halting.

Exhaling through her nostrils, she marched to the door, flinging it open wide. "Yes?"

An astonished Nick Townsend appeared in the doorway. "Hello, Poppy," he said. "Is Heston in? I need to speak with him privately. Something's come up."

"I'll say it has. Do come in, Nick." She cast one final glance at Heston.

"He's all yours, Nick," she said, scurrying into her bedroom.

"Not all of him," Nick remarked.

Mortified, she swiftly shut the door behind her and collapsed in a fit of silly giggling.

***

Aglow with desire, Poppy settled into a cozy, stuffed chair, all the while feeling dazed, awkward, and, frankly, amazed. Through the closed bedroom door, she heard a burst of men's laughter. As the sound died away, she realized something even more amazing.

Her hiccups were gone. Her breathing had slowed. She rose from the chair.

The threat was at bay—for now. Reclining on her bed, she relived each second of the past twenty minutes. But sleep would not come. Gradually, she gave up on her nap and turned on the bedside lamp. Lying alone in her temporary bed, she asked herself the inevitable question.

Am I going to make love with Heston again?

Physically, she was ready. But emotionally?

Heston had practically admitted to many more lies. Involuntarily, she listened to Heston's muffled voice coming from beyond the closed bedroom door. Her gaze moved down the length of her king-sized bed. A king should be sleeping alongside her. She should be sleeping with a king.

All those years, alone—so hard to bear.

Harder to bear were the memories of Heston's love-making, memories that whispered to her within the walls of her padlocked heart. She dropped her face into her hands. For so long, she had craved the feel and taste of him. His kiss, just now, had opened a long-closed door.

Physically, she was ready for Heston's pleasure, as well as her own. Emotionally, however, she was eons away. Even the thought of such pleasure was too intense for her now.

She remembered one particularly amazing round of lovemaking, the night she had conceived the twins. In the sweltering heat of that blustery summer night, Heston had slammed into her, over and over again, harder and harder, harder than ever before, until pleasure had become a boundless, pulsating euphoria. If she had died that night, in that bed with Heston, it would have been okay. Although it would have been a fitting end, she had not died but merely drifted for hours.

Afterwards, as starlight had faded into sunlight, Heston had stood, naked in silhouette against the rising sun. At the height of his manhood, in his forties, he had seemed base, yet supernatural, like an ancient sculpture, come alive, a satiated satyr of perfect proportions—svelte, muscular, and glistening in the sun's rays—pleased with himself, the world, and her. She could almost see him now, as if his presence were somehow with her.

Startled, she glanced at the closed door. It was. At this very moment, he was no more than twenty feet away from her. Her thoughts drifted back into the past.

In dawn's light, Heston had sidled over to the bed, sprinkled her subsiding body with water, and collapsed in abandon beside her, grinning like a proud fool, yet the most beautiful proud fool in the whole world. She had been more in love with her husband at that moment than she'd thought humanly possible. Like an inhabited idol, he had raised his head one last time, lightly brushed her forehead with his bee-stung lips and then rolled over, falling into heavy slumber, all the while clasping her hand in his.

This had been only one of their precious nights together, years ago. It might as well have happened yesterday.

She had watched Heston play that scene, never dreaming that someday he would leave her and be gone from her empty, aching bed and body—forever. Even now, she blamed herself. She had never felt worthy of such splendid ardor. Was she ever really Heston's destined consort? As a young man, he had idolized Montserrat Flynn.

Did he settle for me?

No, she was not ready emotionally. As her reverie dispelled, her fingers clutched at the bedspread. The pliant cloth felt cold, rough, even formidable. She hated it, clawing it with her sharp coral nails. She knew the truth of her own inner rage.

Oh, Heston. How had everything gone so wrong?

No, it was all too much. Too many things had come between her and Heston. And yet—

This could be my very last chance to say yes.

What if Heston dies?

***

Meanwhile, Nick Townsend settled himself on the large end of the sectional couch in the sitting room of Heston's hotel suite. He wiped his brow with a handkerchief.

"Sorry if I interrupted anything," he said to Heston, who tossed him a frosty bottle of sparkling water. "Thanks, man. It was cool earlier, but it's heating up outside now."

Heston sat down, too. "You know what they say. 'It's not the heat—' "

"The hell it's not." Gratefully, Nick took a swig of the fizzy liquid and wiped his mouth with the kerchief. He cast a sidelong glance Heston's way. "I interrupted some hanky-panky?"

"No. Hell, no. Tell me what's going on." Heston faced the window.

"You two weren't getting up to something?"

Heston donned his most serious attitude. "I assure you, man. It's nothing of the kind. Actually, my wife and I had a fight."

"Did you kiss and make up? Is that when I walked in?"

Heston flashed his caps. "Tell me what's going on, Nicholas. Why are you here?" He eyed the savvy security specialist. "Come to think of it, why are you stalling?"

Sighing, Nick set the empty bottle on the coffee table and took out his smartphone. He cradled the phone in his hand. "Because I've got something—unpleasant—to tell you. On a subject a lot less jolly than kissing and telling."

"Lay it on me." Internally, Heston girded for the worst—*whatever that might be.*

"A visitor to the hotel was found beaten. Savagely beaten. Around 8:00 a.m. this morning. Right after we left in the limo, it was."

Heston said absolutely nothing, waiting expectantly. He stared at Nick, inquiringly.

"That's all you got?" Nick gaped at him. "No reaction?"

Heston shrugged. "All right. Did he or she survive?"

"She." His lips formed a straight line. "Ambulance took her. She was comatose."

"Why bring it to me? Who was she?"

"A middle-aged lady. Resides in—Marco Island, Florida. The ID in her otherwise empty wallet gave her name as Marilyn Johnson Kessler." He watched Heston's reaction.

"Why are you telling me about a middle-aged person from Marco Island? Do you think she's my stalker? Was she seen on the movie set?"

"No." Nick leaned forward. "But she had photos of Winner on her phone." Nick's phone jingled in in his hand.

"Then she *could be* the stalker? Maybe Winner is the real target."

"It's possible. Or this lady could've been in league with someone else—someone who does have access to the sound stage." Nick answered his phone.

Stepping to the window, Heston waited until Nick had finished the call and said goodbye. Without turning around, he said to Nick, "If the beaten woman truly is our stalker, I will be greatly relieved."

Coming over, Nick waved his phone at Heston. "This woman. You said you didn't know her."

"I don't."

"Yeah, you do. Take a look." Nick held up his smartphone. A glamor photo of a young, strawberry-blonde model graced the screen. She was attired in a string bikini.

Heston grabbed Nick's phone and stared at the image on the screen. Appalled, he looked at Nick, returning the phone to him. "It's not possible."

"It is," assured Nick. "I just got the word from my men. The woman's real name is—"

"Maude Winston Demming," Heston whispered.

"Well, now she goes by Marilyn Johnson Kessler. Seems she's had a couple of husbands since your marriage ended fifteen years ago."

"A couple of victims, you mean."

Nick clucked. "Caused you nothing but trouble, eh?"

Heston chewed a fingernail. "Maude Winston was my second wife, Nick. She's Winner's biological mother." He plunged into Nick's deep browns. "She's also a sadist—a sadomasochist. I divorced her because of her abuse of our daughter."

Nick located his kerchief again. "We're looking into her history now. Isn't Maude the sister of Banks Winston, that old goat of a satyr, who's rooming right down the hall?"

"Yes. Have you told Banks?"

"How could I? I just found out myself. Besides, I'm more interested in what he can tell me. I'll pay him a visit when I leave here. I'll ask him to verify her identity—unless you want to do it."

"No." Heston's thoughts raced ahead. "Do you believe the attack on Maude last night—is related to what happened to me—on the sound stage this morning? To the three dolls? To the bad poetry?"

"It's conceivable, Heston. But—not likely."

"Why?"

"Because there was no note. Whoever did the deed—I don't think it was our wanna-be rap artist. On the other hand, Maude herself could be the bad poet. Hard to say."

"Could Maude be in league with our stalker? She does have motive. She loathes me. She's always wanted to hurt Ladybug. Look, Nick. If Maude lives—?"

"Barely breathing, so they told me."

"If she does, may I talk to her?"

"We'll see. She has regained consciousness. That was the other thing they just told me. But she's too weak. She's still in ICU."

Heston wrinkled his brow. "Who found her, Nick?"

Nick took an official pose. "A hotel service worker—one of my operatives—found her comatose beside her Chevrolet."

"Chevrolet? That doesn't sound like the Maude I knew."

"She's fallen on hard times, I reckon."

"Ah."

"My man found her in the visitor's parking lot. He'd seen her before—inside the hotel. He's writing up a report—said he'd have further pertinent details for me."

Heston felt lost. "So, in the end, Maude's hatred caught up with her." He was moved, somehow, in a way he could not explain. "Poor woman." He regained his composure. "Not that she deserves pity."

"To tell you the truth, she does. Some plastic surgeon did a number on her looks." Nick tapped his pocket. "I need a smoke."

"Since when? I thought you quit."

"Since I started this case."

"Should try vaping."

"I have. I prefer these." Nick tapped his breast pocket.

"I prefer vaping to those coffin nails." Heston said absent-mindedly. "So, Maude looks bad?"

"Don't look like the same person anymore. If you had seen her, you probably wouldn't have recognized her."

Heston shuddered. "Horrible." Reality was sinking in.

"Something else in her purse, by the way. Religious pamphlets."

"Religious?

"Mm-hmm. Seems she had taken an interest in her own salvation."

"Really."

"Mm-hmm. It happens, man. People change."

"That much?"

"Sometimes. I've seen it before." Nick's voice lowered. "Guilt can do funny things to people." He paused. "She had a gold cross around her neck when my operative found her. Whoever stole her cash and credit cards had the decency to leave that on her."

Heston felt sick at heart.

Nick patted his shoulder "Buck up, man." He pointed a callused finger. "Do not drop your guard. I repeat, do not drop your guard, Heston. This whole thing could be one big set-up. The nutcase we're after could still be out there—preparing to strike again."

Heston nodded. "Don't you mean 'the nutcase who's after me'?"

"I mean," said Nick, opening the door to exit, "bolt the hell out of this door once I'm out of here."

"Will do, Chief. Thanks." Heston closed the door, but he quickly re-opened it, calling down the corridor. "Where's Winner?"

"Don't worry. We're watching her now. She's still at the studio—with Ezra."

"Who's going to tell her about Maude?"

"On it!" Nick shouted over his shoulder, without breaking stride towards the elevator.

"What about Poppy?"

"You're on it," Nick called, stepping into the open elevator car.

Slamming the door to his suite and bolting it immediately, Heston realized he was trembling. In flashbacks, he recalled his long-ago wedding night he'd spent with Maude in New Orleans, where he had been shooting a Civil-War picture. They're marriage had gone downhill from there.

Two murder attempts in one day. Me and Maude.

Emotionally eviscerated, he leaned against the closed door and shuddered violently.

Chapter Thirteen

At the same moment, Hailey Champlain was watching a video screen. Seated on a stack of cushions, she was wearing a pair of thick, black-rimmed spectacles. Her hair was pulled back in a ponytail, a hairstyle which accentuated the dark roots at her hairline. She was snacking on sesame sticks and wine. From her remote perch inside the Grande Suite at the Southern Seas Resort, she was closely observing the movements of Poppy's and Heston's three youngest children as the children met up with one another in the Atlanta airport. They had flown in separate flights.

As she monitored the teens movements, she could hear her brother Adair's snoring. Her brother was snoozing, a mere ten feet away from her, asleep in a recliner. The sound grated on her nerves.

I wish The Monster had volume control. I'll be glad to be rid of that noise.

Hailey increased the audio on her device. Her camera's predatory lens showed the three teenagers at a gaming parlor inside the airport terminal. The Demming kids seemed competitive. They laughed and conversed with one another freely. Hovering over them, three burly security guards—one per child, as far as she could tell—watched out for disturbances in the surrounding environment.

Hailey studied the children closely as they entered the airport hotel. All three well-dressed teens were slim and appeared to be healthy and well-cared-for. The eldest of the three, the boy, was athletic; the two girls, less so, but they were in good shape. The boy had an air of controlled aggression.

That kid looks dangerous. Maybe I should offer him a job.

The girls—whom she knew to be twins—were not a matched set. The taller of the two had clear, pale skin and straight, dark-brown hair. Her facial features resembled Heston's—and Winner's. This daughter, whose name was Sage, was too pretty to be dowdy, but she had a bloodless air about her.

She looks like a bore.

The other Demming daughter, an inch or two shorter than her twin, was a vibrant, freckle-faced redhead, who resembled her mother, Poppy, but whose feathers were finer and body, more elegant. Probably *wild in the sack.* This girl's name was Tegan.

What was the boy's name again? Hailey referred to notes.

Dakota Demming, Sage Demming, Tegan Demming. Not an ugly duckling in the flock.

Our stud, Heston, has done a fine job of it. If only he hadn't sired that bitch, Winner.

Hailey studied the notes provided by her investigator. Dakota was a young man with a reputation for violence. He had been the one who had shot a man at point-blank range on Heart of Fire Key eight years ago. Reputed to seek out extreme adventures. Plays the drums adequately. Attends military school in Maryland. A killer by nature—and soon, by trade.

The twin girls? Again, Hailey perused her notes.

Sage Demming was bookish, even scholarly. Plans to be a marine biologist. Tegan, a bon vivant, was popular with the opposite sex. Apparently, Tegan was the air-head type, the life of the party type. Spends spare time primping and dancing.

That's dead on. Look at the little slut primping in that mirror.

Such pretty girls. She would have to keep Ezra away from both of them, too.

Too bad they may be caught in the crossfire.

247

Hailey laughed.

Too bad for them. Too good for me.

***

Over several hours, the local police crime unit investigated the scene of Heston's near-demise. The show's cast members, including Heston, had left the premises, soon after answering questions from the police. Only Winner, and her new, Nick-appointed bodyguard, had remained at the studio with Ezra.

Vexed over the latest turn of events, Ezra prepared to leave for the day. Returning from the loo, Winner was followed closely by Nick, who seemed tightly wound.

"Got a minute?' Nick said, addressing both Ezra and Winner.

Tired, Winner took a seat. From her vantage point, she could see the security bodyguard, whom Nick had assigned to watch over the premises. She waved at him. He gave a quick nod of recognition but did not wave or smile.

As the show's director, Ezra was still preoccupied with his production. "I think I did the right thing—by postponing the first read-through." He looked to Winner for reassurance.

"So do I," Winner said. "But poor Daddy," she said. "That was one close call. It shook him up."

"It didn't make me feel all warm and fuzzy," Ezra quipped. He did not want the girl of his dreams to know how affected he'd been. *It scared the life out of me.*

"Hesty had a close call, all right," observed Nick, who cleared his throat as if to begin an oratory. "And he's not the only one."

"Another cryptic comment," said Ezra, who was feeling hungry and shaky. *What I would give for a beer and a burger.* "To whom do you refer, sleuth?" he said aloud to Nick.

Nick scowled at Ezra. "Gold, this is no joke. I've got something serious to tell Winner."

"Then tell me, Nick," she said tentatively, as though she didn't really want to hear. She exchanged a worried glance with Ezra.

"Spit it out."

Ignoring Ezra's remark, Nick addressed Winner. "There's something you need to know—and some things I need to know from you."

"Okay." She seemed worried, but she retained her composure.

Nick proceeded. "Win, your father already knows about this."

"About what, Nick?"

"I've just come from the hotel. I told Heston while I was there. I would have liked for him to have joined us—for this conversation—but he's indisposed right now, and I can't waste time."

"Indisposed? How?" Ezra asked. "Oh, you mean recovering from shock."

"That, and—" Nick wiggled his eyebrows. "Let's just say the love bug's been biting."

Ezra scrunched his nose. "You mean he and Poppy—?"

"Seriously?" Winner's approval seemed lackluster, at best.

"On to the business at hand." Nick licked his lips and cleared his throat once more. "Win, a woman was found today—in the early morning hours—by one of my men. She was found near her car. In the hotel parking lot. She had been badly beaten."

Moaning, Ezra maintained his cool. He glanced down at Winner, who looked pale and drawn. He was glad the girl was sitting down.

"Why are you telling me this, Nick?" she asked, monotone. Fondling a strand of her own hair, she began to twist it round her index finger.

"Because—" Nick's eyes flitted to Ezra, and then lighted again on Winner. "That woman was Maude Winston. Your real mom." He spoke in a measured tone. "She's been going by the name of Marilyn Johnson Kessler. We know it's Maude because your uncle Banks came to the hospital and identified her for us. She's regained consciousness now."

"Good," said Ezra, relieved.

Nick hesitated. "Maude doesn't look—the way she used to."

"Her supermodel days are long gone," said Ezra. "She was big when I was in school."

"It's more than age. Something's happened to her face," Nick said, adding, "Banks knew all about that. Seems she and Banks had been in contact recently."

Winner said nothing. She glanced up at Ezra. Ezra looked at Nick.

"She knows her mom was here last night," Ezra said to Nick.

"Knows?" Nick did not seem surprised, not in the way Ezra had expected. But, then again, on the job, Nick liked to maintain his image as an old-school hard ass.

"Yes," Winner responded without expression, continuing to twirl the flaxen strand. "And I don't care."

"Whew. Just got cold in here." Nick thrust his hands into his pockets. "Aren't you even going to ask me how she's doing? If she's dead or not?"

Winner seemed dull, lifeless. "How's she doing? Is she dead—or not?"

Nick bent down closer to her. "She's critical."

Winner did not respond.

"Aren't you going to ask me who did it?"

Saying nothing, Winner shook her head.

"You don't care about that either?"

Again, she shook her head, this time, vigorously. To Ezra's amazement, she slipped her hand into his hand. He felt the warm, tender quivering of it—a dove seeking shelter.

"Nick, give her a break, okay?" Ezra squeezed the girl's hand gently as he spoke. "She has a lot of mixed feelings about her real mother. She's conflicted. And she's just watched her dad—whom she's also conflicted about—suffer through a murder attempt. Cut her some slack, man."

Nick adjusted his collar. "Can't. Sorry."

"Why not?" Ezra demanded.

"You seem to know so much about everything. You tell me." Nick's tone was stern.

Slipping her hand away, Winner said, "Nick thinks I know who did it, Ezra. Don't you, Nick?"

"Now we're getting somewhere," said Nick, visibly relaxing. "I don't want to hurt you, Winner. But I need to know where your fiancé is. Right now. As we speak. Do you know?"

"No."

Exhaling, Nick stepped back. "That's what I thought."

"The jerk split," said Ezra angrily.

"Well, on his way out the door, he left his calling card. A battered woman at death's door. For your information, he stole Maude's cash and credit cards. Once he tries to use the cards, we'll nab him."

Ezra curled a lip. "A real stinker."

Calm, but intimidating, Nick zoned in on Winner. "Help us out, Win."

"Tell him what you know, Winner," Ezra said.

Nick saved her from the act of betrayal. "His name isn't Velasquez. It's Vega. We know that already. Facial-recognition tech. Vega's got outstanding warrants. His ID is confirmed by the conversation video, but the parking-lot video, no. The attacker wore a black mask. Dressed in solid black, too. Wore gloves."

"Premeditated," said Ezra.

Her face contorting, Winner whispered. "I overheard—her—call him Danny Vega. They talked about it. Last night. At the hotel."

Nick homed in on her. "Then you heard their entire conversation at the hotel?"

"I—"

Mission accomplished, Nick relented. "No use in denying it, honey. My operative rode up with you in the elevator afterward. Remember him?"

Winner blanched.

"You look pretty on the elevator's security cam."

"Oh, my—" Winner hung her head.

Nick looked at Ezra. "I know what happened to Maude. I know who did it." He looked back at Winner. "Save me some trouble, Win. Talk to me. What I don't know is why Vega did it. Robbery won't cut it."

"Don't the security cameras have audio?" she asked. "Listen to that."

"As a matter of fact, they do not," Nick replied.

Ezra gaped at Winner.

Tears streamed down her face. "I can't—"

Fuming, Ezra said to Nick. "Can't it wait? Can't you see she's in turmoil?" Gently, he stroked the crown of her head.

Nick's scowl returned. "You two can't add. Has it occurred to either one of you? That this Danny Vega character may be our stalker? Or that Maude may be? Either one of them could have given Heston the booby prize today."

Winner appeared dazed. Her phone chimed.

"Check it out," ordered Nick, hand on the doorknob. "It might be our evildoer. Maybe he's texting his threats now, or it might be your boyfriend—feeling guilty."

"Or both," Ezra noted.

Winner obeyed, fumbling to extract the phone from her handbag. "It's just Poppy. She says, *'The kids are in Atlanta. Will stay overnight at the airport hotel. Arrive Orlando tomorrow 11:35a.m. They can't wait to the do the theme park, so get set! I'm taking them back to Naples right after and you too if you want to come.'* "

She turned to Ezra. "I don't know if I can face all this family stuff alone. Maybe you'd go with us? To the theme park?"

Ezra said knowingly, "Sure, I'll go. Me, and that guy out there. And about a hundred other security guys." He turned to Nick. "You're Security Guy Number One."

"Wouldn't miss it," Nick said, but his eyes were not smiling. "Although, professionally speaking, I must advise you not go,"

Waving a hand, Nick invited Ezra to follow him.

***

Reluctantly, Ezra complied with Nick's request, leaving Winner alone. Once the two men were alone, he snarled good-naturedly at Nick. "What do you want from me?"

"I want you to tell me what's between Maude Winston and Danny Vega."

"How should I know? I wasn't there. I didn't overhear their conversation."

"No, but your lady love did. I'd bet my grandma's false teeth that she told you what they said."

"You'd lose," Ezra lied. He was so in love with Winner he would do anything for her—anything to protect her and anything to have her—if he could drum up the guts. "If she wants to tell you, fine. But I'm not betraying her confidences. Not for you or anyone else, Nick. Not for any reason."

Nick whistled. "That love bug's been getting around," he said. "Guess I'll let things simmer."

"Do your job, detective," Ezra jeered at Nick, walking away in disgust.

"I am. I'm having you arrested." Abruptly, he halted mid-stride and placed a phone to his ear. He moved a few feet away. Out of earshot, Ezra watched Nick talk furtively into the phone. Ten seconds later, Nick hung up.

"Seriously, you did it?" Ezra cried.

"Don't have to," Nick called. "My operative phoned. Maude Winston is out of ICU. I'm going to straight to the horse's mouth." Nick turned and walked away, a new spring in his step. On the way out, he gave a thumbs-up to the stolid security guard, still standing watch over the premises. "Good job, man. Keep it up," Nick said.

***

That evening, the hotel deli was buzzing, as usual.

Nursing his beer, Ezra watched Heston and Poppy interact. Secretly, he was amused. That they were desperately desirous of one another was obvious—to him. But the two of them were far from admitting it. Enjoying a beer of his own, Nick joined in the conversation.

"Yeah, so, here's the thing," Nick said to his companions, Heston, Poppy, and Ezra. "I've had a chance to scan more of the hotel's video from yesterday. I believe that the maid—or someone disguised as a chambermaid—did plant the Heston doll in Poppy's bathroom. Trouble is, after that, the maid gave us the slip. Can't locate her—or him—on the any of the videos."

"A mystery yet to be solved," Ezra mumbled to no one in particular.

"However," Nick continued, "I have learned one pertinent fact, otherwise related to this case."

"Which is?" Heston queried.

Nick cocked his head. "Does the name Daniel Vega mean anything to you, Heston? Or you, Poppy?"

"Daniel Vega?" Poppy echoed. "That name does sound familiar."

Heston grunted his interest. "Vega's a common name in Latin American countries. But it's ringing a bell . . . on the tip of my brain . . ."

"Rogelio," said Poppy, as the name crept into her head.

"And who would he be?" coached Nick.

Heston perked up. "You mean Inez's second husband, Rogelio Vega? Oh, that's right—"

Poppy said, "Rogelio Vega's son is named Danny Vega. He's the one Sasha Bassett was in love with—remember Heston? I remember she called him *El Tigre* because he had a tiger tattoo on his back. Sasha used to think he was so sexy—"

"So sexy she framed you for murder—out of revenge," Heston whispered, half to himself. His eyes met Poppy's. "All because you ruined her relationship with him." Heston frowned, skeptical. "Nick, so what does Danny Vega have to do with our problem?"

"Think about it."

Poppy gasped, grabbing Heston's forearm.

"You're getting it," Nick said approvingly.

"Ladybug's Damian Velasquez has a tiger tattoo on his back. She told me so herself." Poppy swallowed hard. "It could be the same man.

Danny was a real charmer—and a dangerous one to boot. He hit on me once."

"The age fits, too," Heston said, chewing a fingertip.

"And the physical description fits." Poppy scarcely breathed. "So does the pattern of behavior. Danny Vega's the one who beat my ex-husband, Jim Talbot, to a pulp. Put him in the hospital. Then disappeared. The Naples authorities never located Danny. I don't believe Rogelio's heard from his son in years. Oh, another thing that fits! Danny was athletic. He and Sasha played tennis."

"Oh, my—Winston!" Heston said, rising to his feet.

Unconsciously, Poppy rose. "That's why he didn't want to meet us. *Me.*" She placed a hand on each cheek. "He knew I would remember him from the old days."

Ezra caved. "That's why he pretended to be sick at the party—to avoid you."

"You could finger him. Drop a dime on him." Nick chuckled without humor.

"Which I would do—will do now."

"I need to mention something else. It's unpleasant, and, no doubt, hurtful to Winner. But this no game. It's life and death."

"What is it?' asked Poppy.

"Maude and Danny had been lovers, long ago. He stole money from her then and ran off."

"Poor Win!" breathed Poppy. She smoothed her hair with both hands.

"Danny attacked Maude because she had threatened to reveal his past." Nick drained his beer.

"You got that from the horse's mouth, Nick?" Ezra asked. Mindlessly, he fingered an overhanging fern frond. Catching sight of the server, he signaled for a second beer.

"From Maude's own lips. Her brother, Banks, confirmed her story. Maude had told him about her relationship with Danny."

"If I ever lay my hands on that rat Vega—" Ezra growled, snapping the frond.

"You'll have to push me out of the way," said Heston.

"We'll find him," said Nick. "And we'll bring him in for questioning."

"Do you think Danny Vega could possibly be our stalker?" Poppy ventured.

"Let's ask him." Nick's face was impassive, but he sounded skeptical. "But let's keep our options open." He paused and scanned the faces of his companions. "There is another possibility."

"What?" asked Ezra.

"You won't like it."

"Shoot," said Heston.

"What if Winner is secretly conspiring with Vega? What if she took the three dolls but denied knowledge of their disappearance? What if she gave them to Vega, and he planted them, wrote the notes, and so on."

"Why?" Ezra demanded, angry. "What motive would she—or they—have?"

Nick exhaled, shrugging. "Heston's a rich man. If Vega is really a fortune hunter—which I believe he is—he might have seduced her into becoming an accomplice. To snag her inheritance. For all her grown-up beauty, Win is still a kid. She leads with her heart. A con man like Vega could make easy work of her."

Incensed, Ezra exploded. "That's where you're wrong, Townsend. I have faith in Winner."

"So do I," said Poppy and Heston, in unison. Looking at one another, they each blushed.

"What about your housekeeper? And her famous daughter? Do you trust them? They could be in league with Winner and/or Danny Vega."

"That's absurd," Poppy cried. "Lissette has worked for us for years!"

"Maybe you're in league with them," Nick shot directly at Poppy.

"Hey!" said Heston. "Knock it off, Nick."

"Of course, I don't believe you are, Poppy. But it's my job to turn over every fallen log. To see what is crawling underneath."

"Well, you've turned it over," said Heston. "There's nothing there. Now move on."

Nick glanced briefly at Ezra. Ezra bit a lip. *Oh yeah—*

Heston's defending Poppy like any true lover would. It only a matter of time before those two wind up between the sheets together.

***

Fifteen minutes later, Ezra and Heston sat alone in the deli. Poppy and Nick had gone to their respective rooms. Seizing the opportunity, Ezra put Heston on the hot seat.

"You and Poppy are hotsy-totsy," he said nonchalantly. He clicked his tongue irreverently.

"No, we're not," said Heston irritably.

"Trust me, man. You're about to score."

"Watch how you speak about my wife, Gold."

"Okay, but—" Ezra scoffed. "Shakespeare said it best. 'Methinks thou doth protest too much'."

Heston stewed. "Not in this case."

Ezra nodded in exaggerated fashion. "Yeah, right. Uh-huh."

Heston seemed preoccupied.

"Is something wrong?" Ezra probed.

Heston glared. "Why don't you mind your own business?"

"You are my business, Heston. You and your whole family—are my business." Ezra moved closer to the troubled star. "Look, man," he said quietly, "why don't you just face facts? What's between you and Poppy—why, that's true love. Can't you see that? Don't you know it? Don't you feel it?" He tapped his own chest.

Swayed, Heston met his eyes briefly, then looked at the floor. "Maybe I do." He shuddered. "But there's too much friction between us. Too much fighting."

Ezra leaned in. "You know that other thing Shakespeare said, right?"

"Which one? He said a good bit."

"You should know it by heart, Heston. Shakespeare said, 'To thine own self be true."

"Clichés." A scowl of derision crossed Heston's handsome countenance. "What the heck did he know?"

"He knew a lot." Ezra pointed to his chest. "And I know some. I know you two love each other. What's between you and Poppy is true love, Heston. The rubber-band kind. The kind that keeps snapping back no matter what goes wrong in life."

"True Love?" Heston mused.

Ezra sat back. Crossing his legs, he braced one ankle atop his knee. He tugged at his sock, which was receding into the heel of his shoe. He was feeling the effects of two beers. "Yes. True Love." He contemplated Heston. "You know, the *True Love* was the name of the sailboat in *The Philadelphia Story*—the one Cary Grant and Katharine Hepburn sailed as newlyweds. Great film, that. A real 1930s classic. He even called her 'Red.' Can you dig that?"

Heston made a face. "Please don't do your Cary Grant impersonation."

"I promise—if you promise not to do your Katharine Hepburn." Laughing, he jostled Heston's shoulder. "Lighten up, man! Look, you need Poppy. She needs you." Rising, he slapped Heston's back. "Stop wasting time. She's your woman. Take her." Rising and walking to the door, Ezra opened it. "Now, get lost. I have my own love life to worry about."

Heston squinted. "If it involves my eldest daughter, you'd better watch your step, Gold—not to mention your hands and other body parts." He indicated, significantly.

"Rightly said, Daddy-o." Grinning broadly, Ezra strolled towards the door of the hotel deli. On his way out, he lifted his third bottle of beer from the startled server's tray.

"Courage!" he explained, waving the bottle at Heston.

"Been there!" Heston called to Ezra in return.

Chapter Fourteen

Hard at work, in her real-estate office in Naples, Inez Vega heard her phone ring and answered it promptly. To her disappointment, it was not a sales call. Rather, the caller was that tiresome Poppy Craft.

"Poppy, dear. So nice to hear from you. What can I do for you? I haven't quite finished doing the market analysis. For your house on Galleon Drive?"

"My house on—?" Poppy sounded befuddled.

Nothing unusual in that.

Inez tittered. "Yes, dear. Your house—we agreed that I would do a market analysis for you. Have you talked to Heston about signing the listing agreement? Now that you two are divorcing?"

"Oh, no! Don't bother."

"Why not?

"Because I've changed my mind, Inez. We won't be listing the house, after all."

"You are still divorcing Heston, aren't you?"

"Maybe not. We're working things out."

Inez saw red. "Don't fool yourself about Heston, Poppy. I couldn't keep him, and you can't either. Face facts, dear. Heston's a world-class playboy."

"Really, Inez? Well, as a matter of fact, I received flowers. Roses. Guess who they were from?"

"I don't believe you. You made that up. You're lying."

"Think so?"

"Yes!" Inez heard the crack in her own voice.

"Maybe I'd better go, Inez."

"Frankly, Poppy, I don't believe there was a bouquet of roses."

"Well, there is." Another pause. "How are feeling these days, Inez? Mentally? Are you sure you're—back to normal?"

"You mean, am I ready for another stint in the looney bin? Fine! I am fine."

"Good. Because there's something about your stepson that you should know."

"Danny?"

"Yes. That's why I phoned you. To warn you."

"Warn me?"

"Danny's on the run from the police. Another attempted murder. He just beat up Heston's second wife, Maude—you know, Winner's mom— here in Orlando. Just the way he beat my ex-husband, Jim, fifteen years ago."

Inez held her panic in check. "I don't believe a word you're saying, you lying, redheaded schemer—"

"If Danny contacts you, please phone the police. He could be dangerous. You could be hurt—or taken advantage of."

"I'll see you burn in—!"

The phone went dead.

"Me and my big mouth." But Inez couldn't resist a smile. In truth, she wasn't really sorry that she had told off Poppy. The phone rang again. She answered. "Yes?"

"Inez?"

"Danny? Where are you, son? Where are you?" Inez pleaded.

"Jail," said Danny, sounding tired. "I've got to make bail, Inez. Can you help me out, babe?"

***

In their suite on the 16th floor, Nick and Ezra were winding down from the day.

"Forget it, Nick." Ezra moped openly. "I'm giving up on Winner."

Disappointed, Nick felt like yelling and did so. "Come on, man! Where's your *cojones?*"

Ezra looked annoyed. "Leave me alone about it, please."

"I will not."

"Look, man. Face facts. I have. Winner preferred another man to me. She liked that guy more than she liked me." Ezra pouted. "At this point, I'm pushing it. She's already turned me down once. If I keep after her, she'll sue me for sexual harassment."

"Oh, please! Stop whining." Nick howled, the muscles in his face, tight. "Ezra, didn't anybody ever tell you? Sometimes, in life, you have to fight for what you want."

"Yeah, they told me." Ezra skewered him with a glance. "But, sometimes, Nick, you have to *want* what you fight for."

"You're so full of crap," Nick barked in frustration. "You do want her, fool. You love the hell out of that skinny, blonde girl."

Ezra shifted uneasily. "Win's delicate. She's five-feet eight-inches tall, but she's small-boned, fragile like those porcelain dolls she collects—"

Nick got in his face. "What. Ever. You love her. That's the point."

Edging away, Ezra toyed with his smartphone. "Yes. I do."

"And you want to comfort her, don't you? Make her happy she's not marrying that slick jackass?"

"Yes."

"Then go on, man. Go get her. Tell her the truth. Tell her you love her. Tell her how much she means to you. Only do it after you wine and dine her, not before."

"Eh?"

"See, Ezra, your problem was that you came on too strong, too soon."

"I did? I did."

"You asked her to marry you. That's what you said you did."

Ezra lowered his head. "That's what I did, all right."

"Listen to Papa. The ladies like to be wooed. They're skittish. My suggestion is—that you start over at the beginning."

Ezra caught fire. "Tell her she's lucky she's not throwing her life away on a con man?"

Nick sputtered. "I wouldn't. I wouldn't mention that over-the-hill loser at all. Tell her how *you* feel." He poked his index finger into Ezra's chest. "It's not about him. It's about you—you and your sweet lady love. That other dog can go jump in the lake."

Ezra coughed a laugh. "Well, I'm convinced." His facial features twisted. "I'll kill Danny if he tries to get her back."

"Now you're talking."

Sighing, Ezra slapped Nick's shoulder. "Thanks, man."

"You're welcome. Somebody had to do it. I did it."

Ezra laughed, but his laughter was tinged with animosity. "Funny, isn't it? I can see when Heston's in denial, but not my own self." Rising, he strode to the dresser and, opening a drawer, removed his sunglasses and keys. He donned the glasses and pocketed the keys, along with his phone. "I'm out the door, Townsend. Don't wait up."

"I won't." Nick said. "I won't have to."

What you don't realize, fool, is that she wants you just as much as you want her. She just doesn't know it yet. "She's yours for the taking. You just need to believe it."

"Yeah." Ezra strode confidently to the door. "She's mine, all right," he muttered on the way out, slamming the door behind him. "I'll start by asking her out for dinner."

"That's the spirit."

"I love her."

"You take what's yours, Ezzie," Nick said to himself, alone in the empty room. "Life's too short to screw around whining." *Yowee. These artistic types. They make my head spin.*

Rubbing the back of his neck, Nick slipped off his shoes and rummaged through the contents of his mini fridge.

"Man, I need to relax," he proclaimed, opening a bottle of Jack and chugging the contents." He lit up a joint, toked briefly, and doused the flame before it could set off the smoke alarm. Vaguely, he pondered Ezra's hostile outburst. The man had hidden depths.

"I do not understand people. But I try. I do try."

These were the last words Nick uttered before he passed out cold, utterly fatigued. Snoring, he dreamed about the son he'd lost in the war and the wife he'd lost to cancer.

***

Alone with Winner, Ezra girded his loins. "Well, Miss Demming, I understand you're back on the market these days." *But she's still wearing Vega's engagement ring.*

She smirked. "Guess so. I'm not sure yet."

Tally ho. "Have dinner with me tonight."

"You mean—go out?"

Ezra nodded, hands stuffed inside his pants pockets. Slouching, he looked from side to side, as if waiting for a bus. "Date me, Winner." He glanced pleadingly in her direction.

"Are you serious?" She seemed stupefied. "You are serious. I thought we went through all this."

"Well, you could do worse. I have all my own teeth. I own an Aston Martin and a condo in Singapore. And I'll play the fool for a homemade knish. I can be fun at parties. too. But I have to get drunk first."

Winner couldn't stop laughing. "Ezzie, stop it. You don't have to sell yourself to me."

"I don't?"

"No. Of course not. I know you. I know you're a great guy. You're just not—"

"Uh oh. Here is comes again."

"No, don't take it that way. Listen, I'm flattered. But I'm just coming out of a really intense relationship—that went bad. I don't know who I am or what I want."

Ezra threw his hands in the air. "Oh, please, Winner. Cut it out already." He gesticulated wildly, to prove his point. "I wanted to buy you dinner, nothing more."

"No?"

"No. You're getting way ahead of yourself here. I'm not asking for a relationship with you."

"No?"

"Maybe a goodnight kiss. That's as far as I will go. For now."

Winner laughed. "Will you buy me a White Russian, too? I love White Russians."

"For a moment, I thought you meant me. My mother's people fled from Belarus."

"What?"

"Skip it. Bad joke. So, I'm assuming you mean the highball? Mixed drinks, we call them in the upper classes."

"Will you buy me one?"

"Yes. I'll throw caution to the wind."

"Then I'll have dinner with you tonight."

"You will. Okay. Fine. Pick you up at eight."

"K."

"K."

"See you, Ezra."

"Yeah. See you. At eight."

"Mm-hm."

"Don't be late."

"Get out of here, Ezzie!"

"Oh, right." Breathless, he toddled towards the open air. Once out of sight, he spun in circles, chanting, "I'm taking Winner to a fancy dinner," until he fell out, dizzy, into the grass of the park. After a few minutes, reality set in. He sat up, worried.

Where the hell am I'm going to take her?

He took out his mobile and gave Nick a call. There was no answer, so he left his buddy a voice mail. "Hey, Townsend. Winner said 'yes' to dinner. You know so much. Where should I take her?"

Ringing off, Ezra had an idea of his own. *The hotel dining room? Yeah. That would be the safest bet—safest for Win.* Kneeling in the grass, he phoned ahead for a dinner reservation.

Chapter Fifteen

Seated opposite Ezra, in the hotel's elegant dining room, Winner quietly commanded every eye in the house. Her eye-popping pulchritude escaped no one. Tonight, she was clad in a little black dress, sleeveless, cut short at mid-thigh. Black pearls surrounded by diamonds dangled from her porcelain lobes.

"How's the White Russian?" Ezra asked lightly.

Winner licked the rim of her cocktail glass. "Delectable."

"Big word, college girl."

"Design school," she corrected, slightly tipsy.

"Sure that's what you want to do? You're a bright young woman. You can do anything you want. Lawyering, stevedore, tattoo artist—"

"I didn't want to do anything at all but be a wife and mom. I thought I was getting married to Damian—to that fiend—to do just that." Her lips quivered. "You know, it's funny."

"What is?"

"Why I brought us all to Orlando—to announce my engagement. See, Ezzie, I always wanted to be proposed to—well, in front of the Enchanted Palace. Ever since I was a little girl, I dreamed of having my prince, like, get down on one knee and ask me to marry him."

Ezra listened carefully. "Did Dan Vega do that for you?"

Winner's countenance grew sad. "No. He didn't." She waved her hand. "This was as close as I got to my fantasy—the Southern Seas Resort, Orlando."

"You can start over now, Win. You're so close. You dream can still come true."

"I don't care what happens anymore. My life is over." Winner nursed her drink, watching it steadily. Then she raised her silver-blue eyes and he felt as if he might pass out. Recovering his cool, he cracked the first joke that came to mind. "You could start your own business: Inebriated 19-year-olds R Us."

Not listening, she batted her blackened eyelashes. "Ezra, I would be lying to you if I told you I've never thought of you—in that way."

Holy— "What way?"

Winner hedged. "In a sexual way," she said demurely.

"You've thought about me in a sexual way?"

Winner was scandalized. "Shh! Don't yell, please." She crunched on an ice cube.

"What position?"

"What?!!" Winner giggled in spite of herself, covering her face in supreme embarrassment. "Ezra! That's not what I meant."

Ezra beamed. "It's what I meant."

Tilting her head to one side, Winner unleashed a radiant smile. "I meant that—well, I've always found you to be—kind of appealing. Cute. Like I told you."

He stopped breathing. "Not the passion I'd hoped for." But he gazed at her, secretly thrilled. He'd been around enough women to know that 'cute' meant 'sexy.'

"What I mean is—well, you're not bad looking," she offered up.

He raised his martini glass. "Thanks. Neither are you."

Her jaw flew open. Then she laughed into her napkin. "So I've heard."

Delirious, he put down his glass. "Looks aren't everything, Win. That's what cute people like me tell ourselves when we're trying to impress a real-life princess like you."

Winner blushed. "You like me the way I am, Ezra?"

"I love the way you are, Winston." *Everything about you, from the moment I first saw you. I love you. I adore you. I worship the ground you walk on. What position? Oh, tell me, please. What position did you imagine me in? Whatever it was, that's right where I want to be. I would do anything for you, Winner. Anything you want. Name it. It's yours."*

The server approached. "Will you be ordering now, sir?"

"Know what you want?"

"Not yet." Tearing her gaze from Ezra, Winner shook out her blonde mane. "Order for me, Ezzie. Thanks."

"Sure." Studying the menu, he held up two fingers, a non-verbal a request for two more cocktails. The server nodded and went to fetch the drinks.

Fumbling in a charming fashion, Winner rose and meandered into the ladies' room. Every eye in the dining room twitched as her taut body undulated lazily through the intimate restaurant. Her slim, shapely legs seemed a million miles long.

Ezra scanned the room defensively. *She's mine.*

His hackles rose. The stalker could be any one of these jokers. But which one?

The server reappeared. "Another White Russian for the young lady—and your martini, sir."

Fortunately, Ezra had decided what to order before setting foot in the hotel dining room. He rattled off his selections while mentally reliving the image of Winner fanning her face with a cocktail napkin. The flush on her cheeks was driving him wild. As he concluded his instructions to the server and watched the man walk away, Ezra had a realization, while tapping liquid from his martini olive.

Winner has already told me what she wants. Exactly what she wants. What she has always wanted, and where and how she wants it.

Ezra's thoughts raced. She had even told him the position she had fantasized for him. In Winner's proposal fantasy, her prince must be down on one knee when he popped the question.

Oblivious, Winner rejoined him. Quickly, Ezra rose and helped her into her chair.

"Thank you, you sexist thing, you."

As Ezra resumed his seat, he caught sight of Nick Townsend moving nimbly towards their table.

"Uh-oh," Ezra said to Winner. "What's happened now?"

"Breaking news," Nick said.

"What are you? The town crier?" Ezra asked casually, munching a bread stick. "Join us?"

"Just for a minute. This is important." Nick accepted a spare chair offered by the maître' d but declined to order. "Danny Vega has been located, arrested, and interrogated."

Winner scarcely breathed. "Where?"

"Sarasota PD."

"Were they able to *get* anything out of him?" Ezra asked, wiping his mouth.

"Vega denies being Heston's stalker, but he does admit to bludgeoning Maude."

Winner was incredulous. "He does?"

Ezra clasped Winner wrist. "Did he say why?"

Nick kneaded a knee. "Vega was afraid Maude would bring the law down on him—for past offenses—if she told Win, or anyone, the truth about him—or their relationship—his and Maude's. The man was living under an alias because he had outstanding warrants for other violent offenses."

"You were lucky, Win. You would have been next," said Ezra.

"Oh, I'm going to be sick—"

"No, you're not. He's not worth it."

She addressed Nick. "Do you think Dam—Danny Vega sent me those text messages?"

271

"No, not according to what we've uncovered," said Nick. "Our sick stalker did that. I'm getting closer to—knowing who that is, Win. But I need to be sure."

The server approached and set down a White Russian in front of Winner.

"Thank you," she said to the server.

"You old enough for that?" Nick gave Ezra the evil eye. Then he turned to Winner. "Winner, Danny wants to see you. He asked me—to ask you—to get in touch with him."

Ezra flung his napkin on the table. "To visit him in jail?"

Nick brushed breadcrumbs from the tablecloth. "Winner, I'd be very careful if I were you."

Adamant, Ezra cried, "Winner—!"

She patted Ezra's hand. "Not going to happen, sweetie. Don't worry." She looked directly at Nick. "I never want to see Danny Vega—or whatever his real name is—as long as I live."

Ezra relaxed visibly. "You don't?"

"I do not. I am finished with that man forever."

Nick responded. "Guess it wasn't true love for you."

"Guess not."

"Good girl," said Nick, rising. "I'll let Vega know."

"Thanks, Nick." Ezra waved a salute.

"Enjoy your dinner," Nick said meaningfully and left the dining room.

Amazed by the turn of events, Ezra contemplated Winner. He reached inside his jacket.

"Don't you worry, Miss Demming. I believe you're in luck,"

"Oh?"

"I just happen to have some true love right here in my lapel pocket. And it's got your name on it." He grinned charmingly—he hoped.

"Oh, Ezra, that's just too corny—and I adore it." She seemed to be half-laughing, half-crying. The alcohol had taken effect—and probably she had taken anxiety meds in the restroom. She was crafty at slipping them in.

"I never slept with him, you know," she confided woozily. "But I wanted to. And now I don't."

He watched, gratified, as Winner withdrew the glittering diamond ring from her finger and dropped it into her drink. "Poof!" she said. "He's all gone. Just like that." Her fingers refused to snap.

Ezra's instincts told him she was vulnerable, hurting. If he wanted nothing more than to bed her, this was his golden opportunity. For the very first time, he had a clear field.

She might be willing—

But what if Winner turned down his advances? Better to not even try. At least, his dream would remain intact. He flagged the server, ready, all of a sudden, to leave.

Corny. The woman thinks my love-making is corny. Get over yourself, Gold.

Instead of enjoying her second White Russian, Winner started to bawl. Declining food, she asked Ezra to take her back to her suite. Fishing the engagement ring from the glass, he agreed.

All the way up in the elevator, she wailed the loss of Danny Vega, refusing to be comforted, at last admitting to Ezra that she had swallowed a couple of pills on her recent trip to the ladies' room.

After hearing her disclosure, Ezra decided to postpone his goodnight kiss and drove her to a hamburger joint. She ate half a cheeseburger with ketchup and a couple of fries, which he felt was progress. On the way home, she fell asleep in the front seat, her head resting on his right shoulder. She smelled like onions. He drove through the night like a charioteer scaling the heavens.

Oh, yeah. I'm in love all right. Guess there's only one thing left to for me to do.

First, he would need to find an engagement ring of his own. He couldn't use the sticky, discarded one in his pocket, no matter how outrageously fabulous it was. That would be in bad taste.

***

As Poppy slept in her bedroom, Heston slipped out the door of the suite he was sharing with her. He needed privacy to make a call. He couldn't risk that his wife might awaken. He couldn't stop thinking about what Ezra had said to him in the deli, earlier that afternoon: he and Poppy were headed for bed.

Deep in his soul, Heston knew Ezra was right.

But how could he bed Poppy with unconfessed lies still on his conscience? And without bringing her into the loop about—everything? She had demanded complete candor.

Am I willing to accept her conditions?

Seeking counsel, he phoned Reverend Bill, his mentor and sponsor at the church shelter in Nashville.

"Poppy and I are getting closer. But she's insisting that I come clean about everything."

"Oh?" Bill sounded intrigued. "Everything?"

"Yes, everything. That's not possible, Bill."

"Oh." Bill sounded sympathetic.

"Some of my revelations would devastate her."

"Oh, yeah, sure."

Heston elaborated. "Let me give you an example, one you're familiar with. I don't know whether or not to tell her about my recent interactions with Montserrat Flynn."

"You have nothing to feel guilty about on that score, Heston," Bill assured him.

"I know that. But Poppy doesn't. She wouldn't understand."

"I understand."

"You're not a jealous woman."

"Can't argue with that."

"Bill, this time around— nothing sexual happened between Montsey and me, not in the entire time I spent in Nashville."

"The lady suffered from dementia, Heston. You treated her honorably."

"I wanted to help her. Montsey didn't even recognize me. To her, in her condition, I was just a nice man who came to call. I brought her small gifts."

"You had been lovers at one time—"

"Off and on. For years, in my youth and early twenties, even into my thirties—she was a vision of loveliness—but Poppy knows all that. When we married, I swore to her that I would never run after Montsey again. And I didn't! I just found Montsey there, living on the streets of Nashville, in that dreadful mental state. I couldn't leave her there, alone—"

"What were you doing in Nashville in the first place?"

Touching his frontal lobe, Heston recollected. "I had come there on business. It had to do with Kipp's music. Some of the copyrights were being violated. I stayed to work things out with his PRO."

"That's when you saw Montsey on the street—and recognized her?"

"Yes. She didn't recognize me. She called me Tom."

"So, you fabricated an identity for yourself: Tom Roberts, homeless drunkard."

"I was drinking then."

275

"When you brought her to my shelter, that's when you and I first met."

"I had nowhere else to turn. I was in bad shape myself. Wasn't thinking straight."

"Yeah. I see a lot of that."

"Bill. Poppy is right about me. I am a liar."

"We all are, Heston. What other secrets are you keeping from your wife? Confession is good for the soul."

Ashamed, Heston balked. "You want the list?"

"What do you want, Heston?"

"Bill, you think I should tell Poppy the whole truth about my past, don't you?"

Bill hesitated. "I'll tell you a little story, Heston," he said. "Once upon a time, in my youth, I worked for a company. I had lowly job, but I knew people in the upper echelons." Again, Bill paused.

"Go on. I'm listening."

"One Friday, I wanted to take the day off—for personal reasons. I approached my boss and told him the truth—about why I needed to take the day off. I didn't claim illness or a funeral—none of the usual reasons."

"No standard excuse?"

"Right. My boss became angry. I was shocked. I thought mine had been a reasonable request." Sensing the irony, Heston laughed in sympathy.

Bill continued. "Later, I told a mature acquaintance of mine about the incident. She was the administrative assistant to the top man in the concern—and you know what she said to me? 'You told your boss the truth? Bill, never tell them the truth. Tell them what they expect to hear. Tell them what they want to hear. What they need to hear.' "

Heston processed Bill's words. "You're saying—"

Bill interrupted. "What I'm saying, Heston, is that, sometimes, it's better to protect people when they themselves are vulnerable or are in a vulnerable position. You know the truth, in your heart. But you were also given the gifts of discretion, kindness, empathy, love, and leadership."

"I see." Heston digested the nuggets of wisdom. "I didn't expect this advice from you."

"I deal with many people. Sometimes, you've just got to make a judgment call."

"You understand, don't you, that Poppy left me because I lied to her? A lie of omission?"

"Yes."

"But she doesn't know the worst of it, Bill. My biggest lie is one of misrepresentation. I've lied to her—and maintained the lie—for a long time. However, I have now decided that I must tell her the truth about it."

"Then you will. Just be tender."

"I don't mean to be mysterious, but I don't want to disclose it to anyone—until Poppy hears it from me first."

"So do that, and weigh the other, as it comes up. Sometimes, Heston, it takes more courage to suck it up and shut up. That's all I'm saying—if you want to spare someone excruciating pain—pain for which there is no solace."

Heston ruminated. "You're saying I should lie to Poppy?"

"No. I'm saying you should use discretion and consider what is in Poppy's best interest. Sometimes, it's not what you say. It's how you say it."

"Okay, Bill. Thanks."

"Heston?"

"Yes."

"Ask your Creator to guide you."

"Pray?"

"Now you have it."

"Okay. I'll let you go, Bill. I know it's late. Thank you."

"Hey, I've one more question. Was I right about the suitors?"

Heston barred his teeth. "Consider them vanquished."

"Uh-oh," said Bill. "Guess I struck a nerve, King Odysseus, Alien Space Warrior."

Groaning, Heston slapped his forehead. "You looked it up."

"I did an online search."

"Speaking of Odysseus . . . Bill, I have a stalker."

"What?"

"It's a long story. Some lunatic is after me and my family. He tried to kill me this morning."

"What! Are you okay?"

"Physically, yes. None of this has been made public yet. Keep it under you hat, will you?"

"Not a word. "

"Thanks. Hey, I didn't even inquire. How are things in Nashville?"

Bill's tone changed. "I wouldn't know. I'm in Daytona Beach, right now. On a retreat."

"You're here in Florida?"

'Been here for three or days."

"Enjoy. I'll let you go, Bill. I know it's late. I know I'm tired. It's been quite a day."

"Be vigilant, Tommy. By the way, DeAngelo and Rudy asked me to thank you."

"Give them my best."

Ringing off, Heston realized he had to make Decision Number Five, his most important decision to date. He had to tell Poppy about Kipp, but he had to do it gently, in the kindest way possible. There was no time to lose. What if the killer struck again?

What if I die before telling Poppy the truth about our son?

Decision made, he rose from his seat alongside the hotel's lighted pool. Late at night, he was virtually alone, except for the celestial stars shining down from the heavens. Now it was time to return to the suite he was sharing with Poppy.

Should I wake her? Tell her tonight? Wait until morning?

As he walked towards the lobby entrance, a small woman crept out of the shadows.

"Howdy, Heston."

He recognized her. "Good evening, Hailey."

"Heston, will you do me a favor? Join me in the bar. I know you don't drink, but I need a nightcap. And I have to tell you something important."

"Can't it wait? I'm bushed."

"No. 'Fraid not." Her voice became authoritarian. "I need to talk to you now."

He acquiesced, too fatigued to argue. "Lead on, boss lady."

***

Expensive perfume filled the cool, dry air in the hotel's finest barroom, virtually empty except for Hailey and Heston.

"I understand your three youngest are coming tomorrow," Hailey said, her expression bright.

"Uh, yes," replied Heston. "That's why my wife is getting some shut-eye. They descend upon us at 11:35 a.m. Then we're all going to the theme park together. I haven't seen them in years."

"Isn't that dangerous? Considering all that's happened?"

"Yes. But they've so been looking forward to it. My wife doesn't want to disappoint them. She'll be taking them all home to Naples tomorrow night. She believes they'll be safer there. Until we get this stalker situation under control."

"Will Winnie be going to the theme park, too?" asked Hailey. "One big family group?"

"Yes. Ezra and Nick, as well." Good manners required that he include Hailey in the invitation, but instinct prevented him. "Should be fun," he said. "We'll head over right after lunch. Quite an entourage, too—we'll be surrounded by a swarm of bodyguards."

"That's smart. Winnie draws fans like flies. I know you used to." Hailey flashed teeth. "You don't intend to return to Naples after that, do you?"

He felt she was pacing herself. "No. If I did that, I'd be violating my contract with you. Win and I will be staying here, naturally, to work on the pilot."

"Which means the danger will remain here, too," Hailey observed. "More than likely."

He regarded her. "You sound as though you know something the rest of us don't."

Hailey showed her magnificent teeth. "Won't you have a libation, Heston?" She sipped her mojito happily.

"Thank you, no. That, too, would violate my contract with you."

Hailey got down to business. "I do know something you don't know. You see, Heston. My baby brother, Adair, is mentally ill. No one knows it—but me. It's been our family secret."

Heston didn't mince words. "I knew five minutes into my first conversation with your brother."

Hailey poked a straw at the lime slice in her mojito. "See, that's just it. Six months ago, you wouldn't have been able to tell. He's much worse lately." Short, bare legs crossed, Hailey sat across from him in the leather-upholstered booth. She was running her mouth, characteristical-ly, but her defenses seemed down. He was waiting for a clue as to her purpose.

"Sometimes, Adair will take his meds. Sometimes, he refuses. I can't control him."

She appeared to be confiding in him. He wasn't sure what to make of this sudden intimacy, but he listened attentively as she spoke. Basically, he was curious.

What, exactly, does she want from me?

Hailey said, "Remember when Adair told you how he had refused to pressure you? About purchasing Cedric Spicer's paintings?"

"Vaguely." He resisted her attempt to charm him and continued to mask his responses. Something about Hailey's manner did not seem genuine. "Did Adair mention the conversation we had—at the party?"

"Yes. He did. Adair tells me everything."

"Really."

"Say—I heard about Maude. Condolences."

"You did? From whom? Not Adair, surely?"

"From Nicky." Hailey's eyes narrowed. "What about it, Heston? Did you deal the blows? Bully for you if you did. Bitch probably deserved it."

"I beg your pardon?"

"Don't pretend to grieve, Heston. I'm sure you loathed the woman."

"Hailey, regardless, I would never beat a woman senseless. I'm in-sulted that you suggested it."

"Oh? Who did it then?"

"Ask Nicky. He's working the case. No doubt—since you witnessed today's incident—you've learned all about my—little problem."

"Problem?"

"Our stalker." Heston studied her closely.

"I know more about it than you think."

His eyes would not stay open. "Why am I here, Hailey?"

She glanced downward, then back at him. "I wanted to warn you, Heston. About poor Adair—and the danger you may be in."

Heston considered her words. "Why? Are you saying that Adair wishes me harm?" Heston shot forward. "Is he the one who's been doing all these weird things?"

"Heston, I think it's possible that he—"

"He what?"

Hailey seemed to recant. "Maybe I'm wrong. I struggled with this, Heston. Whether to tell you or not. Really, Adair doesn't know much of anything—except how to look in a mirror."

"That's typical of us actors."

"Takes a preening peacock to know one?" Hailey giggled. Then she spoke seriously. "The world doesn't know—the truth—about Adair's condition. I've tried to care for him all his life. To shield him. But when he's malicious this way—"

"Please come to the point, Hailey."

"All right. Where was I? Oh, yes. Truett told Adair and me Cedric's paintings were not that important. He claimed that Cedric Spicer was a minor deity in the pantheon of artists, and always would be."

"Obviously, an astute judge," Heston observed. *She's not the total airhead she pretends to be. She's literate and artsy.*

"What *Vati* didn't know," said Hailey, stopping to sip from her straw, "is that the paintings *are* that important to my brother, so Adair waited. Waited until the shriveled, old prune—that's how Adair put it— was dead and buried, and he became the sole power—as his only male heir."

"What about you? Didn't you share in the inheritance?"

Hailey was hesitant. "I was provided for. That's all. Adair inherited everything. He has immense power now, Heston." She gazed at him sympathetically. "All his life, since he was about twelve, he's been a big fan of yours. In fact, he idolized you while he was growing up. He owns all your movies. He memorized the dialogue in your scenes. His favorite is King Odysseus, Alien Space Warrior. He can recite the entire movie by heart."

Heston said nothing. He waited for the rest.

"Adair knows everything about you, Heston. He used to pretend to be you." Her voice became softer. "Lately, he's—well, he thinks he is you. He thinks he's your character. He can't tell the difference anymore."

"Is he our stalker?"

Wide-eyed, Hailey raised and lowered her shoulders. "Who knows?"

"I think you know."

She continued. "All I know, is that he is obsessed with you. Adair found out some things about you, Heston. I guess that's my point."

Heston's heart skipped a beat. "What things?"

Reluctantly, Hailey reached into her bag and extracted a smartphone. "Watch this video, please, Heston. Does it ring a bell with you?"

In shock, Heston watched the video playing on Hailey's tablet phone. Naked figures in chiaroscuro, voices low and guarded, grainy old videos, images hardly distinguishable.

"That's not me," Heston asserted.

"Oh, honey, it is. Don't you remember this encounter? Many years ago, when you picked up two hitchhikers. Perhaps you don't recall the incident—because you were so high."

He felt sick, queasy in the bowels of his being. He stared at the tablet in Hailey's hands, as the little woman blathered on. "These two young ladies do remember you. Only, they're not young anymore. And they were never ladies, were they? Aging is a trial, isn't it, Heston?"

Heston held his face expressionless.

Hailey continued. "Now the two old girls are worried, trying to live on their measly Social-Security pensions. Your former play pals were only too happy to part with this video of you at your—most potent point, shall we say. For a handsome price."

"Who paid it?"

"Can't you guess? Adair. But don't blame him. He's not responsible for his actions, Heston."

"I'm sure he—or you—paid them handsomely."

"Well, I don't know about that. Adair took advantage of them, yes, didn't cheat them. But he did legally bind them to secrecy. If you give me your collection of early Cedric Spicer paintings—the entire collection, mind you—I will destroy this video. And this—"

To Heston's horror, Hailey conjured a battered journal from her bag. "Just FYI, Heston—Lynne Cordova chronicled some of your early escapades in writing. And Vivian's. Ezra was too good for my wicked stepmother."

Frozen in fear, Heston's lips barely moved. "Where did you possibly get that diary?"

"I didn't get it," Hailey insisted. "Adair did. He hired—*people*—to search for it."

"Search where?" He was barely breathing.

"You know where, Heston. Come on. I don't have tell you that Kipp is—"

Abruptly, he stood up.

"I've upset you," Hailey cooed.

"Who else knows about this, Hailey? You. Adair. Your private investigators?"

"That's all. For now."

"Meaning what?"

"I came to warn you, Heston. Adair has gone ape-shit crazy. He wants to be you. He's trying to take over your whole life. I've tried to talk sense to him, but he's beyond reason."

Dam broken, Heston's thoughts flowed in a thousand directions.

"You haven't told Nick?"

"I have not. I came to you first."

"So, what do you expect me to do about—those." He indicated the video-tablet and the vintage journal.

"Well, I know what Adair wants from you—Cedric Spicer's paintings." She grinned toothily. "Don't ask why. He's got that bee in his bonnet."

"He's got a hive."

She leaned into him. "Oh, give him what he wants, Heston. Please. Otherwise, he might—"

"What?"

"Do something drastic—to your family." She moved away and cast a waif-like glance his way. "You don't know him like I do, Heston. Underneath, he's malicious. I try to humor him. I've tried all my life. Sometimes, I lose patience. You're not the first one. I've protected—others—from Adair's wrath."

"What do you mean by *drastic?* Like dropping a light-fixture on my head to crush me to death?"

Hailey went on without responding. "If you choose to withhold the collection from him, he will post this video—and this story—on the most popular social-media sites on the Internet. You know the ones I mean—"

Heston sputtered. "Adair Champlain is one of the most—"

"Despicable creatures?"

"Pathetic is more like it. Look, Hailey, I could call his hand." Heston hedged. "No one will believe it is I."

Hailey looked ruffled "He'll make sure they believe it. The whole, wide world will believe it! Just imagine, millions of hits. Your big fans will love seeing this side of you, don't you agree?"

Heston went on the offense. "Forget the stupid paintings."

"But the diary—"

"What does Adair plan to do about Kipp?"

"And Kipp's little household? Adair doesn't understand. It's just a power grab on his part—flexing his puny muscles. But the truth could come out if—you don't cooperate."

"Why does Adair want the Spicer paintings?"

"I told you! Adair is crazy."

"So?"

"He's gotten it into his head that Cedric Spicer was his real father. Of course, that's insane, too. But it's the whole point. See, he has you and Cedric and King Odysseus, Alien Space Warrior all confused inside his head. His thought processes are muddled."

"Why don't you have him committed?"

Hailey's eyes flashed hot, then cold. "Heston, you are missing the point. I can stall Adair for twenty-four hours. You have until tomorrow night. After that—I can't make any promises. I'm sorry to say."

Heston got up and stepped outside the booth. "Say nothing to Nick. I'll tell him—in my own time."

"Okay." Too close, Hailey turned away. "It's a shame you're such an old fart now, Heston. Sometimes I get off to your early films. Like this one. Ha-ha. You were one handsome dude, old man. "

Struck by her sudden rudeness, he gaped at her. "You are many things, Hailey. Predictable is not one of them."

Hailey appeared pleased. "Sorry. I'm spoken for."

"Who's spoken for you?"

"Why, Uncle Ezra, of course."

Shaking his head, Heston objected. "I know for a fact that Ezra is not attracted to you, Hailey."

Avoiding his gaze, Hailey chortled. "I don't know what you're talking about." She set one foot outside the booth. "Twenty-four hours, Heston," she warned. "And it's curtains."

"Curtains? That's a bit melodramatic, even for you." He asked her, "Hailey, what about you? Are you—in danger—from your brother?"

"How gallant."

"Or is he in danger from you?"

Reaching up she tweaked his cheek." Twenty-four, stud—"

He grabbed her wrist and thrust her hand away. He stared down at the impish grin, now frozen on Hailey's face. "No dice," he said.

"What do you mean?" she asked, eyes leveled to slits.

"I mean no paintings, no blackmail."

"You'll regret this, Heston." Exiting the booth, she left him with the tab. He signed for it grudgingly. Then he walked back outside to the empty pool area. He gazed up at the heavens.

Blackmail? Blast it.

He thought of Poppy. This ugly business with Hailey had forced his hand.

The cruel truth of Adair's secret video would only add to his list of lies and would decimate his wife all over again. It would be just like seven years ago, when she had found out he had lied to her about having an affair with Lennox Cordova's nymphomaniac of a mother, Lynne—which had led to that inadvertent bedroom romp with Lennox. Oh, that freaking diary.

I told Kipp and Beryl to burn it.

How would Poppy react now, eight years later, when she found out about his drug-induced frolic with the two hippie hitchhikers.

I was just a kid.

A cyclone raged inside his mind. Even though that encounter had occurred many years ago, it was still an episode he had hidden from his wife. All he could remember about it now—was very sketchy.

I don't know—

A thought struck him. Maybe Adair hadn't beaten Maude into a coma. Maybe Hailey had. She was vicious enough. He couldn't stomach the idea of working with her anymore.

I'll have to put Ezra wise—and Winner. And Nick, soon enough.

The main issue was Kipp. Someone other than himself knew the truth now, and it was going to come out, regardless. If Poppy was going to hear the truth, he wanted it to come from him. He wanted to explain to her why he'd kept Kipp's secret all these years.

He would tell her everything first thing in the morning. Then he would make contact with Kipp. Someday he might even confess the whole truth about his relationship with Lennox: that he had shagged her when they starred in the film, *Blue Juniper.* However, first he would need to consider Bill's advice.

Chapter Sixteen

On the following afternoon, Poppy finally had a moment to breathe. The morning had been hectic. The kids had arrived early. Lunch had been a circus.

"I've missed our talks, Poppy," Heston admitted freely, now walking beside her down a bustling lane inside the theme park. "This is first time today we've been able to talk."

Side-by-side, she and Heston wandered leisurely, although still tethered to their teenaged children, who had run on ahead. Free on holiday, the kids were enraptured by the various amusement rides and venues. At the moment, the kids—and their bodyguards—were making tracks for the Enchanted Palace. It's spires and turrets dominated a central square in the amusement park.

Just ahead, Winner strolled alongside Ezra Gold. Winner's presence was attracting the attention of passers-by, but the attention was deflected by Millie, who engaged onlookers and kept them from accosting the actress. Meanwhile, the three youngsters—Dakota, Sage, and Tegan—were busy ignoring their elders.

Strolling along, Poppy listened intently to Heston's ramblings and musings. She felt he was leading up to something. Simultaneously, her antennae were alert for danger. The two bodyguards assigned to her and Heston trailed behind them, and their presence gave her comfort. Somewhere in the park, she knew, Nick Townsend was watching remotely over the entire family group, keeping his distance but remaining ever vigilant.

To Poppy's surprise, Heston caught her hand in his and held it. He talked to her as he strolled the paved walkway. "There's something I must tell you, Poppy. But, first, I need to explain why."

"To set me up?" She tried to sound lighthearted. She was only half joking.

"Just listen. After I lost you, I was adrift—and stunned. I didn't know how to react or where to turn for answers." He squeezed her hand. "I had just witnessed Kipp's extraordinary forgiveness of Gabe Cade. I suppose my consciousness began to evolve."

"How do you mean?" she asked, gently returning the squeeze.

Heston ran his free hand across the top of his head. "It's hard to explain in words, Poppy." He thought for a moment. "I realized my way of thinking about life was all wrong. That everything I'd been taught, everything I'd believed and accepted as reality was—inadequate—to explain what is really going on here on Planet Earth."

She was trying to follow his logic, or lack of it. "How so?" she encouraged.

"I was searching, adrift in spiritual mist. I knew I needed something, some arcane knowledge I did not possess. That was when, well—I interacted with someone—some people—who seemed more attuned to the answers than I was."

"Who?"

"Someone—connected to the Higher Power."

She took her cue. "You were wonderful in the role of the mystical monk. Even I believed you were celibate," she said, tongue in cheek.

He beamed. "You saw the film?" Stopping he turned to face her. He took her other hand, too.

She nodded. "Three times." The corner of her mouth twitched. "Okay. More."

They faced one another at this moment, in the same way they had faced one another, as youngsters when playing London Bridge. He held both her hands in his.

He seemed sincere. Yet his eyes flitted to hers and then quickly, away. He was such a good actor. *It's hard to tell.*

"I suppose I chose that film role because of my questioning."

As she focused on Heston's speech, he dropped her hands and resumed his walk. She kept pace.

He emoted. "My experience in Nepal? Ezra called it my "Razor's-Edge" phase. And he was right, although I didn't know it at the time. Since then, thanks to Ezra, I've read Somerset Maugham's famous novel, seen two film versions."

Carefully, Poppy trod into their shared past. "I know you were greatly affected by playing Paul Gauguin, ten years ago. You took up painting."

"Yes. I was trying to find myself, even then."

"Did the same thing happen after playing the monk? You—"

"Began a spiritual quest of my own. Exactly."

"Isn't that sort of an occupational hazard for actors?"

Heston smiled sheepishly. "Yes, I became each role I was playing. And this time, the role—of a European who found Enlightenment—took me beyond the visual arts into—immateriality."

"You're losing me."

"The ether, Red. Transcendence. Face it. Early on, I was materialistic in the extreme."

He was setting her up for something, but what? She was about to question him further when their conversation was interrupted.

Ezra and the kids stopped to take videos. Stopping in his tracks, Heston again clasped Poppy's hand and held it. Again, she did not withdraw her hand from his. Her heart, as well as her fingers, wrapped around Heston's strong, reassuring warmth. Yet, still, she did not trust his love for her.

She knew him so well. She sensed his next move. As the kids posed with life-sized version of animated movie characters, Heston drew her behind a tree. Readjusting his cap, he put it on so that the bill jutted backwards. His silver-blue eyes sparkled mischievously. His beauty could still take her breath away.

He looks like a kid again.

"Take your cap off," he said.

Unmoving, she regarded him.

"Relax." He inched closer. "I said cap, not panties."

She wanted to defy him, to ask why, but she did not. She knew why. She removed her cap, shaking out her bangs as Heston stepped closer, his ribs now touching the tips of her breasts.

Placing both his hands round the base of her neck, he dropped a soft kiss onto her cautious, waiting lips. Slowly, he moved in, body pressing against hers, his fingers finding their way into her hair. Lowering his head, he caressed a second kiss onto her bare throat.

Moved, Poppy shivered. *Oh, no. I can't . . .*

"Heston." She balked, shaking her neck free and stepping away from him. "Do we really want people to see us—like, m-making out behind a palm t-tree?"

"What people?" he demanded, looking around angrily.

"All these tourists. These fans." She indicated the monitors. "Security." She pointed down the walkway. "Or those cartoon characters—"

"C'mon, Red. You're worried about giant, talking chipmunks? And big, black mice wearing gloves?" He shook his head in feeble contempt.

"Th-there are actors inside th-those costumes, you know," she retorted, aware that she sounded idiotic. "Look!" she pointed. "See that clown? In the yellow fairy-costume? In the turret—over there, at the Enchanted Palace? That's a real person." Edgily, she glanced around.

"And there," she indicated, waving. "Space cadets and giant bananas—and see that dancing elephant?"

Heston shrugged. "I know that. They're actors. I'm an actor, remember. I know what actors do for a paycheck." Emotionally, he withdrew momentarily and made a joke. "That one up in the turret is probably Nick, undercover."

She chuckled, involuntarily.

Heston studied her shrewdly. "Are you really that nervous?"

She did not respond.

"What's making you nervous, Redhead? Danger from our stalker? Or the possibility that I might want to bed you tonight?"

"Stop it, Heston," she said, unsmiling, knees quivering. "Is this all part of the set up?"

"Yes." With maddening finesse, he sidled up to her and whispered in her ear. "But it's okay, Penelope. You and I? We're married." He pointed down the walkway. "See those kids over there? They're ours."

She laughed, in spite of herself, as he caught her around the waist and drew her to him. Clinging to him felt so good, so right, as if the empty place in her life had been filled.

He was a perfect fit—and he knew it.

"You don't play fair," she chided affectionately, resting her chin against his shoulder. "You never did."

"I'm not playing, my love." His lips brushed her right temple. "And I'm about to prove it to you. I'm going to tell you the most difficult thing I've ever had to tell you."

She stepped back. "What is it, Heston?"

"Realize, please, that I have decided to accept your terms—with one condition of my own."

"What condition?"

293

"I'm going to tell you the worst first. Then, if you are still speaking to me, I will begin to tell you the rest. But I will do it in my own good time, as I see fit and how I see fit." He looked her over. "Well, what do you say, Mrs. Demming? Is it a deal?"

"Heston, I—"

He looked at pavement and then met her gaze squarely. "I love you so much," he said.

Ezra's voice chimed out, as the young director rounded the tree trunk, a grin on his bright face. "Will you two knock it off?" He chuckled. "Move it, already. We're headed for the Enchanted Palace."

Instantly, she and Heston stepped apart. Quickly, Heston turned round his cap. She put her cap back on, too, self-consciously fluffing her hair, checking her lipstick—

"Teenagers," Ezra grinned in irony, unable to suppress his amusement at the couple's lack of comfort. He looked at Heston. "Don't forget to give her gum back."

"Shut up, Gold." Heston grabbed Poppy by the hand and dragged her after the kids, who had walked on ahead.

"Mind your own bees-wax," Poppy called flirtatiously to Ezra, as Heston pulled her up the walkway. Laughing joyously, Ezra bounded after them, catching them up and passing them. Happily, he trotted back to Winner's side. They continued idling towards the Enchanted Palace, which loomed ahead, gloriously lit by a rainbow of lights.

"What's gotten into him?" she asked Heston. "He's been acting loopy all day."

"You haven't answered my question, Poppy," said Heston.

"I'm digesting your offer," she replied coyly. Secretly, she was afraid to hear his devastating revelations of past indiscretions. In fact, she was beginning to regret her ultimatum.

Once again, she and Heston followed Ezra and the kids. Heston slipped his arm around her waist. She reciprocated, encircling his waist with her arm. This was the feeling she would be willing to die for, this belonging to him, with him, as part of Heston's very being. Yet, doubts tormented her.

How long would it last? Was Heston acting even now? Giving his greatest performance?

All to get back in my bed?

Up ahead, Ezra and Winner stopped short. They now stood on the drawbridge, at the front of the Enchanted Palace. Poppy and Heston stopped, as well, fifty feet behind. Jaw unhinging, Poppy watched, mesmerized, as Ezra took Winner's hand in his and dropped onto one knee.

Astonished, Heston walked alongside his wife, sharing in her wonderment.

"Shut my mouth, Penelope Susan," he drawled, in his best Southern accent. "He's going to do it. Young Ezra has decided to pop the question to our sweet, little Ladybug."

***

Murder in her heart, Hailey watched from the highest turret of the Enchanted Palace, heartsick, as Ezra dropped down on one knee in front of the palace—and offered an engagement ring to her hated rival, Winner, the bitch.

The bitch! I knew she'd drag him to the Enchanted Palace. That was her scheme, all along.

From on high, Hailey signaled her accomplice: *Take your position. We launch Final Gambit in two minutes.*

Seething, Hailey continued to watch as her hated prey received Ezra's proposal. Winner's step-siblings, the three Demming dimwits, were taking selfies. Trailing behind the crew, at a discreet distance, were Heston and Poppy Demming—holding hands, no less. Heston had rebuffed her offer at his own expense. Let it be on his head, then.

The king and queen are of no consequence. It's the princess who's the prize.

Looking down, Hailey scoured the surrounding terrain. This gambit required risk, but risks must be taken. Various security personnel lurked about. That old reprobate, Nick Townsend, was nowhere to be seen, which meant, of course, that he was monitoring events on a computer screen somewhere.

Or else, he's hiding in the shadows, somewhere in the park—if he can find any in this swirling mob. Heston seems unperturbed. He looks almost silly. His wife looks fish-eyed, as usual.

Would Heston be so calm, so collected, if he knew that his eldest daughter was about to die? That his own life and the lives of his family hung in the balance? That horny has-been was strolling around the grounds of the theme park like one of the peacocks that roamed the grounds, as if everything were hunky-dory—as if it were 20 years ago and he was the handsomest man in the world. His teen-aged children, on the other hand, were entitled to their own frivolity—for a few final moments, before their lives changed forever—or ended totally.

If Hailey's resolve had ever weakened, it never would again. She watched, sickened, as Ezra slobbered over Winner bony hand—and then kissed her cheek.

Her dream has come true—and it should have been mine.

Her tension at a fever pitch, Hailey checked the time. Then she checked her clown make-up. Satisfied that she was unrecognizable, she checked her weapons. She was ready. She looked down at the ground. The bitch was smiling.

Toodles, Winnie-poo-poo. It's been real. If I don't kill you, my trained baby-brother will. If he can't manage it, my secret weapon will.

Folding the wings of her costume, Hailey descended the steep stone steps that wound around the turret and spiraled down to ground level. Once on the ground, she raised the knife and began running towards Winner Demming.

***

Meanwhile, oblivious, Ezra gallantly proposed. "Winner, I love you. Will you marry me?" He presented her with a ring. "This is the only ring I have," he said. "It's my class ring, but I'll buy you any ring you want—"

"Ezra, what are you doing?" Mortified, Winner blanched as she glanced around self-consciously. "Get up, you idiot!"

"Not exactly the response I was hoping for," quipped Ezra, holding fast to Winner's hand. Grimacing, he shifted his body weight but remained on one knee.

Heston turned to look at Poppy, whose brown eyes shined as she watched the romantic scene unfold.

"I knew he had a thing for Ladybug," said Heston softly.

"We all knew," said Poppy. "Except for Win."

On impulse, Heston patted Poppy's restless coiffure. She looked up at him, meeting his gaze.

Oh, yes. The flame still burns.

Confident, he turned his gaze towards Ezra and Winner.

"Please, won't you do me the honor—" Ezra was saying.

Ladybug looked ill-at-ease yet overjoyed at the same time. Bemused, Heston frowned. He would never understand women.

"We'll talk about this later." Winner shielded her face with her hands. Tourists were gathering round. Smartphones were recording. The bodyguards spread out, covering the burgeoning crowd.

Rebuffed once again, Ezra slid the class ring into his pocket and kissed her hand. Then he rose and kissed her cheek.

He did not notice the weirdo running towards him, but Heston did. It was that fairy-princess clown—the same one Poppy had noted earlier, at the top of the Enchanted Palace. Probably an aspiring actor, whose part-time gig was to dress in gold-lame wings. Whoever it was, the person was short in stature.

Suddenly, the fairy-princess clown ran up to Ezra, grabbed him by the arm, and tugged him away from Winner's side. But Ezra resisted, flung off balance. Ungainly, he toppled and sprawled, dazed. With knife in hand, his assailant—lurched towards Winner.

Poppy screamed. Heston bolted towards the fairy clown.

Alerted, two of the bodyguards dashed from the crowd, but fell to ground, as shots rang out. The other bodyguards worked to keep the frenzied crowd of park visitors at bay, but chaos became inevitable.

Scrambling to his feet, Ezra hurled himself at the fairy-princess clown, who, reeling, dipped the knife defensively. To Poppy's horror, Ezra fell onto the knife, penetrating his side. Blood spurted from the wound onto Winner, who screamed, and onto the fairy-princess clown's yellow wings.

Removing the knife, the fairy-princess clown gaped at Ezra.

Spouting blood, Ezra staggered backwards, his fingers clutching at his oozing wound, a look of disbelief upon his face, as he collapsed, moaning in agony, onto the ground. Blood pooled around him. The wicked fairy-princess clown spied Winner, who knelt beside Ezra.

Standing over Winner, the fairy-princess clown dropped the bloody knife and raised an automatic handgun, pointing it directly at Winner.

Like a greyhound, Heston sprinted towards them.

A hard thud knocked him to the ground. He lost his breath. Gasping, he saw a tall, costumed figure looming over him—but this time, he recognized the assailant.

"Get up, Pretender."

Heston knew that voice, too. It belonged to Adair Champlain. Although dressed as King Odysseus: Alien Space Warrior, Adair, like his fairy-princess clown accomplice, was wielding a knife. His face, too, was thick with greasepaint. Heston had the impulse to laugh.

Mad as a freaking hatter.

Staring up into the face of madness, Heston's wind returned. Quickly, he jumped to his feet, wobbling, at first, then finding his footing. Like the fencer he was, he lunged for Adair's knife, ripping it from the hand of the space king, expecting, at any moment, to feel the full weight of Adair Champlain descending upon him. But he did not.

Why not? Where is Adair? Where is the fairy?

"Winner! Run!" he heard Nick shout. Sirens blared in the distance.

"Dack! Come back!" screamed Sage.

Hysterical, Poppy ran to Ezra's side. Kneeling down, she cried out. "Help him! Someone, help him!" Another woman screamed. Poppy spun around.

"Heston!" She shrieked, pointing a finger.

Wheeling about, Heston did not see Winner or the fairy-princess clown anywhere, but he did see King Odysseus, sword in hand, advancing on *Poppy.*

Adair wrapped Poppy in a choke hold, his sword at her throat. Adair throttled Poppy, backing her away from the arriving security police, whose cars squealed up behind Heston.

Gun in hand, Nick ran towards Adair and Poppy, but he was too far away—

In a split second, Heston cleared a park bench as if it were a track hurdle, plowing, feet first, into Adair and sending him reeling, sword skidding across the paved walkway. Staggering to his feet, Adair located the weapon and seized it. Sword in hand, he sprang at Heston, just as Heston turned protectively towards Poppy.

"Go!" he shouted to her.

"Behind you, Daddy!" Sage yelled at the top of her lungs.

Slammed from the rear, Heston fell to earth, as Adair's full weight landed on top of him, at last. Wrestling, rolling on the ground, the two men struggled violently. Finally on his feet, Heston felt a blade enter his back. Seconds later, bullets whizzed past him.

"Heston!"

"Daddy!"

More shots rang out. *Somewhere . . . in the sky . . .*

"A drone!" Nick's voice, far away. "It's targeting Winner! Bring it down!"

Screams.

Automatic gunfire . . . like raindrops pelting the deck of Windswept . . .

Swirling in a vortex of pain and blood, amidst the fervor and noise—the dying sounds—of chaos, Heston Demming floated in darkness—then, brightness—as his vessel turned towards his ultimate destiny, the eternal confluence of the Gulf of Mexico and the mythical River Styx.

Or, could it be the River Jordan . . .

Chapter Seventeen

Enshrouded by an eerie mist, Heston drifted towards a group of people who seemed vaguely familiar. They were burdened-down people, rugged men and hardened women. Within the strange haze, the light grew bright, the mood in the room, solemn. He heard himself speaking to the seasoned crowd. *"Me llame Tomas.* My name is Tom, and I'm an alcoholic." He was his younger, derelict self, at a meeting somewhere in the Dominican Republic, or was it Nashville? The people answered him in Spanish and in English. Wherever he was, he had been here before.

Deja vu? He had done this already.

Then he was no longer at the meeting. Instead, he was floating, ceiling-high, looking down on a tiny, bare room. A man was lying on a steely bed. Heston could see himself, lying down there, surrounded by busy doctors and nurses. He realized he must be in Kipp's clinic, for now he was staring now at good-looking man with golden hair and copper-brown eyes. A circular spotlight shined on him. Heston shielded his eyes from its glare, as the shining man spoke from the circle of light.

"Dad, it's me. Kipp."

"Kipp? Am I sick? How did I get here?"

"Well, it's kind of hard to explain, Dad."

"I was—somewhere else. Now I'm with you." Troubled, Heston reached out. "Don't let them find you, son. Stay hidden; stay here in this foreign land, wherever it is—you've been found out. It's only a matter of time—don't tell anyone who I am. They'll realize you're my son—will blow your cover."

"Dad, don't worry. Nobody here cares that you're you. For that matter, nobody around here cares if I'm me—not anymore—not even Marissa and Perfecto—my days of rock stardom are over."

Heston's eyelids fluttered. "Perfecto? Your medical mystic?"

In a flash, he glimpsed an ethereal figure. He was young, dark-haired, athletic—his dead son, Franco—but surely it was only a halluci-nation. "Frankie?" Franco, too, said something in Spanish . . .

Surely not Franco. It's not possible. Unless . . . unless I'm . . .

"Stay with me, Dad." Kipp sounded distant. "Yeah, Dad. Dr. Perfec-to Logue. You fund his work. Remember? He married my old girlfriend, Marissa. Yeah, they have three kids now."

Heston beckoned. "Kipp, are we in Santo Domingo? I remember, I got blind drunk there once—when you were on call—Beryl was furi-ous—"

Kipp seemed at home in the circle of light. "Urn, not exactly, Dad. We're not exactly anywhere."

Heston struggled for breath. "Kipp, am I in heaven? I need a drink. Kipp, son, do you have any—

"Booze? Sorry, Dad. Fresh out."

An adolescent blond boy appeared in the misty circle of light. He addressed Kipp. *"Popi?"* Kipp turned, shooing the boy away, to beyond the light.

"Later, Shawn. I'm busy with a patient. Tell your mom I'll be late for dinner."

The boy glanced at Heston. *"Ola, abuelo."* Quickly, he departed the circle of light, disappearing into the surrounding mist.

Heston gawked after him. "Was that tall kid Shawnee? How old is he now?"

Kipp shook his golden head, amused. "Your grandson is ten now. He wants us to call him Shawn."

"Beryl—your wife?"

"Happy as a clam." Kipp paused. "And still feisty as ever."

Heston tried to smile.

"It's okay, Dad. Berry and I have a daughter now, too. We spawned since your last visit. You have a beautiful little granddaughter."

"A granddau—?"

"We named her Joy. Joy is three years old. Dad. She's a carrot top like Mom. Got those wide-set eyes, but they're blue. Sky-blue, like Berry's."

Heston breathed with difficulty. "I want to know Joy."

Kipp turned into the swirling haze and called out. "Hey, Joyous. Get in here *rapido.* Come meet your *abuelo.*"

A dainty child with auburn locks skipped out of the mist and into the vortex of light. She was wearing a yellow frock and sturdy white-top oxfords with white socks. Her frail, white legs were dotted with tiny, orange freckles.

"Hello, Joy—" Heston said. Fascinated, he reached out a hand.

Joy giggled, ignoring him. Skipping, she rounded his bed, circling it, and proceeded to skip round it again, and then again, boisterously delighted with her own antics, lost her in a world of her own amusement.

"Settle, Joy," said Kipp, catching her by the shoulders on the third go-round. "Settle." He hoisted her into his arms. She beamed with delight.

"See that man?" Kipp pointed.

Joy looked at Heston. She nodded vigorously, a forefinger in her mouth.

"That's your *abuelo.*"

Astonished, Joy shook her head 'no.'

"Yes." Kipp tickled her. She squealed in delight.

"No, no, no!" she squealed amid peals of silly laughter.

Suddenly, Heston felt faint. The circle of light began to shrink. Oddly, Joy began to fade.

Suddenly anxious, Kipp turned to face him. "Don't worry, Dad. They've got you under control now. I'm almost there. Hang on."

"No, son. Don't—endanger yourself. Stay away—Kipp." But Kipp was ignoring him now, his attention focused on the child in his arms. Kipp, too, began to fade away.

A hand grasped Heston's. "Trust, son. Have faith." Heston looked up into the face of his beloved mother, Kay. He only caught a glimpse. Her lovely face faded into the mist. The light was growing dim.

What is happening to me?

Looking down, he saw that the doctors and nurses were no longer at his bedside. Now Poppy entered. She stood by his bedside. She held his hand—bending down, smoothing his forehead, weeping.

No . . .!

All at once, he felt dizzy, queasy. Agony engulfed him. The thickening mist swirled into a funnel cloud, swallowing up both Kipp and Joy. Disappearing, they seemed oblivious, lost in their pantomime, as light and sound faded away and cold, empty darkness fell across his hospital bed.

***

Isolated from the hectic pace of the Emergency Room, Poppy waited, in quiet desperation, beside Heston's bed in the critical-care unit. Heston was unconscious. She had forgotten about her three adolescent children, who waited restlessly, under guard, in a private lounge on the same hospital floor.

Who could have done this? Why?

As she smoothed Heston's forehead, she whispered prayers of petition. A physician, entering Heston's room, cleared his throat. Poppy looked up. "What's the verdict?"

The doctor drew a deep breath. "We have a consensus. Mrs. Demming, we must perform surgery on your husband immediately. In the area of his spine. He may or may not experience paralysis after the surgery, but he certainly will without surgery, and he will die, eventually. As it is, he has only a thirty-percent chance of surviving the surgery. We need your permission to proceed."

Poppy straightened to her full height. "You have it."

"Good. My Physician's Assistant, Adeline, will assist you with the necessary forms."

"Okay." She asked the doctor, "What happened to the attackers? Are they still—?"

"Don't worry, Mrs. Demming, Our facility is swarming with security agents. One is guarding your door." The doctor thumbed. "As soon as I know more, I'll tell you." He indicated Heston. "Has your husband shown any sign of awareness?" He examined Heston's inert body.

Poppy shook her head. "Not since I've been—"

Heston's eyelids fluttered.

"Heston squeezed my hand!" she cried to the doctor. "He's opened his eyes!"

"Mr. Demming?" The doctor's gaze met Heston's. "Sir, you've sustained a life-threatening injury to your spinal area. We're going to operate. Your wife has given us permission."

Heston blinked.

"Even if surgery is successful, you may or may not retain the use of your legs. We won't know until after the surgery."

"It's okay," Heston said, barely audible. "Too—old to—dance."

"Heston!" Poppy cried. "You're not too old. You will dance. And I'll dance with you."

Heston smiled weakly, squeezing her hand once more.

"Mrs. Demming," the doctor said. "We're going to prep your husband for surgery. "You'll need to . . . leave now." The doctor left the unit. Seconds later, a male nurse entered to prepare Heston for the ordeal ahead.

Poppy lowered her mouth to Heston's ear. "Heston, can you hear me?"

He squeezed her hand. His eyes closed.

"I love you," she whispered. "And I am with you. I'll be right here."

"Kids . . .?" he breathed.

"Fine. All fine. They'll be here, too. We'll all here, pulling for you."

He squeezed her hand.

"Heston, you were so brave today. You saved my life. You were like the returning hero. Except in real life. You came back and saved us all from disaster."

He lay motionless, breathing. "Popp—"

She leaned in. "Yes, Heston?"

"Love—you—"

The male nurse put a hand on her shoulder. "I'm afraid you'll have to leave now," he said kindly.

Poppy nodded, placing her palm across Heston's forehead.

Rallying, he raised a hand, beckoning. "Ki—," he whispered.

Steadily, she obeyed, pressing her lips to his.

"Hey, Pigtails," he managed, eyelids fluttering. "Want to—ride—bikes sometime?"

Memory stirred, Poppy croaked a sob.

"Don't—'sokay. Tell Kipp—I'm waiting—" His voice died out. His hand fell away.

"Mrs. Demming, please—" Gently, the nurse guided her from the room, shepherding her into the arms of a matronly hospital volunteer. They passed the armed security office stationed outside the door.

306

"I know, honey," the gray-haired lady cooed, as she deposited Poppy in a chair in the waiting area. "We'll get you some hot coffee," she said, as the nurse returned to Heston's bedside.

"No, thanks."

"Well, you let me know if you need anything. I'll be right over there." She pointed towards the snack machines.

"Thanks." Poppy sat, dazed. She watched numbly as orderlies arrived, entering Heston's room. Seconds later, they wheeled her husband away on a gurney.

It was too much to comprehend. Her mind replayed the day's events. Heston's final words rang in her ears. "Tell Kipp . . ."

Oh, Heston. You were really out of it. Kipp's been dead for years.

To quiet her emotions, she prayed for the success of the operation—and for her husband's immortal soul. At last, it occurred to her to check the text messages on her phone. Opening her eyes, she looked down the long hospital corridor.

To her relief, she saw Nick Townsend walking towards her. Beside Nick, however, a good-looking, suntanned blond man in early middle age was striding quickly. At that moment, the blond man caught sight of her and stopped in his tracks.

She recognized his face. Poppy's heart slammed inside her breast. Leaping to her feet, she uttered a garbled cry of disbelief as the man approached quickly and embraced her.

"Forgive me, Mom," he pleaded, holding her tightly as she screamed into his shoulder, pounding his back with her clenched fists—until, at last, spent, she rested against his chest and wept, grateful, into his Hawaiian shirt.

"I got here as soon as I could," Kipp said, still hugging her closely. "How's Dad?"

Overwhelmed, she clung to him, speechless.

In the meantime, Nick had located the coffee dispenser and now stood, across the corridor, chatting up the hospital volunteer. Just then, the doctor's PA, Adeline, appeared, device in hand, ready for Poppy's digital signature on the permission forms. An attractive brunette, Adeline wore a white lab coat and heels.

"Your father said to tell you—he's waiting for you." Adeline whispered to Poppy's resurrected son. Kipp's hair was still golden, his copper-brown eyes, alert but gentle, and his stature, athletic—like the former quarterback he was, but his air of command now was tinged with tenderness. Adeline added, "They say you're back from the dead. Your father's anxious to see you," Kipp nodded, as Adeline took a step backwards.

"I can heal. I have a gift," he explained.

She pondered him. "Can you help your father? He's been stabilized."

"Yes. I believe I can."

"Then, in the name of heaven, do it. They're prepping him for surgery now."

"Is he conscious?"

"He was. Not sure."

"Take me to him."

Kipp kissed his mother's crown and gently pulled away.

He followed Adeline through the door marked "Do Not Enter."

***

Kipp whispered into Heston's ear. "Dad? I'm here."

Heston was lying on the hospital gurney. The tiny room was sterile and empty. The smell of futility, of fear and death, hung heavily in the frigid air.

308

"You have one minute, sir. Then we prep your father for surgery." Adeline stepped away, tactfully allowing Kipp a moment alone with Heston. She walked to Poppy's side. Poppy was leaning, in silent shock, against the wall of the ER critical-care unit. She watched, in disbelief, as the scene before her unfolded.

Kipp rose slightly and bent over Heston's inert form. "Dad?"

"Kip—?" Heston whispered, his eyes opening into slits. "Fantasy— dream—was I dead? Are you—*dead?*"

Poppy uttered a tiny cry. The Physician's Assistant placed a hand on her shoulder and squeezed gently. Poppy barely noticed.

"No, Dad." Kipp's lips were pressed again to Heston's ear. "You're not dead. I'm not dead either. We're both alive."

"But—I saw you—you came to me—you spoke—" Heston agonized over each escaping word.

"I don't have time to explain." Kipp took Heston's hands in his. "Dad, can you feel me? Can you feel my energy? Nod if you can."

Heston nodded.

"Good. Dad, you are going to survive this surgery. Do you hear me?"

Again, Heston nodded.

Kipp's intensity became palpable. "Do you believe me? Do you believe you will survive this surgery?" An intense energy—of light, warmth, awe—permeated the atmosphere. An aura surrounded Kipp. His golden hair gleamed. His skin seemed electrified.

The light and energy passed into Heston. "Yes."

"Claim it, Dad. Say 'I believe. I believe I will survive this surgery. I believe I will be with my loved ones again—my family who love me— with Mom who's sitting right over there, crying her heart out over you.' We need you, Dad. We all need you—and we love you. We want you back. Say it, Dad. Say, 'I believe'."

"I be-lieve—" Heston's words, barely audible, seemed to fill the tiny room, alive with energy.

"Then you will," said Kipp. Bending down, he uttered a prayer of sorts. Poppy could not make out the words. Then he kissed Heston's ear, released his hands, and turned to Poppy and the PA. "Let's go, ladies," he said, opening the door to the hallway.

"I'm staying," said Adeline, cynically. "It's my job." She looked skeptical. "I was taught to trust in the science of healing."

"So was I," said Kipp. "When I attended med school. And I do. But I also have faith in faith."

"You're an M.D?" Adeline asked.

"You bet your sweet stethoscope. I completed my internship last spring. Under an alias."

"Where?"

"At a university in the Caribbean. With Dad's help." Kipp gazed fondly at Heston.

Her gray eyes sparkled. "I'd like to have an autograph sometime—or maybe a selfie, with you, Kipp. If you don't mind."

"I'll ask my wife."

From the gurney, Heston whispered. "My son—the rock star doc—"

The PA looked down at Heston. "Your son, the mystic healer."

On impulse, Poppy walked back, one last time, to Heston's side. "I believe, too, Heston." She kissed his lips. "If Kipp can return from the grave, anything is possible." Bravely, she strode out the open door. Following her, Kipp stopped and turned back to his father.

"I'll be with you, Dad. By next week, we'll be fishing for marlin. You, me, and Nick. Maybe the week after. Soon."

"Okay."

"I love you, Dad."

"Love—you—son."

Gently, the PA closed the door behind Kipp as he and Poppy exited into the hospital corridor.

Chapter Eighteen

In a quiet nook, Kipp and Poppy waited together during Heston's surgery. Kipp was keeping an eye on Poppy. His poor mother seemed even more disoriented and emotional than he had expected. He knew, however, that she had just suffered, and witnessed, a violent attack, which compounded her shock at his arrival. Sitting down beside her, he handed her a hot cup of coffee and sipped one himself.

"Mom, are you okay?"

"I don't know."

"Please forgive me for keeping you in the dark."

"Your father knew, didn't he? That you were still alive."

Embarrassed, Kipp nodded. "Dad arranged the whole thing. All those years ago—the plane crash, our presumed deaths—all of it." He could see the rancor on his mother's freckled face.

Dad will survive, but he'll have hell to pay.

Kipp tried to explain. "I was avoiding the law here in the States. Dad helped me elude justice. But I'm not hiding any longer, Mom. I've come back to pay what I owe society and to move on." Yet he could feel that his mother was in no mood to listen to reason.

"Your father lied to me. All those years. Let me believe you—Beryl and Shawnee, too—were dead."

"Forgive him, Mother."

Her brown eyes bored into him. "How could you, Kipp? How could he? What could be more cruel?" She looked at him in anguish.

"Mother, I want a chance to prove my love for you. Please say you'll let me. Please say yes."

"Yes," she said quietly, to his utter astonishment. "Yes." Her expression softened. "But I think I must be furiously angry with you—and

Heston—only, right now, I can't make sense of it all. I reserve the right to yell at you—both." Her breathing was shallow; her brow, furrowed.

He kissed her cheek. "Aw, I want to make it up to you. The kids, too. Think they'll let me?"

"Yes. In time." Quickly, her lips brushed his cheek.

"I want to touch people's lives. It's time." He took her hand. "You saw what happened in there just now, with Dad? I can't keep this gift of healing—this knowledge—to myself any longer, Mom."

No, you shouldn't, honey. You should share it." Poppy said. "You can start with your own sister." Pointing down the corridor, as Winner came into view, Poppy spilled coffee on the linoleum floor.

***

Down the hall, Winner—frazzled, but relieved beyond measure—walked out of Ezra's hospital room. Ezra would live. At the moment, he was sleeping, after his own successful surgery.

In a trance, Winner drifted towards Poppy, who was helping a man to wipe up a spill. Winner addressed her. "Ezzie's going to be okay. How's Daddy?" As the man wheeled around, she studied him. He was muscular, blond, and agile—and strangely magnetic. He seemed familiar. But who was he?

Winner acknowledged his presence. "Hi."

The man said, "Hi, yourself, movie star." To her surprise, he approached her with a cautious ease. "Winston, do you remember me?"

Poppy rose and followed the man, explaining. "Win, this is your half-brother, Kipp. He's alive. He's come to help us. In our time of need."

Uncomprehending, Winner ignored Poppy's comment. "What just happened out there? Who were those lunatics? Does anyone know who attacked us?"

The man spoke in a recognizable—indeed, famous—voice. "Nick's working on it."

Winner focused on Poppy. "I've been with Ezra. He's going to be okay. How's Dad?"

"They're operating on him now." Worried, Poppy gave her a hug. "He's in the hands of Heaven." She seemed so distraught. "Honey, did you hear what I said? This man is—"

"I heard you!" Nerves frayed, Winner pulled away, glaring. "Kipp, where the hell have you been?" Fumbling in her purse, she located the pill bottle, opened it, and swallowed three pills.

"That's not good for you," Kipp observed.

"Bug off. My father and my boyfriend were attacked. My brother's back from the dead. Bug. Off, Mr. Sex, Drugs, and Rock n' Roll."

"Rock. No roll. Dinosaur days." The long-lost Kipp—compassionate and mature—contemplated her calmly. "Look, I'll explain everything to you, Winnie—about my return, at least. Nick Townsend contacted me. Gave me the scoop. Sent a chopper for me." He shrugged. "Now I'm here."

Winner felt as if she were inside a video game. "Where were you?"

Glancing at Poppy, Kipp hesitated. "Caribbean. Beryl's there, too, Win. She's alive. So is Shawnee. Guess what? We have a daughter now, too. You have a niece."

"What?" cried Poppy.

Delighted, Kipp hugged her. "Guess I forgot to mention that. Sorry, Mom. Her name is Joy."

"I can't believe you're alive," Winner whispered, as the drug kicked in. Like her stepmother, she couldn't take her eyes off him. "I can't believe this entire, crazy day! Pinch me, somebody!"

Vaguely, she felt Poppy at her elbow, supporting her, holding her steady.

Kipp caught Winner in his hypnotic gaze. "Believe, baby sister. Believe." Embracing, he gave her a brief bear hug and released her. "You've turned into a real beauty, baby girl."

"Hardly." Feigning modesty, Winner sniffed. "My eyes are all red."

"Patriotic," teased Kipp in brotherly fashion. "Red, white, and silver-blue." He glanced at the ground and then raised his gaze. "I must say, ladies, it's good to be back in the old US of A." His copper-brown eyes brimmed. "You have no idea how much I've missed you guys."

Embarrassed, Winner addressed Poppy. "How's Daddy? Really?"

"Win, it's quite serious. He may be paralyzed—"

Overwhelmed, Winner broke down. "It's all my fault. If I hadn't thrown the stupid surprise party, none of us would be here!"

Ineptly, Poppy comforted her. "At least Ezra's out of the woods."

Kipp regained control of his emotions. "It wasn't his time. People go when it's their time."

"Is it Daddy's time to go?" Winner asked him, frightened.

"Absolutely not," Kipp replied.

"How do you know?" she demanded.

"A little bird told me. I heard from that same bird that my old buddy Ezra's ape over you."

She nodded, sniffling. "Ezzie risked his life to save me. We—he—I—" She broke down.

Kipp stroked her hair. "I get the picture, Ladybug. Don't worry. Go on and cry it out. Let it all go." Instinctively, he embraced both women, one under each arm. "What you say, girls? Let's go find the rest of our family and give them the scoop."

"What scoop?" asked Winner.

"That I have returned," he replied, wounded.

"Oh, that," Winner teased in sisterly fashion. "I thought you meant the news about Ezra. Where are the kids, anyway?" She regarded Poppy.

At that moment, a male surgeon approached, followed by a black-haired woman in a white lab coat. "Mrs. Demming," the surgeon said to Poppy. "Your husband survived the surgery. Unfortunately, I'm afraid we need to talk. As I feared, there have been—complications."

***

Recovering from surgery, Heston rested in his hospital bed. He was not alone in his private hospital room, however. His son, Kipp, was keeping watch over him, listening on speaker phone to Heston's conversation with Nick Townsend. The sound of Nick's gruff voice was reassuring.

Weakly, Heston spoke to the phone. "I want to know what just happened to me, Nick. You know all the facts. Let's have them."

"Not all, Heston, although I do know most of it."

Heston heard the rasp of his own voice. "The clown-princess in the turret. That was Hailey, wasn't it?"

"Yes," Nick replied. "For the moment, all I can tell you is that—well, Hailey's not expected to survive. According to the doctors, it's only a matter of hours; perhaps, minutes."

"The other one—Space Odysseus—the one dressed like me? Adair?"

"He managed to get himself shot by Hailey's drone."

"Drone?"

"My sharpshooter brought it down," explained Nick, "before it could do more harm."

"It was terrifying," said Winner. "When I looked up and saw it—"

"They don't call me 'Nick o' Time' for nothing."

"Thank you, Nick."

Nick went on. "Adair roamed the park for a few hours. Eluded us, but we captured him in the end. Adair's in custody—at a mental facility."

"Tell me the rest, Nick."

"Uh, no. It's not going to work that way. You need your beauty rest. Besides, I have one final loose end to tie up."

"What is it?"

"A third accomplice." Nick sounded amused. "Once I clear up that point—then I'll tell you the whole story. I'll tell everybody, all at once. It'll be easier on me to do it that way."

Heston glanced at Kipp, who was hanging over his shoulder, listening. Heston said to the speaker phone. "We'll be here. Where and when?"

Nick paused and then asked, "When are they releasing you from the hospital?"

"Day after tomorrow," Kipp replied in his stead.

"How about the day after that? I'll come on down to Naples."

"That's three days from now," Heston complained.

Nick ignored the whine. "Around 11:00 a.m.? Assuming my theory is correct—"

"We'll be waiting, buddy," Kipp said to the speaker phone. "All of us. I'll get the family together."

"I'd like the entire Demming household to be present," Nick said.

"Including Lissette?"

"Yes. Everyone. It's important."

"Okay." Heston attempted to adjust his position in the bed.

"You got it, big dude."

Heston had the last word. "Plan to stay for lunch, Nick."

"With pleasure, Heston. Plan on two guests. I'm bringing someone with me—I hope. See you then—if I live." Nick ended the call.

Heston and Kipp exchanged glances. "What the heck does that mean?" Kipp wondered aloud.

"Muddy water will become clear," Nick said. "Say, Heston. I talked to Poppy. She told me the score. Sorry to hear it, man. Know that I'm pulling for you. Anything I can do—"

"Thanks, Nick."

Kipp chimed in. "He'll walk again, Nick. One day soon. You'll see."

Chapter Nineteen

That afternoon Maude Demming was resting in her semi-private room in a nursing facility in Orlando. Recovering from the beating, she was making good progress. Her doctors were pleased.

However, the experiences of the past few days had brought many of her transgressions to light, in her own mind. All the previous night, she had prayed over an important decision. Now, as she sat drinking her green tea and watching the morning news on TV, she could not believe the news anchor's words. He said:

"According to our sources, movie idol Heston Demming has been paralyzed, from the waist down. As our regular viewers know, Demming was critically injured in a near-fatal attack right here in town. Since then, the star has been fighting for his life. Heston Demming is best known for his award-winning portrayals of French painter, Paul Gauguin, and mystical monk, Hugo Laughlin, as well as for numerous roles in block-buster films. Although out of the public eye for years . . ."

Maude turned off the TV and immediately phoned Nick Townsend, who had visited her in the hospital and given her his number.

"Hello, ma'am." Nick's voice sounded calm but inquisitive. "What an unexpected pleasure."

"This is not a social call, Mr. Townsend." She did not want to chit-chat with Heston's old pal.

"What can I do for you, ma'am?"

"I just heard the news. Heston's paralyzed."

"Yes, he is. I spoke with the man himself only a few hours ago. He's coping."

"Mr. Townsend, I want to arrange a meeting with my daughter. Will she be back to Naples soon?"

"As far as I know. Their production has been—well, canceled, I think. Because of all this business with the attack at the theme park—"

"I want to see her. I want you to arrange it for me." She heard Nick inhale deeply and exhale slowly.

"That's a tall order."

"It would mean a lot to me if you would . . . smooth the way for me."

"How are you doing?" he asked. "How's your own recovery going?"

"I'm fine. I've been blessed." She would not be put off. "Will you talk to Winston for me?" Maude heard only silence. "Help me, please. I want to make amends. I want to start over with my . . . baby girl."

Nick inhaled and exhaled. "This is about bearing an olive branch?"

"Absolutely." Then she said, "It's about—I'm a new and different person."

Deliberating, he made a few clicking sounds with his tongue. "Okay. I'll talk to Winner. But you'd better be for real, lady. I'm nobody's patsy."

Maude pressed her point home. "I'm for real."

"Then I'll see what I can do. It's time the two of you got on with the show. Not sure how Heston's going to react, but I'll try to pave the way for you, ma'am."

She could hardly respond. "Bless you," was all she could manage to utter before ending the call. A meeting with the daughter she had abused as a child was the scariest thing she had ever contemplated. It was even scarier than looking at her old 8x10 glossies.

***

The next day, on the tennis court at the Demmings' home in Naples, Kipp and his half-sister had paused for a lemonade between sets. Quibbling, they stood beneath a dark awning and sipped from tall, cool tumblers. Despite the shade and the iced drink, Winner was fired up.

"Of course, I'm not going to marry Dan," Winner shouted. "Not now! Not after everything that's happened. He lied to me. He deceived me. He hurt me! Even worse, he—"

"Okay, okay," Kipp said in his most placating manner. "I was just asking, kiddo. I want to know what you are planning to do—in the future."

"Whatever it is, it won't be with him. I hate Danny Vega."

Kipp took a sip of lemonade. "Hate's pretty intense. Hate can kill you inside. You might consider forgiving him."

"What? Forgive Danny Vega? Never."

"Never is a long time." Kipp shaded his eyes from the sun.

"There's a news flash." Winner scowled at him. She poked a straw at the ice in her glass.

"Sarcasm doesn't look good on you, Win. It's like a color that doesn't suit your complexion."

Suddenly, he had her attention. *I'm speaking her language now. You got her. Now hold her.* "You won't forgive Danny Vega for deceiving you?"

"If I do or don't," Winner said. "It doesn't matter either way. Dan and I are finished."

Kipp considered this statement. "Well, it does matter. It matters—for your peace of mind if nothing else. If you'd half a mind to, you could flush all those prescription pills."

"How?"

"By finding inner peace."

"Oh, brother."

"Look, forgiving Vega doesn't mean you have to take him back. It just means you won't suffer inside for the rest of your life." *She's too young to understand this yet.* He tried another tactic. "You know, Danny Vega is just the first name on your Forgiveness-To-Do List. You've got Hailey and Adair. There's Dad and me. What about your real mom? Are you planning to forgive her?"

"Probably not," Winner said hotly. After a moment, she muttered, "I'll think about it."

"Good." Kipp embraced Winner, who squirmed. "I know it's a lot to ask. I know it's not something you can do overnight. But you can start the process. It may not happen all at once."

"I said I'll think about it."

"Okay, okay. Relax."

"You can't just waltz into my life, Kipp, after eight years, telling me what to do."

He backed off. "Yeah, I can. I'm your big brother. It's what I do."

Winner laughed in spite of herself. "No, I mean it."

"Yeah?" He sidled up beside her and dug his fingers into her waist, tickling her.

Winner doubled over in laughter. "Stop it," she commanded in her best princess voice.

Echoing her laughter, he pulled her to his side. Giving her a quick hug, he released her. "I'm going to tell you something else you don't want to hear, Win."

"Oh, no."

"You need to stop making stupid horror movies. You need to use your star power to change people's lives for the better. You and Ezra both."

"The production has been canceled—for obvious reasons," she remonstrated.

"Follow what I'm saying. You're in a position to do it. Help people. Spread love and truth and light in the world. That's what I'm going to do—what I am doing—no matter what my future holds—be it prison or poverty or whatever. Now that I've earned my M.D., I can go anywhere, help anywhere."

"I'm not you," said Winner. "I don't know who I am—yet." She regarded him. "You and Ezra were friends once, right?"

Kipp shrugged. "Yeah. Best buds. When you were just a kid. What am I saying? You're still a kid." He grinned at her.

"No. I'm not." She faced him, silver-blue eyes twinkling. "I'm old enough to get married. And I have to give Ezra Gold an answer. He'll be here tomorrow for Nick's big meeting."

Kipp chortled, coughing. He dropped her hand. "Are you saying what I think you're saying?" He set down his empty tumbler and picked up his racquet and a yellow tennis ball. He began bouncing the ball. "You've got me on pins and needles here. Tell me about you and Gold. I want to know."

Winner wiped her hand. "You don't like Ezra, do you? You're still holding a grudge."

Kipp said, "You know about—what happened between us?"

Watching him, Winner tilted her head, hand on hip. Her eyes narrowed. "Ezra told me. He said you got mad at him one Thanksgiving."

"After he spilled the beans to Dad, yeah." Kipp frowned. "I was an arrogant punk in those days."

"So, have you forgiven Ezra?" Winner's silver-blue eyes nailed him. "You want me to forgive my birth mother for abusing me as a child, but you haven't forgiven Ezzie—for one little slip-up?"

"Ezzie?"

"Stick to the point, Rock Doc."

Kipp fetched the runaway tennis ball. Perturbed, he rubbed his palm over his eyes and nose. Coughing again, he played for time. *The kid is right. How the heck can she be right? I hadn't even realized.*

322

Physician, heal thyself.

He heard Winner's smartphone ring. She answered.

"It's Nick," she mouthed to Kipp as he stood watching her.

"Winner," Nick said. "Got some news for you." Kipp could hear him.

"What news?" she asked. "I can't take much more."

"Maude Winston. She phoned me. She wants to meet with you. I told her I would ask you. See if you were willing to meet with her."

Winner's features became drawn. She stared at the carpet of green grass on the lawn. Kipp cast a questioning look, but she did not notice.

Winner spoke to Nick. "She was horrible to me."

"I agree," Nick said. "But I've got to ask you. I promised her I would."

"What does Daddy say? Did you phone him first?"

"Yep. Your decision."

Kipp eyed his troubled kid sister. "Winner, what about it?"

Winner looked up. She glanced his way, a flash of fear that he felt, rather than saw. *Poor kid.*

She spoke to Nick. "Okay. I'm free this afternoon. Tell her to come here. I'll give her ten minutes. But I refuse to be alone with her."

Nick's voice was even. "Good girl, sweetie," he said. "I'll let her know. She's back on Marco."

"Okay." Pocketing the phone, Winner faced Kipp. "Maude asked to meet with me. I said okay. She'll be here this afternoon."

Throwing an arm around her narrow shoulder, Kipp gave her a hug. "I'm proud of you." He was about to say, "You followed my advice," but he thought better of it. "I'll be here for you, sunshine," he said instead. "If Maude lifts a finger against you, I'll come running."

Who knows what memories she's wrestling with.

323

"Just remember. Even if I weren't here for you, Winner, you still wouldn't be alone."

"What do you mean by that?"

"You'll figure it out—one of these days." He heard a distant rumble of thunder. "Time to go in."

"Good. I just realized. I don't enjoy tennis anymore. From now on, let's play pickle ball. Okay?"

***

An hour after serving lunch, Lissette stole quietly into Heston's study. She saw Winner and Kipp, sitting together, chatting. Lissette broke in on their conversation.

"Excuse me, Miss Winston. Your . . . *mother* is here. She's waiting in the living room." Lissette tossed her head twice, indicating Maude's presence in another part of the house.

Kipp tenderly patted Winner's shoulder. "I'll be right here. Call if you need me."

"You're not going in there with me?"

Kipp shook his head. "Go on. Face your giants."

Gathering all her strength and courage, Winner walked into the living room. From the back, Maude still looked beautiful. Only when she turned around, revealing her pathetic face, Winner drew back involuntarily.

"Pretty bad, huh?" Maude said to her. Even the voice sent chills down Winner's spine.

Steeling herself, she entered living room. She did not invite her unwelcome guest to sit down, nor did she herself take a seat.

"Thank you for agreeing to see me—so soon after your ordeal."

"You've been through an ordeal of your own." She did not know what to call this woman.

"I remember this room quite well," said Maude airily. "Your father threw me out of it bodily." Her voice softened. "Heston was protecting you—from me." She resumed a light tone. "It's been redecorated. Not my taste, but—"

Winner remained cold. "It's not your home anymore." She heard her mother's sharp intake of breath.

"No. It's not. But you're still my daughter, Winston. Nothing can change that."

"You changed it. Fifteen years ago." Winner's teeth chattered, her rage laced with fear.

"What has changed—is me," Maude said softly. "I'm different now. I've . . . learned what a fool I was. I was—vain. conceited, cocky." She faced Winner squarely. "Now look at me."

Winner looked. What she saw was heartbreaking, and yet, behind the sad figure she caught a glimmer of—hope?

Her mother continued. "After the palsy came, I started attending religious retreats. I knew I had done wrong—a lot of wrong. I realized I needed salvation." She lifted her gaze. "I found it."

"I-I don't know what to say—"

"I wanted to find you, honey—to beg your forgiveness. But a court order prevented me—until now. It doesn't apply anymore."

Winner tried to understand. "So, you came looking for me?"

Maude took a tissue from her purse and dabbed her nose. "No." She sighed. "What happened was this: I spotted Danny Vega in Naples last week. He didn't recognize me, but I recognized him. And I followed him. All the way to Orlando. To you."

Inside, Winston cringed. Her palms felt damp. "Why?"

Rolling her eyes, her mother turned away. "Oh, honey." She turned back, facing Winner. "I don't want to hurt you. Please believe me."

Winner licked her lips. "Hurt me . . . how?"

The woman who was her natural mother took a deep breath. "Danny Vega and I were lovers years ago. For a very short time. About a week. After I had divorced your father."

Winner felt sick. "Oh, my—"

Maude's volume rose. "Before Danny ran out on me, he rolled me."

Winner's heart raced. She grasped onto a chair back. "He what? What does that mean?"

"Stole all my money. Jewelry. Credit cards. Wiped out my bank account. Left me broke, alone, and stranded. While I was high and sleeping it off. I was high all the time in those days."

"I knew he had rolled you. I overheard your conversation with him in Orlando."

Dismayed, Maude threw her hands up. They fell at her side. "When I saw you walk out of that elevator and he kissed you, I thought I would die. It was like the earth had opened up and swallowed me down."

Winner covered her ears. "You don't have to—"

"I knew who you were instantly. I'd been following your career. Collecting pictures of you." She ambled slowly around the room. Her hostility surfaced. "I wanted to kill him, Heaven help me. But I didn't. Instead. I confronted him."

Winner could still hear the hollow words.

Maude gaped, "Heaven has forgiven me. That I know. But—can you forgive me, Winston? Will you forgive me? Do you forgive me? Believe me, I'm still trying to forgive myself—for what I did to you—and your father—and other people who crossed my path. My unborn children—"

"You mean—?"

Daughter and mother eyed each other, as eternity hung in the balance.

"It will take time," said Winner, at last.

"Oh, well." Maude visibly relaxed. "That's another thing I've learned, Win. Things take time. Everything does."

"I can't promise anything."

"Except that you'll try?"

"Yes. Except that."

"It's a beginning," whispered Maude, who suddenly was crying in deep heaving sobs.

Tentatively, abandoning the safety of distance, Winner stepped towards her grieving mother and stroked her forearm. "Don't worry, Mommy. I'm not going to marry Danny Vega. Danny's history."

Suddenly, Poppy's voice sounded down the hall. "Where's Winner?"

Winner heard footsteps running towards the living room. Looking around, she beheld Poppy, who halted, catching her breath, in the foyer.

"Guess what!" Poppy exclaimed. "Your father wiggled his toes."

Chapter Twenty

Heston sat in his wheelchair, outside, alone, on his Port Royal estate's boat dock on Naples Bay. The sky was overcast, so the bay waters appeared slate gray. The marshy odor of the mangroves, far across the expanse of water, reached his nose. It was a good smell, one he'd missed.

The dock seemed empty without *Windswept,* although his children's small pleasure vessels now commandeered much of the dock space. Still recovering from his surgery, Heston felt forlorn, forgotten, and frightened of the future.

During the past few days—transitioning from the hospital in Orlando to the confines of the home he had once shared with Poppy—he had been coming to grips with his condition. Physically paralyzed below the waist, he felt as if each emotion had intensified beyond recognition: his past regrets, his love for Poppy and the kids; the fear of being an invalid forever; the terror of impending old age and the fading of his beauty and influence.

Throughout this ordeal, Poppy had been a brick. He hated having her see him this way—weak, ineffectual, flaccid, unmanned. Like a fool, he had overcompensated.

"You know what I want to do to you, don't you?" He had rasped into her ear the details of his lustful longings.

"My darling," she had responded, stroking his cheek. "Be patient. Please. All in good time."

"Or not," he had replied, his tone, acidic.

Then he had moved his toes. Aloud to no one but the pelicans, he snarled. "Even at this point, my full recovery is a crap shoot." Hellish to admit, he feared he might never again be strong enough to satisfy her.

The past few days, since leaving the hospital in Orlando, had been drudgery, endless rounds of bland meals, shaving, sponge baths, being hoisted into bed and out again each morning. Lissette was a great help, as was the male attendant who helped to hoist him, as well as with intimate routines such as wound cleansing, bandaging, and the calls of nature. Each day Heston had done battle with worry. Whenever he was alone, he fought a tendency to catastrophize.

He tried to implement what he had learned during the months he spent in the ashram, prior to joining Bill's flock. Bill had phoned him two or three times, plying him with spiritual sustenance, for which Heston was grateful. Between Bill and Kipp, he felt he had a fighting chance.

He gulped down tears.

How did I descend to this low point in my life?

In years gone by, after abandoning his acting career, he had taken up metaphysical studies. He had lost interest in painting by then. Instead of expressing his creativity, he had gone inward, searching for his soul.

It was at that time that he had first gone into seclusion on Heart of Fire Key, there reading, studying, meditating, contemplating. Alone, he had had an epiphany, realizing in a flash of insight, that there is but one moment, the eternal now.

At that time, he had realized that his whole life prior to that moment had been lived in the ego. Eventually, desiring to seek knowledge from experts, he roamed the country, the world, always *incognito.* oftentimes scruffy. He had learned to operate in the world as a "normal" human. Because he no longer looked enough like his movie-star image for people to recognize him, he was able to live the part he had chosen for himself, the final one being Tom Roberts.

Through a series of hard knocks, he had come to relate to others as this regular guy. Whenever he'd felt that others were getting too close—

or beginning to suspect his true identity—he would move on. During this period, he did not have sexual relationships. Technically still married to Poppy, he eventually attempted to experience the life of a monk—a spiritual seeker like the man he had portrayed in his last film. Sometimes, he'd lost the battle, but mostly not.

Long enough to know that I don't enjoy celibacy.

Ultimately, he had come to accept that he was both a spiritual and a material being. It was at this point in his personal evolution that Montserrat Flynn had died. It was at this juncture, this moment of epiphany, that DeAngelo had found him praying a prayer of gratitude on the steps of St. Mary's of the Seven Sorrows.

Heston had realized how deeply he loved Poppy and his children. In that moment of clarity—he wondered— whether, perhaps, there was a way to combine his dual nature—by being of service to humanity, the planet, and the Higher Power was a more worthy life goal than the pursuit of fame, material wealth, and ego-driven artistic output—for the sake his aggrandizing his ego.

Shouldn't art express something greater than puny human conceit? Shouldn't it express its true Creator, rather than its human creator? Even be directed to produce what a greater will would have one produce?

His own output, he realized, had always been about glorifying himself or making a buck. Lost in thought, he watched the pelicans roosting on his backyard boat dock. Looking out across Naples Bay, he thought about the lush mangroves and the non-human life that teemed within them, then laughed at himself for over-dramatizing.

I'm starting to sound like Kipp.

The ideas kept coming. Kipp's influence on his thought was apparent. Kipp's own beliefs were becoming his.

Belief . . .

What did he believe about his own life now? Had he been put here to serve the greater good? Had he received the gift of beauty in order to put him in a position to serve the others, rather than himself—like his son, Kipp, had been doing secretly, in microcosm, but now Kipp was going public with his gift. Kipp, too, was a beautiful man, and he had discovered his own goodness, at last.

It's a brave choice my son is making.

Heston knew himself to be in an elevated position of wealth, able to do something not in microcosm, but on a grand scale, for greater good. True, he had done some things already. After Franco's death, he had established the Foundation for young athletes.

See, I've done good in the world. But it's not enough.

That act was his first step on the path to his destiny. Sitting in his wheelchair, he believed he was being tested. What action would he take?

He knew now he had been put here and given these gifts in order to help humanity, indeed all living things, Life itself, to evolve to a higher plane of Love and Understanding. Kipp had discovered this fact years ago.

Now it's my turn, although I don't have Kipp's talent for it.

But as a man with the great financial and public-relations power, he could do something to help humanity evolve to the next level of 'Cosmic Consciousness,' as Kipp would say.

But how? Write? Speak? Pray? Seek truth?

He could preach against the evils of war, violence, bloodshed, hatred, bigotry, injustice. Yet, that seemed so vague. He was a specific person. He needed as specific purpose, a specific goal and a plan to reach it. But any plans he made would be contingent—upon whether or not he would recover the use of his legs. Centering himself, he clutched the handrails of his wheelchair.

If only I had created something real—not make-believe silliness—to glorify my Maker.

Then he realized: he had, inadvertently, created something real. He had created Kipp. And Winner and Sage and Tegan and Dakota and, may he rest in peace, Franco.

Co-created . . .

Realizing this fact, Heston relaxed somewhat.

I'm off to a good start.

Lost in thought, he heard footsteps approached him from behind.

***

"Sun's going down, Dad. Time to come in."

Kipp's husky voice startled Heston into awareness. The hour was late. "Yes. I wouldn't want to miss my prune-juice cocktail," Heston replied.

"Aw, come on. Lighten up, man. This too shall pass." Grasping the handles on the back of Heston's wheelchair, Kipp guided him towards the sliding-glass doors off the kitchen.

"Think so?"

"Know so. I was right before, wasn't I?" Kipp said, stopping. "Besides, I'll tell you a secret. It doesn't really matter what I think. It's what you think—what you believe—and what you do about it—that matters."

"I—"

Kipp walked around the chair and stood in front of Heston. "You've faced challenges and been victorious, Dad. Many times. This is just one more of those times."

"It's a big 'one of those.'"

"Yes, but you're a big guy." He tapped Heston's chest. "In here. Where it counts." He tapped Heston's forehead. "And in here. Where the visioning takes place. Imagination is your thing, Dad. You're a creative artist. Manifesting—well, it should be a piece of cake for the likes of you."

"Hmm."

"Sure. Put it all together—vision, believe, do the hard work required—the physical therapy, the exercising, eating right, praying prayers of faith and gratitude—"

"Oh."

"Just remember, Dad. It has to happen inside you before it can happen on the physical plane."

"It?" Heston felt befuddled. "Maybe I've had too much given to me—*por nada*. Son, I've been thinking of selling Heart of Fire Key. Although I just missed the deadline for accepting a very generous offer. Still—"

Kipp scratched a stubbled chin. "Sure you want to do that, Dad?"

"Don't want me to?"

"Not really. I got plans. Like to run 'em by you."

"Yes?"

"Kind of like to check the place out myself. See if my plans might work—there." He pursed his lips. "It's been a while since I was on the island. The last time I sailed my sloop to Heart of Fire was at least three years ago."

"I'd like to go there with you."

"Great. It's a plan, Stan."

"It's a date, mate—once I'm out of this blasted forsaken contraption." He slapped the handles of his wheelchair and grimaced ferociously. Defiantly, he wiggled his toes and laughed.

"After my court date, we can discuss the timing." Grasping the handles, Kipp wheeled the chair back down the dock, onto the paved pathway around the tennis court and, at last, through the kitchen's back door. "Hey, Dad, Winner's real mom came to visit her today. They . . . kind of . . . reconnected."

"Will wonders never cease?"

"No, never, Dad. Not as long as you keep believing they're possible. Hey, Dad . . . there's something I need to tell you about the diary."

"Forget it, son. It's too late."

In the kitchen, Lissette was talking on the phone. "Oh, here he is," she said, handing the phone to Heston. "It's Mr. Nick. I think he's figured out the whole thing. He wants to explain everything—who did it and why they did it. He's confirming his lunch appointment with you tomorrow. He wants us all to have a big meeting," she babbled, as Heston tore the phone from her hand and slapped it to his own ear. "Even me," she said to Kipp. "I wonder why?"

***

On the morrow, at 11:00 a.m., sharp, eleven anxious people seated themselves in Heston's study. choosing their seats from various sofas and chairs, crowding the intimate space. Each person faced forward, towards Heston, who, as head of the household, sat ensconced in a wheelchair behind his own massive desk. Nick Townsend was standing at his side, slightly in front of the desk. Nick, too, faced the assembly, dead on.

"Thank you all for coming today," Nick said to the apprehensive group.

Hurriedly, Winner rose from her seat. "Nick? May I say some-thing—to everyone—before you go any farther?"

Reluctantly, Nick let loose the reins. "Sure, cupcake. Go ahead."

Turning to the group, Winner spoke. "I want to offer all of you an apology. Especially my father. If not for me, and my stupid surprise

334

party idea, none of you would be here. None of this would have happened." She indicated Heston. "My dad wouldn't be paralyzed." The words were hard for her to say. "I'm sorry." She addressed Nick. "That's all I wanted to say. It's all my fault."

Dignified, she resumed her seat beside Ezra on the couch. Ezra's arm wrapped round her sleeveless shoulders. Relieved that her little speech had gone as planned, Winner settled in to listen to Nick's comments.

"Win, I'm sure we all appreciate your sentiments," said Nick, indicating the group assembled before him and Heston. "But I beg to differ. This was not all your fault."

"Here-here," said Heston, catching her eye and nodding.

Nick proceeded. "On the contrary, Winner, you, as much as anyone in this room, are a victim of a murderous plot concocted by a troubled mind. And I think," he emphasized, "that we all know who I mean."

"Adair Champlain," said Ezra, beside her, his voice resonating.

"Not a bullseye, Gold," Nick countered. "But close." He looked to the back of the room. "You know who I mean, don't you, Tropica?" The sultry singer was seated beside her mother, Lissette. Lissette studied the floor.

"Yes," said Tropica. "I know who."

Nick addressed the gathering. "That's why I brought Tropica with me today. She and I have come to an agreement." He turned to Winner. "Her future depends on you now, Win."

"Me?"

Nick spoke to Tropica. "Tell us your story, please, young lady."

Belying her usual agility, Tropica rose awkwardly from her seat, as if gravity were a force too strong for her to overcome. Supportive, Lissette squeezed Tropica's hand, then let go.

335

"I'll tell you guys what happened to me," said Tropica. "Not that's it's any excuse. It's not. I made the choices. But I hope you'll understand why." She looked at Heston. "I'm sorry, too, Heston. I had no idea—"

"Just explain," Nick prompted her from the front of the room. All heads remained turned in Tropica's direction. Tropica swallowed hard.

"Hailey Champlain came to me. Wait, that's not right. Hailey summoned me. Like a lackey. Around the first of November. She wooed me, I guess you might say."

"Seduced you?" asked Ezra. "Hailey liked girls—and boys."

"Hailey liked you, Ezra," Tropica replied evenly. "Only you didn't know it."

"What? Forget about it." Ezra withdrew his arm from Winner's shoulders. He leaned forward in his seat, his elbows propped on his knees.

"Hailey was obsessed with you, Ezra. She had been since her childhood," Nick said.

"You're nuts."

Tropica went on. "You were oblivious, Ezra. She was infatuated with you. When she realized you were seriously in love with Winner, Hailey lost it. She decided to destroy Win." She looked pleadingly at Nick. "But I didn't know what her purpose was. Honestly, when—"

"When what, Felicia?" asked Heston in a low baritone.

"When she told me what she wanted me to do."

"Which was?" asked Poppy, seated in the front row, near the big desk.

Eyes filled with pain, Tropica glanced down at her mother. Her gaze returned to Poppy. "Hailey ordered me to steal the dolls from Winner's collection. She knew about the dolls. Win had described them to her. She had buddied up to Winner by then. Taken her barhopping in New York.

By hook and crook, she ended up producing Ezra's series and everything."

"On purpose," added Nick. "To gain access to Ezra—and Winner."

"I thought Adair Champlain was the nut case," yipped Tegan. The nubile, adolescent redhead sat squeezed in between her twin sister, Sage, and brother, Dakota, who appeared to be bored.

"He had a lot of his own issues, Teggie," Nick responded carefully. "But Hailey—"

"Despised Adair," whispered Tropica. "Only I didn't know that either." Tropica's struggle to express herself seemed excruciating. "I told Hailey Winner was my best friend. I refused to steal the dolls. I told her my mom's job would be in jeopardy—if anyone found out."

"But you had access," Poppy said, putting the pieces together. "You joined us for Thanksgiving. That's when you swiped the first two dolls, isn't it? Then you returned here—right before coming to Orlando—to visit your mom—ostensibly. And that's when you stole the third doll from Winner's bedroom. You knew right where it was."

"You were here the day I buried it under the bed," said Winner to her childhood friend.

"So that's how she knew," Kipp said, applauding. "I was wondering."

Tropica blurted out, "Poppy, Hailey blackmailed me. Isn't that what you call it?" She looked to Nick, who nodded in the affirmative. She continued, now petitioning Winner directly. "Oh, Win, I'm so sorry. I had to do it because—get this, Win—Hailey threatened to murder my mom—if I didn't."

Tortured, Lissette stifled a cry. Poppy regarded her worriedly.

Kipp interjected. "You believed her?"

"Yes!" cried Tropica. "Why shouldn't I have? See what she did to Heston—and Ezra—and what she was planning to do to her own poor brother! I would have been a fool to doubt her. Hailey Champlain scared the living shit out of me."

"Language," said Dakota, idly playing with his own shoelaces.

"Fe, what was she planning to do to Adair?" Winner asked.

Nick took over. "Have a seat, please, Tropica. I'll take it from here." Trembling, Tropica resumed her seat. "Before I go any further, I want to be sure that all of you to know Hailey Champlain is dead."

"Dead?" A buzz went round the room.

"Quiet, please." Nick said. "After mounting the attack at the theme park, Hailey fled the police. She ran back to the Enchanted Palace and up the stairs of the nearest turret. Once there, she jumped."

"But why?" Winner demanded, sickened by the thought.

Nick turned his attention to Dakota. "Want to tell them why, son?"

Without looking up, Dakota continued to play with his shoelaces. "I ran after her. She ran up the turret staircase. I ran right behind her. When she got the top, I didn't stop. I almost had her, but that's when she jumped."

"Honey," Poppy put a hand to her mouth. "Why didn't you tell us?"

"He told me," Nick said. "What Dakota just told you was true. What he left out was the part where he stopped to pick up her weapons. He was pointing the gun at Hailey when she jumped."

The group reacted in stony silence. No one knew what to say.

Nick pushed ahead, sharing the results of his investigation. "I've discussed the whole affair with Adair yesterday. I've come up with a theory." Nick pursed his lips.

"Where is Adair?" asked Ezra. "I assume you have him stashed somewhere."

"Adair is in custody. Right now, he's in psychiatric lock-up. In a secure facility."

"Can what he said be trusted?" Poppy asked.

"No, but I have concrete evidence that confirms the salient facts. Hailey kept notes on her electronic devices. I've got a warrant and was able to search her writings."

"So, what exactly is your theory, Nick?" asked Heston. "About Hailey's motive?"

"My theory is that Hailey was stricken with guilt, remorse, and fury—during the attack itself—when she realized that she had stabbed Ezra instead of Winner—and that Ezra had thrown himself under her blade to protect Win. That's when Hailey dropped her weapons and rushed back up the stairs to the turret of the Enchanted Palace and jumped."

Silence blanketed the assembly.

Lissette rose. "We need coffee. I'll make some."

"Sit down, Lissette. You're still part of us. Listen to Nick," Heston said.

Lissette sat down.

Approving, Nick carried on. "See, folks, it was like this. Little Hay-Hay had hatched a big, evil plan. But it was about more than just possessing Mr. Gold here. Though, to be honest, I haven't yet figured out why she found him so attractive in the first place."

"Kiss my ass," growled Ezra, scowling.

"Language," cried Dakota and Tegan in unison. They pulled pinkies. Tegan giggled.

"The poor kid," Ezra muttered, to no one in particular. "I had no idea—oh, hell. Maybe I did. But I tried not to encourage her. I wasn't attracted to her. She used to fawn over me. Vivian thought it was cute—"

"Now I get it," said Winner. "When I think back on the things Hailey said and did—she was hot for you, Ezra."

Ezra snorted.

"But, Ezzie, you weren't the only prize," Nick said, "No, Hailey's plan was to gain control over the entire Champlain fortune—which is ginormous—and to have Ezra—and to rid herself of the duty to her needy baby brother. To be free. In other words, ladies and gents, Hailey Champlain was a woman who wanted it all."

"What's wrong with that?" asked Tegan bluntly.

Heston lectured his daughter. "Everything, Teggie. Hailey tried to steal and kill her way to happiness."

"Whick never works," observed Kipp.

"Sure as hell didn't work this time," Ezra said. Leaning back, he took Winner's hand in his and squeezed it.

She squeezed back but did not smile. As her eyes met his, she felt her cheeks flame. Ashamed, she turned away from his intimate gaze. Outside the window, blue sky and white clouds, green grass and mani-cured shrubs—*so serene.*

"You were onto Hailey from the beginning. Eh, Nick?" Heston asked, commanding Winner's attention once again.

"You were sleuthing? We thought you were—attracted to her," said Poppy.

"That's what I wanted y'all to think," Nick said knowingly. "That get-up of hers? Looking like Winner? Dressing like her. Cozying up to her. Strange. To me, it was a big, rippling red flag. Something isn't right here." He smiled. "So, I spent some time with the woman—feeling her out. Got what I needed and—"

"And solved the case," said Sage, who had listened raptly to the en-tire proceedings. "Handily done, Mr. Townsend."

"Thank you, Sage-girl. I wish I had figured it out before the roof caved in. But the whole thing was pretty sinister, and I'll tell you how." Nick wasn't finished. "See, Hailey wore that get-up for more than one reason. It was also part of her—let's call it seduction—aimed at Adair.

340

Adair was obsessed with Heston and Heston's character, King Odysseus: Alien Space Warrior. And without his meds—which Hailey controlled, by the way—Adair couldn't tell reality from fantasy."

"Which was what Hailey wanted?" asked Heston. "Is that what you mean?"

"Yes. Her first goal was to eliminate you, Heston, and then Winner. That's because she was framing her pathetic, delusional brother for your death—and she wanted Winner to be caught in the crossfire. That way, Hailey herself could not be blamed. All the guilt for the two murders would fall onto Adair."

"Adair was Hailey's fall guy?" Kipp quipped.

"I don't understand," said Poppy. "If that's true, then why did she participate in the attack itself?"

"All I can do is theorize—based on the science, of course, and Hailey's written notes—but I think Hailey lost control of herself at the last minute. Take it with a grain of salt, but Adair told me yesterday that Hailey had convinced him to kill Heston. Hailey's notes and the device itself indicate she had arranged for the drone to shoot at Winner. She had arranged things so that the drone would be attributed to Adair. Hailey had a high IQ. She wasn't the dumb bunny she pretended to be. She just wanted us to believe she was an airhead. It was part of the frame."

"I was a marked man, regardless," Heston said, half to himself.

"You bet your life, you were." Nick speculated. "Maybe the pressure on Hailey became too great. Could be that her bizarre behavior was caused by psychotropic drugs. Forensics says she was loaded to the gills that day. No prescriptions in her name, however."

Ezra leaned against Winner. "I told you abusing that shit can be dangerous," he whispered.

Tropica spoke up. "People that rich can buy all the drugs they want, anytime," she said meekly. "I know personally—Hailey was having wild mood swings. I tell you, she was one scary broad."

"Rest in peace," said Lissette, making the sign of the cross.

"Amen," Kipp said to Lissette.

Nick checked his time on his smartphone and then continued. "All that cutesy junk? Spider-Girl was spinning her wicked, little web."

"Why did she dress like me?" asked Winner. "If she hated me so much. Why not Poppy?"

"Isn't it obvious?" said Heston. "She wanted to attract Ezra. Ezra was attracted to you."

"There was something fraudulent about Hailey," observed Poppy. "I picked up on that." She shook her index finger. "You know, I'll bet she got that idea from watching Adair imitate Heston."

Ezra spoke up. "All this stuff supports my own theory, the one I've never mentioned to anybody."

"Which is what?" asked Nick.

"That it wasn't Adair's father—Old Truett III—who brutalized him as a boy. It was his sister."

Nick whistled. "Neat. I concur."

Ezra tilted his head. "Hailey always claimed that Truett had been responsible for Adair's mental problems."

"Little Hailey was piece of work," said Kipp. "Tragic soul"

Nick pointed his way. "She knew all about you, Kipp. I've looked through her files."

Heston interjected his own thoughts. "She knew Kipp was alive." He caught Tropica's eye. "She tried to blackmail me with the knowledge—the same way she tried to blackmail you."

"Wow," said Tropica.

"Hailey had a third motive, too, Nick, for bumping me off. She wanted my Cedric Spicer canvases. I told her they weren't for sale."

Nick looked smug. "Know why she wanted them?"

"I'm afraid to ask," said Heston.

"One of the reasons Hailey did not inherit along with Adair was because she wasn't really old Truett's biological daughter."

"No. Stop." Poppy buried her face in her hands. "I don't believe it. No wonder Wallace left him." She noticed Nick looking puzzled. "Wallace was my partner. We owned an art gallery. He and Cedric were—an item—in their younger days. Cedric was bisexual." She glanced at her children, who were all ears.

Ezra was in denial. "Cedric Spicer was Hailey's father?"

"Indeed," Nick confirmed. "She'd had her DNA tested. She was convinced he was."

"The old tomcat. He got around, didn't he?" Heston mused. Restless, he rolled his wheelchair back and forth. He appeared to be growing stronger. "In a nutshell, Nick, please. Give us your blow-by-blow account of the crime. Then we'll eat lunch."

"Good. I'm ready." Nick said, accepting the challenge. "Here's the way the crime came down, people. About six weeks ago, Hailey gets her bright idea. Then she starts to move. She agrees to produce Ezra's pilot, and gets Adair to finance it, but only if Adair stars. Ezra agrees. He has already enlisted Winner."

Ezra shook his head. "I should have known."

"Hardly," said Heston. "Hailey was shrewd—and a pretty good actress herself, I might add."

"Indeed she was," said Nick. "She'd studied acting. Anyway, our little chick continued to hatch her plan to off Winner, her competition. She wooed Tropica. Had her steal the first two dolls from this house during Thanksgiving dinner. Then, when Heston turned up out of the blue, Hailey saw an opportunity to rid herself of both Winner and Adair at the same time. Her scheme evolved."

"This is priceless," Sage commented, thoroughly engaged. Beside her on the sofa, Dakota yawned.

"Be that as it may," Nick said, eyebrow arched. "Hailey got creative. Keep in mind, Hailey made Adair believe it was his idea. Setting him up to take the fall. She plays into Adair's fantasies about Heston and Odysseus, and convinces Adair—while she's manipulating his medications, mind you—that he is the real Heston Demming, the real Odysseus, and that our Heston was the pretender, the phony Alien Space Warrior. All the while, she's trying to attract Ezra's attention, all by imitating Winner."

Winner shuddered in disgust.

"Not even close," Ezra reassured her.

"Then," Nick continued, "Hailey goes into action. She insists Ezra offer Heston a role in the series—on Heston's private island."

"Insists?" Heston said. Grimacing, Ezra waved a hand dismissively.

"Using an underwater-craft, she takes Adair to Heart of Fire Key and has him act out his fantasies while he plants the first mutilated doll—the Princess Daphne action figure. Then they leave the island by night and re-board their waiting ship, which I happened to see in the fog."

Heston tuned to Kipp. "I thought it was your sloop. Scared me senseless 'cause I wasn't alone."

"In between all this, she's sending violent, obscene text messages to Winner."

"You traced them?"

"No. Hailey's notes told the story. After each text, she would toss the cheap phone into a river, bay, or whatever."

"Devious."

"See, Danny Vega wasn't part of Hailey's plan, but she knew about him. She had your whole family thoroughly investigated by the best private eyes money can buy. That's how she knew about—" Nick stopped talking and glanced at Heston. "Anyway" he resumed, "that's how she knew about Kipp's being alive and about the party and Win's trysts with Damian and so on."

Poppy looked puzzled. "What about the flower wreaths at Franco's grave? Wasn't Hailey sending those, too?"

"Absolutely," replied Nick. He glanced at Winner. "That was part of the frame she was arranging for Adair. According to the florist, those were sent by Adair Champlain, but Hailey's records indicate she sent them."

"Did Hailey send me roses?" Poppy asked.

"No," said Nick. "That was Adair, in one his delusional episodes—when he believed he was Heston and you were his wife."

"Wouldn't you know," said Poppy smugly.

"Once everyone had registered at the hotel in Orlando, Hailey bribed a chambermaid to plant the second doll—"

"Daddy as Odysseus," injected Winner.

"Yeah, and this time, Hailey was buttering up Winner, while secretly plotting her death, and she was kissing up to Ezra, trying to entice him—uh, romantically."

"Spare me," said Ezra.

"At the party," said Heston, "Adair threatened me, in a veiled way."

"All facilitated and encouraged by Hailey," replied Nick.

"Then what?" asked Kipp. "This is fascinating, even though I wasn't there."

"I think it was around that time," said Nick, "that Hailey must have learned about you being alive, Kipp. That's when she had Tropica steal the third doll, the pop-idol doll. And she was becoming more and more anxious about Ezra's infatuation with Winner, so she upped her game. Once she had the doll, she took Adair to the movie studio—to which they had access, as producers. There, they planted the doll and arranged the light-drop. Listen, folks. Hailey was something of a digital genius."

"But the falling light missed me," said Heston.

"I yelled, remember?" said Ezra. "You stepped out of the way."

"She missed you on purpose with that light fixture. She wanted to scare you, Heston—scare you into talking. You didn't cooperate. So, Hailey went full-blown: the drone attack. It was an easy thing to arrange from her vantage point, the Grand Suite on the 16th floor of the hotel. Much easier than picking you and Win off one at a time."

"Stop!" cried Tropica. "This whole thing makes me sick." She rubbed her forehead.

"Sorry, Tropica," said Kipp kindly. "I have one more question. Who made the offer to buy Heart of Fire Key from Dad? Was that Hailey, too?"

"Oh, that. Yes. No. That was Adair. Beneath a corporate shield. All part of Hailey's frame up."

"Poor Adair," said Sage.

"He can be lucid, when he's taking the right medication at the right times, which is what he's doing now and will be doing from now on. He'll be incarcerated for life but heavily supervised. He's not responsible for his actions."

"He was easy to dupe. Poor fellow," Heston observed.

"One final note," said Nick. "In case you're wondering, the Champlain empire will be turned over to distant relatives. The rest you already know," said Nick finally. "By the way, when Maude showed up, and Hailey caught wind of the fact that Winner and Danny were history—leaving the field wide open for Ezzie—I think that's when Hailey freaked out, started OD-ing on the psyche meds. Just my speculation, but that's what makes sense, considering the facts of the case."

Winner looked sheepish. "I think I even gave her some." She slapped her own forehead. "Idiot."

Nick contemplated Winner. "Ms. Demming, about the only question left to be answered is this one: are you going to forgive your Best Friend Forever over there, or are you going to press charges against her?" He indicated Tropica, who huddled in the back of the room.

"Charges?" Winner gaped.

"For theft and accessory to attempted murder, Ladybug," said Heston. "That's what Nick is implying."

Nick nodded, a serious look on his face.

Winner gazed across the room. Tropica was crying. Her hands covered her face. Winner looked back at Nick. "No. No charges." She looked at Poppy. "If a powerful, crazy person had threatened to kill Poppy, I would have done the same thing Fe did."

Moved, Poppy sniffed.

"Good girl," Heston whispered under his breath. Kipp caught her eye and grinned, thumbs up.

"May we go to lunch now?" Poppy asked both hosts and guests.

"By all means," said Heston

Winner's tummy growled. "You guys may not believe this—but I'm actually hungry."

"On the terrace, everyone. Follow Lissy, please," Heston announced, adding in a low voice, "And I refuse to eat any more gelatin."

As the group stood and dispersed, Nick approached Winner, who had risen from her seat and was holding Ezra's hand.

"Win," said Nick, "there is one more question you need to answer for me."

"Oh? What's that, Nick?" Winner asked. "Good job, by the way."

"Are you going to put this poor fool out of his misery and marry his ass?"

"Meaning me?" Ezra growled.

"Oh, Nicky," Winner began. She felt a tap on her shoulder. Turning, she beheld Tropica, who embraced her, blubbering like a big, sultry baby. Looking over Tropica's shoulder, Winner caught sight of Ezra's face.

Silently, as the room cleared around him, Ezra mouthed the words, "I will make love to you." Indicating his hidden bandages, he added, aloud. "It's just a matter of when." Then he sauntered from the room.

***

Six days later, in his private suite at the Edgewater Beach Hotel in Naples, Ezra sat nursing a glass of wine. Winner was curled up beside him on the loveseat. She no longer looked like the kid, even though she was wearing pink flannel pajamas and fuzzy bedroom slippers. At Ezra's invitation, on the previous evening, she had joined him in the suite. Still, nothing had happened between them, except that they had slept together in the same bed and spent the day on the beach. Now evening was falling.

She, too, was sipping wine. "You were the real target of the stalker all along, Ezra. Not me, not Daddy, not Kipp—but you. Hailey Champlain was obsessed with you."

Ezra scratched his chin. "I don't want to talk about it."

"She must have had a reason."

He adjusted his shirt collar. "I don't know. I was a man. I was there. I was kind to Hailey when no one else was."

"Maybe she found you attractive. Did you lead her on?"

"No! Let's forget the whole thing. Let's talk about your ill-fated romance. What do you say?"

"If you insist." Winner pondered her past. "Obviously, Danny Vega wasn't like you. He wasn't nice all the time." Provocatively, she stretched out her legs. Her fuzzy slippers brushed the leg of his trousers.

Is Ezra going to make good on his promise?

"I'm not nice all the time." Ezra rubbed her ankles, then withdrew his hand. "No, you're right, Win. He was a loser. He hurt you. What if you hadn't found out? He would have kept on hurting you for the rest of your life."

"Wow. That's true."

"Things between you would have gotten worse and worse. He might have killed you in the end, or one of your kids. You're not still carrying a torch for that guy, are you?"

"He paid attention to me, Ezzie."

"Yeah. Negative attention, Winner, the very thing your therapist has warned you against, time and again. You've told me so yourself." He leaned in, across her bent knees, and took her hands in his. "Winner, what you need—and deserve—is a man who loves you as you are—not some badass who's looking for someone to maim."

"Maim?"

"Yeah. Danny wanted to cripple you. He paid attention to you because he needs a victim to control. You were his willing victim. Do you get this at all?"

"I'm starting to," She whimpered. "Ezra, don't be mad at me."

"Oh, honey." Dropping her hands, Ezra stood. Pacing the floor, he rubbed the back of his neck. Turning around, he faced her. "How can I get you to see what I'm talking about? What do I have to do?"

"Ezra?"

"What?" He stopped pacing.

"Will you make love to me? Like you said? Are you—healed?"

"Oh—expletive! Double expletive." He ruffled his hair with both hands. "Winner, look—"

"You don't really want me, do you?"

Frustration overcame him. "Want you? Want you? I'd rather ravish you than do anything in this world. Oh, the things I want to do to you— but they're good things, Winner. Well, maybe not good. But things to make you *feel* good, not bad." He calmed himself down. "If I take advantage of you now, that puts me in the same league of users as Vega."

"Even if I want to be used?"

"Especially then."

Winner rose and walked to the mirror. She contemplated her own reflection, then turned to Ezra, who was leaning against the wall.

"Danny criticized everything about me. He hated everything I did, everything I said, everything I wore, the food I cooked, all the music I listened to. He hated my friends, my family, my opinions, my acting, my hair styles, my lovemaking—"

"No way."

She buried her face in her hands. "I'm so ashamed."

"I thought you told me you and Danny never—"

"Well, I mean, we kissed—and stuff like that." She howled in anguish. "Oh, Ezzie. I'm not the innocent babe you think I am. Not by a long shot. But I promise you, I never had intercourse with Danny Vega."

"I believe you."

"You do?"

He threw up his hands. "Winner, I'm the man who won't hurt you." He patted his own chest. "I'm the man who will be good to you. I trust you. I believe in you. I want the best for you. Are you hearing me? Earth to Princess Daphne. Come in, please." He paused to consider. "What would Captain Kirk do in a situation like this?"

Standing near the window, Ezra stared out at the stars. They were shining down on the mangrove swamp and the waters of Naples Bay. Somehow, in those few beats of silence, awareness dawned in Winner's mind. She tossed a throw pillow at his back.

"Yes."

Picking up the pillow, he tossed it onto the loveseat. "Come again?"

"Yes," she said. "I hear you now, Ezra. I don't know why, but—what you're saying makes—weird sense. I mean, it all fits."

He ran to her and hugged her to him. "Thank the—"

She returned his embrace. For a moment, they stood holding one another in silence. She liked the texture of him. He was solid, hairy, masculine, cuddly. She could feel the pounding of his heart, the rhythm of his breathing, the goodness in his soul, the truth of his manhood.

"Ezra?"

"Huh?"

"I accept your proposal of marriage."

Ezra touched his forehead to hers. "In that case, sweetie—"

"Yes?"

"I will make love to you right now." He kissed her lips.

She responded.

I like it.

She wanted him.

He pulled back, again touching his forehead to hers.

"Why did you stop?" she asked, breathing hard.

Taking her hand in his, he placed it strategically. "Are you very sure?" he asked. "Can you go through life with a name like Winner Gold?"

"Absolutely," she replied, unzipping his shorts as his kisses resumed.

Victorious, he guided her to the bed. Then he took her down.

Winner enjoyed her own victory, too. For the remainder of the evening, a single thought flickered in her mind, as she took her fill of Ezra Gold.

I knew I was going to love being married.

Chapter Twenty-One

Deep in conversation, Heston, Kipp, and Nick huddled around the driftwood bonfire they had built on the beach at Heart of Fire Key. The co-mingled scents of sea air and wood smoke hovered around them. Stars filled the night sky. One week had passed since Nick's revelations.

"I feel sorry for Adair Champlain," said Heston. "He was Hailey's pawn."

"Her victim—all his life," said Nick. He finished his cigarette and tossed the butt into the fire. "Last one," he announced. "I'm quitting again."

"Good man," said Heston, smoothing the blanket beneath him. He stretched out, full-length. "I rarely smoke anything."

"Most of all, I feel sorry for Hailey," said Kipp, seated on the ground beside Nick. "She was tortured soul. I wish I could have helped her before—there was no turning back."

"She should have been the star, not Adair," said Nick. "She was a better actor, but you're right, Kipp. She wasn't really as frivolous as she seemed. Maybe she didn't have the sense of play to be an actor. That's what it takes—I've decided—to be a pro."

"Acting is more than play," Heston retorted. "Much more. It's closer to religion than to show biz—in its essence."

"Performing in any capacity is," Kipp offered. "Being on stage. Like, center stage is the most intense."

Heston nodded. Light and shadow from the flickering flames played across the facial features of his two companions. Deep in the night, his thoughts were running deeper.

"Y'all channeling again?" Nick chided restlessly.

"It's not channeling," said Heston. "It's more like communing."

"With the Oneness," said Kipp, soft and low, barely audible above the ocean waves and crackling fire. "When you're onstage—commanding the stage—like when I'm singing a solo—it's like the whole energy of the universe is concentrated in you at that very moment, and—you're like—this—*prism* that shoots light energy out to everyone in the audience."

"That's not channeling?"

"No. It's much bigger. It's prayer, but not petitioning. It's—everything, all at once, surrounding you, immersing you, going through you."

"Coming back to you, too," interjected Heston. "From the audience . . . and the Higher Power."

"It's the Higher Power coming through you."

"Animating you," said Heston.

"Yeah!" Kipp beamed. "And add music to the mix? Whoa!"

Pocket knife in hand, Nick whittled a piece of driftwood. "If you ask me, acting is job like any other. Grown men paid to dress up like kids, pretending to be other people."

Kipp burst out in laughter.

"It's a living," quipped Heston.

"Too bad Ezra couldn't join us," said Kipp. "He and I—we made up, you know."

"Good," said Heston. "Ezra loves you."

"But you couldn't pry him away from Winner with a crowbar," Nick pronounced.

Heston tossed a stick into the fire. "He's writing a new script."

"Yeah?" Kipp asked, watching the stick catch flame. "No more werewolves and vampires? I hope."

"No mummies, either. No, it's about a pop star who saves the world."

"Clever," Nick said snidely. "You producing it, Heston?"

"Probably."

Nick harrumphed. "You artistic types don't know when to quit."

Kipp side-bumped Nick affectionately, as Nick shaped the piece of wood. "You don't fool me, Nicholas. You're an artist at heart." He nodded towards Nick's busy hands. "Everybody is. We're all co-creators, all aspects of the Creator."

"We are?"

"That's why we're here, man."

Heston rolled over and propped his head." The Reverend Bill might have something to say about that."

Nick said, "And he'd be right. Ain't one, but two. Heaven and hell."

Contemplating world views, Heston stretched his long legs towards the bonfire, feeling warmth on his now-functioning legs and feet. He was still cherishing the miracle of the return of feeling in his lower body. The three men contemplated without speaking. Heston broke the silence.

"Acting as we know it has evolved—descended from ancient men reenacting a hunt or doing a rehearsal for a successful hunt around a camp-fire—just like this one here. They'd dress in costumes, animal skins—"

Kipp applauded. "Yeah, it's spiritual in its beginning. From the Stone Age 'til right now. And going on into the future."

Nick admired his own handiwork. "So, you were paying attention in theater-history class. Eh, Professor?" He glanced Heston's way.

"Nice work," remarked Heston, staring at the tiny sculpture in Nick's hands. It seemed to dance in the flickering light.

"Greek theater was a high point, wasn't it, Dad?" Kipp asked, prodding for more.

"That was thousands of years later," Heston replied. "Men in masks acting out sacred dramas and comedies of myth and lore in outdoor amphitheaters. It was the origin of theater as we know it today." Curling up, he retracted his feet. "Sorry. I don't mean to sound so dry."

Nick carved as he spoke. "Well, I kind of see your point."

Heston sat up. "Anyway, I'm tired of Greek stuff. I never want to hear about King Odysseus or Princess Daphne again as long as I live."

"Suits me." Pocketing the knife and the small carving, Nick rose suddenly. "I'm going to the lagoon. Going to check my traps."

"Okay, man," waved Kipp, as Nick, brandishing a small flashlight, disappeared into the night.

Once Nick had departed, Heston turned to Kipp. "I hope you're grateful to Nick. Nick is a fine fellow."

"He knows how I feel." Kipp craned his neck, gazing up at the stars. "Hey, Dad. Since tonight's my last night as a free man, I'm glad I get to spend it with you." Shadows flitted across Kipp's face. His copper eyes revealed his apprehension.

Heston looked away. "Get set, boy. The media are going to eat you alive. After all, you're rising from the dead. About to ride the whirlwind."

"I'm all set—except I need to phone Cecily Hodges in the morning. I promised her an exclusive interview—before they put me in the pokey."

"She'll appreciate that. She's in love with you, you know. Wanted nothing to do with me."

Kipp hedged. "Yeah? Well, I'll have you know Beryl has my heart. If it weren't for Beryl—"

"What?"

"I might have become a priest. Or a monk. *Mira,* a hermit, living on top of a rock in the desert."

"Seriously?"

"Yes. Seriously." He looked into Heston's eyes. "Look, I hear what you're saying about Reverend Bill—about oneness versus duality."

"Okay."

"Dad, I need clarity. Who knows? I may become a minister. I do want to share the good news. But the way it was really intended, not the way it's often presented."

"Really?"

"Uh-huh. The way I believe it was meant to be interpreted, but I've got to pay my debt to society before I can spread the word."

"Yes. It's important to seem legitimate."

Kipp glared at him. "To be legit, Dad. Not to seem it."

"Right, son. I stand corrected."

"To be—a teacher—I have to first come clean with my family, myself, my public." Kipp stared into the flames. "I want to share what I've learned, so I've got to face the consequences of my actions first."

"What if you're in jail—for a while?"

Kipp shrugged. "I'll start a prison ministry. Been done before."

"I see."

"Do you, Dad?" Kipp regarded him affectionately. "I can preach love wherever I am, to whomever I'm with."

"Doctor Demming," Heston said, "You can preach love while you're setting a broken bone or bandaging a cut."

Resting on one elbow, Kipp stretched out. "Dad. Have you ever thought about, well, rebuilding that little church over there?" He indicated the ruined chapel.

"I don't know."

"We could attach a medical clinic to it." He chuckled. "If I'm here, I mean. I'd like to start my own mission. I've learned a lot over the past few years with Perfecto."

Heston squinted into the distant future. "Is that the plan you mentioned a couple of weeks back?"

"Yes. I hate to admit it, but I was thrilled when that corporate offer fell through."

"The sale wasn't meant to be," observed Heston "For one thing, I didn't reply in time. Then, when Hailey and Adair dropped out of the picture, the board of directors lost interest."

"I get it."

"I could list the property. Put it back on the market."

"No, Dad! Don't please!"

"You want it?"

Kipp became enthusiastic. "I want to use it."

Heston caught his son's fire. "I could rebuild the chapel while you're serving time."

Kipp leapt to his feet. "Beryl and Shawnee can help you, Dad. I'll help in any way I can."

"All right then. Will you help me with Dakota? I can't reach him."

Another son I've managed to alienate.

"Yes. Dakota needs spiritual help," Kipp agreed.

Encouraged, Heston approved. "Then Heart of Fire Key is no longer for sale," said Heston. "I bequeath it to you, Noel, my first-born son. Start your monastery, hospital, whatever you want, here."

Kipp became exuberant. "Dad, that's amazing." He lowered his gaze, then looked at his father. "I'll draw students and seekers from all around globe."

Heston grinned. "Maybe a few musicians and artists, too?"

"And writers," Kipp said, kicking sand onto an escaping spark.

"Maybe your mother would finally come to like this place," said Heston.

Kipp snapped his fingers. "Maybe Beryl and Shawnee could come, and live here—on the island—while I'm in the slam? Get things going?"

"Might work."

"Thanks, Dad," Kipp said hoarsely. "I will make you proud one day."

"I couldn't be any prouder of you than I am right now, son."

"You know, Dad, I've always been a big fan of yours."

"As have I, of yours, son."

The two men warmly embraced, quickly releasing one another in embarrassment.

Kipp kicked more sand. "Not that it's any of my business, but have you and Mom—uh, reconciled?"

The heat from the fire was too hot on Heston's face. He stepped back. "You mean, in the bedroom? No. Not yet. But soon."

"Mom loves you, Dad."

"You think?"

"And now she knows it. When we almost lost you—permanently— she got in touch with her true feelings."

"I only hope that someday—she'll forgive me—totally."

"Dad, one of life's great lessons is self-forgiveness."

"Son, are you preaching already?"

"Yes!" Laughing, Kipp clapped his hands.

"I was afraid of that," Heston teased as he looked around for more wood to throw on the bonfire.

"Our main job in life is not to find love," Kipp said softly. "It's to create love and express it. That's why we're all here on earth—I believe. To co-create love."

"You're not convinced?"

"I'm just an interpreter, Dad, in flux. Right now, this moment? That's how it seems to me." He looked away. "So strongly, that I'm going to bet the rest of my life on it."

"By teaching people to forgive?"

"That's my motto, Dad: Forgive. Teach. Forgive. *Ad infinitum.*

"Don't forget heal. Obviously, son. You have that special gift."

"I understand things in a way others don't seem to," Kipp admitted unreservedly.

Heston played his hand. "Boy, are you ever going to explain to me what happened—after I was attacked—when I was drifting between life and death? How did you come to me telepathically? Or did you use some other faculty? My father—your grandfather—was interested in such things. I don't know much about them."

"You know more than you think, Dad. It's related to that acting thing—what we discussed with Nick."

"You're talking about belief? Multiple realities?"

"Inner knowing, Dad. All is one, Dad. We're all part of the great Ongoing Creation." He raised his hands star-ward. "Change and trans-formation are the ultimate expression of Divine Power," Kipp rhapso-dized. "Our job is to realize and unite with the ever-exploding joy."

"I wanted to stay there." Heston spoke sincerely, his heart aglow. "Maybe I'll visit that retreat of yours one day, Noel, my son."

"There's only one King, Dad—and I don't mean rock n' roll, and I don't mean Odysseus. '. . . the truth will set you free.' "

***

As Heston and Kipp conversed, Nick slunk into their halo of fire-light, back from checking his traps. He held a bucket of scrambling, doomed crustaceans.

"A good hunt," he said, lowering the bucket for inspection.

"Gratitude," said Heston, taking note. He placed sticks of wood onto the glowing embers, and the blaze flared and crackled.

Kipp rose to his feet, shook loose the bucket from Nick's grasp and cried, "Compassion," tossing the beasts from the bucket onto the sandy beach. Returning the empty bucket to the astonished Nick, Kipp seem relieved. Reaching down, he picked up a large wooden stick and waved it in the night air. With wand in hand, Kipp stood mesmerized by the leaping flames. Humming, he began to dance around the blazing bonfire.

As Kipp broke into a singing chant, Heston soon joined in the dance, moving as best as he could. The wind, blowing in from the sea, began to rise, fanning the flames high.

"Survival," said Nick, setting the empty bucket on the ground. He frowned, hands on his hips. The waves of heat and heady sea air seemed to lift him from his body, onto another plane of existence.

For a moment, Nick stared at his companions, watching their antics in awe.

"Crazy artistic types," he muttered, as he, too, began to dance around the bonfire, joining Kipp and Heston in the ancient worship service.

***

Two weeks elapsed.

Inside the caretaker's cottage on Heart of Fire Key, Heston and Poppy were spending New Year's Eve by themselves. Late that night, uninvited and unannounced—but expected—Heston entered Poppy's darkened bedroom, silhouetted by starlight shining in the window.

"May I come in?" His voice was guttural.

"Of course." Her own voice sounded timid, rather than confident.

Entering, Heston left the door open behind him. Smooth music filtered in from the other room.

In the darkness, Poppy felt him slowly advancing. Lying between the sheets, she slipped out of her pajama bottoms—and waited, as he rounded her bed. Moonlight and starlight from the window streamed across his prowling form.

If you're teasing me, Heston, I'll die from it. Please don't be teasing me . . .

She could see that he was dressed in a sports shirt and shorts, the same clothes he had been wearing earlier in the evening. Hand on the bedpost, he stopped and stared down at her. Even in the darkness, she could feel the intimate caress of his gaze, as it ran the length of her naked body, hidden beneath the top sheet.

"What do you mean, 'of course'?" he asked snidely.

"Even if I weren't your wife, Heston—which I am—I wouldn't have the audacity to deny you."

He laughed. "No?"

"Not now. Not after you risked your own life to save mine."

"Poppy, I'm prepared to meet your terms. I'm ready to tell you the rest of my secrets."

She heard the quiver in her own voice. "Deal's off, Sean Heston. I no longer wish to know your secrets."

He sat down on the bed. His hand found her left calf, stroking it, squeezing it, merely a film of bed sheet between his flesh and hers. He leaned forward.

"What matters to me, Penelope, is that there is no one else in our bed. Just me—and you. That's the way it's going to be from now on."

"You're laying down the law?' She loved him so much it made her clench inside. It had always been thus. "A royal decree?"

"Yes." He stretched out beside her, lying down on his side, propped by one elbow. "All suitors will be turned away. Understood?"

Poppy's heart thudded. "Aye, sir." *I've put them all on notice.*

His fingers laced her breasts, thumbs toying at her nipples. She did not stop him; merely, she waited in silence for what she hoped was coming.

Please . . .

With bent knuckles, he softly traced a line from her right breast, across her chest and up the side of her neck, to the lobe of her left ear, sending shivers across her body like tremors foreshadowing an impending earthquake.

"H-He's—"

"Mm-hmm?"

His fingertips traced her hairline. Lightly, he combed his fingers through the wisp of hairs at her temple. His eyes, glinting in the darkness, watched the fine strands as they floated back into place against her burning cheek.

She watched him watching. She studied him. He wasn't as agile as he once had been, nor, as perfectly beautiful, but *now* he was *hers*. She grew bold with desire. She wanted to—

"Heston."

"Yes."

"It's just you and me from now on? That's what you're saying?"

"That's what I'm promising—and demanding." He moved his face closer to hers, brushing his lips against the damp skin of her cheeks and forehead. Sliding his body onto hers, he kissed the bridge and the tip of her nose. Bringing his hands to her face, he cupped it and stared, unmasked, into her wide-open eyes.

"I mean it, Red," he said. "If you are going to be my bed partner for the rest of our lives, I need to know that I'm the one and only thing in it. No one on your mind, in your heart, or—in here." His hand traveled down her core and pelvis, his fingers, suddenly, finding their way inside her.

She cried out.

"No one but me. Understood?"

". . . Ah-ha . . ."

"It's been a while," he noted. "Good to know I'm still welcome."

Oh, you arrogant—

"So you love me, do you, Pigtails?"

"Yes!" she cried out loud. "Always. And forever."

Coiling her arms around his neck, she moved beneath him, positioning herself, accepting his open mouth into hers. The taste of him had never changed. It was as it had been in elementary school. Neither had his scent. myrrh and orange-blossoms surrounded her, capturing her mercilessly, taking intimate possession of her senses, her entire being.

Take me, now, Heston—I'll say anything . . . "You are all I need. All I'll ever want. You are my husband, my returning hero, my king . . ."

Ready, Heston ripped off his shirt and opened his fly. Raising his torso— his arms straight, palms flat against the mattress—he stared down at her, his eyes filling with silver-blue wonder, like a rising tidal wave in a turbulent sea, deepening and swelling with power and magnificence, tempered only by maturity.

She, too, had aged, but, great actor that Heston was, he did not show surprise, nor was his enthusiasm lessened. Instead, he spoke tenderly, his colossal prowess undeterred.

"I love you, Poppy Demming. You are my one true wife. You are the love of my life."

"Oh, Heston, I love y—"

Hoisting himself atop her, he drove his love into her with a fierce hunger, a thirst, an eternal need for dominance and union that could be sated by the acquiescence of true love only.

When he climaxed, eventually, she knew, with absolute certainty, that he had meant what he'd said—that she was the only woman in his bed, his head, his heart, his soul—just as she had always imagined it could be, ever since the night they'd first made love, all those many years ago beneath the generative light of heavenly stars.

And on this latter-day Eve, far from Shark Bay, that same generative starlight was seeking out and enlivening generations of Demmings who had been, were being—and would be—fostered by the guidance of their ancestors' deep abiding love for one another and, in spirit, for them, as well, and for the Divine in all—although, not without a little more drama and controversy to keep things interesting.

Aloft in the heavens, the stars beamed down their ever-generative healing light, each and every one of them busily co-creating love.

Epilogue

Six weeks later, Heston received a gift from his son. Kipp's song, *Want You Back Now,* had been written behind bars. Kipp had dedicated the song to his birth parents and requested that his dad record the song and release it. Heston did so. Later, Tropica's cover version became a huge hit.

The lyrics read as follows:

Title: Want You Back Now
Verse 1

We were destined
Heaven knew it
Then I walked out
Really blew it
No excuses
Crazy stupid
But all's not lost
Gonna undo it

Chorus

Want you back now
(I'm) Keeping my vow
(I've) Changed somehow
Falling down
On both knees
Let's make peace
Forgive me, please
Want you back now

Oh, babe
Want you back now
Come on
Want you back now

Verse 2

We'll start over
Got to do it
Hey, this love thing
Something to it
Seen me crying?
I can prove it
Look in these eyes
Been going through it

Chorus

Want you back now
(I'm) Keeping my vow
(I've) Changed somehow
Falling down
On both knees
Let's make peace
Forgive me, please
Want you back now
Oh, babe
Want you back now
Come on
Want you back now

Bridge

Open your heart
Don't try to hide
Real life is hard
Dig deep inside

Chorus

Want you back now
(I'm) Keeping my vow
(I've) Changed somehow
Falling down
On both knees
Let's make peace
Forgive me, please
Want you back now
Oh, babe
Want you back now
Come on
Want you back now

About the Author

Tina Murray is the acclaimed author of a captivating series of glitzy, romantic mystery novels, the Heston Demming series. Murray's steamy, yet spiritual saga chronicles the life and loves of handsome movie-superstar, Heston Demming. In Murray's stories, the sexy actor struggles to tame his passions and torments. While he copes with fame and fortune, he searches for his lost soul, amid the hidden ruins of a secret past. Although he travels the world, Heston's home base is upscale Naples, Florida, where author Murray has lived, intermittently, since her teen years, and knows well. An actress and artist, she also lived in New York and Los Angeles. Returning to college as an adult, she earned both her bachelor's degree and master's degree from the University of Miami. After a tour in real estate, she returned to graduate school. She now holds a doctorate in art education from The Florida State University. Her hobbies include genealogy and songwriting.

She belongs to the Romance Writers of America and the Florida Writers Association. She was present at the inception of the Carnegie Writers.

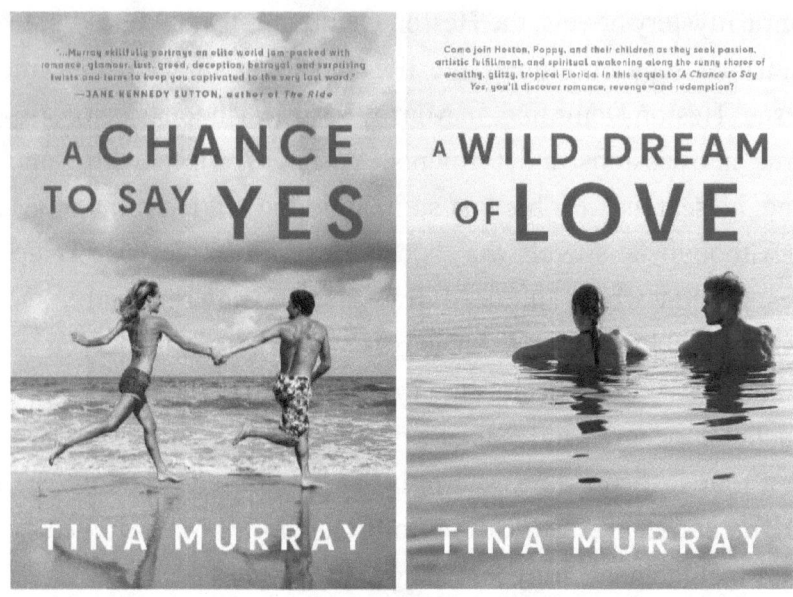

Now Available!

NINA ROMANO

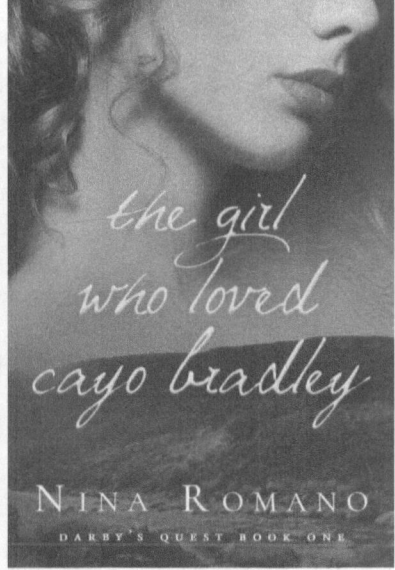

For more information
visit: www.SpeakingVolumes.us

Now Available!

BETH GROUNDWATER'S
CLAIRE HANOVER MYSTERIES

For more information
visit: www.SpeakingVolumes.us

www.ingramcontent.com/pod-product-compliance
Lightning Source LLC
Chambersburg PA
CBHW030808260626
47169CB00001B/235